D0053530

Music

of

Falling

Water

ALSO BY JULIA OLIVER

Seventeen Times as High as the Moon
Goodbye to the Buttermilk Sky

JOHN F. BLAIR, PUBLISHER   WINSTON-SALEM, NORTH CAROLINA

Music

of

Falling

Water

Julia Oliver

Published by John F. Blair, Publisher

Library of Congress Cataloging-in-Publication Data

Oliver, Julia.
Music of falling water / by Julia Oliver.
p.   cm.
ISBN 0-89587-238-2 (alk. paper)
1. Rural families—Fiction. 2. Missing persons—Fiction. 3. Sisters—
Fiction. 4. Alabama—Fiction. I. Title

PS3565.L477 M87 2001
813'.54—dc21

2001025301

Design by Debra Long Hampton

In

memory

of

Ola David Parker

and

Howard Arrington Parker

Prologue

The early-spring meadow is a softer green than the money in her new pocketbook. It's too soon for swimming, but a dip in the cold, cider-colored pond will fortify her for the journey ahead. She takes off everything but a thin shift, wraps the garments around the purse, and places the bundle in the fork of a weeping willow tree.

The big wheel draws her like a magnet and groans like a lover as she mounts it. When she reaches the top, she can hear the triumphant whistle of the train that will bear her away. But the sound of her own voice, calling to the solitary figure whose back is to the window, is lost in the ever-present music of falling water.

1
A Little Jaunt

THEY COULD BE POSING for a photographer. In his lawn-party suit and straw boater, Jason stands beside a touring car that lusters with a sheen of disuse. Regally erect in the front passenger seat, his wife, Lola's sister Gertrude, is attired for serious motoring in a mauve pongee duster and a high-crowned, bird-winged hat. Jason's checkerboard-patterned suitcase and the smaller piece of Lola's matched set are secured by a luggage gate on the driver's-side running board. Alas, this curbside vignette won't be framed or cornered in an album; the only camera is in her head.

Lola and the other faculty members have assembled their classes on the portico for dismissal. At the sound of the bell, Jason strides through the onslaught of fleeing students to relieve her of her satchel. His greeting is cheerful and perfunctory, hers to the point: "What's up?" Both are lost in the din. He propels her into the backseat.

She kisses the air near Gertrude's cheek and asks where they're going.

"Let it be a surprise, Lola." That evasion suggests the destination is Crystal Springs, a resort that's more their cup of tea than hers, where the mineral waters are labeled as though each is distinctive—Freestone, Magnesium, Arsenic, Chalybeate, Black Sulphur, White Sulphur, Alum—though all taste like off-color eggs smell.

Jason presses the starter button. The engine gurgles, then comes to life. Gertrude adjusts her veil and hands a swath of chiffon to Lola. "So your hair won't whip about," she explains unnecessarily.

Pedestrians pause to gawk as the sleek black Packard with the blue midsection lunges into the thoroughfare, almost sideswiping a Maxwell. Gasoline fumes mingle with the gamy aroma of leather and Gertrude's cologne, a not unpleasant combination. Lola's bedraggled shirtwaist will be comfortable for traveling. A neutral breeze reflects the seasonal limbo; autumn hasn't arrived in Alabama, but the oven that was summer has cooled. Might as well be optimistic about situations she has no control over, such as how she will spend this mid-September weekend of 1918, and a war that's put love on hold.

Though he was against entering the foreign conflict (as was President Wilson, in his reelection campaign), her brother-in-law has become a staunch supporter of the cause. Jason chairs the local Selective Service board, supports the Liberty Bond drive, gives generously to the Red Cross Fund, and wishes the steel in his 1917 Twin Six had gone into weaponry and helmets. He has decreed it their civic duty to patronize the electric trolley system and the new motorized taxicabs; except on Sundays, the automobile that was designed for cross-country travel seldom leaves the porte-cochere. At this time on a typical end-of-the-work-week afternoon—which this is not, since they're going somewhere, and also, it's Friday the thirteenth—Lola would be aboard a brown-and-yellow streetcar, headed for the drugstore on the first downtown corner.

Her chum Maggie will be miffed that Lola has left town for the weekend without informing her. They usually take in a matinee on Saturday. Since her ensign husband put out to sea soon after their honeymoon, Maggie has worried she'll be a widow before her time, with no grave to visit. Once you've plumbed the depths of conjugal passion, it's terrible to be deprived of that bliss, so Maggie says. Lola can only imagine.

She had set her sights on Robert Castleman when she was seven and he was nine, soon after she came to Felder to make her home with the Jason Howards. By the time Rob took special notice of her, Lola's dance card was full. And she wasn't the only girl he had an eye for. He didn't press his case until early last summer, after he had graduated from Washington and Lee and begun his career in the family confectionery. (Castleman's Candies are sensuously advertised throughout the Southeast: "Mouth-watering Kisses, Wrapped by Modern Machinery, Always Sanitary.") They had been out together on four consecutive evenings when he asked her to be his steady girl. "You should have asked me years ago," Lola said. "We've wasted an awful lot of time."

Rob soon discovered he couldn't sit behind a desk amidst the aromas of roasting peanuts and simmering chocolate when there was a war to be fought. He joined the National Guard, the country's "second line of defense," and enrolled for Officers' Candidate training at Marion Military Institute in the gentle magnolia town where she would begin her senior year of college. When she had returned to her all-female campus last September, Rob was a newly commissioned second lieutenant about to be dispatched with the rest of the 167th Infantry on eight special trains to Camp Mills, New York. There, Alabama's citizen-soldiers were assembled into the Forty-second Division, an exclusive group of twenty-eight thousand federalized National Guardsmen from over half the states and the District of Columbia. In early November, the Alabama troops were among the last of what would become known as the Rainbow Division to be deployed overseas.

Rob's first letter—from "Somewhere in France"—expressed chagrin that he hadn't accepted Lola's offer to go all the way on their last night together (because he wasn't the sort of fellow to risk getting his girl in trouble when he wouldn't be around to make an honest woman of her). The letter also contained a proposal of marriage that made her blush. Lola's fiancé was half a world away when his parents ceremoniously presented her with a family ring, a large, rose-cut diamond surrounded by opals. They approved of her decision to keep this treasure in its velvet box until Rob could place it on her finger. Lola didn't tell them that, according to her sister Rhoda, it was bad luck to wear opals unless they were one's birthstone. Rob was not pleased that his mother had taken the ring business upon herself. He assured Lola, in double underlining, that he would find the perfect circlet to commemorate their engagement as soon as he got to New York.

"Hold him to it," Maggie said, splaying the fingers of her left hand and admiring the diamond solitaire she'd told Lola at least a dozen times was purchased at Cartier the day the store opened.

The Rainbow legions were sent forward to relieve and assist Allied troops in the trenches near the French town of Luneville. From February through June, Rob's outfit participated in sporadic skirmishes in the Lorraine sector.

During the Champagne-Marne Defensive, what Lola had not allowed herself to think about happened. (Rhoda used to say, "Watch your thoughts. Whatever you think strongly about will come to pass.") The German assault had been expected for days. When it didn't come by July 14, French and American soldiers celebrated the Bastille anniversary with champagne toasts to their leaders. At midnight, the German bombardment began. The *Felder Herald* quoted an Alabama doughboy's description of the battle near the Butte de Souain: "The shelling sounded like a tornado. Our machine gunners and rifles were picking them off, but the Huns kept coming. We stood face to face with an army of great force and dogged determination. To their sorrow, we didn't give in. The Boche opened up with those guns, thousands of them, that illuminated the earth. Incendiary shells detonated with bursts of flame and filled our trenches with horrible, choking fumes, setting the woodwork and boxes of ammunition ablaze. It was an unremitting roar the rest of the night."

On July 15, as Lola was reading in the side-yard hammock, she looked up to see an apocalypse of jagged orange flames against a black sky. The official telegram that came to Rob's parents interpreted her ominous vision. Her sweetheart had been struck down that very day, but he had not been killed. *Wounded* can have a lovely sound when it's not preceded by *mortally*.

Rob underwent surgery in a military hospital to remove shrapnel from his left thigh. A few weeks later, he was sent to a convalescence camp outside London. Lola is jealous of the female volunteer who met his train at Waterloo Station and drove him to the camp—also of Do-Nut Girls, the nurses who helped save his life, and flirty French women (though she could never begrudge him that springtime leave in Paris).

Jason is optimistic, or pretends to be, that the war will end before Rob is deemed fit to return to the Western Front. Lola focuses not on that possibility but on his homecoming, her flag-waving self perched among the sea gulls on the dock in Hoboken, New Jersey, when his ship arrives. For their private reunion, Lola pictures the Astor Hotel suite that she, Jason, and Gertrude occupied on a visit to New York City three years ago, the highlight of which was Mr. Irving Berlin's sprightly operetta *Watch Your Step*, viewed from a gilded bow-front box in the magnificent New Amsterdam Theater. But Rob and Lola won't be taking in Broadway revues. As she removes a traveling suit of jade-green crepe de Chine (her own design, to be executed by Gertrude's dressmaker), Rob sheds the most presentable of the half-dozen khaki uniforms his father ordered from Brooks Brothers. . . .

Jason blows the horn and brakes sharply as another driver cuts in front of the car.

"That was a bit close," Gertrude observes.

"You couldn't be in better hands," he assures her.

"We know that, dear. Lola and I have the utmost confidence in you."

Lola wishes Gertrude would not speak for her, but it's true, she has the utmost confidence in the man who's been a surrogate father to her. Right now, she would like to hug his scrawny neck, what there is of it above that high, rigid collar. "Would you like for me to spell you at the wheel?" she asks.

The reply—"Not at present, thank you"—doesn't surprise her. Jason usually has an excuse to keep her from driving this favorite possession, which may be the last of its breed, as the Packard Company currently turns out engines for the military's land, sea, and air vehicles.

On Market Street, the hub of Felder's economic activity, traffic becomes more congested. As they cruise alongside wagons, carriages, and sturdy Model Ts like a yacht among rowboats, members of the police department's mounted and bicycle squads weave in and out, tooting whistles, adding to the confusion.

The twelve-story First National, Felder's tallest building, looms over seven other banks and a dozen hotels. Alabama's third-largest city (boasting a population of nearly sixty thousand, according to the Commercial Club's latest bulletin) has twenty restaurants and seven cinematized theaters. The elegant Grand still features a pit orchestra and live vaudeville; the Orpheus has higher-toned stage plays. Felder Fair, the two-story-plus-mezzanine department store, occupies a prime corner. Among the smaller retail merchants are dressmakers, milliners, haberdashers (Classy Clothes offers men's finest woolen suits for ten, fifteen, and twenty dollars), greengrocers, butchers, tobacconists, jewelers. One hole-in-the-wall establishment "Cleans & Blocks Men's Felt Hats, Also Curls Ostrich Plumes." The Van Deusen Company's banner—"Proud Distributor for Stutz Automobiles," it reads—overshadows the carriage-and-surrey showroom. The most impressive facade on the boulevard belongs to S. H. Kress, the store with the greatest variety of merchandise and the longest lunch counter in town.

They're nearing the ivy-bearded building where Jason's offices look out on a towering, double-basined, cast-iron fountain erected in 1885, two decades after the South's defeat in the War Between the States; it is a euphemistic symbol of Felder's economic rebound from that devastation.

Pollard Street intersects with an alley of Victorian row houses that have seen better times, the exception being a prosperous, discreet brothel on the corner. The real red-light district is near the station complex, where the Hut, a canteen sponsored by the Red Cross, offers a respectable alternative to military travelers with time to pass between trains. Lola and Maggie are among the volunteer hostesses who provide conversation and refreshments two nights a week. Gertrude is not comfortable bantering with strangers of the opposite sex, even those who are pledged to defend her. She does her bit by knitting mufflers and rolling bandages. Gertrude also rigorously complies with the voluntary food-rationing program. Mondays and Wednesdays are wheatless; Tuesdays are meatless; Thursdays are porkless. Gluttony is permitted only on weekends. Lola sighs with anticipation of the groaning board that awaits them in the airy dining room of the Crystal Springs Hotel.

Jason almost misses a turn, and a screech of Airease-inflated tires prompts another reminder from Gertrude that she and Lola have entrusted him with their lives. The North District commences with a block of cotton factors' offices and warehouses. Next comes a half-mile of manufacturing plants rendered ghostly with gray dust; Felder is the largest distributor of fertilizers in the nation. Hightower's Livery Stables (whose newly stenciled gold-on-black sign urges "Hurry, Hurry! Record

Shipment of Horses!") faces the Metropolitan Stockyard, a series of open stalls under a corrugated tin roof, where cattle, hogs, and sheep call out to passersby like orphans seeking parents.

Farther along is the Remount Depot, where mules and horses are processed for the army. The quadrupeds are sent to Camp Sheridan, the infantry post near Montgomery, to be trained as mounts and draw horses for ambulance and artillery wagons before being shipped overseas. In an early letter from the front, Rob wrote, "A horse muzzled by a gas mask is a pathetic and ludicrous sight. Poor beasts had no idea what they were being trained for. But then, neither did many of their human counterparts." Lola closes her eyes and gives thanks for at least the millionth time that he's removed from the action, and that the Germans have ceased the air attacks over England.

The city ends abruptly as the brick-paved street gives way to a scraped-gravel road. Jason leans forward to peer through the windshield, as though Creek warriors or Kraut soldiers lurk in the woods on either side, ready to pounce upon travelers. Gertrude's cameo-like profile, usually inscrutable, becomes more so.

They have bypassed Union Station, where more than two thousand freight cars and sixty passenger trains arrive daily. (The statistics are from a classroom lecture Lola has prepared.) So much for her assumption that the car would be left beneath the shed and they would board a shuttle that would deposit them within the hour at the bucolic resort. She taps Jason on the shoulder. "Now may I learn where we're going?"

He replies offhandedly, "We should reach Hackberry Hill before sundown."

"Use the time to nap, Lola," Gertrude says in her reprimanding voice. She means Lola is not to ask why they are headed, of all places, to Hackberry Hill.

The falling-out came about in the usual way, over who gets what when someone dies. Fourteen years ago, Gertrude and the husband she'd acquired the previous summer returned to her former home with a two-fold purpose—to divide her late mother's possessions with her sister Kathleen and to collect Lola, the orphaned minor child. Jason had admonished Gertrude to keep in mind that his house was well appointed and that transporting large furniture from Hackberry Hill to Felder would be impractical as well as unnecessary. But her eye immediately lit on the upright piano with a broken music rack and a keyboard minus most of its ivories. It made Lola sad just to look at the thing. According to Rhoda, Papa had brought the instrument home from one of his mystery trips, along with a Graphophone that didn't work and an unstrung mandolin inlaid with abalone-pearl and numerous cracks. Mama had traded the latter two items to an odd-jobs man in lieu of wages.

After a brief consultation with Jason, Gertrude announced, "We would like the piano. Mr. Howard and I wish Lola to have the advantage of musical instruction."

Kathleen had no objection.

Lola said, "The piano should go to Rhoda." Seeing Gertrude's frown, she added quickly, "I suppose we could keep it 'til she returns."

Had they known where she was, Gertrude and Kathleen likely would not have invited that sibling to take part in the choosing. Rhoda had broken their mother's heart when she ran away from home almost a year earlier.

Gertrude pouted but didn't argue when Jason, who was the executor of his mother-in-law's will, decreed the other large pieces should stay in the house built by the sisters' grandfather, where Kathleen, her laconic husband, George Craven, and their young son, Harold, would remain in residence. George would continue to manage the planting, harvesting, and gristmill operations. The arrangement worked to everyone's advantage, so Jason saw no reason to change it.

After that, the choosing didn't go well. Gertrude and Kathleen

11

bickered over a dented gold bangle with their mother's name, Lucy Margaret, engraved in script so small it was barely legible. Before the first hour was up, they were addressing each other through intermediaries: "Lola, please inform Gertrude this reticule was Grandmother's before it was Mama's, and Grandmother promised it to me"; "I don't wish to be obstinate, Jason, but Kathleen knows Mama intended for me to have the reticule and her jewelry." Gertrude got the pearls and the bracelet, but Kathleen dug her heels in about the bugle-beaded purse. The tension between them was such that further disposition of the contents of their mother's wedding trunk was abandoned.

The Howards and Lola were driven to the train station a good hour early. George left them on the loading platform with the piano and some hastily packed crates of silver and china. (Gertrude had managed not to accept any pewter or crockery.) Lola spent the time admiring a small box of paper-wrapped coloring sticks—"Crayolas"—that Jason had brought her. The gift was supposed to take her mind off the fact that she was leaving the only home she'd ever known. He had no idea how relieved she was to be going. There was also a tablet of drawings to be colored, but she wasn't about to dent those lovely points on the first crayons she'd ever seen, much less owned.

Now that what she had long awaited was happening, Lola felt a conflict of loyalty. When Rhoda returned to Hackberry Hill, she would be surprised, maybe even mad, that Lola wasn't there waiting for her. Kathleen had a strange look, as though she didn't really expect Lola would go, when it came down to it. But she didn't say, "Remember, if you get homesick, you can come back," or "I'll write to you," or even "Goodbye, Lola. Have a nice life." At least George tweaked one of her braids, which was the most attention he'd ever paid her.

The rift was exacerbated when Kathleen ignored Gertrude's prompt note expressing regret that "unpleasantness saw fit to rear its ugly head between us." Her next missive chastised Kathleen for not keeping up her end of the correspondence. That one brought a response in large block letters—"FOR GOD'S SAKE, GERTRUDE, PLEASE LEAVE ME ALONE"—on a penny postcard Tru feared was read by every postal employee in Hackberry Hill and Felder, as well as by her housekeeper, who placed it, message side up, on the hall table.

Two years later (in 1906, when Lola was going on nine), Jason told Gertrude it was time to let bygones be bygones and look in on her relatives. She could hardly refuse.

It was a teeth-shaking ride. The rail route between Felder and Hackberry Hill included high trestles over rocky streams. Fearing the train would hurtle off into one of those swirling branches, Lola was surprised when it came safely to a hissing halt at Hackberry Hill's Louisville & Nashville Depot. A stucco building with arched windows and a red-tile roof had replaced the plain board-and-batten shed. Jason wondered aloud what the railroad magnates could have been thinking of, erecting a Spanish Colonial Revival edifice in a town inhabited by descendants of English and Scots-Irish settlers. That didn't get a rise out of his companions. Gertrude was swooning with motion sickness, and a cinder smaller than a flea had lodged in Lola's eye. The pain was intense until Jason removed the speck with a corner of his handkerchief, urging through his spicy Sen-Sen breath, "Chin up, Lola. Put on your most radiant expression for the relatives."

Her sisters acknowledged each other on that occasion with cool reserve. Lola thought it a good sign that Kathleen had come to meet them, and in the surrey; Kat knew Gertrude preferred that dilapidated, canopied conveyance to the more practical buckboard. Lola wondered if she was supposed to bob a semi-curtsy, as Gertrude had instructed her to do when greeting Felder dowagers. She decided not to risk it. Kathleen might ask her who in the world she thought she was, to be putting on airs. To accommodate Jason, Lola kept the tears inside her eyelids and grinned so fiercely the corners of her mouth felt stretched.

Kathleen greeted Lola as though she'd seen her the day before. Restrained by rompers starched within an inch of their life, little Harold hid his face beneath his mother's arm. Lola knew that such shyness wouldn't have been tolerated by their mother, but Kathleen didn't make an issue of it. The new baby, Ray—short for Rayford, after his mother's father—slept in a basket, his tapioca cheeks jiggling whenever the contraption hit a bump in the road, which was frequently. Jason did all the talking on the ride to the house. He pointed out Hackberry Hill landmarks as though those born there had never seen them: the wood-shingled Grange Hall; the red-brick post office, its flagpole rising from a bed of aspidistra; the graded school, built as a house of worship by a handful of Episcopalians before they joined forces with the more numerous Methodists to construct a Methodist-Episcopal church on land provided by the sisters' grandfather. Most of the buildings had porches and second stories where the proprietors' families lived. Storefronts were painted earth shades of brown and sky shades of blue. The dentist's sign was shaped like a molar. The red stripes on the barbershop pole had partially flaked off, so that it resembled a well-licked candy cane. Three physicians were listed on the entrance sign of the Hackberry Hill Hospital, another new construction since Lola's time there. The only name she recognized was the one at the top: Peter Whitney, M.D.

"Looks more like a barracks than a hospital," Jason said. "As I recall, a blacksmith shop was on that corner. One of two such establishments."

"The other's still in business," Kathleen said.

"It's a sure sign of progress that the community requires only one horse-shoeing operation now. Here, as in Felder, automobiles and trucks are fast gaining over buggies and wagons."

The two-story brick hotel hadn't changed. Its flimsy balcony was used only for draping banners on important occasions, such as Confederate Memorial Day. In front of the hotel were a long watering trough and a chain-linked row of hitching posts. Rhoda said the chain was to keep those little iron horse heads from running away. Lola wanted to ask Kathleen if she'd heard from their runaway sister, but she didn't want to see Kat shake her head or give her cause to make a derogatory remark about Rhoda.

Behind the town, winding trails led to homesteads and farms of varying sizes. The largest tracts, the Whitneys' and theirs, were on the other side of the highway. Dr. Whitney's property was designated "Whippoorwill Plantation" on a pristine gatepost sign, though Lola had never heard anyone other than his wife refer to it by the name. The house had verandas—his wife called them piazzas—on all sides and was tiered like a wedding cake; its uppermost level was a small, square room with lots of windows. Although she'd never been in that room, Lola could imagine its view over cotton fields, hay meadows; and wooded sections, all laid out as neatly as a quilting design. Their land would appear haphazard in comparison. As they neared the place where the road divided, the gristmill glinted in the sunshine like the iridescent mica nuggets she and Rhoda had gathered on the creek bank the day Rhoda got herself baptized.

Jason said, "Lola, you may not know that your great-grandfather built the mill of river rock. For many years, it was a prosperous family enterprise as well as a valuable community service." From the highway, the gristmill, which was closer to the Whitneys' house than to their own, looked like a substantial residence. The doorway's marble lentil, inscribed "Holloway's Mill, 1845," wasn't obvious from that distance, and the cumbersome waterwheel was out of sight, though thinking of it at that moment made it visible to Lola. The paddle buckets were edged with bright green moss that looked and felt like velvet ribbon. Rhoda must have told her that. She had never been close enough to the wheel to touch it.

The latticed porch of the house she'd chosen to leave was masked by a dense mat of parrot-green foliage. Bell-shaped blue flowers peeped out from trowel-shaped leaves like the eyes of children playing hide-and-seek in the folds of heavy draperies. "Good heavens, Sister," Gertrude exclaimed. "Mama's morning glories have got out of hand."

Kathleen shrugged. "They hold the hot sun off."

"Of course, the vines planted by your dear mother hold sentimental value as well, but we mustn't allow them to pull down the porch," Jason said. "I'll take up the matter with George."

Lola entered with her eyes tightly closed and groped her way until she bumped into a wall. She opened them at Gertrude's reprimand and found the ceiling was lower than she remembered. The plank floor groaned with unfamiliar inflections. The smells were different. There was no hint of Mama's flour-and-cinnamon aroma, no stench of bandaged seepage wafting from Papa's room into the kitchen, no essence of Rhoda. "You don't smell like us," Kathleen had taunted her. It was true. Whether she was perspiring or had just bathed, Rhoda exuded a musk of deep woods and water lilies. The house relented and allowed Lola a cumulative whiff of pine-knot fires stoked over the years in the front rooms' fireplaces.

The moment she entered the parlor, Gertrude spied a faded green moire-bound set of *The Decline and Fall of the Roman Empire* and said, with an imperiousness that made Lola wince, "Lola should have these. She's become quite bookish under Jason's tutelage."

Kathleen bristled, "My boys may be quite bookish when they learn to read."

Jason averted that crisis by agreeing with Kathleen that Papa's Gibbon should remain with his grandsons, as Lola was welcome to his set of the same books—which, he didn't remind Gertrude in front of Kathleen, had gilt-edged pages and leather bindings. He did remind his wife that the purpose of this visit was not to resume choosing.

Unfortunately, his intention—to reestablish the bond of affection among close kin—wasn't accomplished. Kathleen and Gertrude were cool to each other; George was nervous; Jason was too hearty, which made him seem condescending; and Lola was miserable. As George drove them back to the station, Lola kept her eyes closed and concentrated on counting to five hundred slowly, by which time they would have passed the mill. She didn't want to imagine Rhoda swimming in the pond or cavorting on the waterwheel.

On their return to Felder at the end of that long day, the rosy-brick facade of Jason's Georgian-style domicile smiled in the dusky twilight like a welcoming face. Lola embraced the lamppost beside the entrance gate and sobbed with relief. She had not been left at her birthplace. Jason asked gently why she was crying, but she was too mortified to explain. Gertrude gave her a goblet filled to the brim with whiskey and sugar to take to bed, as though she had a bad case of croup. As she drifted off, Rhoda's teasing voice whispered, "Don't be a crybaby, Lo. There's nothing wrong with you but a touch of Americanitis."

After breakfast the next morning, Gertrude invited Lola to join her in her special nook, which is furnished with a carved prie-dieu made of ancient wood from a Garden of Gethsemane olive tree—or so she chooses to believe—and a rickety, polychrome Louis XIV bench. These pieces belonged to Jason's mother, Alfreda Quincy Howard, who had the grace to die and vacate her artfully assembled domicile at just the right time— that is, six months before her only offspring met Lola's eldest sister and was smitten by the love bug. This lady—so lifelike in her full-length portrait over the mantel that Lola used to worry she would fall out of the frame and crack her head on the fireplace fender—also had the grace not to hang around in disembodied form. To this day, Lola has never felt her presence, nor, she's sure, has Gertrude, or they would be living elsewhere. Tru has no truck with the spirit world beyond the boundaries of St. Anne's Episcopal Church. She never attended seances or Ouija board parties when such were the rage. Kathleen might not care much for psychic phenomena, but she had to put up with it; Grandmother moved back into the Hackberry Hill house the day after she was buried.

Rhoda could distinguish the scrabbling sound the old woman made as she opened cupboards and drawers searching for her wedding ring from the activity of squirrels in the attic.

Gertrude perched gingerly on the French bench and indicated Lola was to sit at her feet. As Lola waited to learn why she was summoned, Gertrude gazed with satisfaction at the bay window's view of the garden. During her predecessor's tenure, the rear yard had been a formal maze of heat-struck boxwoods. In her only radical change as the new chatelaine, Gertrude got rid of that suffering shrubbery and installed a variety of roses, most of them named as though they were human: Madame Alfred Carriere, Duchess de Brabant, Mary Wallace, Baltimore Belle, Alister Stella Gray. The other sex was represented by Rambling Rector, Archduke Charles, Graham Thomas, and Dr. W. Van Fleet. Gertrude and her ancient, coal-colored gardener whispered encouragingly to each. It never occurred to Gertrude that this might be witchcraft.

Without turning her gaze from the window, Gertrude said in her club-presiding voice, "I have decided you must forget everything connected with Hackberry Hill."

Whole scenes from that place replayed behind Lola's eyelids much of the time. The hall clock, its square face embellished with Roman numerals and a leering profile moon, was a metronome in her head. She heard the plangent arpeggio of water rippling over the rock dam and the roar of the aroused wheel. It had occurred to Lola that her brain might burst from the overflow of converging sounds and sights. But forget everything? "How in the world am I supposed to do that?"

"I'm sure you will find a way. Jason says you are quite intelligent." Gertrude spoke with an edge of disapproval, as though intelligence were a character defect.

"What about the good parts?"

"I have asked you not to whine, Lola."

"I'm sorry." She wanted to use her hands to knead serenity back into

Gertrude's face. Lola found her lovely to look at when calm. Gertrude never allowed herself to lose her temper, but sometimes when an innocent remark struck her a certain way, her face reacted as though it had been slapped.

"A euphonious tone of voice is as important as the content of one's speech." Gertrude added hurriedly, as though she wanted to get on with the important activities of her day, "When dealing with memory, any attempts to separate good parts from the rest could end in confusion. Confusion creates chaos. Therefore, you must concentrate on banishing that time before you came to live with us in Felder. It was only your first six years, Lola. If you refuse to allow this portion of recollected experience to intrude on your thought waves, it will all fade away."

As though to protest that specious statement, framed images suspended by frayed, tasseled cords from the ceiling molding in the Hackberry Hill house materialized on a wall of Lola's mind. The most startling was the primitive oil-on-board portrait of Grandmother as a big-eyed, barefoot child in a long white dress, holding a single flower; the itinerant artist's name and the price, four dollars, were noted in one corner. A wing-shaped water stain on the ceiling hovered over the pastel rendering of Grandfather's sister Meteoria, named for the shower of stars that fell on Alabama as she was born in the early-morning hours of November 13, 1833, and who died in the yellow-fever epidemic of 1855, a week before she was to be married. With even lateral ancestors such as this star-crossed great-aunt vying for a place in her head, Lola feared there might not be room for multiplication tables, the declension of nouns, the conjugation of verbs, the memorization of stanzas, oratory, preludes, fugues, etudes, and sonatinas. She needed every inch of brain space to accumulate wisdom and culture, not as a repository for distracting detritus. Her guardian sister knew what was best for her, and Lola knew where her bread was buttered. She vowed to obliterate the first six years of her life.

"Wonderful, dear. The subject is closed; we will not say any more about it." Gertrude's countenance resumed its taut-sheet smoothness. A fly swatter trimmed in tatting lay across her lap. Languidly, she smashed a housefly on the window sill, then unlatched the screen and nudged it over the edge.

Within a few weeks, like chalk marks on a slate, Lola's early life was erased. Whenever she slipped and mentioned an incident or a person from the forbidden place and time—even their mother, whose youthful miniature, framed in silver, had the place of honor on Gertrude's dressing table—Gertrude assumed a formidable expression, like the schoolmarm she would have become had not Jason rescued her from such a fate: "Bring yourself to the present, Lola." Eventually, an inner censor took over, and there were no more slips.

In the years since, Jason has never mentioned this project to Lola, although he contributed to its success from the outset by devoting time and attention to the development of her mind. Gertrude saw to it that Lola's afternoons were filled with ballet, elocution, china painting, and piano lessons. To Gertrude's disappointment, sight reading and keyboard facility did not come as naturally to Lola as they had to their missing sister. The piano pedagogy ended when the teacher assigned her J. S. Bach's "Three-Part Inventions." In Gertrude's view, musical counterpoint was the height of rudeness—all those voices speaking at once, and not in harmony. Also, perhaps, she thought it prudent to disassociate the girl from the instrument that was a reminder of the forbidden time and place.

Having arrived together, the Chickering and Lola were brought up to snuff simultaneously. The piano got a new music rack and ivory veneers, and the cabinet was refinished. Lola was drilled in table manners and other etiquette, and her knees and elbows were pumiced. The clothes she came with were given to the local orphanage. Although Gertrude let her keep the pinafore Rhoda had bequeathed her, she explained that this dress protector was unnecessary, as Lola would never have to wear a frock more than once between launderings.

Lola had a set of Dolly Dingles to bring out when company came to play, but she didn't want to share those store-bought paper dolls with pampered, perfect girls who looked just like them. She soon lost interest in changing their tabbed dresses and let the Dollies loll about in their shifts. At night, in shoebox beds with their eyes open, the cardboard girls became Rhoda and Lola. In her goose-down bed with the carved mahogany posts and pink organdy canopy, Lola allowed herself to wonder where the real Rhoda was sleeping. Before she banished her past, she had conflicted feelings about whether she would want to leave her comfortable, secure situation for a nomadic existence, should Rhoda ever make good on her promise to come back for her.

For the first several years she lived with the Howards, Lola kept a wary eye on Gertrude's midsection, which never varied in circumference and was kept firmly bound in the latest style of tubular corset. She treasured her status as the only child in the house, although she knew if Gertrude ever expressed a desire for a baby, Jason would see to it she got one.

There is much that is enigmatic about Gertrude. She briefly sets aside her differences with Kathleen once a year, at the most appropriate time to be assertively Christian. A large tin of marzipan or glacéed fruitcake is posted to Hackberry Hill in early December with a card inscribed, "Merry Christmas and Best Wishes for the New Year, From Mr. and Mrs. Jason Howard III and Miss Lola Holloway." She includes sachet pillows or Coty's talcum powder for Kathleen, suspenders or knickers for the boys (she guesses at sizes), and work gloves or cotton handkerchiefs (not linen, and never monogrammed) for George. Gertrude tucks in a note containing the highlights of the previous year, abundantly capitalized: "Jason was Elected to the Vestry for the Fourth Time; Lola was

Valedictorian of her Graduating Class and Chosen by her Peers to Reign as Maypole Queen; Gertrude was Awarded two Blue Ribbons in the Rosarian Division of the Horticulture Fair and Elected Vice-President of the Bluestockings."

Kathleen retaliates with a splintery crate of pecans, which, as Gertrude pointed out the first time, is not entirely a present, since the orchard belongs also to her and Lola. She added, "But one should never look a gift horse in the mouth."

Jason laughed. "I've never heard you use that country expression before, my dear."

She's never used it again.

Although Kathleen does not write to them, an envelope addressed to Jason in penciled, labored handwriting arrives every few months from Hackberry Hill. Dinner is under way before he announces casually, "George Craven has sent a report." He takes a folded sheet of blue-lined tablet paper from a vest pocket, opens it, and peers at it through steel-rimmed spectacles, as though searching for something he might have missed on the first reading. Satisfied that is not the case, he refolds the paper and tucks it back inside the pocket. "Everything seems in order. As usual, there is no profit to be divided. George extends his and Kathleen's best wishes to all of us."

The clink of silver and crystal that came to a stop with the name of George Craven resumes, and Lola pushes the shadowy images away before they get a foothold.

2
Crossings

THEY HAVE NOT ENCOUNTERED another motorized vehicle since leaving the city limits of Felder almost an hour ago, although several animal-powered conveyances have moved deferentially to the side for them. There has to be some practical purpose for this visit. Is there a prospective buyer for the homeplace, and Jason wants to inspect the property before setting a price? Or has George bungled things to such an extent it's time for an inspection?

Whatever the reason, Gertrude would have tried to beg off. Jason may have bribed her with the latest model Victrola, which plays two-sided discs, or the marvelous, newfangled Kelvinator home refrigerator. Or perhaps he simply put his foot down and overruled her, which every now and then he does. Not having brothers or sisters, he has never understood how siblings can bear not to love each other unconditionally.

As soon as the destination is revealed, a Pandora's box of Lola's earliest history—with its good parts and what Gertrude dismissively refers to as "the rest"—begins to creep back in friendly fragments, like unruly dogs begging for another chance to be housebroken. She closes her eyes, not to nap as Gertrude advised, but to give the jumble of memory and imagination free rein by providing a blank projection screen. After years of not permitting her thoughts to dwell on there and then, it's as though she is viewing faded glass slides through a new stereopticon. The doctor's phaeton, nimble as a dragonfly, spins along the narrow road that links his land and theirs and both to the highway. She sits beside him on the narrow, leather-padded bench seat. He's giving her a ride home from school, and they're singing a jubilant song. The scene shifts abruptly to another day. She enters the house alone, wondering what mood she will encounter. The first thing to catch her eye is Grandmother's blue-and-white spatter-ware bowl. Though Mama's frequent use of the word *poverty* has made Lola think a beast lurks just beyond the door, that tub-sized vessel heaped with tomatoes, corn in the husk, okra, crookneck squash, purple eggplant, pole beans, and fat yellow onions—or, in the cooler months, pecans, black walnuts, chestnuts, scaly-barked hickory nuts, pears, crab apples, winter greens, and sweet potatoes—is reassurance they won't starve. Though Mama's hazy image isn't fleshed out, the swishing of her skirt sounds like paper being wadded up to toss into the fireplace. *Stop*, Lola commands, *this gate's been latched too long*. If she cannot recall her mother's face, how will she discern what is real? Best to focus this daydream on Rob, whose features Lola knows as well as her own.

But it's Rhoda, not Rob, who emerges from the shadows and pushes aside a curtain of weeping willow branches that droop like an upended mop over the millpond. They are on the bank. Rhoda swings her, by her arms, into the water. Minnows the color of the water and tadpoles the size of shotgun pellets slither around her. Water blips up her nose painfully. She can't touch bottom; her arms and legs flail like marionettes operated by someone else. She wonders, *Am I drowning?*

"Of course not. Didn't I promise not to let you drown? Make believe you're a puppy, Lo."

She knows nothing about puppies—Mama doesn't like dogs because they bark and bite, suck eggs, and kill chickens. At the moment she thinks she is about to disappear forever, Rhoda hauls her out with a stalk of sugarcane and bestows nonchalant praise. "Excellent! Now you can dog-paddle with the best of them. Next, I'll teach you the sidestroke."

Her mother went to her grave not knowing Lola could swim. Learning to survive in the water would have been a serious, punishable infraction of one of her rigid rules: Lola was never to go near the pond and the ponderous wheel. Had the transgression been discovered, her palms would have been rapped with a ruler. Rhoda would have received worse punishment, as Lola had been assigned to her. The nearest in age though nine years older, this sister was determined to drill some notion of self-reliance into Lola. When Lola dashed onto the highway chasing a rabbit, Rhoda took her behind the barn and forced her to take a good look at a split-down-the-middle hog that was suspended head-down from a pole strung between two maple trees, its blood draining into a bucket. One of the men who were never there long enough for the girls to have to learn their names would hack chunks from the vat-scalded carcass for bacon, ham roasts, spare ribs, and chops. The lips, snout, eyelids, and ears would be ground into sausage. The tasty nuggets in fried cornbread would be the pig's intestines. Mama would scramble its brains with eggs for a special supper, and the dainty little feet would be pickled in brine and sold at the market as a delicacy. Rhoda explained, matter-of-factly, that if she got in the way of flying hooves and wheels, she would look like that hog. But at least, she assured Lola, she wouldn't be eaten.

The only way to glimpse anything of the world beyond their noses was from high up in a tree. Rhoda taught her the right way to climb. "Pretend you're a monkey. Test each branch to be sure it won't give under your weight. And never look down." When Lola cracked her collarbone in a fall from the hackberry tree that Grandfather renamed the town for, Rhoda said, "Damnation, Lolabut. I told you not to look down."

"I didn't until I started to fall." Although the pain was worse than any she'd had before, she was too scared to cry. A lopsided shoulder couldn't be hidden from Mama.

Dr. Whitney overlapped wide strips of sticky tape around her chest and across the hurt shoulder while she sat on his lap and gazed upon his full head of hair that was the color of chewing tobacco and wished he were her father instead of the coughing stranger who, to spare the family his germs, kept mainly to himself in the room off the kitchen. She told Mama she had climbed the tree without Rhoda's knowledge, but Rhoda got a pear-branch switching anyway, for letting Lola out of her sight. Rhoda's legs were crisscrossed with red stripes that took more than a week to heal.

At the beginning of that summer, Lola's last in Hackberry Hill, she was almost six; Rhoda was fifteen. Gertrude was nineteen, on the cusp of marriage to a man ten years her senior; Kathleen was seventeen and would be married soon herself, though she didn't know it then.

Lola tried to stay attached to Rhoda even when it wasn't necessary. She got foot blisters from walking three miles to the Gypsy camp where Rhoda traded rabbit tobacco to have their fortunes told with a greasy deck of cards. Lola's was that she would see the world before she settled down; Rhoda's was that she would become a dutiful mother. Rhoda said the woman had their futures mixed up, and that they should therefore swap. Though she would have given Rhoda her right arm, Lola refused to exchange her future. Another time, they slipped off to Turtle Creek on a Sunday afternoon so Rhoda could get herself baptized. But Lola didn't tag along when Rhoda sneaked out one night a few months before she ran away. From a window of the room they shared, Rhoda accessed the tree that Lola had fallen from. Yes, it was the tree that Grandfather had renamed the town for, which in Rhoda's opinion was a grievous sin. Rhoda was in her bed when Lola awoke the next morning. Lola thought—or pretended to think, because she could never tell on her and didn't want the burden of knowing—that she had dreamt her sister's escape.

✹

Jason has left the main road to follow a crudely painted sign: "Hatchet Creek Ferry half a mile straight ahead." The offshoot turns out to be anything but straight. It winds past tall, queenly trees with orbicular, silver-bottomed leaves that rustle like crisp paper bills. There was a copse of these cottonwoods on the Indian knoll that Rhoda proclaimed was hallowed ground. In a strong wind, they would sway like dancers.

They have coasted almost to the edge of the creek. Jason economizes on fuel by not activating the pedal on downhill slants. Now, he's out of the car, flashing his cigarette case, about to share a smoke with the taciturn ferry operator. Lola wishes she could join them. Jason is aware that she lights up on occasion. Not in Gertrude's presence, of course. Actually, not in his presence either, though she expects that to change in the near future. Her brother-in-law is a progressive-minded man who's in favor of women's equality as long as his own creature comforts aren't threatened. He agrees with Lola that women should have the right to vote, but he hasn't reached her level of indignation that after years and years of suffragism, the battle is not yet won.

Gertrude whispers to Lola that the barge doesn't look substantial enough to carry a motorcar as heavy as this one.

"The distance across doesn't appear to be much over a hundred feet," Lola whispers back. "That fellow is giving the matter careful consideration. He's sizing up the automobile as though it's a woman."

"He looks as though he's sure of his capabilities with women, so I

27

suppose we can trust him to know the capabilities of his conveyance."

"That's the spirit." Lola cherishes such rare glimpses of Tru's quirky sense of humor, which she never realized the other had when they lived in Hackberry Hill. It amazes Lola now how little she knew Tru then.

The man and his son—a youth who gazes at Lola with such lust she feels she should acknowledge the homage—roll the car onto the flat-boat. Gertrude is nervous about remaining in the car, so Jason escorts his charges to a bolted-down, straight-backed, uncomfortable oak bench with a crude cross motif carved on each side.

"Traveling by church pew should be a divine experience," he quips softly.

"Not if it's stolen goods." Gertrude doesn't bother to lower her voice.

Jason doesn't let her have the last word. "Think of it as being sal-vaged, which our Maker would approve of, being in the salvage busi-ness Himself."

Propelled by the current and a cable, the craft begins to float slowly along a diagonal route. To Jason, this is high adventure; he strides about asking questions, nods vigorously at the answers. One of the men prods the water with a pole, as though the tranquil waterway is a sluggish beast of burden. The barge's surface is less than a foot above water level. As the craft gains momentum, the women's shoes and the hem of Gertrude's duster are spattered. "I can swim well enough to save both of us," Lola tells her. "We're not crossing an ocean."

"It's a strange body of water nevertheless."

"Not so strange. This part of Hatchet Creek resembles Turtle Creek, which spawned our pond. According to Rob, who's fished in lots of them, Alabama creeks are like families with so many double first cousins they're hard to tell apart. He says Georgia streams have a characteristic look, too. Remember how Mama used to say that when she crossed the state line into Alabama, the sky became a paler blue, the pines had droopier needles, and the buzzards that congregated on fences had scrawnier necks than any she'd seen in Georgia?" Lola thus reveals that her bottled-up memory has popped its cork.

Gertrude sighs with reproach or resignation or sadness. "I don't recall our mother ever saying anything of the kind."

As they near the opposite bank, something flashes through the trees. A deer—but for a second, Lola could swear it's Rhoda.

After showing her how to climb between the strands of the barbed-wire fence that separated their meadow from the church graveyard, Rhoda introduced Lola to David and Dwight, their brothers whose brief sojourns on earth had occurred in the interval between Rhoda's birth and Lola's.

"I kissed each one before the coffin lid was closed and nailed in place. Both times, it was like kissing statues. Their faces were cold and hard, where before they had been soft as pillows." Rhoda pressed her lips on the stone face of the fat-cheeked cherub, already missing part of its nose, that topped David's tombstone. When she kissed the hard little rump of the lamb that marked Dwight's grave, Lola laughed, and was reprimanded: "It's not wise to make fun of the dead." She talked to all the kin who were buried there, and also for some of them, such as Grandfather, who was represented by a tall granite obelisk. "He didn't fear anybody, not even God Almighty," Rhoda said. "But once he crossed over, he saw the error of his arrogant ways and repented."

"Wasn't it too late?" Lola asked.

"There's a short grace period right after you die in which you get a chance to say what you're sorry for and have your sins washed away." Rhoda believed he was especially contrite about one of his compulsive actions. As county justice and postmaster in the late 1860s, Grandfather had decided to change the name of the village, then called Sehoy. He reasoned that the map of Alabama was dotted with too many words from the Muskogee language, whose practitioners had been moved to

29

Oklahoma three decades earlier. He intended his English surname to become the town's new title, but his friend and neighbor, the old Dr. Whitney, claimed his forebears had arrived on this frontier a few years earlier than the Holloways. Why not call it Whitneyville? Grandfather's response was that people would think the town was named for the Yankee credited with solely inventing the cotton gin (though there was evidence to the contrary). Rhoda had heard the younger Dr. Whitney and their own papa, Rayford Holloway, reminisce about how Grandfather then picked the name of a tree that grew close to his house— an ugly tree with a warty trunk, messy berries, and a dense mass of asymmetrical, wedge-shaped leaves—"in appreciation of the bountiful shade it provides for my afternoon naps." Papa said *Hill* was tacked on to *Hackberry* for alliteration; Grandfather considered himself something of a poet, as well as something of a historian. Lola and Rhoda eavesdropped as Papa described his father to Jason as "one hell of a man. Although some were of the opinion he was a first class son of a bitch." Minutes before, Jason had asked for Gertrude's hand in marriage. Having granted that request, Papa decided he could be himself around the man who would be his son-in-law. And being himself included the use of salty language.

"Why does he want her hand?" Lola asked.

"That's an expression. He knows the rest of her comes with it."

Shortly before she left, Rhoda reminded Lola that David and Dwight were still among them. They didn't speak through her because they didn't live long enough to learn to talk. "They've risen to another level and have sprouted wings. You mustn't be afraid of them. They're just curious about the family they might have grown up in. So if you ever get to where you can see them, act as though it's perfectly natural, which it is."

She explained that the only way Lola could expect to see angels or ghosts was to cultivate sight ability. Lola decided that would not be one of her goals. She wouldn't mind an occasional glimpse of the brothers, but she didn't care to see large, dark shapes on the walls or hear the thump of Grandfather's walking stick on the stairs or smell coffee when it wasn't being made, as Rhoda did.

Kathleen said Rhoda was a fanciful liar and Lola was the only one who paid her a whit of attention. "She's going straight to h-e-double-l."

"Then I'll go there with her." Lola could not imagine life, or an afterlife, without Rhoda. And she liked hearing about the baby brothers, even if it was mostly fabrication.

"David has forgiven me for giving him the measles, but Mama never will," Rhoda said. "In her mind, I killed him."

"Mama would never think such a thing. She knows you couldn't help it if someone caught your measles."

"She's meaner to me than to the rest of you."

There was nothing Lola could say to that, because it was true.

In the amber haze of waning afternoon, the ferry has unloaded its passengers and their automobile. Back on the highway, Jason keeps both hands on the wooden steering wheel, as Gertrude prefers, and whistles a tune from *The Mikado*. He's anxious to get past the uninhabited countryside that lulls Lola with its monotony. When her mind becomes blank again, Rhoda returns to reconstruct a picnic.

Mama was frugal with her White Leghorn hens' thin-shelled eggs, which could be sold at market. The family dined on omelets made with wild duck eggs Rhoda gathered on the tiny island. On this occasion, she had furtively hard-cooked a half-dozen of the prized domestic variety and restuffed the halves with a mixture of mashed yolks and artichoke-root relish that had been a Christmas gift from a Temperance Society lady. Such scheming usually got Rhoda in trouble. When Mama discovered the relish had been opened without her authorization, she would know who the culprit was, and Rhoda's palms would be stung with lashes from the wooden yardstick that hung on a nail in the pantry.

They sat on the flat marble tablet over Grandmother's grave. Lola's only memory of the woman was when she was laid out for viewing, her eyelids weighted with silver coins to keep them closed, her hands with their twine-like veins crossed over her chest. Grandmother hadn't departed willingly. Her death rattle had gone on for four days. "There was an argument over whether to bury her with her wedding band or take it off her finger before the casket was closed," Rhoda said. "Mama was for leaving it on, but Papa said gold was too valuable to bury. Since the corpse was his mother, he got the final say. The ring came off."

"Where is it now?"

"No telling. Papa probably lost it in a game of chance when he was off on a toot."

"He wouldn't go off on a toot."

"Sure he would." Rhoda's derision rang like a bell. "He used to leave for a week or more at a time before you were born. His illness is what keeps him home now."

"You make him sound bad."

"Well, I didn't mean to. Lola"—now and then, Rhoda used her real name, rather than some alteration—"promise you will not repeat what I am about to tell you."

Lola crossed her heart and hoped to die.

"You and I were not meant for this family. I was supposed to go to a place far away from here, where it snows half the year. I've seen that snow in my dreams. Up close, it's like sugar. From a distance, it looks like whipped cream."

"Was I supposed to go there, too?"

"I don't believe so, Lo." Rhoda sucked the juice from a stalk of bitterweed, then spat it out. "It stands to reason you were meant to go to the doctor's house, because his wife had the whole church praying about her empty womb, and Mama wasn't asking God to send her another baby."

Rhoda had seen cows calve and had witnessed Lola's advent into the world, as well as the births of the doomed male infants. She'd been with Mama to deliver babies. Gertrude and Kathleen were never chosen to accompany Mama on her midwife excursions into the backwoods, nor did they wish to be. Mama's price for delivering, which she waived in cases of extreme poverty, was a fifty-cent piece or a couple of jars of honey; the Holloways didn't keep bees. Despite Rhoda's firsthand knowledge of how babies came into the world, the power of myth was convincing enough for Lola; the blue crane that glided aloofly over the pond had dropped Rhoda, then her, down the wrong chimney.

If she had Peter Whitney for a father, Lola could have her own Red Goose real leather button-ups and not have to wear scuffed shoes handed down by one or more of her sisters. After Rhoda told her she was supposed to be his child, whenever Lola saw the doctor's buggy, she would see herself sitting up there beside him. He would enjoy having a young daughter to keep him company on his rounds, especially one who was as eager to please as she would be.

For all her talk of celestial beings and the afterlife, Rhoda did not worry about what God thought of her. When Lola peeked during church prayers, Rhoda's face would be turned toward the nearest window as she strained to see through a murky pane of rainbow glass. She wasn't looking heavenward, but toward the distant mountains she was determined to go beyond someday. On one occasion during the offertory hymn, she hurried out behind the stewards with the collection plates, her hand over her mouth as though she might regurgitate. When church let out, Rhoda and a couple of boys were in the cemetery smoking rabbit tobacco. For punishment, she was tied by her hands to Mama's tall bedpost until supper.

No one in the family but Lola knew that Rhoda sold the weed, after curing and drying the leaves from the patch that flourished behind the barn; she had pocketed four wooden nickels from those boys. Not that she had much time for commerce. Her worst chores were scouring the chamber pots and scrubbing the privy bench; the one she least objected to was churning. She developed strong shoulders from pushing the dasher up and down as the cream thickened into clabber. Lola's first assignment was to press pats of freshly churned butter from a tin mold. When she could turn out tiny yellow mounds with the flower design crisply defined, she was promoted to setting the table and cutting quarter-sized rounds from dough Gertrude had put through the ringer of the beaten-biscuit board. Kathleen chopped and hauled in wood for the stove and fireplaces, helped with the washing and ironing, and milked the cow. Rhoda wished she could milk, so she could talk to the cow and learn its secrets, but Mama wouldn't allow any swapping of chores. Before she escaped—first to college, then to the haven of marriage—Gertrude set the table, assisted with the cooking, feather-dusted, tidied, and swept. Her most unpleasant assignment involved reaching under the warm bottoms of disgruntled hens. She preferred the discomfort of a clothespin clamped on her nose and Kathleen's accompanying ridicule to the stench of the chicken coop. Now, the Howards' Felder neighbors keep chickens, but Gertrude has washed eggs and dressed hens delivered to the back door.

Mama protected her oldest daughter from the sun as well as from hard work, as she believed a peaches-and-cream complexion, along with Gertrude's sweet disposition and her aura of having led a sheltered existence, would attract a suitor of good breeding and high moral character, who would provide her with a gentler way of life. Sure enough, it happened. Mama did not plan Kathleen's, Rhoda's, or Lola's futures. As to whether she would have got around to them if circumstances hadn't interfered, Lola prefers to give her the benefit of the doubt.

Rhoda didn't like her name, which came from an aunt of Papa's who died on the way to Texas in a covered-wagon brigade. The rest of the girls were named for closer connections. Gertrude was called after Mama's mother, who went to her grave without seeing her Alabama grandchildren. Kathleen was for Papa's mother, Miss Kitty. Rhoda said Mama flaunted superstition to name her last daughter for her own little sister, who had succumbed to diphtheria after less than three years on earth; according to Rhoda, that Lola might have come for her namesake when she reached the same age. Rhoda liked flower names. She planned to change hers when she was old enough to Rhododendron, after the wild shrub that looked like blobs of bright pink paint against the pale green of springtime woods. After swimming, they would spread their petticoats on rhododendron bushes to dry. When they put those garments back on, they would peel off the wet bloomers and lay them out. Not even Rhoda dared to swim buck naked, as boys did. "You could change your name to Gladiola," she suggested. "That sounds better than Lola."

By this time, Lola had learned to cultivate her own streak of stubbornness and her own fictions. "Baby Lola might be my guardian angel. I don't want to hurt her feelings."

"She can't be your angel. She's buried in Georgia, and angels, like ghosts, can't cross state lines," Rhoda said.

"How do you know?"

"Mine told me so."

"What's your angel's name?"

"It's confidential. That means it's not for you to know."

Rhoda and Lola bickered good-naturedly, but Rhoda and Kathleen had altercations that went from hair pulling to biting to wrestling, all executed in complete silence, as though they were trained in mime. At the end of one such episode, when they were spent and calm, Kathleen said, "You're too weird to be from around here. Ever wonder where you came from?"

"Wherever it is, Lola comes from there too," Rhoda retorted. Lola was glad Rhoda didn't tell Kathleen that the long-legged crane had dropped the two of them down a Holloway chimney by mistake, then had taken up residence in a tall pine near the pond to watch over them. Kathleen would have made great fun of that fantasy.

Rhoda's favorite spot was the knoll at the back of the cleared land, where Indian arrowheads and spear points were scattered about like rocks. Papa told her the place was a tribal burial mound. Rhoda dug up a bone and subsequently decided it had been part of someone's arm, as her arm started to throb and didn't stop until she reburied the relic. The rise provided a view of the house and the privy, both of which got a coat of whitewash every other year; the carriage house and the four-crib barn were stained the color of dried blood. The chicken coop and the tin-roofed cotton gin had weathered to a pigeon color. From this vantage point, the pond and the falls were hidden, and the stone mill, its cypress wheel clinging to one side like a folded wing, seemed distant, of another landscape.

"From here, it looks like we're rich as the Whitneys'," Lola said.

"Get that notion out of your head," Rhoda retorted. "We're what's known as land-poor, which is a notch above being sure-enough poor."

Behind them were woods that had the underbrush burned off every few years in a blaze like the picture of hellfire in Grandfather's Bible and the church with the bell steeple that Rhoda said Lola must climb on her seventh birthday. But they were both gone before that date came.

Standing on tiptoe and facing another direction, Lola could see the doctor's house, which reminded her of a picture in a nursery-rhyme book that Rhoda wouldn't read aloud because she'd rather make up stories than recite nonsense. Before she left, Rhoda taught Lola to read and do simple sums, so she wouldn't have to waste a year at the start of her formal education. As it turned out, Rhoda wasn't around to take her to school the first day, so it was up to Lola to convince the schoolmaster that she should be put up to second grade.

The unknown world beyond the horizon hadn't begun to tantalize her as it did Rhoda. But that is not to say Lola was complacently homebound. She stayed on tiptoe mentally, poised for flight from a nameless danger at any moment. The atmosphere of unease, of tension at the boiling point, was as palpable in that house as the haze of smoke that snaked from the wood stove through the doorways.

The hollow-eyed man in the room behind the kitchen was a caricature of the vibrant father her sisters had known. Mama's wrath could erupt with the suddenness of a tornado. Her hand would slap a face, then calmly resume its stitching or kneading. All of them—even Gertrude on rare occasions—caught the force of Mama's disapproval or of some anger they never intended to spark. Rhoda provoked her the most. Despite that clash of will and temperament, Rhoda told Lola more than once she admired their mother for having risen above crushing disappointments—marriage to a man of misfortune and the loss of male offspring who could have been put to better use than daughters. After Papa died, Mama bustled about with renewed energy, supervising the older girls' activities and those of George and the men she hired to work a week or less at a time. The bravado didn't last long. While Rhoda was making her plans to escape forever, Mama was about to take wing in her own way.

Gertrude's engagement was the most auspicious event of the period when Lola awoke each day knowing Papa was not going to get well (though that fact was never mentioned). The gloomy atmosphere was temporarily dispelled when her firstborn fulfilled Mama's ambition by bringing home a man who always dressed as though it were Sunday.

The first time Lola saw him, Jason came briskly down the steps of a train. Then, with the kind of gallantry she'd not yet come across even in books, he assisted Gertrude in her descent. Lola and Mama clutched each other's hands tightly as they watched this impressive sight.

Lola wished they had come to meet Gertrude and her man in a trim buggy like the doctor's, not in a lumbering, two-bench contraption harnessed to a pair of heavy-footed draft horses named by Papa, to Mama's consternation, Demon Rum and Whiskey. It was a school day, so Rhoda and Kathleen were unavailable, but Lola pretended she had been chosen over them for the honor of accompanying Mama on this momentous occasion.

Mama had scrimped for years to get Gertrude certified at Peabody, the teachers' college in Nashville, but when the time came, she hadn't accumulated enough money for a semester's tuition. She accepted it as divine intervention that Gertrude's only option for higher education was the normal school in Troy, Alabama. Soon after her arrival there, Gertrude was invited to spend a weekend at a classmate's home in Felder. Jason Howard, who had recently lost his mother (his father having died some years earlier), was invited to tea at the house where Gertrude was visiting. The first time he saw his future wife, he thought she was an angel. Imagine his delight to learn that this lovely, ethereal creature was actually of this earth! He related the anecdote as soon as he introduced himself to Mama and Lola. (Gertrude said later she had every intention of making that presentation but was too dizzy from the train ride to remember her manners.)

Mama touched her hair and fingered the lace fichu at her throat, as though Jason were her beau instead of Gertrude's.

Later, Rhoda said, "Well, stars above. Tru managed to turn coincidence to her advantage. I'd never have figured her for being so crafty."

Lola didn't confide to Rhoda that she had a presentiment the moment she laid eyes on him that this fine specimen of manhood would prove to be her lifeline as well as Gertrude's. Lola sat beside Jason as he drove their buggy back to the house from the station. (Mama asked him to, so she could sit behind with the daughter she'd not seen for some time and had sorely missed.) Lola noted that the competent hands on the reins were smooth and uncallused. At that moment, she resolved to marry someone from the same cut of cloth. Her husband would have a high, dome-shaped forehead and a long, prominent nose, just like the man who would soon be her brother-in-law. (However, as luck would have it, she found Rob, who is movie-star handsome.)

Jason did not want to put off their marriage until Gertrude completed requirements for a teacher's certificate she would never need, and Mama found no fault with that reasoning. Although he preferred his wife to remain in the not overly educated state in which he found her, Jason spurred Lola toward academic achievement. It was his idea that she complete the baccalaureate program with majors in two subjects.

"Now what?" Lola had asked him at the graduation reception last May, brandishing her ribbon-tied roll of sheepskin.

She expected him to say something like, "Now you come home and wait for your young man to return and marry you." In which case, she could counter with, "Let me work for you in the interim."

What he said was, "I've secured a position for you as an instructor in Latin and civics at the Felder High School."

She should have seen it coming. "If I had realized I would end up as a teacher, I wouldn't have studied so hard."

Jason said gently, "Helping others acquire knowledge is a noble occupation. Your life will always be richer because of your having been a serious and inquiring scholar during the formative years. Surely, you realize how very proud we are of you, Lola."

"Then allow me to continue as a serious and inquiring scholar by reading the law under your tutelage."

"Dear girl, that's out of the question. My dog-eat-dog profession is unseemly for a woman." He then repeated, more strongly, "Absolutely out of the question."

Lola's next idea was to sign up with the Red Cross, whereupon Jason gleefully informed her of a new rule that prohibited volunteer service overseas by women who were married or engaged to members of the armed forces. Realizing her resolve to become active with the women's suffrage movement, Jason offered a compromise. He would not object to Lola's being among the banner-bearing marchers on the streets of Felder—though so far they hadn't rallied enough supporters to make an effective showing—but she mustn't expect him to condone her participation in any parade on the avenues of the nation's capital. He feared the Washington suffragettes would follow the Brits' example. For years, those women had chained themselves to railings, refused to pay taxes, staged hunger strikes, even bombed the home of the chancellor of the exchequer. One was killed when she threw herself beneath the king's horse during a derby race. It took such desperate measures to show the men they meant business. Now, finally, British women over the age of thirty had been granted limited franchise. So whenever Jason blustered about what she could and couldn't do within the movement, Lola responded as Gertrude did whenever he threw a roadblock in her path: "We shall see."

Paradoxically, since he does not wish her to make significant decisions without consulting him, Jason has taught Lola the importance of taking a stand. "Not choosing is a choice," he's fond of saying. It was he who decreed she would have the say about where she would live after Mama died. He explained the options. Lola could leave the only home she'd ever known to reside with him and Gertrude in Felder, or she could remain with Kathleen and George in the Hackberry Hill house. After pretending to consider the matter for almost a minute while she silently counted to fifty, Lola declared her preference was to live with him and Gertrude. He probably took that to mean she felt closer to her senior sister than to the second-eldest, but at the time, Lola had no sense of real connectedness with either. She simply knew she could not stay on in a house where she would be constantly reminded of the sibling she had loved with abandon, who had abandoned her.

3
Starts and Stops

WHEN JASON RELATED THE GIST of Dr. Whitney's long-distance call, Gertrude went into her swoon position. One hand flew to her forehead, the other to her chest. At least she remained upright. "Please promise me you won't involve Lola," she said.

"My dear, she's already involved, as are we. The three of us will go today."

"I'm not up to the train ride."

"We'll take the car."

"We could have mechanical failure!"

"Had her checked over thoroughly earlier this week, and she's in great shape." Jason tends to think of his automobile in the feminine gender. He added cajolingly, "Emily Post and her son were the first to motor the Lincoln Highway across the country, from New York to San

Francisco. The esteemed authoress pronounced it a great adventure."

The eyebrows relented; the frown relaxed. Gertrude's mouth curves pleasantly most of the time and quite alluringly on occasion. "How far is it by automobile?"

"Less than seventy miles. We'll be rolling on a regraded route." To anyone but Gertrude, he would have added, "Thanks to Senator Bankhead and the Good Roads Association."

"I'll go if you agree Lola may be spared the ordeal." Like some unskilled lawyers Jason contended with, his wife sometimes acted as though she had bargaining power when she didn't.

"Gertrude, I've made up my mind." When he used that certain tone of voice—not harsh or strident, but calmly authoritative—nine times out of ten, she would capitulate without further protest. "Peter Whitney said he would tell Kathleen and George to expect us sometime in the afternoon. I'll contact the school and ask that Lola be relieved of her duties at noon so she can come home and get some things together."

"Please don't arouse the curiosity of that nosy headmistress. I'll pack for Lola. Couldn't we pick her up at the regular dismissal time and leave from there?" Usually the picture of poise, Gertrude was thoroughly agitated now; a pulse in her throat fluttered as it does at the peak moment in their lovemaking.

Thinking of the heady pleasure she seldom denied him, Jason agreed to this request. "Of course. Starting out at three o'clock is later than I would like, but we should make Hackberry Hill before dark." He couldn't resist adding, "You might pray that we do so."

Gertrude said tartly, "I'll pray the crisis dissolves before we arrive and that this excursion will be nothing more than a wild goose chase." She tucked a stray wisp into her smoothly rolled topknot. "That is not a country expression, by the way. Elizabeth Hawke used 'wild goose chase' in a paper she presented to the Bluestockings."

"Ah, yes. Mrs. Hawke should know the habits of geese."

42

The little joke was wasted. Gertrude informed him, archly, that her friend was the most literary member of that elite group.

Jason's own prayer is that Lola not disintegrate as she did several weeks ago when he told her the Castlemans had been notified that their son had been wounded in action. Lola was furious that she, who was "closer to Rob than anyone else in the whole damned world," hadn't received a telegram from the War Department, but had to learn of it thirdhand. She had reason to be upset, so he didn't reprimand her for swearing, although he wished she hadn't cut loose like that near an open window.

When Lola came to live with them, she had tried to please, to measure up to the standards Gertrude set for her. The colorful but unacceptable exclamations disappeared along with the scabs on her elbows and knees. For the first year or so, she was the perfect youngster. Then, without warning, the plucky self-reliance dissolved into near infantile dependence, and she began to have insomnia and nightmares. The physician diagnosed the condition as "unnatural depression." The argument could be made that depression in a child is always unnatural. Childhood should be the happiest of times; Jason's own certainly was. He was surprised to hear Gertrude inform the doctor that her own serenity was due to a fortunate spell of amnesia that simply erased her early years. She then asked the aghast fellow for a panacea that would banish Lola's "unsettling recollection," which, Gertrude attested, had attained "photographic proportions." It was the most intellectual-sounding pronouncement Jason had ever heard her make.

According to the pharmacist, the prescription contained nothing other than sugar, talc, aspirin, and dye. Eventually, Gertrude took matters into her own hands. Jason has never asked how she exorcised their ward's demons, but once the black cloud lifted, Lola became the delightful, sunny creature she was meant to be. Except for an occasional, short-lived outburst, the girl has remained on that even keel. What awaits them today in Hackberry Hill may cause her some emotional turbulence, but there's no way out of it. Jason wishes there were an option, that his youngest sister-in-law might be spared whatever awaits them. But at twenty-one, Lola is old enough to take these lumps with the rest of the family.

Now that she has joined the ranks of wage earners, Lola insists on paying her room and board. Jason will not deny her such a character-building gesture, although he would prefer not to be compensated financially for the continuation of her vitalizing presence in his house. A year from now, Lola will be in her own domicile. As a wedding gift, Robert Castleman's father intends to buy the couple an electrified bungalow in Clover Dell, Felder's fashionable new extension, where the streets are canals of mud.

The first time he saw her, Jason was captivated by the child who cupped her hand near his ear and whispered so her mother and Gertrude wouldn't hear, "Godamighty, Mr. Howard, that's one humdinger of a necktie." Later that same day, in the garden adjoining the Holloway house, he had a first glimpse of his future wife's other siblings as they were absorbed in hanging a birdhouse. At his approach, Kathleen ducked her head, too self-conscious to speak, but Rhoda extended a hand for him to shake, as though meeting someone wasn't the least bit out of the ordinary for her.

In the company of her sisters, Gertrude seemed to shift away from him. None of the four resembled another particularly, and except for Lola's obvious attachment to Rhoda, they were not affectionately close. Yet the nexus was obvious to him: they were links in a chain. At dinner that evening, this quartet of nymphs appeared to regard Jason with a singular disdain—because he was an outsider, or a man, or both.

The matriarch was formidable. Miss Lucy ordered her daughters about as though they were hired staff. Although Rayford Holloway's persona was appropriately that of congenial country squire, Jason detected in him a penchant for self-indulgence. Apparently, the man had enjoyed his invalidism—being doted on by his wife and daughters—for some time before the lung disease was advanced enough to sap him.

When Jason returned to Hackberry Hill to be married, he was met at the station by George Craven, Lucy Holloway's employee who would also become a Holloway son-in-law, although Jason had no idea George was courting Kathleen (*courting* being a euphemism for what the fellow was really up to). As they rounded the curve toward the house, Jason cast an admiring glance toward the impressive stone structure that housed the family's gristmill—and encountered a startling sight. Rhoda was attached to the waterwheel. "Good God. Isn't that dangerous?" he asked his companion.

George sighed. "It is if her mama catches her at it."

Suddenly, the girl leapt into the pond, swam a few strokes, then waded the rest of the short distance to the bank. She must have had something on, though she appeared not to. A dark, wavy mane of unbound hair hung about her face and shoulders like a cloak. As she gazed brazenly at them, Jason had the impression he could have his way with the girl. Not that he ever had a lascivious thought about Rhoda Holloway. Quite the contrary. He found her almost boyish physique and bold demeanor more than a little off-putting. And of course, he was enthralled with Gertrude; the promise of that luminous flesh rendered him impervious to other physical attraction.

It had been apparent from his initial visit that Rhoda was cut off from the well of maternal affection. After their marriage, Jason asked Gertrude why Miss Lucy disliked one of her daughters. She assured him he was mistaken; her mother was especially tolerant of Rhoda, considering the latter's "antics."

"Such as?" Jason pressed, assuming she meant mischief of the nature he had witnessed.

Gertrude declined to be specific. "Rhoda is an embarrassment to

Mama. I hope you won't consider me disrespectful, but I don't care to discuss my family's problems and shortcomings with you."

"Damn it." Jason swore for the first time in the presence of his wife. "I'm in the family now."

"The fact is, Jason, although you are my husband in the eyes of God and man, you are not and never will be my blood kin." She took a deep breath and continued. "As a matter of fact, neither is Rhoda. That she came to our family as a foundling was never spoken of again after the day she arrived. Kathleen was quite young at the time, and Lola hadn't been born, so they don't know. It's one of the few memories that survive from my childhood."

Jason was touched that Gertrude shared this information with him. Shortly thereafter, Rhoda ran away from home, and Gertrude asked him not to tell it about that she had a sister whose whereabouts were unknown. He certainly didn't, but as the senior male connection of the Holloway family, the squire having died before Jason married the eldest daughter, he considered it his duty to try to find the girl. A discreetly worded plea was posted at intervals over the next several years in metropolitan newspapers: "R. H. from Alabama: Please get in touch with your brother-in-law, J. H. Your sisters G., K., and L. love you and miss you very much." Neither this notice nor the one of Lucy Holloway's demise that Jason placed in Montgomery, Birmingham, Atlanta, Savannah, Columbus, Nashville, Chattanooga, and Memphis periodicals produced any results.

In retrospect, it occurs to him now that he should have offered to take Rhoda in when he married Gertrude. Subconsciously, he must have feared that adolescent female would cause tension in his new household. With Lola, the situation was different. After Lucy Holloway died, it never occurred to Jason Howard not to extend to his youngest sister-in-law the shelter of his home and heart. By that time, Rhoda had run away.

Peter Whitney was cryptic this morning in relaying information that would travel over wires and through headphones: "I wanted to alert you that significant evidence has turned up here regarding a missing person." Despite the static, Jason sensed a ripple of emotion in the voice at the other end, which he found curious; as a physician of mature years, Whitney should be an old hand at conveying bad news. Jason inferred immediately that the missing person was Rhoda Holloway, and that she was dead or in some terrible trouble, neither of which should be discussed over the wires. He asked no questions and assured the doctor they would come to Hackberry Hill right away. Gertrude regards notoriety as she would the bubonic plague, so Jason must do his best to keep any family scandal, if it comes to that, out of the newspapers.

Driving in flat, uncongested territory requires minimal mental concentration. He could spend this time silently arguing both sides of a pending litigation. *Oh, God in heaven, is that sizzling coming from beneath the bonnet, or from a swarm of cicadas?* Alas, it's not the latter. He presses the clutch and brake pedals too quickly while simultaneously turning the steering wheel. As the car jerks to a halt, Gertrude bounces a bit. But she doesn't comment.

Lola says, as though she's been asleep, "Have we hit something?"

"No. I'll just have a look at the engine."

The engine looks as he thought it would: thirsty. Jason checks the running-board kit. He had the red and white containers—gasoline and oil—replenished this morning. He would have thought the fellow would have the courtesy to fill the blue one with water. "Gertrude, did you include a bottle of water in that hamper?"

"No, but there's sugared tea. Will that do?"

As he mutters a string of oaths not fit for ladies' ears, his wife presses her hands over hers. From the back seat comes the joyful spontaneity of Lola's laughter. Then, realizing the seriousness of their plight, she offers to hike back to a farmhouse they've just passed. Jason must quickly decide what's the right thing. If he goes, the women will be left in a stranded vehicle without male protection. The alternative is for him to stay with Gertrude and send Lola.

He hands her the canister and a dollar bill. "Offer the money, but don't force it. People like to help other people out." He watches her start off briskly down the road. It's only a hundred yards, give or take a few. Then Gertrude hands him her opera glasses, which heaven only knows why she brought today, if not for this very purpose. For one crystallized moment, Jason is overwhelmed with love for these females God has brought into his life. Gertrude has made it possible for him to keep Lola in his sights as the girl climbs the steps to the rickety porch of a house that's never seen paint. But the five minutes she disappears from view—presumably, she's been invited inside—seem like an hour. Lola is far too outgoing and trusting for her own good.

She thrusts the thing toward him as though she can't wait to be rid of it. "I'm glad we don't have to drink it. This water was hauled from a well that a woman fell headfirst into and drowned. She was under the influence of alcohol at the time."

"That isn't humorous," Gertrude says.

"No, it's not," Lola agrees. "It's downright sad."

Jason doesn't ask whether she's telling the truth. "Did whoever gave you the water take the money?"

She retrieves the folded bill from a pocket and gives it back to him. "Nobody was at home. I helped myself, and as I leaned over that well to lower the bucket, I thought how easy it would be to fall in, down, down, down, headfirst—"

"Damn it to hell, I should have gone myself."

"You should have seen to the water supply before we left," Gertrude says reasonably. "Then no one would have been in danger of drowning in a well. At least, not any of us."

A few uneventful miles later, Lola opens the hamper and finds small plates, napkins, and a tray of watercress sandwiches. The dark green leaves on the small rounds of buttered bread look like clover and will taste of the riverbanks where the cress flourishes. A capped jug and glass cups are also in the wicker carryall that's stashed beneath the jump seat. She passes the tray and two plates, with napkins, to Gertrude and asks, "Dare I try to pour while we're moving?"

"Best not. We'll quench our thirst at the next stop."

"Which may as well be now," Jason says. "According to the odometer—a wonderful instrument that is, too—we're almost halfway, at which point I'd planned to take a rest stop." The car comes to a standstill gently this time, like a wound-down toy. The incessant cacophony of insects, birds, and fenced-in cattle takes over when the engine noise ceases. The real countryside is not as subdued and quiet as gilt-framed landscape paintings in hotel and bank lobbies would have you believe.

When the tea party's over, Gertrude and Lola head for the bushes. Despite her hobble skirt, Gertrude sets a brisk pace. Jason stands behind an open door of the car simultaneously relieving himself and smoking a cigarette.

As though shopping for a Christmas tree, Gertrude selects a bell-shaped cedar with ground-touching branches. Lola stands guard while her sister goes first. After much rustling of garments, then a cozy, rainlike sound that lasts for several seconds, then garment rustling in reverse, Gertrude emerges, her face flushed with relief and exertion. Wordlessly, she hands Lola a packet of wiping paper. Gertrude thinks of such amenities.

Lola calls out, while taking her turn behind the bush, "Do you expect to find the old house much changed?"

"I haven't given it any thought." She is determined to play the game of out of sight, out of mind until the last possible minute.

A clump of dandelion weed tickles Lola's most private parts, and she wonders if Gertrude encountered the same sensation.

When Lola emerges, Gertrude remarks, as though the other had protested the idea of interrupting this road trip for such a worthy purpose, "Now, that wasn't so bad, was it?"

"No, indeed. It was thoughtful and considerate of Jason to allow us to relieve our bladders."

Gertrude misses or ignores the sarcasm. "Yes," she sighs. "He is most thoughtful and considerate."

"So are you, dear Tru." That's not sarcasm. As they stroll arm in arm to the car, Lola says, "I hope we never get on real outs with each other."

"For heaven's sake! Of course we won't," Gertrude replies, as though the idea is preposterous. "But I do wish you would remember, with that fine mind of yours, that I don't care to be called 'Tru' in public."

"I'll try. Though as you know, I have a talent for forgetting." Lola's inclination is to add, but she doesn't, "Right now, my fine mind is avidly retrieving all sorts of stuff you insisted I forget."

Jason's head is once again beneath the raised hood. The sight reminds Lola of a cartoon in a salacious book Maggie found in her father's library: A physician is mostly hidden by his female patient's voluminous skirt; the woman's face has a contorted expression; the caption is "Oh . . . OOh . . . OOOH!"

Gertrude and Lola haul themselves into the car without Jason's usual gallant assistance. Moments later, whistling a tune from *Pirates of Penzance*, he starts them off again. Lola can tell from the set of his shoulders and the way he grips the wheel that he's not thrilled to be making this trip. Gertrude is as resigned as a tethered hen who knows her destination is a big black pot. But Lola is buoyant with expectation. Her intuition tells her she's in for a surprise. Maybe Rhoda's come home with a rich husband.

4
Answered Prayers

THE IMAGES CONTINUE TO FLOW in a manageable stream, like the water that trickled from the pump she had to stand on a stool to operate. . . . Before she was born, there were miscarriages and still-births, plus the two male infants who lived long enough to get names. Despite what Rhoda had told her—that having lots of babies wore out a woman's brains, as well as her bones—Lola got up her nerve to ask Mama if she would please have one more. She wanted to move past the onus of being the youngest, which, in her perception, equated with that of runt in a litter of pigs; everybody knew the runt had to suck hind teat. Mama answered firmly, "No, indeed. I am through with all that."

Rhoda said "all that" meant sleeping with Papa. When he decided to become bedridden, Mama moved him out of his own parents' tall four-poster into what had been the servant's quarters behind the kitchen.

According to Rhoda, Grandmother's cook, Elvira Perkins, who lived with them until she died, was one-quarter Creek Indian and the color of egg-plant. She would dip turkey feathers into a silver liquid and paint the parts in their hair to ward off head lice, and she could make fish drunk enough to catch by scattering the pounded root of a plant called devil's shoestring mixed with buckeye powder on the water. Rhoda said Elvira could speak real African mumbo jumbo; Kathleen said Elvira made it up. Mama prepared Elvira for burial, which was in the Holloway family plot, because the woman had no living kin. Rhoda vowed that, someday, she would see to it Elvira got a tombstone.

Mama treated her broken husband with dutiful solicitude. Before breakfast each morning, she changed his leg bandage, replacing the dark-stained cloth strips with clean, boiled ones. Rhoda offered to relieve her of this ritual, but Mama said she would take care of her husband's needs as long as she was able.

At the time, she was sewing Gertrude's bridal gown from linen sheets that had never been unpacked from the trunk she brought with her from Georgia. She soaked the sheets in water tinted with blueing powder to remove the yellow tinge of age from the fabric. The gown had to be pure white or people would talk. She went back to the trunk for a mother-of-pearl comb to fasten to the veil she had made from a lace curtain. Lola watched as she prized up the rusty hinges and raised the domed leather lid, releasing the bitter scent of mothballs. Among the treasures were two almost identical dolls with china heads. "The year before you were born, your papa brought these to Kathleen and Gertrude," Mama said. "You can hold them." She fluffed up their taffeta dresses before placing the dolls in Lola's arms. They were stiff, unpliable. Lola had rag dolls stuffed with sawdust that were easy to love. The best of the lot was a two-headed reversible. One side had a white sock-face and yellow yarn hair. Flip the skirt upside down and there was a black face in a bandanna kerchief, with thread-tacked gold hoops where her ears would be. She didn't care enough for the strange, china-head dolls with their shiny, dead-white faces and tiny feet to be disappointed when Mama placed them back inside the trunk.

Lola asked Mama where Rhoda's doll was.

"She lost it the very day she got it. I would have taken a switch to her for being so irresponsible, but your father said not to." Mama sighed. "He was inclined to be far too lenient on that girl, which is certainly not character-building."

That night, Lola asked Rhoda about the doll Papa brought her. They were in their bedroom, where a window faced the church graveyard. This was the window Dwight and David brushed their duck-sized wings against if closed, and entered on whim if open.

Rhoda's face darkened like an eclipsed moon. "It's a convoluted tale."

Lola shivered with expectation. "That's the kind you tell best."

"Aren't you going to ask what *convoluted* means?"

Lola took a wild guess. "Twisted?"

"Close enough. I may get mad as hell telling it."

"Just remember the convoluted tale is not my fault, and don't take it out on me."

"All right, but don't interrupt. I'll start with when Papa left to go on the trip. He said he had business in Montgomery, and Mama said that was a likely story, meaning it was unlikely, as he hadn't had business in that city since he didn't get reelected to a second term in the legislature. Then he said he was going, by God, and she could like it or lump it. Of course, Mama stopped speaking to him. I begged Papa to take me with him, and I think he might have, except for the fact that she was so peeved. He was gone a whole week. Every night, I prayed he'd come back soon and bring me something. When he returned, he had three cardboard boxes in his valise, each wrapped in pink tissue paper and tied with yellow ribbon." There was enough moonlight from the curtainless window to put a gleam on Rhoda's face. The rise and fall of her voice was mesmerizing as she narrated the story Lola knew wouldn't end happily. "Gertrude was going on twelve. Kathleen was nine. I was seven, the youngest, since David had died and you hadn't been born. That's why you got left out when Papa brought us the dollies, Lo."

Lola experienced the envy she often did where Papa was concerned. Although she hadn't been around when he took his other daughters for rides on his saddle horse or read them poetry by Keats and Shelley, she could imagine. In a wrinkled, dusty suit that he'd worn every day of that week in the busy capital city, Papa rides up their road on his spotted gelding, which had been brought to the train station by a hired man. The wind lifts his wavy, light brown, almost shoulder-length hair. The handles of his valise are looped over the saddle horn, wrapped-up surprises are inside that scuffed bag. His trio of daughters, in pigtails pulled so tight their foreheads look stretched and paper-stiff gingham dresses, cluster about him as he dismounts. . . .

But this was Rhoda's story. "I brought him a glass of lemonade. Gertrude had baked sand tarts, his favorite sweet. Kathleen had done nothing to welcome him home. Guess which one of us got the first present?" She didn't wait for Lola to answer. "It didn't have her name on it, but the second he held a box up, Kat grabbed it. Then he assured Gertrude and me, 'There's one in here for each of you.' Mama was so relieved to see him. I think she feared he intended to leave us for good."

"He would never!"

Rhoda's expression let her know how naive she was. "Papa hasn't left because no woman has tempted him strongly enough. It doesn't mean he hasn't dreamed about going."

Around the time Rhoda was telling this, a black crust the size of a big housefly had appeared on his leg. Ever since Lola could remember, he had coughed with what neither he nor Mama would ever admit was tuberculosis. Lola pictured him as a healthier, younger man who resisted the wiles of those temptresses in Montgomery to return to the females he loved dearly, his own wife and daughters, bearing costly gifts.

"He pulled me onto his lap," Rhoda resumed. "I said 'Damn, Papa, those are mighty fine new suspenders.' He laughed, but Mama sent Gertrude to get the soap to wash out my mouth."

"Tell about Kathleen's present." Lola didn't want Rhoda to get side-tracked recounting the mouth-soaping, which wasn't anything unusual. She herself had barely learned to talk when she was made to lick a bar of soap for saying "horse's ass." No one could imagine where she learned the phrase, not even Rhoda, who told Lola, "That's when I realized you had potential."

"He went shopping in an emporium next to his hotel. Emporium is a fancy word for a fancy store. Say it, Lo."

"Em-po-ri-um."

"It's spelled like it sounds." She waited.

Lola broke it down by letter and got it right the first try.

"Excellent. I do believe you have a talent for spelling, as well as for grasping the sense of a word. Papa bought the dolls on impulse, which means he hadn't planned to."

"I-m-p-u-l-s," Lola said, hoping to elicit more praise.

"Wrong. You left off the e. His intention was to buy Mama something, and he did that first. Her gift was the hair ornament that she's never worn. If he had presented me with it, I'd wear it constantly."

"Why won't she?" Mama would look like a queen with that high comb tucked into the soft pile of silver-streaked black hair that perched on top of her head like a nesting bird.

"It was a way for her to get back at him for taking the trip."

Lola found that amazing. Mama's power was such that she could even punish Papa.

"The Sunday after he came home, Gertrude asked her why she didn't wear her gift to church, and Mama said perhaps she would later, but to this day, she's never placed it in her hair."

"She's found a use for it now. She sewed it to Gertrude's bridal veil."

Lola had told Rhoda something she didn't know.

"Oh, shoot. That comb will be Gertrude's from now on."

"You'll get to wear it, too. She means for the wedding gown and veil to be for all of us, not just for Gertrude."

"Why should I care? I'm never going to marry."

"You will, too," Lola said. "All girls get married." Except the old-maid twins who finished each other's sentences and brought them sugar-dusted teacakes that Mama would throw out later, because the Sullivan sisters were peculiar and didn't have high standards of cleanliness.

Rhoda read her mind, as she frequently did, though Lola never learned to read hers. "You and I are not going to live together forever, like Miss Minnie and Miss Mattie. I look forward to being alone. Anyway, juicy little peach that you are, you'll be married off. In a few years, boys will be panting around you, Lo."

"I don't believe I care to be married. I'll find something else to do with my life."

"Good thinking."

"Please finish the story."

"Where was I?"

"Kathleen tore the tissue paper off—"

"And grabbed the doll out of the box and skipped across the porch with it. I was near to wetting my drawers from anticipation. Papa took the next box out and handed it to Gertrude. I'll say this for Tru, she thanked him before she even looked to see what he'd brought her. In fact, she said, 'Thank you, dearest Papa,' two or three times." Rhoda never missed a chance to mimic Gertrude's measured, precise enunciation, but Gertrude never took Rhoda to task for hurting her feelings. Sometimes, she tried to take up for Rhoda to Mama, although never very vigorously.

Rhoda threw her heavy rope of hair from one side of her neck to the other and hoisted her dress above her knees. "Finally, it was my turn. Papa handed me the last box. I can't describe the pleasure of having a store-wrapped gift to open. I was slow and careful untying the ribbon, because I didn't want to yank a knot in it; I wanted to press it between the pages of a book and keep it forever."

"Do you have it still?"

"No. Don't interrupt again."

"Sorry. You were opening your present."

"I held my breath as I lifted the box lid. The doll that looked out at me from that box was the ugliest thing I'd ever seen." Her voice thickened, as though someone else were articulating through her. "It had on a skimpy cotton dress—not a ruffled, shiny dress like the others—and worst of all, it had a wooden head. I said to Papa, 'Are you sure this one is for me?' and he said, 'Who else would it be for?' But it wasn't his fault that I got it. He didn't know which doll was in which box." She picked up a small rock and tossed it from one hand to the other. "Mama said, 'It's just as well Rhoda got the one with an unbreakable head. She's too rough for a fragile doll.' "

Lola wished she could put her hands over her ears and not hear the rest.

"I took the box out back to the woodpile and placed that ugly creature on the chopping stump. Then I lifted the ax and brought it down across the neck. That little head crunched and rolled off like an apple."

"Was it like killing a chicken?" Lola dreaded the inevitable day when she would be ordered to wring the neck of a live pullet. Kathleen and Rhoda were old hands at it. Even Gertrude had to master that skill.

"Not exactly. Although for a few seconds, it seemed like I had decapitated a real person. I buried both parts on the Indian knoll."

"Did anybody see you?"

"No. They were still listening to Papa tell about his trip. Mama even forgot about washing my mouth out. Later, when Kathleen asked me where my doll was, I told her it was none of her damn business. When Papa asked, I said I had lost it in the woods. He told me not to worry, he'd get me another, but he never did."

Lola was stuporous with sympathy. "How could you bear to watch Gertrude and Kathleen with theirs?"

"As it happened, I didn't have to. Gertrude was past the age to play with dolls, and Kathleen was no more a doll person than I was. Their fancy girls stayed on the chest of drawers between their beds. I admit I thought about taking them out and chopping their heads off, too, but I soon got where I didn't care about them one way or the other. When Mama decided they'd been gathering dust long enough and put them in the trunk, it was as if she had buried them alive. Like finally she was on my side." A wistful smile flickered across her face.

Rhoda was clever enough to invent stories. Lola had to know whether this one had any truth to it. The next day, as Mama bent over her sewing and Lola sat beside her snapping beans into a colander, she asked, "Was Rhoda's doll just like the ones Papa brought Gertrude and Kathleen?"

"I don't recall what hers looked like, only that she was careless enough to lose it right away."

The next question was risky. "Why did Papa go to Montgomery that time?"

"The devil called, and he was foolish enough to listen." Mama bit off a long strand of thread and squinted as she poked it through the needle's eye. "The train fare, the hotel accommodations, meals at fine restaurants, tickets to the opera house, those fancy presents, and heaven knows what else he's never told me about—it all took savings we haven't been able to replace."

"Well, I hope he had himself a fine old time."

Mama snatched a string bean from Lola's hand, broke it into four parts, and hurled them into the bowl. "You'd do well to put your attention on what you're doing, instead of on what's past and doesn't concern you. Keep the pieces uniform in size and pull the strings off as far as they'll go. If there's one thing I can't stand, young lady, it's a pot of messy-looking beans."

She didn't go inside the room with its dank, dark smell of impending death. Except for the vision concocted of him as a younger man, Lola's memory of him is mostly olfactory. Her father's fetor was a blend of tobacco, whiskey, medicine, and slowly rotting flesh.

Papa's funeral took place a month before Gertrude's marriage. Lola was spared the ordeal of having to press her lips to his forehead, as the others did in dutiful farewell kisses. While Mama and her sisters mourned, she felt only guilt for not knowing him well enough to love him as they did, Rhoda most of all. Lola had seen Rhoda ranting, raving, cursing— what Mama called "acting out the devil's bidding"—but she had never seen her shaken as she was that day when Mama came out of Papa's room and said to the four of them, whom she had assembled in the parlor hours before to wait with dread for this very pronouncement, "Your father's struggles are over." Lola, Gertrude, and Kathleen sobbed as though they had rehearsed, but Rhoda turned without a sound and ran from the room, out the front door, and around the side of the house. Lola watched her clamber over the Indian knoll and enter the woods.

Rhoda was the only one of them who remained dry-eyed during the funeral, but for weeks thereafter—until she climbed out the window and made her escape—Lola heard her weeping in the night, in the bed across from hers.

Despite the fact that the household was officially in mourning, Gertrude's nuptials went ahead as scheduled. Rhoda said Mama, who was normally a stickler for the way things looked, would not risk losing Mr. Howard by postponing the big event. Dr. Whitney escorted

Gertrude down the aisle, but it was Mama who spoke the firm "I give her" to the preacher's question.

Rhoda refused to be a bridesmaid, although Mama had made her a wide sash of pink taffeta ribbon like the ones Kathleen and Lola wore over their white dotted swiss Sunday dresses for this special occasion.

To Lola's surprise, Mama didn't prevail over Rhoda's intention to stay beside Papa's grave while the rest of the family was inside the church getting Gertrude married. Kathleen attended the bride as maid of honor. Lola was thrilled with her role as flower girl; the doctor's wife provided a silver basket of rose petals for her to scatter behind the bride and groom. The sanctuary had been transformed by Temperance Society ladies into a magical woodland chapel. Garlands of longleaf pine and magnolia branches tied with clusters of honeysuckle and primrose were strewn over the pulpit, the sides of the pews, and the communion rail.

A reception at the home of the bride was not appropriate, since it was a house in mourning, but Mama couldn't deny Jason and his contingent of out-of-towners some follow-up festivity. Before the pump organ wheezed to a stop, two ladies hurried out a side door to place a lace cloth on Grandmother's dining-room table, which had been transported on the buckboard to a shady spot of flat ground behind the church. Pitchers of mint-sprigged lemonade were poured over a block of ice in Mama's cut-glass punch bowl. The wedding cake—in the shape of two intertwined hearts, baked and frosted by Gertrude—was placed at the other end. Lola took a big slice of it and a cup of lemonade to the side of the church, where Rhoda was stretched out on the ground next to Papa in the space reserved for Mama. Her eyes were closed, knees up, muslin drawers exposed. Lola said, "I brought you some refreshments."

Rhoda's smile came out like unexpected sunshine. "I hope the punch is spiked. Don't even try to figure that out. It's over your head."

"No it's not. *Spiked* means somebody put nails in it."

"Lord, have mercy. Will I ever get you educated? *Spiked* means the punch is laced with rum or bourbon." Rhoda sat up. Dead leaves and moldy pine straw clung to her hair. For an eerie instant, it looked to Lola as if Rhoda had risen from a grave.

"Well, this lemonade hasn't been spiked with anything but mint," Lola said. "You should come around back. The Temperance ladies brought toasted pecans, cheese straws, cucumber sandwiches, and three kinds of cookies. Plus Mama's chicken salad. Mr. Bascomb is tuning his fiddle. He's set up a stand with a stack of real sheet music, not the hymnal. The preacher said it was all right to have dancing. Please come, Rho?"

She wouldn't budge. "Go back and cut a rug. If you see anybody sneak a swig from a pocket flask, pretend it's me that's getting high." Rhoda picked up slang from magazines she read at the lending library. There was no money to spend on books, especially the throw-away kind. Lola's sisters looked forward to the arrival of a new *Consumer's Guide* from the Sears, Roebuck & Company, "The Cheapest Supply House on Earth." (As though to make up for that girlhood deprivation, Gertrude subscribes to *Ladies' Home Journal*, the *Saturday Evening Post*, *Collier's*, *Good Housekeeping*, *Vogue*, and even the rather racy *All-Story Magazine*. The latter, in 1912, introduced Lola to the thrilling saga of "Tarzan of the Apes." Gertrude peruses rather than reads these periodicals and never discards an issue.)

Lola figured out for herself that "cut a rug" meant dance up a storm. On the shady, grassless, swept ground behind the Hackberry Hill Methodist-Episcopal Church, Gertrude's frock-coated bridegroom led her in a sedate foxtrot to the tremulous bowing of "I'll Take You Home Again, Kathleen." Kathleen's face was as pink as her sash; she didn't want anyone to get the idea she thought that doleful song had been written about her. Lola whirled alone, like a spinning top, to "Turkey in the Straw." It was the only way she knew of to get high for Rhoda.

George Craven made his way from the sandy ridges in the

northernmost part of the state as though he had a compass set straight for the Holloway place. Rhoda said the man who stood hat in hand at the back door looked rougher than the Gypsy knife sharpeners and trinket sellers Mama told them never to speak to, yet she hired this stranger on the spot. Mama was too shrewd to be taken in by his proud look and rugged masculinity. She must have realized that beneath the Heathcliff exterior was a humble man who was eager to work. George proved to be almost as much an answer to her prayers as Jason was.

By the time Papa was incapacitated, productivity was at a standstill. He had never mastered the routines of milling and getting a crop from seed to bale. His policy, according to Rhoda, was not to tell employees what to do, but to allow them to figure it out. In this respect, he did not take after his own papa. Grandfather could attend to his holdings and hold public office at the same time. He died in full saddle, or almost; he'd just come in from inspecting the fields when he dismounted and dropped dead. "Apoplexy!" shouted the old doctor, the stethoscope plugging his ears, so he didn't realize how loud he talked. "God's will," sighed the preacher. "Damn fool," muttered the widow, Miss Kitty. "Ate too much at dinner, then went back into the hot sun without his afternoon nap."

Papa had studied at the university in Tuscaloosa, then read law with a judge in Montgomery before returning to Hackberry Hill to ply his profession. The office space Grandfather procured for him—a back room of the post office—became a gathering place for men who passed through town and stopped long enough to join the smoky game of chance Papa always had going. Apparently, no one was concerned over this improper use of federal property. After Papa got himself elected to the Alabama legislature—Grandfather was dead by this time—he closed his law practice, decided not to plant cotton that year or any other, and ordered several hundred pine seedlings from the Agriculture Department of Alabama Polytechnic Institute. The twigs arrived tied in bunches like kindling. Kathleen and Rhoda helped plant them. They dug the holes with table spoons in plowed-up fields where cotton had been the only crop for over fifty years. Papa could now brag to his colleagues in the statehouse that he was in the forestry business. Many a Texan, he liked to explain, had made his fortune in timber; it wasn't just cotton out there. The county record books contained the scrawled letters G. T. T.—for "Gone to Texas"—after the names of enterprising agrarians who had left these parts in the 1850s. Mama reminded him that Alabama was not a magical land like Texas; it would be years before those little switches produced a drop of turpentine, much less were ready to be cut for lumber. But Papa's optimism that they were finally on the path to prosperity was so infectious Mama bought herself a new sewing machine.

George had been there only a few months when Papa died. He proved himself adept at operating the gristmill and also the plantation gin when farmers with small crops brought their wagonloads. He wasn't too hard or too easy on the wanderers Mama hired to help out, and even when he had to do it all himself, he didn't complain about the pay. His atrabilious expression gave no hint of what turned out to be a shy, easy disposition. He slept in the mill and ate on the back porch. After Gertrude married, Mama invited George to take meals with the family. Several weeks later, he made a bigger leap in status. Stammering and blushing, he asked Mama's permission to marry Kathleen.

"That seems a sensible idea," she said, her voice laced with resignation and disapproval. The ceremony took place the next Sunday during the morning service. Kathleen did not wear the white wedding gown or the fancy comb and veil. The minister asked George and Kathleen to approach the altar together. Their vows were witnessed by a captive congregation. Jason wired regrets that he and Gertrude, who had not fully recovered her equilibrium after their honeymoon trip to Niagara Falls, would be unable to attend. Mama again said a firm "I give her" to the preacher's question, but there was no festivity afterward, not even a wedding cake, and nobody gave Lola a basket of rose petals to scatter behind the bride.

At least Rhoda graced this occasion with her presence. She had stuffed her pockets with wild daisies; during prayers, she plaited the stems into a flower ring and set it on Lola's hair. "Let's swear to each other we will never marry lunkheads like George Craven," she whispered. Lola hoped no one in the pew behind them heard that.

On the way home—she and Rhoda walked, while Mama grimly drove the buckboard that carried the newlyweds—Lola asked Rhoda why she didn't like George.

"Because he's a piece of cow pie."

"And *Craven* is a sinful name," Lola said, to be agreeable.

"How so?"

"It's a sin to make a craven image."

"The Bible word is *graven*, with a *g*. Say it."

"*Graven*, with a *g*. Will you marry somebody like Gertrude's husband?"

"I won't marry anybody I have to call Mister."

"That was Gertrude's idea," Lola said. "I heard him tell her, just before they left for their honeymoon, that she should address him by his first name now that they're man and wife."

"Gertrude's gone forever. You've lost a sister."

Lola didn't want to talk about loss and forever. "You didn't finish saying why you don't like George." Kathleen's husband wasn't as impressive-looking as Jason, but he was presentable when he was cleaned up. He wasn't Lola's idea of cow pie.

"I just don't, that's all. End of discussion."

Before a month passed, two things happened: Kathleen's stomach swelled like a rain barrel, and Rhoda confided in Lola that she was leaving. "I will not stay around here and listen to the racket an infant will make in this thin-walled house," she said. "It's been too crowded since that man moved in."

"George doesn't take up any more space than Gertrude did."

"At least Tru was quiet. You never even knew she was around. He makes his presence so obvious. I hear his boots clumping up and down the stairs, and at night, through the wall, I hear him going at it. When those bedsprings creak real fast, that's him humping away."

"What's humping?"

"When he puts his penis in Kathleen's you-know-what."

"Oh."

Rhoda sighed. "Aren't you going to ask me what a penis is?"

"All right. What is it?"

"The thing he pees with. Its other function is to make babies. A man's thing looks exactly like a horse's, only smaller. It has other names, too, but you don't need to know those."

"If he's already made a baby inside Kathleen, why does he keep on humping?"

"That's the way men are. They don't do it just for babies, they do it because they like it. Kathleen might as well be chained to the hitching post. She has to stay here for the rest of her life. But I don't."

"When are you going?" Lola asked the question only to humor her. Not for a second did she believe Rhoda was serious about leaving home. She wasn't old enough to go to college or get married. She didn't even have a fellow.

"Any day now."

"Can I come, too?"

"You're too young to earn your way in the world, and I can't support us both. Not for a while, anyway." Rhoda smoothed a strand of hair off Lola's puckered forehead. "You better stop wrinkling your brow. Those worry lines will set, and you'll look like an old lady before you even get titties. Someday, I'll come back for you."

"Are you going to Georgia?"

"Farther than that. I may travel to the state of Missouri and take in the sights of the St. Louis World's Fair before I head for New York or Chicago or Canada."

"Don't leave me!" Lola wailed, suddenly realizing she might be serious.

Rhoda laughed, throwing her head back so that her storm-colored hair touched the ground where she sat. "You'll believe anything, Loquacious."

Rhoda had fooled her into complacency, so Lola didn't watch for signs of her leaving. But she knew something was wrong by the way the rooster crowed that morning. Rhoda's cry for freedom was in that raucous call. Her bed was made, the covers pulled tauter than usual. Lola closed her eyes and saw Rhoda running down the road in the moonlight. When she opened them again to the bleak emptiness, Rhoda's pinafore was spread across the back of the chair with an unsigned note pinned to the bib: "I won't have any more use for this. Wear it and think of me. Remember all I've taught you, and take care of yourself until we meet again." The doors to the wardrobe stood wide open. Rhoda's three dresses and both sets of her underwear were gone.

Although Lola had her own pinafore, she took immediately to wearing Rhoda's, which came below the hems of her dresses. The ruffled straps slipped off her shoulders.

"That ungrateful girl will have some answering to do when she comes back," Mama said tersely when Lola showed her the note. In the sugar bowl where the household money was kept, Kathleen found a scrawled note: "I'm taking one-fourth as my rightful share."

"Rhoda never did one-fourth of the work around here," George said, looking at Lola.

"I've been tidying up and collecting the eggs since Gertrude left." One thing she'd learned from Rhoda was to stick up for herself.

Kathleen said, "Lola will earn her way soon enough, helping take care of the baby."

Rhoda did not return within the week, as Mama predicted she would. After a while, Lola stopped straining to see past the bend in the road. Mama was making infant day-gowns, and more as a way to spend time with her than from any desire to learn the skill, Lola asked for instruction in how to sew. Under that supervision, Lola embroidered rows of feather stitch and chain stitch down the facings of the garments and tried not to prick her fingers, which were too small for a thimble; Mama had warned her not to get bloodstains on the cloth.

"How come Gertrude doesn't have a baby?" Lola asked. Although she dutifully wrote to Mama each week, they had not seen hide or hair of Gertrude since she and Jason (whom Lola now thought of as the possessor of a penis) departed Hackberry Hill by train the day after their wedding.

"I expect she keeps busy with her social activities and church work and running that fine house." Mama wet an end of thread with her tongue, cocked her head to one side, and concentrated on getting the thread through the eye of the needle before she added, "The Lord's plans for Gertrude may not include children just yet."

"I'll bet you and I have to take care of Kathleen's."

"Do not say 'I'll bet.' Perhaps the Lord intends for you and me to be responsible for the child that will be born in this house."

"I don't believe the Lord's given it much thought." Lola was more assertive now that Rhoda wasn't around to assert for her. "If He had, He'd give an infant to the doctor's wife. Rhoda said she's near about past the age for birthing now."

"That girl didn't know everything." Mama spoke as if Rhoda were in the past; as though she might be packed away in the trunk with the china-head dolls.

"I love Rhoda." Saying it helped to quell the chill in Lola's heart.

"Then pray for her."

Mama didn't show much piety herself anymore. Their church attendance was erratic, and when they went, they didn't stay to socialize after the service. She had stopped attending the Temperance Society meetings, too. Lola figured the sudden reclusiveness had as much to do with Kathleen's hasty marriage as Mama's embarrassment at Rhoda's leaving. The nosier ladies paid calls as though there had been another death in the Holloway house. Their faces registered more shock and disapproval at the dust balls in the corners of the front rooms than at the new bride's too-obvious condition. Mama had lost interest in keeping the house ready for inspection.

Kathleen griped to Lola, since she didn't dare complain to Mama. She couldn't be responsible for all the washing, cooking, and ironing; Lola would have to do more. She had already suggested Lola take over her chore of milking the cow. Lola resented Kathleen's bossing, although heaven knew she was in need of guidance. Mama appeared to be shrinking. She drew her shoulders in and kept her head tucked; her mouth pursed inward so her lips were hardly visible. She was trying to blend into the surroundings, to make herself as unremarkable as Grandmother's primitive pie safe with the perforated tin doors, when she should have identified with the stately walnut highboy that had come with her to Alabama.

"Did you miss your mother after you left home?" Lola tried to think of questions that would elicit some response.

"I miss her every day of my life. I never got back to see her. She was laid away before I learned of her passing."

"We could visit now," Lola said. "Hell, Mama, we could up and move to Georgia! You could sell this place to Kathleen and George."

That "hell" slipped right past her. "They can't afford to buy it," Mama said. "And I have no close ties left in Georgia. Just some distant cousins."

Lola thought it might be nice to meet those cousins, but there was no use trying to talk her into it. Mama wasn't going anywhere but to an early grave. Lola's heart ached, knowing her mother was willing herself to die. She wished she could talk to Mama about Rhoda, and to Rhoda about Mama.

Dr. Whitney would have delivered Kathleen's baby, but Mama didn't want to be beholden to him any more than they already were for his treating Papa without charge. The plan was that a midwife whose husband brought his corn to George would assist Mama. The midwife's compensation would be in free milling.

Elated to see the doctor's buggy come bouncing up their road again, Lola watched as a black driver got out and helped Mrs. Whitney alight, then climbed back onto the seat.

"Hello, Lola," the lady said, offering an appropriately sympathetic smile to the half-orphaned child who opened the door to her. "I've brought your mother a special treat." She handed Lola a bowl covered with a starched white napkin. "This is the first year our imported fig tree has borne fruit. Figs are considered a delicacy, you know."

Lola didn't know. That was the first time she'd ever heard of, much less seen, figs. "Thank you," she said, adding, as Mrs. Whitney proceeded to come in, "Mama's lying down." That was true, though it sounded wrong. Mama had never rested before bedtime until recently. Now, she went to her room after lunch and stayed there until time to start supper.

"I hope she's not ill."

"No, ma'am. Just resting." Lola thought Mama was practicing up for death.

"What do you hear from Rhoda?"

Mama did not acknowledge that Rhoda had run away; Kathleen and George seemed to have forgotten Rhoda ever existed; Lola was desperate to tell someone. "Not a word. We have no idea where that girl is."

But Mrs. Whitney wasn't the someone to respond to this news. She smiled vaguely. "Is Kathleen here?" She was determined to pay a call, to justify the trouble of getting dressed up. Her gloves of sheer netting revealed small, seashell-colored hands that had never held a hoe or a rake—or even a broom or a dustpan, most likely. Lola wondered how the doctor's wife kept busy. She didn't know there was such a thing as a thoroughly idle woman until she met some of Gertrude's Felder friends.

"Kathleen's out back," she said.

"I understand she's expecting. Is she pleased?"

"No, ma'am, not especially."

"Really! I'll go and speak to her."

Lola didn't offer to accompany her. The lady couldn't miss Kathleen, seated in a cane-bottomed chair with a headless hen across what was left of her lap.

Hardly a minute passed before Mrs. Whitney came back inside. "Well," she huffed as she hurried through the house to the front door, tying her bonnet strings with trembling fingers. "I never meant to imply that she was incapable of mothering an infant."

Kathleen gave Mrs. Whitney time to leave before she came in and slammed the defeathered fowl on the kitchen table. The hen's pale, plump thighs seemed weirdly human. Lola visualized Jason gazing with love at a naked, pale-thighed Gertrude.

"What nerve," Kathleen muttered. "As though we're the kind of people who would give up our own flesh and blood."

Mrs. Whitney had offered to adopt the child Kathleen was carrying. George heard about it at supper. Between mouthfuls of biscuits and gravy, he asked, "Did she offer to pay for it?" Mama kept her head down as she twisted her mouth and made her face scrunch up like an apple doll's.

"I didn't permit the conversation to continue."

"Damn right," Lola said.

"You'd be wise to unlearn those cuss words, Lola," George said, after glancing around to see whether Mama or Kathleen would do the chastising. Mama appeared not to have heard, and Kathleen didn't care. But George had no authority over her. Lola felt as though she'd been cut loose from her moorings, and it was scary.

The night of the birthing, Kathleen screamed like the Whitneys' peacocks. The sound seeped through the pillows Lola had pressed to her ears. Mama came out of her reverie long enough to help with the delivery. She emerged from the room with blood on her arms and apron and said, without enthusiasm, "It's a boy." George named the baby after his father.

Little Harold cried day and night; the midwife said Kathleen's breast milk didn't agree with him. They traded corn grinding for a nanny goat, and the midwife taught Lola to strain the goat's milk through cheesecloth and drop it in the baby's mouth from a coffee spoon. Mama made a sugar teat from a handkerchief, but Harold wanted the real thing. He would root around like a pig for Kathleen's breasts, even though what he found there unsettled his stomach and came back up. Kathleen despaired. Maybe she should have let the doctor's wife have him. The doctor would know how to treat a sickly child.

This time, George was the one who was outraged. "My boy stays here, or else I'll take him back where I grew up."

Mama put her hands to her throat, as though George had threatened to choke her. Kathleen began to cry. Lola was trying to force the goat's milk down a sleepy Harold, who opened one eye and gazed at her as if he needed to know something. She told him, with a look of her own, what it was he needed to get straight right from the start: she was not going to be his mother. She needed mothering herself. Lola missed keenly the way things used to be: Rhoda, making her laugh and imagine the impossible, like how it would feel to climb a rainbow or dive to the bottom of the distant ocean where King Neptune lived; Papa, at the head of the table, telling droll tales she didn't understand but pretended to; Gertrude, wafting in and out of the house as though she'd come to pay a social call; Mama, being firm and take-charge, instead of vague and quivery.

Mama wouldn't hold the infant. She said her hands shook too much and she might drop him. She had begun to shuffle like the black-face actors in the traveling tent show Rhoda and Lola had sneaked into. Mama made no effort to do anything other than a little pot stirring and mending.

Soon after Kathleen remarked that she should have let the doctor's wife have the baby, that lady stopped by with a roasted ham bigger than what the Holloways had at Christmas, its surface fat crisscrossed with a brown-sugar glaze and studded with cloves. It occurred to Lola that she meant to offer this wonderful gift in exchange for little Harold—he and the ham were about the same size—but Mrs. Whitney explained she'd come out of concern, because she had heard their mother was still ailing. She showed nothing more than a polite interest in Harold. "I am going to get a child very soon," she confided.

"Well, I'd never have guessed it," Kathleen said, staring enviously at the woman's tiny waist.

"My husband has made arrangements. We will open our hearts and home to a foundling."

Lola wished she could shrink and become that lucky infant.

Harold finally took to the goat's milk. He still cried a lot, but Lola could tell from the determination on his face when he wasn't crying that he was not going to give in and join the babies in the cemetery plot.

Things went pretty well until the day she found Mama lying on the couch with her eyes and mouth wide open. Lola patted her cheeks and begged her to say something, but Mama gave no sign that she heard. When she realized her mother was dead, Lola called out the name of the one person who could have comforted her. Kathleen had to slap her face to make her stop yelling for Rhoda.

The doctor sent a telegram to Jason, who brought Gertrude to Hackberry Hill on the train. By the time they arrived, some women with hardy constitutions—not the smelling-salts ladies—had bathed and powdered Mama and brushed her hair. One of them got out the black taffeta dress Mama had worn in public from the time Papa died; she'd even worn it to Gertrude's wedding. Recalling the ominous swish of that heavy skirt, Lola said, "I'd rather think of her spending eternity in the lavender lawn dress she used to wear to Temperance teas." Kathleen said she'd rather that dress, too, because it was the color of summer twilight and flattered Mama's complexion. That convinced Gertrude, who wanted their mother to look her best when she met her Maker.

They laid her out on the crocheted counterpane of the bed she'd slept in since her first night in that house—and, for as long as Lola could recall, by herself. Then the women drank coffee from cups that were used only for funerals and teas and declared that Lucy looked so natural, just as though she were asleep. This was not true. Lucy Holloway looked as marmoreal as the statues in the cemetery. God had turned a disobedient woman in the Old Testament to salt, and He had turned Lola's mother, who had never consciously disobeyed Him, to marble. At least Lucy Holloway got to rest on that bed for the last time longer than her husband or Miss Kitty did, because she had chosen a cool month in which to die.

They took her away in the coffin George stayed up all one night to finish, to lie in state in the church. Lola cried enough to get the sorrow outside herself, all those tears she never finished shedding when Papa died. She refused to believe she had lost Rhoda. It was after the burial, after they'd finished singing all the verses of the hymn Mama loved best,

"I Come to the Garden Alone," that Gertrude and Jason each took one of Lola's hands and didn't let go until they got back to the house. She sat between the sister she had known the least and this sister's husband, whom Lola scarcely knew at all but whose mixed aroma of shaving soap and tobacco and breath drops she found so comforting. She prayed as hard as she could that they would take charge of her until she was old enough to be on her own.

Jason said, "You have two options now, Lola." As the mentor he would prove to be, he explained that the word *options* meant alternatives, which meant choices. "You may continue to live here with Kathleen and her family, or you may make your home with Gertrude and me in Felder."

Gertrude said, as though she had memorized her part, "Should you choose to accept our invitation, Mr. Howard and I will come for you when the school term ends." She spoke in the precise and measured way that Rhoda had mocked as put-on talk, but to Lola, that day, Gertrude's voice was like honey spooned over bread.

Jason added the magical words: "You would be as our own child."

What she truly wanted was to be somebody's child. Lola wished the move could take place right then; the school term had over three months to go. It was mid-February, and the ground was silvered every morning with a fine sheen of frost, though the pear trees thought it was springtime and were putting out hard, tight buds. She gazed with a new feeling of detachment at the backs of Kathleen and her husband on the wagon just ahead. Over his mother's shoulder, Kathleen's baby stared at her forlornly, as though he knew she would not be a continuing presence in his life.

Gertrude held her parasol over Lola and herself. She said, "I'm sorry we couldn't notify Rhoda. She should have been here." Gertrude must have forgotten that Rhoda did not react to situations like other people. She might have refused to come inside the church for the service. Lola had dared to hope that Rhoda would be waiting for them at the freshly dug opening next to Papa's grave when they emerged from the church.

Later, after Gertrude and Jason left, Kathleen said, "Rhoda managed to avoid another family funeral."

"It likely didn't occur to her when she took off that her mother would pass away anytime soon," George said.

"Are you taking her side?" Kathleen said sharply.

"I don't see that there are sides to be taken. I was pointing out that your sister, who apparently has left for good, had no way of knowing her mother passed away."

The idea that they might get into an argument dismayed Lola, but not as much as hearing the words "left for good." What good had come of her leaving?

Lola wondered if George missed Rhoda's hanging around the mill, where she had no business being, but she didn't dare ask him in front of Kathleen. Not long before Rhoda ran away, on an afternoon when there was no wagon waiting with a load of corn and the wheel was idle, Lola had watched her without the other's knowing. Rhoda was perched on the sill of the top-level window, just above the wheel. From her hiding place, Lola heard Rhoda laugh, the mean one that grated like kernels of corn being pulverized between the grinding stones. Then, "I want my wages." The words traveled clear as a bell.

From inside the mill, George must have said, "What wages?" Mama had never paid her daughters.

"I work like a man, I should be paid like one. All I ask is the price of a train ticket." Then, after he likely asked where she was going, "I haven't decided. But it'll be far away."

His next remark must have infuriated Rhoda. She shouted, "Stop trying to sound like you're in charge around here! You don't own one inch of this place."

But George was in charge. Mama had allowed him to be.

The water moved gently below the wheel, breaking in little *blurp* sounds like fish make when they come to the surface. Above and some distance beyond this pool, the waterfall made enough racket to distract Lola from what she feared would become unpleasant. She went back around front and scrambled up the bank and through the cattail rushes, not bothering to watch out for duck eggs and snakes. She found a more distant spot behind the oleander hedge, where, by parting the branches, she could see Rhoda sitting on that window sill as she hurled her shoes—probably her stockings were stuffed inside them—across the narrow pool to the bank. Rhoda took her time climbing down from the sill to the wheel; Lola watched fearfully as she found her footing. She could see George leaning from inside the same window, likely telling Rhoda to be careful or to get off. The wheel began to move gently under the pressure of Rhoda's bare feet. She pirouetted, waving one arm as she leaned at an angle over the water. When she jumped in and began to swim to the bank, Lola left. She didn't want Rhoda to catch her spying.

At supper that night, Rhoda and George never so much as glanced at each other. Lola hoped Rhoda would tell her about the argument while they waited for sleep in the moonlight-bathed shadows of their room. Instead, Rhoda repeated a fantasy Lola had heard from her before: Sleep was a foggy mist that came through the window screens and swirled their bodies around like leaves or feathers; the mist would waft them from their beds and over the tops of the trees and let them practice being angels while they were still alive. On this occasion, Lola didn't want to hear about the supernatural and the great beyond. She wanted to talk about the here and now. "Rho," she whispered, gathering her nerve to broach the subject, "how did you make the wheel turn today when you were dancing on it?"

Rhoda didn't accuse her of spying. She said, "It's not how much I weigh, or how physically strong I am. I could make that old wheel spin like a windmill if I really concentrated my mental force on it."

"No, you couldn't," Lola scoffed.

"Oh, yes, I could. I can do whatever I make up my mind to do. You can, too, so be careful what you aim for. Now, tell yourself you're going to have wonderful dreams and a wonderful life."

When Lola awoke the next morning, Rhoda was gone.

Little Harold was in Lola's care from the minute she got home from school until he was put to bed after his supper. One afternoon, she laid him on a firm pillow in the pull-wagon and carted him off to visit the dead babies. "One of them was about your age," she told him. Harold blinked as though he understood what she was saying, so she assured him he was in robust health now. The milk she squeezed from the nanny goat was agreeing with him. Rhoda had done more than anybody gave her credit for, Lola thought, as the demands on her own time increased. The months of waiting until her own leave-taking were filled with anxiety as well as anticipation. Despite their reassurance as they departed after Mama's funeral and in letters since that they would be back for her as soon as school let out for the summer, Lola worried that Jason and Gertrude might change their minds.

She took flowers from Mama's garden to her grave. Some of the prettiest ornamentals (Rhoda said that was what you called blooming plants that didn't provide food) dug up from the woods and the riverbanks had curious names: butter-and-eggs, four-o'clock, Johnny-jump-up, ragged robin, bachelor's-button, kiss-me-at-the-gate, preacher's tongue, passion-flower. The last commemorated Christ's suffering on the cross; Lola sensed, from Rhoda's susurrant pronunciation of it, that *passion* was a divine word with powerful ramifications. The hollyhocks and sunflowers against the fence were like overgrown children relegated to the back row for a school program. (She and Rhoda had slept with bags of sunflower seeds under their pillows to bring good luck.) In the garden's prime, the mainstays were low-growing blue phlox, larkspur, tea roses and sweetheart roses, orange nasturtiums (whose leaves could be used in salad), elegant daylilies that closed up before the sun went down, and the multicolored zinnias that thrived in the most ordinary soil, yet looked as fragile as rice-paper parasols. On that day, all Lola could find in the garden to take to the grave were bluets smaller than a fingernail and wispy pink valerian, whose root was used to brew the tea that drugged Sleeping Beauty. One dose and that girl didn't wake up for a hundred years; she couldn't remember the whole story, and Rhoda wasn't around to provide the details.

Since Lola had last been there, the stonecutter had carved Mama's name and dates beneath Papa's. Lola couldn't think of anything else that would interest her. Mama was never one for gossip or small talk.

"Your grandmother has settled in by now," she said to Harold. Her next remark was addressed to the sky: "If you know where Rhoda is, please figure out a way to tell me." A wisp of wind came at that minute and picked up the trailing end of a clematis vine that adorned the low iron fence around the family plot. *Rhoda is with the wind?*

A few days later, the green tendrils exploded with yellow blossoms the size of monarch butterflies. Papa provided that answer, she reasoned. Mama had planted the clematis, but the result was more his style— flamboyant. Rhoda was the daughter who best loved him, and even Lola, who had known him the least, was aware that Rhoda held the special place in his heart.

In spite of the thick mustache and sideburns, there was plenty of kissable space on the doctor's face. One afternoon as she walked home from school, he reined in his flirty, spotted mare and tipped his hat as though she deserved such courtesy. "Good afternoon, Lola. You're looking fine today."

"So are you, sir."

"Come ride the rest of the way," he said, and gave her a hand up.

"Thank you. How is Mrs. Whitney?" She asked not so much from politeness as to initiate conversation, which she craved. Kathleen had become as silent as Mama used to be.

"She's quite well and occupied at the moment, thank you. We have a baby now."

"Oh. Where did you get it?" There was no orphanage in Hackberry Hill.

He answered as though she had a right to ask. "An unfortunate young woman had to put her newborn up for adoption."

"Is it a boy or a girl?" Whichever, she was jealous of it.

"A girl. I hope she'll be as charming as you."

Not knowing how to acknowledge a compliment, Lola ignored it. "What's her name?"

"Her birth mother asked that the name she gave the child be retained, and I have honored that request. Our daughter is called Daisy. As it happens, that is also the name of my own grandmother."

"Does the real mother visit her?" She was aware that her curiosity was perilously close to impertinence.

"No, she doesn't live in the area. And it will be better for Daisy to grow up believing my wife is her only mother."

"That doesn't seem fair to the one who went through the pain of birthing her," Lola said, recalling Kathleen's travail.

"Child, as you have learned, life is not always fair." As though to dispel the gloom of that pronouncement, he began to whistle a cheerful tune to the rhythm of the horse's trot, and Lola sang along. . . . It strikes her as strange that, in this flow of recollection, she can't come up with the song; she couldn't have known the lyrics to many back then. What she does recall is a feeling of harmony that was strong and life-affirming.

As soon as the buggy stopped, she jumped down to secure the horse to their hitching post. The doctor walked with her to the house. The front door—which Lola was glad to find Kathleen had left unlatched for her, as she didn't always remember to—squeaked like a rodent caught in a trap. George had asked Kathleen to oil the hinges; she had retorted that oiling hinges was not woman's work; and there the matter stood. Lola called out a yoo-hoo.

Kathleen appeared, shouldering a string mop as though it were a rifle. "Good afternoon, Doctor," she said, trying to sound prissy like Gertrude and to Lola's surprise coming pretty close, "How nice of you to stop by. Would you like a glass of cool water? I just drew a bucket."

"Thank you, that would be nice." He lowered himself to the couch, although Kathleen hadn't remembered her manners enough to ask him to sit down. Lola ran to the kitchen to get him a glass of water and returned to an awkward silence. Kathleen's face was tight with suspicion. She must have thought the doctor had come to bargain for Harold.

Lola cleared the air. "The Whitneys have got themselves a baby."

The doctor jumped in as though he'd been waiting for the opening. "Yes, Coralee and I have adopted an infant. Which brings me to the purpose of my visit. I understand your child has no need of your milk now, and I'd like to make a humble request." He looked at Kathleen's face, not her bosom, but he must have noticed her supply was sufficient to make two widening circles on her dress front.

"So the word is out that I couldn't nurse my own infant." Kathleen's eyes flashed in anger. She reminded Lola of Mama.

"I don't believe it's common knowledge. The midwife told me because I asked her if she knew of a nursing mother with milk to spare. I hope you will consent to wet-nurse our little Daisy during this crucial time."

"Can't the woman who gave birth to her do that?"

"She doesn't live in the vicinity. We're being serviced now by someone who has informed me she must stop at the end of the week. Of course, I would pay you for this invaluable accommodation."

Kathleen relented. "I'll give it a try. Maybe my milk will agree with another baby."

Dr. Whitney didn't wait for her to change her mind. He pressed a bill into her hand and dropped a couple of coins and a sucker into Lola's pocket. Having another infant around would mean that Lola would have to spend more time taking care of the one they already had, but she was glad they were going to help the doctor.

As he sat on their stiff, old horsehair couch that day, it took all Lola's will power not to crawl onto his lap.

Despite her envy, Lola took to Daisy Whitney. The affection she didn't bestow on her nephew—because she would be leaving him soon and didn't want him to become too attached to her—Lola lavished on the diminutive stranger who was brought daily to be nourished at Kathleen's bountiful breasts. The doctor would deposit Daisy in the morning and retrieve her in the afternoon. He brought Kathleen a suction pump and glass bottles with rubber nipples so he could take home a supply to tide them over until he brought Daisy back the following day. George was pleased about the money Dr. Whitney was willing to pay. Kathleen complained of the routine and threw a shoe at George for comparing her to a brood mare, but she admitted this infant was easy to have around. Daisy hardly ever cried. From her padded wicker basket, she observed whatever was going on, and her face lit up like a little moon at the sight of Harold, though he appeared to disdain her altogether.

Coralee Whitney required a period of recuperation, as though she had given birth. Occasionally, she would ride with the doctor to bring or pick up their bundle of joy. She held the baby awkwardly and seemed to regard Daisy as if she were a different species, a kitten or a puppy. Lola began to perceive it had been more Dr. Whitney's idea than his wife's to take on this waif. Rougher men like George needed sons, but Dr. Whitney, like Papa, was the kind of man who would take to daughters.

Lola didn't know how she knew this. Rhoda wasn't around to tell her, although she still felt Rhoda's presence. She could look out the bedroom window and think she saw Rhoda running across the meadow, squeezing water from her petticoat and the heavy braid of sodden hair that swung like a rope over one shoulder. If she asked, Rhoda would say, "Well, Locus-Pocus, where does it look like I've been?" In the pond, of course, and wearing only her undergarments. She would spread these on bushes to dry enough that she could put her dress back over them. If Mama caught her in wet clothes, Rhoda would get a switching, unless Papa came out from his self-enforced quarantine and forbade her to strike Rhoda. . . . And then Lola would remember that both Papa and Mama were in their graves and Rhoda was God knows where, selling rabbit tobacco or telling fortunes or playing a tinny upright with a traveling nickelodeon. At one time, Rhoda had aspired to become the wand girl who pointed to the lyrics projected on the big white screen in a real theater. Lola couldn't get a clear vision of those scenarios—not like the one she had of Rhoda coming home dripping wet and strewn with pond-lily vines.

Kathleen's milk dried up suddenly. Daisy was put on canned sustenance and no longer brought to the house. Lola was beginning to admit to herself that she sorely missed that tiny girl when Dr. Whitney stopped by one afternoon. He was disappointed to find Kathleen wasn't home; she'd taken Harold with her to the lending library. He said, "I came to ask your sister if I might engage you as a companion for Daisy on Saturdays and after school during the week."

Lola accepted for herself, assuring him she didn't need anyone's permission. At supper, when she explained that the doctor would pay her to play with Daisy at his house, Kathleen said, "The wage goes into the sugar bowl." That didn't bother Lola. She had no opportunity to spend money.

George said, "Why can't the doctor bring his infant here, like he did for you to nurse her? Then Lola could take care of both that kid and ours at the same time."

"I don't like hiring my little sister out as though she's a servant, and I wouldn't, except that we need the money." Then, to Lola's relief, "I prefer for her to go there, rather than have that child brought here again." That settled it.

❧

"I remember when you were the size of Daisy," Dr. Whitney said the first time he came for Lola. Daisy bounced in her lap as he gently flicked the whip to maintain the steady trot. "Once, you had a severe case of the winter croup, and your sister ran all the way to fetch me. When I arrived, your mama was holding your head over a steaming kettle on the stove, thumping you on the back to get that mucus up and out of your chest, and it worked."

"Which of my sisters came to fetch you?"

She wanted to hear the name spoken in his rich, calm voice, but he cleared his throat before replying. "Rhoda." It came out thinly.

Lola told him, without planning to, "Did you know she's joined a circus? Last week, I got a postcard from her. She's learned to swing on the high trapeze and ride an elephant."

The doctor sat up straighter and cracked his whip smartly across the flank of the horse, causing the buggy to jerk forward. That was the only reaction the man registered to what he must have realized was a fiction born of grief.

"I made that up. We've not heard anything from her," Lola admitted. He patted her on the shoulder but said nothing.

That day, before he brought her home, he vaccinated her on the leg for smallpox. Lola took pleasure in the scratching pain and the resultant fever, because the doctor had shown concern for her welfare. Kathleen was relieved he didn't charge for it.

She enjoyed those times spent with the cherubic Daisy in the doctor's quiet and elegant house with its seductive aromas of medicine and spicy cooking and flowers. At first, his wife would greet Lola before retiring to her room; then she didn't bother to appear at all. The housekeeper, Hettie, whose shy little daughter clung to her skirts, brought the baby to her.

Lola wonders if she'll have an opportunity to renew her acquaintance with Daisy Whitney this weekend. The girl would be approximately the same age Rhoda was when she left. Lola tries to imagine Rhoda as she might look now, at the ripe old age of thirty, but the picture doesn't come.

5
The Arrival

KATHLEEN STANDS AT THE TOP OF THE STEPS and watches the big motorcar, two spare tires clinging to its rear like a bustle, move sedately toward the house. Her lazy geese, not used to such alarm, lurch into each other and flap their wings experimentally. Jason climbs out and walks around his automobile as if admiring it—though probably he's checking the tires for damage from the potholed road.

"Show-off," George mutters, moving out of the vine shadows to join her.

"He deserves to indulge himself for putting up with Gertrude all these years." Her charitable opinion of this brother-in-law has come about grudgingly. The first time she saw Jason Howard, he stood out in their austere household like the china dolls Papa bought for them too late. Gertrude was as puffed-up as a pouter pigeon over her conquest. In rare accord, Kathleen and Rhoda refused to be impressed by the fancy Dan with a carnation in his lapel and spats on his shoes. But they did their best, as Mama had instructed, to pass collective muster in her prospective son-in-law's eyes.

Mama was at her happiest sewing Gertrude's wedding gown while Papa was dying in the next room. Kathleen also had reason to be pleased over the upcoming nuptials. With Gertrude gone, she would have a room to herself. Privacy was a luxury like chocolate and oranges; she never knew how delicious it was until the brief bit she had of it ended with her own marriage a few weeks after Gertrude's. Sometimes, when she's in the black hole of despair, her husband implores, "What's got you down, Katie?" And she wants to say, "Living close with you," but something stays the whip of her tongue. When she's right again, she looks on him fondly and thanks God she hasn't chased him away, because there are times when his closeness shields her from despair. George is a dependable man, solid as the trees he turns into tables and coffins. There's art and magic in the way he does that; he taught himself. Though he's never hinted at it, Kathleen knows George has thought of leaving her and this place, but he hasn't the courage or the cruelty to follow through.

This first glimpse of her sisters causes Kathleen a moment of physical pain. Her eyes sting as though assaulted by a dust storm. Her breath seems stuck in her breastbone. Gertrude, not quite as slender as when they last met (twelve, thirteen years ago?; Kathleen has lost count), gets out of the automobile without showing any flesh above her ankles, then turns to supervise Lola's emergence. Kathleen could have passed that one on the street and never recognized her baby sister. Grown up, she still looks a bit undernourished, which Kathleen supposes is fashionable for city women. Jason, lugging two dusty grips, leads the procession up the walkway. George stumbles as he descends the porch steps, so self-conscious his natural grace of movement has deserted him. Kathleen remains where she is, her arms crossed, afraid her throat will constrict and she will croak like a frog.

Lola calls jovially, "Kathleen, we're here!"

"So I see." Her voice works, and she finds that her legs will move. When they reach each other, neither having hurried, Gertrude touches cheeks with Kathleen, then backs away quickly and inquires "Sister?" to be sure she isn't greeting a stranger. Lola gives her a firm handshake, a frankly curious smile, and a hug that catches Kathleen off guard. After George relieves him of the luggage, Jason puts both hands on her shoulders and kisses her cheek. Mama didn't bring them up to show affection or affectation, and whichever Jason's gesture indicates, Kathleen doesn't choose to acknowledge it.

"Lola hasn't been told anything's amiss," Jason whispers while his large, homely face is near hers. Lola has turned her effusive attention to George. No wonder the girl is cheerful; she has no glimmer of what's behind this reunion. Then Kathleen recalls that Lola was by nature a Pollyanna, always trying to put a sunny slant on things.

When Jason invited Lola to live with them, he became Kathleen's benefactor as well as Lola's. Lord knows, at the time, she had enough to contend with—a new husband, a sickly baby, the responsibility of running a house for the first time, the shame and disappointment at not finishing school. Lola must realize Kathleen did her a favor by making no effort to keep her here. She's escaped the drudgery of country living. Kathleen's sons have worked beside her or their father since they were little things. Now that she sees the opportunity for maternal loving is almost past, she softens their load however she can, mainly by slipping them spending money. It's a relief not to have a girl in the brood, because her lot would have been a rough one.

Kathleen does the house chores in her own time, in as slipshod a manner as she wishes. She doesn't have to set a standard for a daughter to follow. After they married, George tried to order her about, because he thought he was supposed to. When he saw how it got her back up, he stopped. Her husband doesn't look down on women as a category, as other men seem to. The four of them live in quiet here, as used to each other as a den of bears, saving their speech as if talk is too valuable to waste. But she never feels lonely in this quietness. In some manner she does not try to comprehend, it's as though one time is superimposed on another. Grandmother, Mama, and Papa are still around, as are the children she and her sisters used to be.

These familiar phantoms don't bother her, except for Grandmother. Miss Kitty can be a nuisance, though on occasion she has guided Kathleen to objects she thought were lost. Sometimes, when George and the boys have left (breakfast having been accomplished in complete silence except for the blessing George recites, as though it is a poem, in his bell-like mountain voice), she half-expects Mama, her skirts grazing the floor like broom straw, to emerge from the back room with a wad of Papa's sodden, rank-smelling dressings, or Papa himself, leaning on Rhoda for support, his booted foot coming down on the plank floor harder than the slippered one: ka-PLUNK, ka-PLUNK. The sound reminds her of the way Mama used to shout her name in summons: "Kath-LEEN, Kath-LEEN!"

The waxed-lily version of Gertrude that's emerged from the automobile reflects an otherworldly vibrancy, as though she is a numinous twin of the sibling with whom Kathleen shared a room but never confidences. Now, Gertrude acts as though she's a legitimate guest and it's up to Kathleen to entertain her.

Kathleen doesn't know how to behave around company, since they seldom have any. The days of calling to leave engraved cards on a tray must be past. She's never had cards with her married name and has never had the habit of paying purely social calls, nor does anyone drop in on her. Coralee Whitney used to, though Kathleen gave her no encouragement. Gossip has it Coralee's given up the pretense of sociability now that she has found a more dependable solace. Such information is free in the marketplace of Hackberry Hill's Main Street, which is part of the highway that connects them with the outer world. Along with twine, Borax powder, kerosene, and seed packets from Wallace Hardware; talcum, rose water, paregoric, and glycerine soap from Johnson Drugs; notions, cloth, and apparel from Mercantile Dry Goods; and coffee, sugar, flour, baking powder, and hoop cheese from Hill's Grocery, Kathleen acquires the information that Dr. Whitney, saver of life and limb, is doping his wife to insensibility. Such a tidbit might be of interest to visiting kin, but why tell them of a neighbor's scandal, when there's enough of their own to contend with?

After the prolonged greeting, they troop inside, the floorboards of the porch and front hall creaking ominously beneath three extra pairs of shod feet. Gertrude looks around what George calls the best room as though she has never seen it before. Maybe she's surprised that the parlor hasn't changed much. Except for the absence of the piano, which she took, and the unobtrusive addition of two of Kathleen's paintings, the room is as it was when she lived here.

George reminded his wife earlier today, when they learned the Felder relatives were coming, that they have other reasons besides his taking Lola off their hands to be grateful to Jason Howard. The man has never shown an inclination to divide the land or alter their status here. But Jason's consideration and affability don't lessen Kathleen's resentment of his wife. She and Rhoda were in the fields getting sunburned and callused while Gertrude's complexion remained pale and smooth. What bothers Kathleen even more is that the senior daughter was always able to tune out the insidious insults Mama and Papa inflicted on each other.

Gertrude sheds a gossamer coat and dislodges a hatpin with a diminutive, enameled pansy on the end. The hat comes off without disturbing a hair of her swirled pompadour. She will remain a Gibson girl to the end of her days. Lola smiles, as if she knows what Kathleen is thinking. Gertrude finds hooks for the hat, the parasol, and the coat on the hall tree, then turns to ask, in her musical voice—Rhoda used to say Gertrude's speaking pitch was the E above middle C—"Sister, shall I help you with tea?"

Kathleen could remind Gertrude who has the silver service and the Haviland cups and who was left with heavy, graceless furniture that seems to have taken root beneath the floor and crockery that chips but refuses to shatter into pieces that could be thrown away. But having promised George she will remain calm and civil to these people who are play-acting at being their loving kin, Kathleen deflects, rather than attacks. "We'll have coffee with the evening meal, which is close to ready now."

Jason asks, "Would there be time for me to give George a quick spin in my automobile?"

She concedes that supper can hold 'til they return.

After the men leave, Gertrude leads the way to the kitchen and carefully rolls the sleeves of her dress up several inches above her wrists. She removes an apron from a peg and examines it before tying it in place over her dress. She takes a cup towel from the cupboard drawer and tucks that into the belt of Lola's dress, then starts to turn up one of the girl's sleeves.

Lola says, "I can do that myself."

"Well, be careful of those lace cuffs, dear."

"If you're of a mind to help, you could set plates on the dining-room table," Kathleen suggests to Lola. "We're having standard fare, but to fancy things up a bit, I'll ladle the chicken and dumplings from a tureen on the sideboard."

That last is for Gertrude's benefit. "I didn't intend for you to go to any extra trouble for us," she says, which the three of them know is not so. She adds, with more curiosity than concern, "You look as though you're not feeling well, Sister."

"I'm tired as usual by this time of day."

"Do you have a servant?"

"No, I don't care to spend money that way." Help is cheap enough that she could afford someone two or three days a week. The fact is, Kathleen doesn't crave the companionship such an arrangement would bring. She and the other female would begin to share the details of their lives, the shortcomings of their husbands. The alternative would be to treat the person who was doing her laundry as an inferior, and Kathleen wouldn't be comfortable with that either.

"Do Peter and Coralee still have that family of loyal retainers?"

"Indeed they do. The Whitneys have always existed several notches above us. Don't tell me you've forgotten that."

Gertrude raises her eyebrows and her voice simultaneously. "They may have been more comfortable in circumstance, but I never considered the Whitneys above the Holloways in station."

Lola looks from one to the other as though she expects fireworks to start. She must have forgotten the way they used to deal with tempers here. Their mother's rule was that unpleasantness had to be resolved outdoors, never where she could see or hear it. (*Unpleasantness* was Mama's word for other people's rage. She didn't acknowledge her own.) Even Gertrude had a special pecan tree with low branches where she would sit to sob out her anger. Rhoda and Kathleen worked off grievances by inflicting bodily pain on each other. They used their fists and knees, like boys. That was Rhoda's idea. Good, solid hair pulling would have been enough for Kathleen. If Lola had stayed here, even without a sister near enough her age to fight with, she'd have found it easy to vent her frustrations. She could have climbed trees or jumped in the hay or swum in the pond or found a clear space in which to yell as loud as she wanted to. Or maybe she would have taken up sketching and painting pictures, as Kathleen had, and found that boredom and despair could be made to disappear for hours at a time.

The girl had learned a lot about taking care of herself while she was here. Rhoda trained this little sister as she might have a pet dog, which they never had. The retriever Papa hunted with was not allowed inside the house and conveniently died soon after Papa became incapacitated. George thought Mama had poisoned the dog, like she did stray cats. She had no use for animals that didn't pull their weight.

As she moves around the table setting out plates and silverware, Lola takes up the subject of the Whitneys. "I hope I see Daisy while we're here. Remember when I used to help take care of her?"

"As I recall, it wasn't for long," Kathleen says. "Daisy's quite the young lady now, fifteen and full of herself."

"I teach girls that age. They're either too vain or dreadfully unsure of themselves. Of course, my male students have the same characteristics. The shy boys are so appealing I have to remind myself not to touch."

"That was a very careless remark," Gertrude observes. "It's not as though you've had years of experience. You have only been in the profession for two weeks."

Lola laughs. "Well, now that secret's out." Then, to Kathleen, "Who do I think I am, to be telling you about boys! Where are Harold and Ray?"

"They're supposed to be pitching hay, but I suspect they're watching your horseless carriage cruise about the place."

"Jason will give them a ride tomorrow." That expressive voice must be the result of elocution training, Kathleen surmises. Gertrude's reason for wanting the piano was so Lola could have "lessons." As if life doesn't provide enough.

"The motorcar's returning," Gertrude announces, as though she's the only one who can hear it. "Shall I put the dough in the oven?"

"Let me." Lola grabs the pan from the biscuit board and heads for the stove, her skirt rippling prettily to reveal firm, shapely legs (ballet lessons, most likely) and a tricot-edged silk slip. "I'll be extra careful so as not to singe my cuffs."

Kathleen smiles. The baby sister has learned to take Gertrude with a grain of salt.

George whistles through the screen door, his way of letting her know it's time to eat. From the back steps, he rings the bell to summon the boys. Seconds later, they sidle in, reeking of youth and perspiration, timidity and good will. Harold and Ray shuffle their feet and grin as though they're tongue-tied. Observing these ungainly, unmannered, grimy, beautiful sons she has produced brings tears to Kathleen's eyes. Lola calls each by name and pumps their hands as if she and they are men. Gertrude's acknowledgment is to suggest they "might wish to wash up for dinner." Recognizing the voice of authority, they bound off like good hunting dogs.

After the boys reappear in clean shirts and trousers, faces and hands scrubbed, hair parted in the middle and slicked down with water, everyone sits at the table in what could pass for harmony. Jason accepts George's invitation to ask a blessing. He begins with something that sounds Episcopalian and concludes with a special request: "Heavenly Father, help us to deal intelligently and compassionately with the thorny issue that has brought us together this day. In Christ's name we pray. Amen."

Lola exclaims, "That's the first I've heard of any thorny issue. Jason, please tell us—or me, if I'm the only one who's in the dark—what is going on?"

"Ah, this smells divine, Kathleen." Jason chews and swallows before he responds to Lola. "We will leave the matter, which may have aspects of unpleasantness, until after dinner."

Unpleasantness. Mama's word again. If she's among them now, Mama is just a bystander. Another erstwhile family member is the star attraction at this reunion. But thanks to Jason for insisting they dine before dealing with her, Rhoda doesn't manage to spoil anyone's appetite.

Frequently, Gertrude has to bite her tongue to keep from reminding Jason and Lola that if not for her, they would have no connection whatsoever with each other. She finds it especially irritating to watch Lola feign intense interest in subjects she has no need to fathom, such as foreign languages, politics, the machinations of war, and the law of the land. Although he enjoys their "lively exchange of ideas," as he puts it, Jason did not choose for his lifelong companion and helpmate someone who places intellectual accomplishment above femininity. Nor, as Gertrude was compelled to warn Lola before she left for college, would any other man worthy of his salt choose that kind of woman. Gertrude still recalls the terror of being sent off to an institute of higher learning in the expectation (Mama's, not her own) that she would find a husband within the first year. Of course, she aspired to the safe haven of marriage, but she could not imagine undertaking anything so serious as seeking her soul's partner without her mother's constant guidance. Fortunately, Gertrude didn't have to initiate the search. Jason found her. He moved into her orbit with the most honorable of intentions. She truly believes the union was made in heaven, as shortly after they became formally engaged, she dreamt she had been present at her mother-in-law's passing (which occurred several months before Jason met Gertrude) and that the lady said, "Gertrude Holloway, I bequeath to you my son, with my blessing. Your intuition will prevail when his judgment errs." When she related the dream to Jason, he laughed as though she'd made it up. "Doesn't sound like her in the least," he said.

She could not have asked for a more considerate, affectionate, and amiable companion, but the times when she has managed to change her husband's mind have been very few indeed. She was unable to persuade him this morning, after he received the telephone call from Dr. Whitney, to spare Lola this unpleasant business. At least he agreed not to tell her anything while they were en route. Lola would have plied him with questions he didn't have the answers to; both would have become overwrought; and the turmoil might have provoked a mishap on the road. As it is, they arrived safely, Jason's keen faculties and Lola's equilibrium intact and Gertrude's nerves not terribly frazzled.

The run-down condition of the house dismays her. Kathleen has not kept the threadbare curtains out of sentiment (as Gertrude might have been tempted to, because their mother made them). She could have purchased a bolt of unbleached muslin and stitched new draperies on Mama's Singer, unless she's got rid of that machine. At least George and Kathleen have not been burdened with a disgusting number of children. Those strapping sons are rather overwhelming. Thank heavens she doesn't sit between them at dinner, as Lola does. What table manners! Lack of, that is. And why is she surprised? Kathleen never paid attention to Mama's attempts to refine the sisters.

Soon after they were married, Jason complimented Gertrude for having acquired polish "on her own." She informed him that she had acquired the correct ways of doing things from her mother. Unfortunately, by the time he met her, Mama was beginning to show a lapse of attitude. If she were here and still in her right mind, she would send Kathleen's young ruffians to dine in the kitchen, so that the visiting kin would not have to watch them shovel food into their mouths as though they were stoking a fire.

During dinner, Lola says to Gertrude, "Can you believe Harold is coming up on sixteen? He'll soon be going to college."

After swallowing an overcooked morsel of chicken—at least she hopes it is chicken, and not one of those huge geese that all but assaulted the automobile when they arrived—Gertrude says, "Time does fly," and wonders where on earth the money will come from for this bumpkin to be educated.

As though she's heard that unspoken thought, Kathleen remarks, "Dr. Whitney's put ideas in his head about the university. Harold understands he would have to help pay his own way by working part-time during those years."

The boy nods vigorously. At that moment, his face reflects an intelligent demeanor. It is conceivable that this grandson could have inherited Papa's exceptional brain power—whatever part didn't go to Lola. Gertrude is inspired to offer encouragement: "God helps him who helps himself, young man."

"Aunt Gertrude, would you please tell me the source of that quotation?"

"I'm afraid I don't know," she admits, disconcerted by his intensity. She almost says it came from the Bible, but although she reads that book each day, she can never come up with an appropriate spiritual aphorism and state its source in conversation.

Lola laughs the way she does whenever men are around. "Harold was teasing. He doesn't care where you got the quotation."

"Actually, I would like to know," the boy says earnestly. "But I don't want to put you to any trouble, Aunt Gertrude."

He looks so distraught that she assures him, "You've not put me to any trouble. Either I recall or, as in this instance, I do not."

Jason says, "How are your grades, young man?"

"He leads his class."

"Ah. Excellent." Jason does not approve of Kathleen's answering for her son. He turns a shoulder in her direction. "How much longer have you of high school?"

"Two more years." The boy supplies that information.

"Two more years, *sir*." Jason rebukes him firmly but gently. "That's a habit you would do well to cultivate, Harold."

"Yes, sir."

George says, his voice cracking, most likely due to its lack of use, "We don't have visitors often enough for the boys to learn how to act around them. He'll remember from now on."

"I'm sure he will." Jason would have been a marvelous professor. "When the time comes to make application for admission, I may be of help. The president of the university is a personal friend. Now, let me see if I have you two straight. Since you're Harold, you must be Rayford." He moves his level, piercing gaze to the younger boy.

"Yes, sir, pleased to make your acquaintance, Uncle Jason."

Kathleen flushes with pleasure at this one's response. She is thrilled to have these sons to display; their robust good looks offset the rustic manners and attire. But Gertrude can't bring herself to acknowledge that maternal pride with so much as a glance. She was still endeavoring to get to know her husband when Lola came to live with them. She has often wondered if she and Jason might have been blessed with offspring had they not undertaken, so soon in their marriage, the serious responsibility of rearing her youngest sister. Not that it wasn't the right thing to do. Heaven only knows how Lola would have turned out had she remained here.

At that moment, Kathleen pushes her chair back with unnecessary noise. To Gertrude's further annoyance, she starts to scrape and stack the plates at the table. Nevertheless, laying her napkin aside, Gertrude rises to assist. Lola leaps up as well, knocking her water goblet over in the process. "Oh, rats," she says. "Sorry. I'll get a towel."

Kathleen rolls the same napkins they have just wiped their mouths with and places them in the pewter rings, to be used again. She says, "Ray, take the scraps to the hound." In a softer voice, she tells the older son, "You may go to your books now." Gertrude is not surprised Kathleen favors her firstborn. Their mother was partial to her first child, with good reason. Gertrude's only goal during her formative years was to live up to her mother's expectations, and she believes she has accomplished it.

Jason and George retire to the porch, presumably to discuss what has brought them here. Before the kitchen work is done, Kathleen dismisses her sisters rather curtly. When they are beyond the swinging door, Lola puts her arm around Gertrude's shoulder and whispers, "Make the best of it. You've done well so far."

"I will continue to try." But she is not in harmony with this house. She yearns to be back in the Felder residence with the Persian rugs and her late mother in-law's jewel-toned damask draperies, which, thanks to the double linings, have survived the harsh Alabama sunshine for at least four decades and may not need replacing in Gertrude's lifetime.

The impression that she is an observer here, rather than a participant, is buoyant and freeing. She would like to share this insight with her husband, but that won't be possible tonight, as they will be in the low-ceilinged room under the eaves that she used to share with Kathleen. In the nighttime quiet of this house, conversation can travel from one room and floor to another, perhaps even from one time to another. Of course, she does not believe in the supernatural in the way Rhoda claimed to—all that ridiculous talk of cherubim flying in and out of the windows, and Grandmother wandering about. Unlike some of her flighty acquaintances, Gertrude has never been tempted to attend table movings. If voices from bygone days are trapped in these walls, she does not wish to hear them. Not Papa's; not even Mama's; and especially not Rhoda's.

One thing George hopes to learn this weekend is whether or not he and Jason Howard have anything in common other than marrying sisters and the embarrassment that their women don't get on well together.

He has to agree with his wife that Gertrude is the greater cause of it.

According to Kathleen, that one was putting on airs when they were children. There was only one princess in the house, and that was Gertrude. Kathleen still reads the dictionary like some folks do the Bible, because her papa convinced her and Rhoda that memorizing words and their meanings was the way to get educated. But Gertrude got to go to college.

Kathleen had a fully developed woman shape when George first laid eyes on her. It wasn't long before he'd lain down with her. The loving has gone on quite satisfactorily, else he might not have lingered, as Katie's not easy to live with. He knows firsthand, as Jason doesn't, how the Holloway family scrapped with each other back then. Kathleen didn't make a pretense of being upset when the sister nearest her in age disappeared. She's never said whether she is suspicious about what happened between him and Rhoda, and he's let that sleeping dog lie. As for what really occurred, he's not sure that most of it wasn't his imagination. Except he can't rule it out as never having happened.

When George came to work for them, Mrs. Holloway had him move into the gristmill. Alone at night in that stone building with the wind whispering around it, he had lustful thoughts. He'd not been acquainted with many females outside his own family and neighbors. But he remembered all of them—cousins, teachers, old-maid aunts. What he would do is undress these women in his mind, 'til he could see the dark or light thatch between their legs and the brown or pink tips of their bosoms. To his shame, he even thought of Miss Lucy that way. That lady was full of brimstone. Energy sparked off her. Her husband was sapped—not much life force left, though you could tell he'd once had it in spades. He could see the woman of the house was frustrated from lack of a man, but she'd have come after George with a rolling pin if he'd ever put a venturesome hand on her.

He never intended to get anything going with Rhoda. She wasn't one of those he undressed in his mind. She teased him in a way she meant to be insulting that George recognized was a kind of flirtation. Most likely, she scared off boys her own age and wanted to see if she could attract a member of the opposite sex. George was randy enough to get excited when she'd brush up against him, but to his credit, he always backed away.

Until the one time he didn't. He had taken ill at work. After dosing him with a brackish liquid that smelled like deep roots and damp earth—her own concoction—Mrs. Holloway told him to go to bed and sweat it out. About sunset, she sent Rhoda down to the mill with a jar of soup. Knocked out by whatever the woman had given him, George was lying on his stomach on the cot when the girl climbed the steps to the loft. Rhoda was slender as a reed and wiry. Except for that mass of hair, she might have been a boy. He felt her hard little breasts against his back, her breath on his neck. When he awoke alone on sweat-soaked sheets, the fever broken and his head clear, he hoped it had been a dream. But you lead a horse to water, he's going to drink, even if he's down-in-the-mouth sick and half delirious. The next day, as George was leaving the main house, Rhoda followed him. He told her for God's sake to leave him alone, that she wasn't old enough to be carrying on like that. She said age had nothing to do with it, but that he shouldn't worry, as she had no intention of coming back for more.

As it happened, George had already taken a genuine fancy to Kathleen, who, being a couple of years older than Rhoda, was old enough, in his opinion. When they met in the hayloft (never in the mill), she was quiet and eager, a quick learner, a real sweetheart. After the first couple of times, Katie became expert at hoisting her skirt and petticoat and peeling down those drawers and stockings. If there was time, he would pleasure her some first. Seeing her clench her hands to keep from crying out thrilled him more than the sound would have.

The fun hadn't gone on long before Kathleen missed a monthly bleeding, then another. She was too scared of her mama to tell her, but the woman realized what prompted George to ask to marry her daughter. Mrs. Holloway wasn't happy about the match—she'd always shown a distance with George—but she was practical. She got them married right away, and George moved into the house, where he was assigned a narrow bed in Katie's room that was just big enough for one person, which didn't make him feel like he was anybody's husband. He was not invited to call Mrs. Holloway "Miss Lucy," as her other son-in-law did, but she treated George with some respect, because, her husband having passed on, she'd come to rely on him as the man of the place.

The lady did him and Kathleen a great favor by not lingering long once she lost her usefulness, and George was glad of a chance to do something special for her. Mr. Holloway had an expensive coffin of burled walnut with sterling-silver handles. He showed it to George soon after he came to work there, and related what Kathleen said was likely a true story: He bought the box in New Orleans and let it be known, on the return journey, that he was escorting the body of his dearly beloved wife, who had died on their holiday. The fib got him much sympathy, especially from a fine-looking widow whose table he shared in the dining car. Kathleen said if ever her mother had gone with her papa on one of his trips, one of them would have come back in a coffin. When the man's time came, George helped stuff him into it. When it was apparent the widow wasn't long for this world, George made her one from the best of a stack of heart-pine planks that had been in the carriage house no telling how long. (His own mother was buried in half of a hollowed-out tree trunk; once they placed her inside, she seemed attached to it, as though she and the tree had taken root, thrived, got diseased, and died together.) He didn't have time to trim it out, but each nail was driven with gratitude, and he waxed the pine box 'til it glowed like honey.

With Miss Lucy gone—he could call her that now—and after Jason and Gertrude took the youngest girl off their hands, things began to come together for George and Kathleen. Lola should have realized that Katie had her interests at heart when she didn't urge her to stay on here. That worked out fine. Lola got advantages, and Gertrude got to feel good about doing right by her little sister. As he pointed out to Kathleen last night, Jason has never given them any trouble. When the gristmill activity dropped off by more than half in one year, he agreed with George that the operation could be phased out. The pecan orchard makes its yield about every other year, and even though the figures aren't in the black yet, George has felt more prosperous since Jason gave him the go-ahead and the wherewithal to get into beef cattle a few years back. Some hereabouts who still plant all their acreage in cotton and corn thought he was crazy to get into cattle, but now they're impressed with his thriving herd of Herefords.

As they were riding in the fancy car this afternoon, George almost laughed when Jason said the cattle looked "quite content." Jason reacted as though George's response—"All those dumb beasts know of contentment is rutting and eating"—were a sidesplitter. He did have some suggestions and pronouncements. If George had not investigated the feasibility of piped-in, running water, he should do so at his earliest convenience. The "antiquated" outhouse, the chamber pots, and the copper bathing tub that must be filled and emptied by hand are, in Jason's view, "outmoded relics of the past."

Since Jason didn't bring up the real reason for his visit, George didn't either. It wasn't George's idea to call the Howards, and Kathleen wasn't pleased that the doctor took it upon himself to do so. "They should know," George nonetheless told her. In fact, both he and the doctor are relieved that Gertrude's husband has come to take charge in this grisly matter. George gets almost physically sick just thinking of it.

Now, having supped well—Jason put away two helpings of Katie's blackberry cobbler dressed with thick cream—the brother-in-law has settled himself into the chain-hung cedar swing George made. It was his suggestion that the men retire to the porch, which, in his opinion, is going to collapse beneath the weight of those God-awful vines if it doesn't rot first. "I'll have Ray thin them out again," George says.

George pulls his chair up close enough that anything they say won't waft in through the screen door and the open windows. The women have finished cleaning up after the meal and are in the best room sewing and reading, not talking. He likes looking in the window at the tops of their bent heads; women's hair, especially when it's thick and burnished, is their best feature, at least of those that show. The boys have made themselves scarce.

They're two men trying to be comfortable with each other.

Jason opens a silver cigarette case marked with curlicued letters too fancy to make out, though George assumes they're his initials, and says, "Try one of these. There are costlier brands, but in my opinion, Will's Gold Flake is the Commonwealth of Virginia's finest tobacco product."

It could be the Commonwealth's rock-bottom worst and George wouldn't know the difference. The case looks like something a lady would carry. He could never walk around with such a thing in his pocket, much less brandish it in the presence of another man. He feels inadequate in choosing from a dozen identical cigarettes, which seems to be a life-or-death matter, but he manages to extricate one without pinching his finger on the spring wire that holds them in place. George wishes he could accept the simple offer of a smoke without being clumsy. Jason appears not to notice. He lights George's fag, and then his own, with a metal contraption that spurts blue fire.

While the little torch is doing its work, he says casually, "Peter Whitney told me there is new evidence about a certain disappearance. I'd like to hear what you know before we talk about it with the women."

Kathleen wrote down what she and George decided he should say, and George has learned it. Even so, he's glad to be in the dark by the lattice and not with his face full-lit, as Jason's is, by the window glow from inside lamps. To George's relief, the memorized sentences roll out as though he had oiled his tongue. "Last weekend, my boy Harold took it upon himself to clean the waterwheel and the adjacent gears while the water level was still low, following a late-summer dry spell. Harold's bare feet touched what turned out to be a pile of human bones."

Jason sighs, as though he's been told there's a touch of blight on the pecan trees.

"Harold bagged up the bones and took them to the doctor." George takes a deep drag on the cigarette. He's reached the end of the planned part. Kathleen told him just to answer Jason's questions from that point on, but Jason is silent, so George plunges on. "We didn't know anything about it until Harold asked to take some of my tools over to the doctor's, where he was putting the skeleton back together. Kathleen was provoked that Doc knew before we did that mysterious bones had been found in our pond."

"Who got the idea the remains could be Rhoda's?"

"Seems to me the doctor mentioned the possibility. But Kathleen told me she immediately thought of Rhoda when he said it was a female of around fifteen to eighteen years of age. There was something about a tooth. Doc offered to telephone you. I figured he'd call you last night."

"He contacted me this morning at my office. Business lines are more secure than party lines, and although my residence is on a private circuit, he didn't know that. Of course, the switchboard operators can hear what's said, so he was wise to be cryptic. I have informed Gertrude that something has turned up to shed light on Rhoda's disappearance. I thought it best not to tell Lola anything until I knew more. I don't have to tell you how devastated that girl was when Rhoda disappeared." Jason shudders, as if he could shake it all off. "This is a devilish turn of events, George. We must deal with the situation as best we can, not ruffle the women's feathers any more than necessary. Tomorrow, we'll sort it all out and give the skeleton a proper burial."

George doesn't try to hide his surprise. "A burial?"

"As I recall, there are plenty of unused spaces in the family's cemetery lot."

"If you want a coffin, I have one in the barn."

"Now, that's thinking in advance, to keep a coffin on hand."

"I like to build things, and burial boxes are easy to sell. Usually,
soon's I finish one, it gets snapped up." The woodworking has been more
than a hobby for several years now. It's never occurred to George that
Jason would be interested in what he does with his spare time. Now, it
occurs to him that Jason may not think he's entitled to any spare time.
"This mess of bones could be buried in a burlap bag, but I expect the
women will insist on a regulation container for the family plot." Kathleen
has more sentiment about that graveyard than she does about her living
kin. She says she goes there to paint and think, but when she returns
from those visits, her eyes look as though she's been with a man, and
she speaks in a preoccupied way. George used to follow her to reassure
himself she wasn't meeting someone.

"Yes, I expect you're right." Jason is watching the sky, which in the
last few minutes has turned from a writing-ink color to black as road tar.
The big, coin-shaped moon looks pasted on. "It's awfully dark, despite
that harvest moon."

"The curtain drops in a hurry around here."

"It's as though the stars have bypassed Hackberry Hill."

"Well, most everything else does."

Jason says gloomily, "May as well tell the girls now."

Kathleen searches George's face. Did he say it as planned, or did he
mess up? George smiles, and she relaxes. Gertrude glances at Jason as
though surprised to see him here. Maybe she thought she left him in
Felder. He does look out of place in this house, but so do she and Lola.

That one looks up from a book with a smile on her face, like she expects to hear good news and won't tolerate any other kind. George is glad Jason doesn't ask him to repeat everything and irritated that Jason assumes it is his place to do the telling now. He aims it straight at Lola, very matter-of-factly: "We have come here to give Christian burial to what may be the remains of your sister, which were found in the pond."

The book clatters to the floor. "What are you saying, Jason? The remains of my sister? Please tell me you don't mean Rhoda!"

"My dear, of course I mean Rhoda. Your other sisters are alive and present."

"No!" The girl wails and wrings her hands, like women are supposed to when they get upset, though this is the first time George has ever seen one do it. As Gertrude coos, "Shh, shh, take deep breaths," Lola gets herself under control enough to ask, "How long have the remains been there?"

Jason turns to George. "Did the doctor give an opinion as to the time of death?" As though it's a matter of hours and not years.

"I'll let Harold answer." The boy is sitting on the lowest tread of the stairs, a hand clasped on each knee, waiting for the chance to speak, but he's not the kind to jump right in. Sometimes, like now, George is so proud of Harold he could cry like a woman.

Harold rises before he begins, and his voice comes out full and sure. He could be a preacher, and in a lot less time than making a doctor would require. People would respect him just as much, too. Preaching ran in George's family for a while; two of his great-uncles stood in the pulpit. "The doctor estimated the bones had been on the bottom of the pond for anywhere from five to twenty years," Harold explains. "They were all together, beneath the wheel's gears, between two good-sized rocks that likely were left over from building the pilasters that hold that edge of the mill above water."

Kathleen says, "Rhoda would prance about in her bare feet on the waterwheel, pretending she was a dancer like Isadora Duncan. Fear wasn't in her. She thought she was invincible."

"But she was never careless." Lola is scrubbing her eyes with her knuckles to get rid of those tears fast, like she used to when she lived here. Miss Lucy didn't allow bawling. "She knew how to balance herself, and she was an excellent swimmer."

"She was a daredevil," Kathleen insists.

"Shh, Sister. We must be careful how we refer to the departed," Gertrude puts in.

"The term *daredevil* is not a reference to Satan, my dear," Jason says.

"But if the shoe fits, one must wear it."

Harold shoots his father a perplexed glance. George shrugs. These aren't his kin.

"It doesn't make sense. Rhoda, dead in the pond, when she's supposed to be in New York or Chicago or Canada?" Lola's chin trembles.

Kathleen puts a fist to her mouth, not to stop sobs but to keep herself from saying something she'll wish she hadn't.

Jason places a hand on the girl's shoulder. "Try to see the revelation in a positive light. Finally, we have the relief of knowing where Rhoda has been all this time, and the consolation that she did not run away from home and family."

"Some consolation. I'd rather think of her as alive and well, leading the life she intended, far from here. If she didn't run away, then someone must be responsible for her being on the bottom of the pond all this time."

"She has not been there all this time," Gertrude says without looking up from her knitting. During this serious talk, she has not missed a stitch; the yarn is the color of army uniforms. "Rhoda has been in heaven from the moment she took her last breath."

"In a pig's eye." George tries to stifle Kathleen with a glance, but she ignores it and looks as though she has plenty more to say.

Jason says sternly, "It is not our place to judge Rhoda. Our mission is to accept the logical conclusion that these bones are all that's left of her earthly body and to put them to rest at the first opportunity, which will be tomorrow. In order to be refreshed for that busy day, I suggest we retire for the evening. May I inquire as to the sleeping arrangements?"

Kathleen informs him the boys will bed down in the mill tonight, so the Felder folks can have the upstairs to themselves.

Gertrude murmurs, "We wouldn't dream of putting the boys out of their rooms."

Jason overrides the demurral. "That is most considerate and accommodating, Kathleen. George, what time do you usually arise?"

"Five." He pushes it back a half-hour.

"Please give me a wake-up call then."

"I'll poke the ceiling below you with the broom handle, the way I wake the boys." He's not about to rap on the door like a servant.

Kathleen tells the women, "You'll find water in the pitchers on the washstands. The necessary jars are beneath the beds, same as always."

Lola asks, "Is the outhouse still out there?"

"Hasn't fallen in yet," Kathleen replies.

"We maintain it." Harold is being modest with that "we." He sees the privy is supplied with a sack of lime, a tin cup, and paper rolls, and every couple of weeks he scrub-brushes beneath the holes in the plank seat. There's nothing a black widow spider likes better than a bite of human backside.

Lola rises. "I'll look in on it."

"There's a lantern hanging by the back door," Kathleen tells her.

Jason looked in on it during the afternoon ride. When he emerged, buttoning his trousers, he mentioned that he'd grown up with a privy at the alley end of his family's city lot, but as soon as Felder got a water-

works and chlorination, they'd installed "a glut of bathrooms, three upstairs, two down" and did away with the "eyesore." "But our outhouse
wasn't surrounded by attractive planting and latticework, as this one is,"
he added. "These cannas and gardenia bushes are quite lush, no doubt
because of the proximity of human feces."

"More likely, it's the manure Ray works around the plants," George
said.

"Manure, as in cattle dung?"

"As in chicken shit."

"Ah. Thank you for the clarification."

Now, Jason guides his wife up the stairs. As though the landing's a
pulpit, he turns to bestow a benedictory good-night.

"I wonder how Doc will take to this burial business," George whispers to Kathleen as they head for their privacy.

"Not happily. He's probably counted on keeping the skeleton in his
office for decoration." Inside their room, she puts her arms around George
and murmurs, "I hate this."

"You hate this?" he teases, as he aims his trusty member, through
their clothing, toward its rightful niche.

"You know what I mean." Kathleen pulls away from him. She can
put her mind on only one thing at a time. But once they're between the
sheets, George is confident she'll warm up to the idea.

6
The Bone Discoverer
and the Doctor's Daughter

LOLA'S HAIR GLEAMS LIKE THE COAT of a sorrel horse. (She told Harold she'd just as soon he not call her "Aunt.") His mother's hair is a lighter shade of brown, without any red in it, and Aunt Gertrude's is pale as wheat. Lola's skirt is several inches shorter than Aunt Gertrude's, and she has well-developed calf muscles. Harold has been noticing details about females since Doc lent him a book on human anatomy.

She used to haul him around in a wagon when he was a baby. If she hadn't gone to live with Aunt Gertrude, Lola would be like his older sister now, and she would have been company for his mother, who has a lonely life.

Daisy will admire the way Lola dresses, and how friendly she is. She plans to come over with her father tomorrow to pay a condolence call, which Harold's mother says is fancy talk for being nosy. But Doc is neither nosy nor fancy-talking. He said the Cravens and their relatives should have a chance to discuss this matter privately before he meets with them to answer any questions.

Harold doesn't understand how they could just greet each other— his parents and his mother's oldest sister and her husband and the youngest sister who didn't finish her growing up here—as though it were a normal occasion. The fact that they've stayed away for so long makes this visit anything but normal.

He has to get used to the idea that he has three aunts. The one who left before he was born he'll never know in person, yet Harold feels as though he relates better to her than he does to the others. Rhoda was the age Harold is now when she climbed out a window and disappeared. She must have wanted to see something of the world; so does he. If the war's still going on when he's old enough, that will be his ticket out. Harold may volunteer for an ambulance corps in order to get medical experience at the same time he's serving his country. Rhoda didn't have the excuse of a war to leave home. It was scandalous back then for a girl to think she could tap into freedom same as a boy. It still is, Harold reckons.

He had never even heard the name Rhoda Holloway until it was connected to the bones he found. His mother's not one to reminisce about when she was growing up. He has no experience with blood relatives beyond his parents and brother. A few weeks back, as he was examining drops of his own blood through a microscope, he was startled to hear Doc say, "Harold, it's time you began thinking of Daisy as though she's your sister." But how would he think of a sister? Harold's cheeks heated up with embarrassment at his ignorance. He was glad his eyes were involved with the instrument as Doc went on: "In fact, Daisy is your kin. You may not be aware of the fact that your grandfather and I were related. My great-uncle married your great-grandfather's sister. Yes, that's it, more or less. Do you hear from your aunts, Gertrude and Lola?"

"Only at Christmas."

"They were lovely girls."

Harold repeated the conversation to his mother. She likes for him and Ray to pass on anything they hear. She laughed when Harold told her he was supposed to think of Daisy as his sister because their families were related. She said, "That's ridiculous. Daisy was adopted as an infant. Even if she were the Whitneys' real child, any kinship between the doctor and Papa wasn't close enough to keep you and Daisy from being sweethearts. What does he think, that you might dishonor his precious girl? I'm going to give that man a piece of my mind next time I see him." She gets mad at the least slight to him or Ray or Pop.

"Please don't do that, Mama."

Most of the time, she cools off as quickly as she gets mad. She said, "Coralee put her husband up to telling you that stuff, because she has better things in mind for Daisy than marrying you."

"I haven't given a thought to marrying anybody," Harold said truthfully.

"Good. Keep thinking that way. Actually, the doctor gave you some sensible advice, since you seem determined to hang around his house. If you think of Daisy as your sister, you won't give in to some irrational urge to jump in the hay with her. Please tell me you haven't already."

"No, ma'am. Of course not. We're just friends." The reason he spends time at the Whitneys' house is to be around the doctor, who shows him how to improve his mind and lends him reading material. He will never forget the man's saying, at least a year ago, that Harold had "the talent, tenacity, and temperament to become a dedicated physician." Tonight at supper, Uncle Jason said he could be of help when it's time for Harold to make application to the university. He nearly fell off his chair with surprise and gratitude.

Maybe when he has a medical degree, he'll be good enough to be

Daisy's husband. But for the time being, he's doing like her papa wants him to, keeping a distance. No more wrestling around with her on the ground, which makes Harold want to pin her down and lie on top of her. He hasn't shared with Daisy what her papa or his mama said on the subject, but he did tell her that she's not to hug him anymore until further notice.

"Further notice? Well, how long will it be 'til you decide to give me this further notice?" Daisy yelped, frowning unattractively.

"When I'm sure I'm going to be a doctor. After I've had enough training to see whether I can make the grade."

"Oh, pooh, that's too long a way off. We'll see about that." Most of the time, Daisy's nothing like her mother, who's nervous as a bird. But then, according to Harold's mama, she's not their real daughter. Of course, Daisy doesn't know this about herself, or she'd have told him.

After her mother retired for the afternoon, Daisy climbed the stairs to the third and last landing, which opens into a small room full of windows at the topmost level of the house. Her father calls this place "the widow's walk." Her mother used to come up here for the view, until it began to bother her that the glass panes didn't get washed on the outside except when the house was painted. The doctor refused to ask any of the men who work for him to climb that high. The rains do a passable job of cleaning off bird mess and smashed bugs.

Daisy was sorry to see a smear of fresh blood on a window, which meant some poor bird had quite recently flown into it, probably a cardinal. According to Hettie, a redbird sees its reflection and tries to mate with it. *Boom, squash, ugh.* Daisy hoped she wouldn't come across its mangled body on the ground below.

The river isn't visible from any other level of the house, but from this room, it appears to be just beyond the woods instead of a couple of miles away—what her father calls an optical illusion. He and Daisy come here at night to look at the heavens through the telescope. She likes to hear him tell how the stars came to be, even if there's no truth to the legends. But she cannot commit to memory the names and locations of the major constellations. Poor Papa. His only child is not a natural scholar like Harold.

Sometimes, she comes up here to catch a glimpse of Harold as he goes about his chores. But on this occasion, she came to watch for the Cravens' kinfolk to arrive. Keeping one eye squinted and the other focused through the brass tube on scenery that didn't move was boring, so she left her post a couple of times. By five o'clock, Daisy was beginning to think those brief absences had caused her to miss the big event. Then, at half-past –the downstairs hall clock's chime can be heard all the way up the stairwell—an automobile bigger than any around here zipped along the Cravens' road, stirring up dust as though it were scandal. The car had doors the color of jaybirds. Her heart started thumping as though Queen Mary's royal coach were paying a visit to Hackberry Hill. As if that would ever happen here.

Actually, it might. General Andrew Jackson, before he became president of the United States, came through a little over a hundred years ago whipping up on the Indians. When the Marquis de Lafayette stopped at Lucas's Tavern on his Alabama travels (as the governor's guest, which bankrupted the state treasury), Papa's grandmother presented him with a bouquet. Long before either of those famous men, the explorer Hernando De Soto made camp on the river. Papa has an ancient Spanish dagger he found wedged deep in the trunk of a tree when he was a boy.

Papa said she can come along when he calls on the Cravens and their visitors tomorrow, but Mama objected. "If you insist that Daisy accompany you," she said, "don't expect me to."

Papa said, "How can you be so rude to Gertrude?"

That "so rude to Gertrude" sounded catchy. Daisy laughed. Mama began to weep—which she does at the slightest provocation—and accused Daisy of making fun of her like those Holloway girls used to.

Papa said, "Coralee, Gertrude has never been anything but kind to you."

Mama would not back down. "When I first came here, Lucy Holloway made it clear she didn't care to be friends with me, so I don't care a fig about renewing my acquaintance with any daughters of hers."

At such moments, Daisy feels sorry for both of them, but sorrier for Papa. Mama looks down on most everybody, yet gets her feelings hurt when people don't pay special attention to her. At school, when Daisy will be sure to overhear, they say her mother is a lunatic. Mrs. Craven never asks her about her mother. Mrs. Craven is kind of weird herself. Daisy wishes Harold's mother would suggest she call her Miss Kathleen. Maybe she should call her Cousin Kathleen, now that Papa has decided they're related. Ha, ha. Even though he told Daisy that with a perfectly straight face, she took it as kidding. Sometimes, Papa plays little tricks on her that aren't really funny, but she has to pretend they are. When she realized he didn't intend this as a joke, she said, "Harold has always been my best friend, and that's not going to change just because he's all of a sudden my fourth or fifth cousin."

Papa said the friendship didn't have to cease, but he expected them to observe certain rules, such as no handholding, hugging, or kissing. "Don't worry," Daisy reassured him. "Harold sees to it there's no touching at all between us." Harold quit arm wrestling with her almost a year ago, and during the summer just past, he announced that she couldn't swim in their pond anymore, because there'd been a fish kill and the water might be contaminated; he wouldn't want to be responsible for her getting typhoid or malaria. Daisy wouldn't put a toe in that pond for the world anyway, now that she knows someone was dead on the bottom of it for as many years as she is old. The poor drowned thing may be a girl who would have been another aunt of Harold's.

Tomorrow, Mama will stay in her room with a blinding headache in order to have a real excuse not to pay her respects. Papa will give her a double dose of nerve tonic like he does on Sundays, because the Sabbath is supposed to be a peaceful day, and Mama must be all-the-way calm in order for Papa and Daisy to leave her at home alone while they attend church.

To call on the Cravens and their company, Daisy will wear the new frock she ordered from the Best & Company catalog; for the first time, Mama allowed her to choose for herself, so of course, she selected something without smocking or puffed sleeves. The dress is plaid taffeta in three shades of blue, styled with a cinched waist that flares out into a peplum It makes her look as though she has a shape.

As she watched, one man and two women got out of the car. The hatless lady had to be Lola, who, according to Harold, used to play with the two of them when they were babies. When Daisy asked Papa about that, he was vague. "Hmm. Yes, I do recall the youngest Holloway girl did help care for you for a brief time, just before she went to live with the Howards." Lola's skirt was well above her ankles and swingy, and her hair was bobbed in the new style. The other one looked like a magazine illustration from another time.

That much Daisy got through the spyglass. These people were bound to be sophisticated. Just last week, during geography, the teacher described Felder as "a progressive city of industry and cultural refinement." Papa says he'll take Daisy there sometime, and they will stay in a fine hotel. But he hedges about setting a date. He won't leave Mama, and she won't go anywhere.

Daisy asked Harold why he and his folks never ride the train to Felder to see these relatives. His response was they wouldn't be welcome at his aunt Gertrude's, as she and his mother don't have much in common. Well, now they have that skeleton in common.

Papa ordered her not to discuss Harold's discovery with her "companions." What companions does she have, other than Harold and Ray, and Hettie and Torey? The girls at school like to be invited to her house, but they don't like her, so she's stopped asking them over. They're jealous because she's the doctor's daughter and because they think Harold is her boyfriend. Daisy can't help it that her house is bigger and better than any of theirs, and that Hettie and Torey are there to keep things up to spit. Daisy is not required to do anything except her lessons, but not a day goes by that she doesn't offer to shell peas or snap beans or feather-dust. Hettie has been more affectionate to Daisy than her mother has. Papa used to read to her every night, and then all of a sudden, she was not allowed to sit in his lap anymore. He no longer pats her on the head, now that she's nearly as tall as he is. Maybe that's why she yearns to touch Harold whenever she's around him.

Harold found those old bones and brought them to Papa, who glanced inside the bag and said in his preoccupied way, "Hmm. What do we have here, a dog or a deer?"

"Dr. Whitney, I believe these are human remains," Harold said solemnly.

Papa perked up. "Then we'll put them together, see what we have."

Some months ago, he had given Harold a medical book with illustrations of the various parts of the body (including, Daisy knew from peeking into the tome, several of the male organ). Papa told him to study it carefully. Harold walked home with her after school for the next two days after discovering the bones, but as soon as they were in sight of the small building behind the main house, he would break into a run—he was that eager to get to his project in what Papa used to call "the infirmary." For the last few years, it's been a "laboratory." Mama never liked having contagious or dying patients on the premises, and there's no need now that there's a hospital in town.

Papa was just as absorbed by this undertaking as Harold was, but he wanted Harold to have the experience of doing most of the assembling himself. When Daisy took a plate of Hettie's oatmeal cookies out to them that first day, Papa dismissed her with a look. She didn't care to watch that gruesome activity anyway. Yesterday, as they came out of the laboratory together, Papa had his arm around Harold's shoulders. Daisy wanted to yell bad words. It looked like Papa cared as much for Harold as he did her. More, maybe, because Harold shares his passion for medical science. Papa came to the kitchen door to say he was going to give Harold a ride home. Daisy asked if she could come, and he said, in the voice she knew not to argue with, "Not this time. Your mother might need you. You haven't told her anything about the skeleton, have you?"

"No, sir. You told me not to."

"It's just that I prefer to tell her myself."

"When?"

"Tonight."

After the dusty Ford clattered off, Daisy went out back for a really good look through a window. Papa keeps the door to his laboratory locked, but he seldom bothers to pull down the window shades. What she saw was truly unearthly. This amalgamation of knobby, cleaned bones—Harold had scrubbed years of mud off them—had personality. The creature seemed as relaxed as though she reclined on a bed. She'd been revitalized by all the attention; Harold and Daisy's father had held her, stroked her, gently put her back together. The skull was placed almost sideways, so that it faced the window and appeared to scrutinize Daisy as carefully and coolly as that one did her. Daisy had a sudden desire to cradle the pitiful head in her hands and croon to it. Then, just as suddenly, she wanted to run from the horror of it, which is what she did. She flew to the house and into the kitchen. Hettie said, "Sugar, you look like you've seen a—"

"Haven't seen a thing," she said quickly. She thought she should protect the privacy of the female creature who was a guest here, even from Hettie.

Papa makes house calls until all hours. Even though Mama reminds her it's a breach of etiquette, she and Daisy often begin the evening meal without him. They did so last night. Daisy had gone to the kitchen to replenish the water pitcher when he came into the dining room. The swinging door was ajar, so she overheard him tell Mama that the bones of a young female had been found beneath the mill, in the pond.

Despite Papa's attempt to reveal the information casually, so she wouldn't get agitated, Mama dropped her fork and wailed, "Promise me you will stay out of this, Peter. That pond is not on our property."

"I'm already into it. Harold Craven brought his discovery to me. Have you forgotten I'm the coroner? I have offered to inform Gertrude's husband, Jason Howard. The Cravens have no telephone."

Daisy came back into the room as Mama threw her napkin down and left the table. As usual when she carried on like that, Papa continued to eat. He would go up and look in on her later, at which time she would be sound asleep, having ingested something from her hidden supply of pharmaceuticals, in addition to the potion she gets at Papa's direction. Mama is very manageable for someone afflicted with chronic hysteria. The diagnosis came in a letter from a physician in Memphis, after he'd studied Papa's description of Mama's condition. But it was Papa who figured out how to treat her.

"Are you going to ring up Mr. Howard right after supper?" Daisy asked, as she brought him a slice of the pecan pie Hettie had baked that afternoon. Papa buys more pecans than they can possibly use from the Cravens. He probably hopes that money will go into a college fund for Harold.

"No. I'll call him tomorrow at his office." Mama used to criticize Papa for procrastinating about most things outside his medical practice.

She said it took her years to get Daisy, and when Daisy asked her if that was Papa's fault for procrastinating, she said, yes, as a matter of fact, it was. There is much Daisy doesn't comprehend about the human reproduction cycle, even though she's gawked aplenty at the lurid diagrams in Papa's books.

After Mama went upstairs last night, Papa suggested he and Daisy retire to the library and play dominoes. She loves to be with him that way, their heads almost touching across the game table that has a checkerboard inlaid in the top of it. They turned the blocks of ivory over, so that all the dots were hidden, and each chose seven. "Harold's grandfather taught me to play this game," he said. He produced the double-five starter, marked his ten points in crossed Xs under his initial on the scorepad, and added, "That man would always insist on placing a friendly bet. He thrived on games of chance."

"Harold doesn't. He considers card games and dominoes a waste of time."

"I'm glad to hear it, as the love of gambling is bound to be in his blood."

"Would it be better if Harold didn't take after his grandfather at all?"

"I didn't say that. Rayford Holloway was a fine man with a keen mind. But he had his weaknesses."

Encouraged by this unusual conversation, Daisy said boldly, "Papa, I feel a pressing need to know more about that lost girl."

"Who?" Papa racked up another five.

"Rhoda Holloway."

"If you have the double four, you can make yourself fifteen points. How do you know that name?"

She played the double four. "I heard you tell Harold that's probably who's in your laboratory, and that she was his mother's lost sister. So, what was she like when she was alive?"

"Young lady, that kind of curiosity is morbid. Maybe your mother's right; you have no business going over there with me tomorrow."

She resorted to tremulous pleading. (She can actually make her chin quiver and her eyes water at will. Torey says she should go on the stage.) "Please don't deprive me of this opportunity. I do so want to meet Harold's visiting kin. How can I learn about the world beyond Hackberry Hill if I don't get some exposure to it?" Last year, Daisy had overheard him tell Mama, "She should have some exposure to the world beyond Hackberry Hill." Mama said she would die if he sent Daisy away to school. Daisy doesn't want to be sent anywhere yet. But when Harold departs for college or the army (*Please, God, let this war end before he gets drafted*), she might as well leave, too.

"If I take you, you must promise not to talk unless you're spoken to, missy." His attempts at sternness make her smile. Papa is the gentlest of creatures.

She decided to skip school this morning so she could wash her hair and get Torey to wet-plait it into a lot of braids; it takes hours to dry that way, but the result when it's let loose is a cascade of crinkly waves, the next best thing to naturally curly hair, which, alas, she does not have. While she was occupied in that time-consuming vanity, Daisy planned what she would say. She must not speak to an adult first, but she should have some responses in mind, in case one of them should address a remark to her. She told Papa at breakfast that he wouldn't have to take her to school because she had a slightly sore throat. Fortunately, he was too distracted to verify the condition.

If only she could stop thinking about the dead girl. Last night, after dreaming she was Rhoda Holloway running in the moonlight toward that creepy, old mill with its poisoned pond, she woke up drenched in sadness.

Not long before he died, Rayford Holloway told Peter Whitney he regretted giving up his practice of law early on "to devote myself to wresting a livelihood from this demanding soil." Like his father and grandfather, Peter had followed two paths simultaneously, as agrarian and physician. But it would have served no purpose to remind his friend of that.

An intelligent man who enjoyed stimulating conversation, Rayford was not inclined to be industrious. By midlife, he settled complacently into a physical lassitude that bordered on hypochondria. His daughters took after their mother in that they sparkled with energy.

Like Peter's wife, Rayford's was an import. Rayford's father had met Lucy's father in a military hospital where both were sent for injuries incurred at the greatest slaughter of the Civil War, the Battle of Antietam Creek in the neutral state of Maryland. Rayford's marriage was arranged by this pair of former Rebels over mint juleps made with corn whiskey, consumed on the veranda of a ramshackle mansion that General Sherman hadn't deemed worth the trouble to torch. Soon after the young man and his father returned from that matchmaking expedition to Marietta, Georgia, the latter died. Rayford honored the commitment and married the girl he'd seen only once and never so much as kissed.

After the wedding, Rayford turned his new bride over to his mother for breaking in. Peter's father wrote to him, "Rayford Holloway has got himself a fine-looking Georgia peach who carries herself haughtily but doesn't seem averse to hard work." The exacting rules of good wifery laid down by a formidable mother-in-law bridled Lucy but did not sap her spirit. When Peter found Coralee, his father warned him, "Seldom does an orchid thrive in a country garden. Lucy Holloway is the rare exception. It's likely not to happen twice in the same area."

He should have listened. Peter's mother was both infuriated and intimidated by what she called Coralee's "air of condescension." Perhaps, had his mother lived longer, she'd have shaped his bride into what was expected of her, as Miss Kitty did Lucy.

Both Coralee and Lucy had been used to a gentler way of life before fate landed them here. If Coralee hadn't been determined to present herself as near-royalty, and if Lucy hadn't been occupied with pregnancies, miscarriages, children, learning the land operation, trying to keep her husband grounded, plus midwifery and backwoods medicine that bordered on witchcraft, these two women might have consoled each other and become fast friends. As it was, while Lucy settled into the roles expected of her, plus those she chose for herself, Peter's lonely, spoiled, idle wife found companionship in elixirs and tonics.

Rayford Holloway's mother didn't take to her bed as matriarchs usually did in their waning years. When she realized she was failing, Miss Kitty began to spend all day, every day, in a high-backed rocking chair placed, with her foot-pedaled cuspidor, in the wide hall, where she could see the comings and goings. Shortly before she died, Miss Kitty told Peter the best thing she could say about her only son was he'd provided her with a bunch of good-looking, able-bodied granddaughters who could fetch and tote. After her mind started to go, she developed an attachment to her late husband's pistol. She took it from beneath her pillow when she awoke in the morning and kept it with her until she went to bed that night, when it went back beneath the pillow. Rayford assured Peter the gun wasn't loaded, but the latter found it unnerving to place a stethoscope on a woman who rocked back and forth with a pearl-handled revolver in her lap. He observed that the grandmother clearly had a special fondness for Rhoda, as did Rayford. Both were dead when that unfortunate girl needed them the most.

Peter marveled that Rayford allowed Lucy to run his business without relinquishing a drop of his authority over her. Once he established himself as an invalid, all the man had to do was tap the floor with his walking stick, and his wife or a daughter would scurry to do his bidding.

Peter has observed that George Craven is a steady worker and no man's fool. In recent years, there's been slightly more of an aura

of prosperity about the Holloway place. It was either extremely patronizing or downright generous of Jason Howard to allow Kathleen's husband to manage the property after Lucy died. He doesn't know Jason
well enough to say which, but he expects to after they've spent some
time together analyzing the sad business that has brought the man here.
Jason indicated on the telephone that Gertrude and Lola would come
with him. Peter looks forward to seeing those girls, especially the latter.

He's relieved that Coralee won't be going over there with him. She
requires more and more sedation, and it saddens him that Daisy observes her mother's worsening condition. For her own sake, he should
send the girl away to school, but this village, like most small Southern
towns, has fine, dedicated teachers, and Daisy is not a born student. No
matter—she's the darling of his heart. She has adjusted well to the solitude here, never having known anything else. He'd like it if his only
child would determine to pursue a nursing vocation. Daisy has helped
Peter on occasion in the laboratory, though she has a tendency to pale
at the sight of free-flowing blood or exposed wounds. That weakness
would be corrected in her first weeks of training in a big hospital, such
as the one in Richmond that prepared her father.

Neither Kathleen nor Coralee knows their children are related to
each other. Not that the kinship would be a hindrance; marriage between first cousins was not unusual a generation ago. Harold has indicated he wants to become a physician, and Peter plans to encourage
him in this pursuit, to the extent of financing his schooling, if his parents will allow it. Should the boy desire to return to Hackberry Hill,
Peter will take him on as an assistant.

When the Holloway girls occasionally strayed onto their turf, Coralee
would shoo them off as though they were ducks. As the oldest three
matured, Coralee was insecure enough to be resentful when she knew
Peter was over there playing dominoes with Rayford.

When he first brought Coralee here, she was as sprightly and enchanting as a butterfly. And, it turns out, as fragile. Women who grow up in this environment tend to become strong in body and in character. Lucy Holloway realized early on she had to become capable in ways she had never dreamed of, and did so. But even strong women have breakable hearts, and after Rayford died and Rhoda left, Lucy's spirit snapped. Her dying was accomplished as though she made up her mind one day to start the process and get it over with in a certain length of time.

In her unfathomable despair, Coralee perishes in smaller increments. If she had close relatives he could send her back to, he would have done so long ago, but his wife's only brother was taken by consumption and their parents died of meningitis, all in the first year of her marriage. Coralee's constitution is amazing. She never has a head cold.

Peter is delighted at the prospect of showing Daisy off to the Howards and Lola. He wants them to know his daughter, as she will take her place among them eventually. Even now, not knowing of the connection, they can't help but be impressed by Daisy's charm and comportment. That is, if they can focus their attention on anything but the revelation that the runaway has been found—or what was left of her, after the silent scavengers that inhabit the pond meticulously disposed of hair, cartilage, ligament, and flesh.

7
Sleeping Arrangements

THE MINUTE THEY GOT HOME FROM SCHOOL, their mother told them the visitors would require the upstairs. "You boys can spend the night in the mill." She tried to make it sound like a treat. "All by yourselves, no grownups around. Won't that be fun?"

"Not if we get ate by gophers," Ray said.

"*Eaten*, not *ate*. Keep your lantern wicks turned up; the light should scare away anything that's missed the poison." Then her face turned anxious. "Harold, maybe you should take a gun." Ray's brother, Mr. Responsibility and three years older, can be trusted with firearms. Ray would be liable to shoot off his own big toe.

"Wouldn't want to waste buckshot on rats. We'll take the tomahawks," Harold said.

Ray's tomahawk is just like Harold's, only smaller. Pop made them.

Ray's only used his once, to hack the tail off a squirrel he killed with a slingshot. He asked his mother to sew that tail on a cap for him, so he could be Daniel Boone, but she said, "Here's the sewing box. Thread a needle and do it yourself." He ended up just hanging the squirrel tail on a nail in the barn. The way Harold wired those bones together was like sewing, but Harold doesn't mind doing girl things.

Ray has never spent a whole night in the mill before, although Harold and some other older boys took him down there one Halloween when he was six or seven. They had rigged up a plot to scare him to death, and damn near succeeded. Unbeknownst to Ray, Fred Batson had sneaked off to put on his sister's dress and bonnet. Suddenly, something in female garments appeared on the stairs and piped in a high, artificial-sounding voice, "Whoever trespasses in my house is in mortal danger!"

The others pretended to be scared. Ray really was, because he didn't know it was Fred.

"I am the Holloway ghost," the voice continued, "and you boys are trespassing on my property."

"No, we're not," Harold said. "We have a right to be here."

"If you do not leave, someone will become a victim of the Holloway curse. I urge all present to flee the premises immediately." With that, Fred slithered away in his rustling skirt and came back in his own clothes, pretending he'd gone to pee out a window and had missed the ghost's appearance.

Jack Hudgens said, "God-dawg it. Wonder who's gonna get visited by the curse?"

"The curse is what girls get once a month," Buck Norris spoke up. "So it can't be me. Say, Ray, do you reckon you might be a girl? Maybe we ought to pull down your trousers and see."

Harold swung the lantern to shine on Buck's face. "Don't make fun of my brother."

Buck said he was sorry. "I don't know what made me say that. Why did you say one of us would have bad luck, Fred? You were supposed to say, 'Don't make a mess in my house, boys, and I won't haunt you,' or something along those lines."

"What I said came as a surprise to me, too," Fred admitted. "I nearly panicked trying to get that dress off. I felt like if I didn't hurry up, I'd be stuck in it as the real ghost of the Holloway mill."

"There isn't any real ghost," Harold said.

Then Buck said, "Let's go back to your house and throw some horseshoes."

Harold let Ray hold his hand on the way.

Here they are again in the spooky, old mill, but this time, it's just the two of them. Despite what Mama said, the flames from two kerosene-soaked wicks don't make a lot of light. This is one dark-as-hell place.

Harold spreads his pallet on top of the cot where their father used to sleep. Pop bunked out here before he married their mother and got to move into the house with the family. "Oh, sure, I'll be glad to take the floor. Why not? Don't mind if I do," Ray says, dropping his quilt roll to the splintery floor.

"Sorry, I wasn't thinking. You take the cot."

"That's all right. I don't want it." Ray knows Harold would give him the shirt off his back. As Mama says at least once a month, there isn't a selfish bone in Harold's body, and Ray has to agree, even though it makes him mad when she compliments his brother.

Now, they are both lying down. Harold's breath keeps a different rhythm from his. Ray has often wondered how it would be to have a twin brother who did everything the same way he did, who breathed in and out when he did. He and Harold are way too different, and not just in age, to be twins.

There isn't anything to do but go to sleep. The cot creaks as Harold turns over; the sound is like a kitten mewing. Maybe, Ray thinks hopefully, there's a resident cat that keeps the place free of mice and rats and possums. He seems to remember Pop's saying a tabby took up here and had kittens while he was living in the mill, and he liked having the company. But if that cat and her babies got into the poison pellets, then what he hears could be a ghost kitten.

Harold says, "I can't sleep on this rickety thing." He takes his bedding off the cot, spreads it on the floor beside Ray's, then arranges himself on it as carefully as if he's laying his own corpse out for burial. Harold is not one to flop around. Ray can't see his brother's face, but he's glad Harold is within touching distance. They used to sleep in a room together, when Mama kept one upstairs bedroom ready for company that never came. Then she decided each boy should have his own space, and Ray moved across the hall into the room that had been Mama's younger sisters' when they lived in the house. Even though it looks the same as the other one—low-ceilinged, with nooks and crannies under the eaves— he often feels like he's trespassing on somebody else's territory. He'll feel that way more than ever now that he knows one of the girls who lived in his room is the skeleton.

Nighttime noises are louder here than they sound when you're inside the house. "One of those cows has insomnia," Harold explains. "If I knew which one was making the racket, I'd give it a bolus to make it go to sleep."

"Where would you get a bolus?"

"Dr. Whitney would give it to me. He keeps a bottle of different sizes and kinds in his bag."

"He's a kinda strange fellow, isn't he?" What's strange is how little Ray knows the man his brother spends so much time with. Two or three times a week, Harold gets up extra early to get most of his chores done before school, so he can go to the doctor's backyard office in the afternoon and look at books that have pictures of naked people.

"No, he's not strange. The doctor is just a really good person, through and through," Harold says in a way that makes Ray want to sock him. Ray used to pick fights with Harold, but the latter called a permanent truce two or three years ago, when he broke Ray's nose after Ray surprised him by jumping from a tree onto his back. Ray was hoping to crack a few of Harold's ribs on that occasion, but instead, he got his just desserts.

"You gonna marry Daisy?" he asks.

"What gave you that idea?" Harold sits up and stares at Ray, although it's too dark for them to read each other's faces.

"Just seems obvious that's the direction you're headed. You could move into that fine house and take over her old man's business."

"My plan is to practice medicine in missionary hospitals before I settle down. I want to see something of the world."

"What do you think I ought to do when I grow up?" This is a question Ray could never ask anybody but Harold. And he couldn't even ask Harold in daylight, because he wouldn't want to watch him struggle to come up with a satisfactory answer.

But he doesn't strain with the effort now. "Do whatever you think will make you happy, Ray."

"What will make me happy is if I own this land that no one calls a plantation anymore, or even a farm. It's either 'the homeplace' or 'the Holloway place.' I've never heard it called 'the Craven place.' I'd plant cotton clear to the front door, like they used to, and have a big sign with CRAVEN CROPS where anybody riding by on the highway would see it. If you marry Daisy and take her off to Timbuktu, then maybe I could get hold of her land, too."

"Wouldn't that be biting off more than you could chew?" Harold is taking him more seriously than Ray intended.

"Not if you'd sell it to me at a reasonable price."

"I can't promise I will marry Daisy, or that she'll have a land dowry."

"Didn't Pop get some of our place when he married Mama?" Ray knows that's not true; he asks the question to keep Harold talking. Ray wants to fall asleep to the sound of a familiar voice, so he won't start paying too much attention to the strange sounds.

"No. He doesn't own any of it."

"What kind of dowry did he get, then?"

"Nothing I know of, except his livelihood. He thinks of this place as ours, because Uncle Jason lets him run it without interference and doesn't require us to pay rent on the house. Pop's never complained about the way Uncle Jason treats us."

Harold looks for the best in people and situations. Even though he's jealous of Harold, it is impossible for Ray to hate his brother for more than five minutes at a time. "If you go to a foreign land, would it be for the rest of your life?" He can't imagine his own existence without Harold in it.

"Probably not. Even if I didn't come back here, I would never abandon our parents in their old age. When the time comes, I'll offer to take them to live with me, but they'll likely want to stay on here. With you."

Ray hasn't meant for things to get planned out that far. "I may not choose to remain a rube myself. I'd like to see some of the world, too, especially Gay Paree."

"You'll get your chance if the war goes on a few more years."

"Shoot, I hope it does. I want to kill off some of those Huns. I heard Uncle Jason tell Pop he believes it will be over soon, that the old sissy Woodrow Wilson was right in the first place, we should never have got into something that wasn't any of our business."

"Uncle Jason called the president a sissy?"

"Naw, I threw that in free of charge."

"Uncle Jason's worried about Lola's boyfriend being wounded."

"Bet she's worried, too, wondering whether a whole man is coming home to her."

"He took a hit in the upper leg. It's not as though his injury will make him unfit for marrying."

Ray can't pass up the opportunity to turn that into a joke: " 'Oh, Lola, my love, my turtledove, forgive me for not telling you sooner, but my pecker got blown clean off, and I had to leave it over there.' 'Never you mind, sweetheart, we can make do without.' "

"That's not funny."

"Nothing's funny anymore. I haven't had a real falling-down laugh in I don't know when." Since Harold is already irritated with him, Ray decides to ask what he's been dying to for some time. "Have you done it with Daisy?"

Harold sighs like an old man. "I haven't done it with anybody. And you better not have, because you're too young to know what you're doing, but not too young to get a girl in trouble."

"If I reach the age of sixteen without taking a girl to the hayloft, I may shoot myself." But it's not going to be easy. The girls Ray knows won't even let you kiss them.

"Don't let yourself think about it so much." An exaggerated yawn lets Ray know that Harold's not interested in any more conversation.

"I got to ask you something else."

"What now?"

"Do you believe there's a ghost who walks around in the mill and can be seen from the road when the moon's bright?"

"Heck no."

"They say she wails right pitifully. Maybe she's the one crying, and not a cow."

Harold groans. "Anybody who can't tell a cow from a ghost has no business thinking he can revive a dead plantation. We have to get to sleep. Pop said he would wake us up early."

"Won't that be unusual," Ray mumbles, and socks his pillow a few times. He lies there and listens to Harold's breathing change to where it's almost in harmony with his own. Two banjos twanging away. Damn,

Ray thinks, I wish we were twins! They'd be equals in every way, and closer to each other.

He says his prayers silently, thinking it might be well to get a word in before any more trouble comes.

⌾

Ray wakes in alarm to a swishing noise, as though a broom is sweeping the floor. "Brother," he whispers, "somebody's in here with us."

Harold doesn't answer.

"Leave me alone, whoever you are," Ray croaks.

A breeze that smells of mossy tree stumps and decayed flowers swirls past him like a mini-tornado. He doesn't dare close his eyes again. He sees the bluish dawn roll in beneath the door like spilled milk. At the first cock-a-doodle-doo, he nudges Harold. "The ghost of that bone girl you put back together was here."

Harold swims up from watery depths and surfaces with the most beautiful of the new words caught like seaweed in his throat: nouns that might be names of musical instruments he's never learned to play—*mandible, clavicle*—and names of girls he will never meet—Ulna, Tibia, Fibula, Patella. His favorites are the sweetly mysterious: *pubis, coccyx, sacrum, ischium*. He opens his eyes with great reluctance. "It was your imagination," Harold tells his brother. If she were going to appear to anyone, it would be to him, her discoverer.

⌾

Gertrude mounts the stairs. Jason steps up beside her, places an arm firmly around her armored waist, and whispers, "Hold on, my dear. This climb is steeper than most." As his lips graze his wife's ear to impart the message, Kathleen, watching from the kitchen doorway, hopes Jason isn't laying the groundwork for later activity. The beds in the room she's assigned them were not made for coupling.

Having lived the first nineteen years of her life in this house, Gertrude knows how steep the staircase is and how narrow the treads.

133

She ignores her husband's command to hold on. She ascends without touching the oak banister her mother made her feel shame about all those years ago. The child she was then wanted to know how straddling and sliding down that wide, slightly rounded handrail, which was so much fun, could be naughty. Mama rapped her palms with a ruler for asking and threatened to wash her mouth out with soap. The shameful incident occurred before Gertrude learned that doing her mother's bidding promptly, efficiently, uncomplainingly, and without questioning the wisdom of it was all that was required to keep her in Mama's good graces. She grew up without ever being made to suck soap, as Rhoda so crudely put it.

The landing creaks as though in welcome. "I haven't come back to stay," she says.

"Of course you haven't."

"I wasn't speaking to you, Jason."

"Then to whom?"

"Myself."

"Ah." Her mystique would exasperate most men, but Jason is titillated by it. Making love to Gertrude is never predictable. Sometimes, she behaves like a virgin. At other times, she overwhelms him with an ardor that almost surpasses his own. Her only request is that the act be accomplished in complete silence, with no voicing of emotion, "in order to keep it sacred."

Jason has never before seen her girlhood bedroom. The night after their marriage, they were assigned the only double bed in this house, a massive four-poster in the master bedroom. He is glad Kathleen has displaced her sons for them, rather than herself and George, although he would like being near the only bathroom.

Gertrude gingerly turns the white porcelain doorknob, as though she expects an animal to slither out. The suitcase that Jason purchased in Paris on his grand tour twenty years ago, that she filled with their changes of apparel and toiletries this morning, has been set in the middle of the floor by one of George's sons. "Here we are," she says, as though reassuring the handsome, old bag it has not been abandoned.

"My dear, I find your girlhood room quite charming. Let me guess which bed was yours. I can imagine you in the window spot, your hair spread across the pillow. . . ."

Before her husband finishes that poetic thought, she says, "When I was quite young, I had this room to myself. My parents slept in the room across the hall then. Kathleen stayed with them until she outgrew the crib, then she was moved in here with me. I slept in the bed by the inside wall, in order to be closer to my dear mother."

"And is that the bed you prefer tonight?"

"Yes." Not for sentimental reasons, but because she doesn't want him to watch her face age in the full moon's light, which streams through the uncurtained window by the other bed.

Jason steps behind the open door of the wardrobe to remove his clothes—unfastening the one-piece union suit and garters seems to take longer than usual—and put on the nightshirt she packed for him. She turns her back to him before beginning the tortuous process of unbuttoning and unhooking. Neither is used to disrobing before the other. In the Felder house, they have separate sleeping apartments. When approximately once every two weeks Jason knocks softly on Gertrude's door at half-past nine, both are attired for bed. In deference to her modesty now, he appears not to watch (but does) as she efficiently peels away the layers. When the corset comes off (Gertrude has ignored the War Department's request that women stop buying corsets in order to conserve steel), the red marks made by those metal stays on her pearlescent skin make him wince. He gets a flashing glimpse of her naked back, which bells out below the waist like a luscious pear, before she turns to face him in one of her high-necked, long-sleeved gowns that remind him of infant baptisms.

The Spartan room beneath the eaves, which at first seemed uninviting, now radiates an aura of intimacy. A colorful oval rug of braided strips of cloth hides much of the floor. The only other adornment—a darkly framed, pastoral print of a buxom young woman with a flock of geese—hangs on the wall opposite the beds. Jason wonders if the room's current inhabitant—one of the adolescent boys sent elsewhere for the night—ever mentally undresses the female in that picture in order to work up a nocturnal lather.

A cushionless window seat and a ladder-back chair present the only opportunities for sitting. Gertrude's Aubusson-carpeted boudoir is equipped with a velvet chaise longue, a pair of armless, sateen-upholstered ladies' chairs, a brocaded love seat in the French Victorian style, a wing chair slip-covered in English chintz, a tapestried Chinese Chippendale bench at the foot of the bed, and a puffed taffeta vanity stool. Jason's mother, a gregarious woman, held salons there during her long, terminal illness. Gertrude considers this abundance of fanny space to be purely decorative. She would never entertain visitors in her private quarters. In fact, she does not relish being a hostess even in the public rooms of that house, although whenever he requires her to give a dinner party, she accomplishes the feat (the *fete*) with a bravado that passes for elan.

"The program of last Sunday's service is in my valise. As I recall, it contains a passage from St. Mark's Gospel, which I shall read aloud as a bedtime devotional," Jason says, as if offering her a nightcap. He leads her to sit beside him on the bed by the window, as though he is guiding her to theater seats. He reads at a faster clip than usual and doesn't analyze the Scripture afterward. Gertrude then kneels for her own bedtime prayer. Jason stays where he is. He never gets on his knees except in church, where leather hassocks are provided for that purpose. As her lips move silently, he finds that most responsive part of himself aroused by the unintentional pressure of her elbow against his thigh. As soon as she whispers "Amen," before she can rise, he grasps the globes of her breasts, which, despite the fullness of her garment, are rendered startlingly visible by moonlight that seems electrified. "Lie down with me," he says in the quiet, imperious voice she always obeys.

It has not occurred to her that Jason might assert his rights here, in her mother's house, as though they are in a hotel! At least the act won't take place in what was her own virginal bed.

She keeps her eyes closed until the corn-shuck-and-cotton-stuffed mattress ceases to crackle beneath their activity. After counting silently to two hundred—time enough for him to sink into a stertorous stupor—she arises, tiptoes across to the other bed, and reaches beneath its muslin dust ruffle for the chamber pot that looks absurdly like a soup tureen. As she squats within three feet of her snoring husband, she says another silent prayer, this one of gratitude for the convenience of modern plumbing in the Felder house—chain-flushing commodes; marble lavatories; elegant, porcelain, claw-foot tubs. She has become so accustomed to these amenities she never gives a passing thought to how her life was without them.

After Gertrude replaces the domed lid and pushes the container back to its hiding place, it occurs to her that she should look in on Lola. She supposes the girl has used the pretext of visiting the privy after dinner as a chance to smoke.

Gertrude opens and closes the door softly. No matter how sexually satiated he is, if he doesn't get a solid eight hours of shuteye every night, Jason Howard is cross as a bear the next day. She taps lightly on the door across the hall.

"*Entrez*," Lola chirps.

Gertrude does not approve of the fad of spouting French idioms and phrases as tribute to allies who might prove to be untrustworthy in the long run. She says, "I wanted to be sure you were in for the evening."

"Well, as you can see, I'm not out dancing." Lola is wearing the skimpy shift Gertrude packed. The girl has no decent nightgowns. She sits cross-legged among a scattering of papers on a maple bedstead of more primitive carpentry than the pair in the other room. Gertrude notices that Lola's breasts are the size and shape of orange halves—nowhere near as voluptuous as her own. Lola's fiancé might be chagrined to find himself shortchanged in that department. "Why are you staring at me? Don't tell me my shoulders are burned. I haven't been near the sun in weeks."

"I most certainly was not staring. I was thinking that we must see to appropriate lingerie for your trousseau."

"Maggie's offered to shop with me when the time comes. Don't be offended, Gertrude, but nightgowns like yours, with tucks and ribbons and billowing sleeves, are simply antediluvian. This is the age of come-hitherness."

"It's been my understanding that civilized men prefer to discover what's beneath the trappings in the normal course of connubial events"—Gertrude takes a quick, fortifying breath, as the choirmaster taught her—"rather than have it all so blatantly apparent. The garment you have on leaves little to the imagination."

"Shall I take it off? Then nothing will be left to your imagination. By the way, this bulging tummy represents Kathleen's supper. I assure you I'm not the least bit pregnant."

"And I assure you that tasteless remark is not the least bit humorous."

Outbursts of hostility between them are rare. Lola, surprised at the other's heightened temper, says thoughtfully, "Being here has caused us to regress to the scrappy children we once were."

"I was never a scrappy child." Gertrude sits on the edge of the bed Lola occupies. She looks at its empty twin and asks, though she knows the answer, "Is that where Rhoda slept?"

"It is. If those little boys ever flew in the window, they would land on Rhoda, not on me."

"What little boys?"

"The baby brothers who died. Rhoda used to say—"

"Rhoda used to say whatever came into her head. I am amazed that Mama allowed you to be so much under her influence."

"Mama had other things on her mind besides my welfare," Lola says. "Rhoda had my interests at heart more than my own mother did. She taught me to read before I started school."

"I thought Jason was responsible for your learning so prodigiously."

"That's true, but because of Rhoda, I wasn't a complete ignoramus when he took over. I hated it tonight, when the consensus of opinion around the table seemed to be one of relief that she's been dead all this time. To think that all those years, she wasn't living life to the fullest somewhere else . . ."

Gertrude says, "I'm not up to conversation so late in the evening. I'll say good night."

Lola jumps up, scattering papers to the floor. "Please don't leave. Sleep in here with me, Tru."

"All right." This way, she doesn't have to go back across the hall and lie awake, listening to the unfamiliar sounds of a sleeping male. As she pulls back the tea-dyed coverlet on the bed that had been Rhoda's, a long-ago musk of woods (rotting leaves, dried-out pine needles, molted feathers) and fields (cotton packed into husks they once thought were elfin caps, corn tassels they pretended were human hair) emanates from the bedding. She asks Lola politely, "Will you be putting out the lamp soon?"

"Just let me get this stuff back into the satchel. I'm too keyed-up to concentrate on grading papers anyway."

"Jason has promised me we will leave as soon as this business is concluded tomorrow."

"I didn't say I was anxious to leave."

"Well, I am. There was no necessity for you and me to make this trip."

"How can you say that, Tru? Rhoda is our sister."

"Oh, dear. Now you're upset. I knew it would be terrible for you."

"What's terrible is that she was allowed to stay lost. Why didn't Jason use his connections to find her?" Lola's cheeks are as crimson as if rouged.

"He tried. There was no trail to follow."

"Which should have made him all the more suspicious."

"I'll ask you not to criticize my husband."

"I didn't intend to," Lola says contritely. "I would never blame Jason for anything that's wrong with this family. He was right to insist that we come with him today. Kathleen and George have been hospitable, and their sons are delightful. Surely, you approve of Harold and Ray."

"I don't know enough about boys in general to have an opinion about any in particular."

"These two happen to be your nephews."

"That connection does not require me to forge an emotional tie to them." The kerosene lamp is extinguished except for a lingering smell of scorch. Gertrude's voice floats in the darkness. "Don't forget to say your prayers, Lola. The silent ones are the most powerful."

"I know. I learned about silent prayer from Rhoda."

8
Saturday Morning

"AH, THERE IS NO MORE BLISSFUL AROMA THAN THAT OF BACON FRYING."
Jason, in his thin-soled, pointed-toe lawyering shoes, has entered the
kitchen soundlessly. The egg falls from Kathleen's hand and shatters with
a sound as puny as a chick's first cheep. The colorless fluid seeps through
a crevice between floorboards, possibly onto the pea-head of one of the
speckled guineas that stroll beneath the house and call out, "*Pot-rack!
Pot-rack!*"

Kathleen considers whether it would be cannibalism of a sort, for a
guinea to feed on a chicken egg. There stands before her a man who
might appreciate such a hypothesis, but she's too unpracticed to spring
it on him. By the time the right phrases come (mellifluous jewels of
words, faceted with syllables, prismatic with meaning), the moment to
speak them has passed. She used to check books of poetry out of the

lending library. Now, she mainly reads art books and novels. Yet she cannot imagine telling this man that she reads anything at all.

"Sorry, Kathleen. Didn't mean to startle you." Gertrude's husband, a familiar stranger, moves as though to help her as she scrapes the splattered yolk with a spatula into the dog-scraps dish, then backs off when he realizes she's efficient at such things. He gleams ruddily, as if he's been scrubbed all over, although he had to make do this morning with the bowl-and-pitcher arrangement and a sliver of soap. He has on the same suit as yesterday, with a fresh high-collared shirt. His white buckskin shoes are covered with a film of road dust. Kathleen didn't think to provide him with a shoebrush, nor did Gertrude remember to pack one for him, apparently.

Something about this affable, self-confident man tells Kathleen he needs reassurance as much as the rest of them. She says, to make him feel better about the mess, "Ray's hound will be thrilled; this is one hen egg he won't have to steal." Kathleen cracks the rest of a dozen shells and coaxes their contents into the sizzling, larded skillet. While scrambling them, she adds, "I hope we didn't wake you too early. I never have been able to get breakfast ready without making noise." Never has tried to, as a matter of fact. Kathleen vents her resentment at having to prepare meals for hungry males by slamming pots and pans around. George and the boys are so used to the racket that they don't see it as protest.

"I was fortunate enough to wake hours ago, much to my visual delight. That view of the sun rising over distant hills was spectacular."

"I've seen so many, a sunrise doesn't seem special," Kathleen says, implying she's a good farm wife who's up at first light. It's none of his business that when she goes outside at morning's first blush, it's not with hoe or scythe or milk pail, but with mail-ordered tubes of paint, palette, brushes, sticks of charcoal and colored chalk, and a sketch pad of thick paper. She doesn't paint horizons or roses on velvet or magnolia blossoms on china. She sketches gnarled tree roots that have burst through the ground like arthritic knuckles.

Jason looks as though he knows what she's thinking and will make a thoughtful comment. But what he says is, "Gertrude will be down soon," as if in apology. Well, more power to her. Kathleen would be lazy as the devil if she had his wife's pampered life.

She doesn't ask him to help himself to bacon or a biscuit from the pan she's wrapping in a cup towel to keep warm. The solemn purpose of this gathering calls for the breaking of bread together, in some semblance of unity. Though not in the dining room this time. Kathleen has set the kitchen table and has instructed George to sit, as usual, at the head. She intends to give her husband any advantage she can think of, to keep Jason from usurping more authority (although George was more than a little relieved when Peter Whitney informed him yesterday morning that Jason would come right away and "decide how best to proceed"). Wherever she is, in heaven or hell or in between, Rhoda must be enjoying the trouble she's caused. *Bitch.*

They thought she was leading a life so exciting or sinful or both that she couldn't take the time to drop anyone a line and say where she was. A thumb of the nose to all of you, she so much as said by her leave-taking, which killed Mama same as if Rho had stuck a knife into her flesh. And poor Lola! That child used to trudge to the highway several times a day to look for Rhoda. Kathleen didn't want to be responsible for the baby sister. Once she was gone, the house was cleared of everyone but herself and George and their infant, and that seemed right at the time. She hadn't realized that Lola would not come back for visits. Some city people want their children to spend the summer months in the country, but Gertrude said it would be better for Lola not to have her routine disrupted by a change of household. Kathleen accepted that decision without any protest, not through meekness, which is not her nature, but because she puts a high value on simplicity.

Jason has moved into the hall. He looks up the stairwell, takes a gold watch from a vest pocket, holds the dial up to his ear, winds the stem, steps back to corroborate the time shown on the face of the hall clock, crosses his arms, taps a foot. Time is important to him, and Gertrude is wasting it. Will he chastise her in front of everyone, or later, or never? Kathleen thinks never. He knows Gertrude is not to be dealt with sternly. Too much man-handling and she would retreat into a permanent fog, and he'd be stuck with a completely nonfunctional woman, instead of one who's only partially off-kilter.

Lola whirls into view astride the banister, her pleated skirt above her knees. "Sliding was against the rules," she tells Jason, as he helps her dismount and pretends not to be shocked at this performance, "but Rhoda and I used to come down the stairs this way whenever Mama wasn't around. Gertrude and Kathleen didn't. They were good girls."

Kathleen never thought sliding down that hard wooden rail was fun. She's nonplused that Lola remembers her as a "good girl" and includes her in the same league with Gertrude. She doesn't know what to make of this grown-up Lola. They must have had a devil of a time getting her to conform to their strict rules. Kathleen braces for an embrace that, to her relief, doesn't come.

"I slept like the dead," Lola says dramatically, then, "Poor analogy. I should have said I slept marvelously. It was so peaceful to be summoned into wakefulness by one king-of-the-hill rooster instead of a neighborhood full of them, all trying to outdo each other, which is what we have. Also, in Felder, the noisome approach of the early-morning milk wagon sets a block's worth of pent-up dogs to barking."

"Our neighbors on both sides keep poultry," Jason informs Kathleen. "That will change with proposed legislation to disallow livestock in residential areas within the city limits." She can tell from his expression that he had a hand in the proposal.

"Will dogs be prohibited, too?" Kathleen asks. Mama could not abide a loud dog. Ray's liver-spotted hound hardly ever barks. Maybe Mama, in her floating, invisible form, restrains him.

Jason says, "As a matter of fact, dogs are not included in the proposal. Perhaps we should amend it to do so."

"Dogs are not considered livestock. You'll never get people to give up pets," Lola says, then explains to Kathleen, "Gertrude feels about dogs the same way Mama did. We had a Persian cat until it mauled one of her canaries. Where is everybody? I'm famished."

As though summoned by that remark, they begin to arrive. Gertrude waits out the three-abreast entrance of the boys and George, who reek of outdoors and the carbolic soap they've just washed their hands with at the pump. George nods a greeting all around as he scrambles past Lola and Jason to claim his rightful place at the maple trestle table he made as Kathleen's Christmas surprise two years ago. Kathleen has not put a cloth on the surface that he polished with linseed oil and his bare hands to the color of November leaves. She hopes Gertrude will ask what happened to Mama's table so she can tell her it was chopped up for firewood. To his wife's surprised relief, George looks as though he is master here, resonating a dignity she didn't know he possessed. Gertrude sails in. Jason puts a restraining hand on her arm while the boys stake out their usual places. Then he steers her to the chair next to Harold and seats Lola beside Ray, himself on Gertrude's other side. That leaves Kathleen the end of the table opposite George—not her usual place, but the proper one for the hostess. Jason is a smooth organizer.

George does her proud again by not relinquishing to Jason his prerogative to say grace. As soon as they're all seated, he intones sternly, "Bless this food to our use and us to thy service, amen." Kathleen relaxes.

The napkins come out of the rings. Gertrude scrutinizes hers before placing it in her lap. One more meal to go after this one, and then, God willing, they'll take their leave. Lunch will be a picnic in the cemetery, either before or after the burial. It's been a long time—a very long time, as Kathleen will remind her if she gets uppity—since Gertrude has visited the family graves.

George spoons grits onto plates, to be passed down the table. After everyone has a plate, Kathleen starts the platter of bacon and the covered biscuit tray. Gertrude turns the lazy Susan until she can reach the jelly compote, then inquires, presumably of her hostess (although she hasn't yet acknowledged Kathleen this morning), "Is this pear preserves, made from Mama's recipe?"

"The pear trees died after a cruel frost some winters back, and we've never replanted. But the tough, old quince bush at the corner of the garden always bears fruit."

"Quince." Gertrude winces as she spoons a small glob onto her plate. She separates a bite-sized portion of biscuit, butters it daintily, then dabs it with jelly. None of this smearing the whole thing at once.

Harold sends his mother a reproachful look. Why hasn't she impressed on him the importance of table manners? *Just one of those things I haven't yet got around to,* Kathleen smiles back. She says, "I don't recall that Mama followed a recipe. She boiled the fruit down with sugar and lemon, which is how I do it. Rhoda called this jelly 'quivering quince.' " Everyone chews softly and listens. Not used to having the floor, Kathleen hears herself begin to ramble like a hybrid rose gone wild, climbing beyond its trellis into branches of nearby trees, narrating as though she is the only one present who knows these characters: "The mention of pears reminds me of the time Mama defied Grandmother by refusing to batch up any more soap on the place. She ordered a dozen-sized box of Pears Pure Castile, which, according to the pharmacist, was the best. The next time Rhoda was made to lick a bar of soap for some infraction, she said to me, 'Yum, yum. This store-bought kind is better than licorice. Want a taste?' And I was stupid enough to say yes."

The anecdote falls flat, except for Lola's sad smile of commiseration. At the mention of Rhoda's name, a pall of apprehension settles over the table. Gertrude gives no indication she remembers anything about Mama's ever defying Grandmother, or that her own delicate skin was ever subjected to the strong concoction brewed in a three-legged iron pot, which was also used to scald dirty laundry and render hog fat into lard.

Jason clears his throat, gazes at the navel of melted butter in his grits, and ends the awkward silence by changing the subject. "Consider, if you will, this marvel. Corn was planted, harvested, shucked; then the kernels scraped from the cobs were granulated into cereal, which was cooked and is now being consumed, all right here." Although Jason stops before adding "on our place," George's ears flatten against his head like an animal sensing danger.

Harold, bless his heart, takes this moment to remind everyone, "Dr. Whitney said he'd be dropping by early this morning."

"I hope Daisy's with him!" Whatever Lola says is infused with enthusiasm. Where does that bubbly nature spring from? Not from Mama. Maybe she gets it from Papa, who, until he took to his bed, had a glimmer of fun in his eye and a lilt in his laughter. She adds, "And his wife, of course."

"I doubt she'll come. Coralee's a complete recluse now," Kathleen says, then turns to Gertrude. "It may be fashionable in Felder for women to withdraw altogether, but such behavior is not considered normal in Hackberry Hill."

She replies, "Such would not be considered normal or fashionable in Felder. We have no recluses that I know of."

"My dear, you're forgetting Gladys Baker." Jason explains, "Mrs. Baker hasn't been outside her house, not even to church, in over a year."

"That's because she is ill," Gertrude says reprovingly. "The rector brings Holy Communion to her. The wine, wafers, linens, and chalice are in a small leather case. It's a very tidy arrangement." She taps the corners of her mouth with her napkin, as though making sure that she herself is a tidy arrangement.

"The rumor is the lady stays home because she's a tippler," Jason informs the table at large. "You're not to repeat that, Lola."

"Heaven forbid that I would dare."

"Daisy is Harold's girlfriend," Ray blurts.

"What he means is, Daisy is my friend, and she's a girl," Harold clarifies.

"Well spoken, young man." Jason nods approvingly.

"They used to swim in the pond together," Ray persists.

"Skinny-dipping?" Lola asks.

Harold blushes. "No, ma'am. She asked me to teach her to swim. She had never learned."

"Rhoda taught me to swim when I was four," Lola says.

"And nearly drowned you in the process." Kathleen relishes the meanness of her remark.

"But I didn't drown, and because of that early training, I'm confident in the water now." But Lola's voice is not confident as she adds, looking from face to face, "Am I the only one who misses her?"

George says equably, "It's hard to go on for years missing someone who left on purpose, and with such—"

"Obdurate disregard." Kathleen picks the words out of the air. Jason regards her in amazement. "Papa got me in the habit of learning to spell, pronounce, and define half a dozen new words a day. He said it would be as useful as an institutional education, which was his way of telling me not to expect one. Rhoda and I tried to outdo each other in dictionary learning. Maybe that's why it took with me, because I'm not studious by nature. . . ." She's rambling again. She presses her napkin to her mouth.

Jason says kindly, "I'm impressed that you took your father's excellent advice to heart. Truly impressed, Kathleen."

Lola takes the last bite of a biscuit and brushes crumbs from her hands onto her plate. "What's to be done with the remains?"

"When everyone is finished, you and I shall clear the table."

"Damn it, Tru. Those aren't the remains I'm talking about."

"Jason, please," his wife implores.

"Please what?" He pretends not to know what she asks of him.

"Please remind Lola that swearing will not be tolerated in Mama's house any more than it is in ours."

Little Sister is not intimidated. "I withdraw the 'damn,' but I'm entitled to my say. I do not want what might be Rhoda to end up in a file cabinet."

"That decision could be up to the doctor," George says. "Peter Whitney is the coroner. He'll know what the rules are."

"How can there be any rules for this unique tragedy?" Lola's eyes shine even in distress, like agates from Ray's sack of marbles. Kathleen is thinking what pigments she would mix to come up with that variegated color—the base a medium sepia, with touches of ocher and raw umber. Blessed with Papa's eyes and Mama's cheekbones and auburn hair, Lola is a blend of their best features. No one attempts to answer her question, but Jason's brow is furrowed as though he's thinking hard.

The doorbell rings; Peter has arrived. Everyone jumps up, glad to get out of the kitchen. Half an hour ago, they were enticed by the appearance and aroma of just-cooked food. Revulsion comes with satiation. Remnants of stiffened grits and congealed eggs are smeared across the plates; wadded napkins lie on the table like felled doves waiting to be retrieved. Kathleen informs Gertrude, "I'll take you up later on your offer to clear the table." She seems surprised, as if she's already forgotten the interchange. Gertrude's eyebrows are usually raised, so that she appears to be supercilious or perplexed even when her face is in repose. How does Jason stand it?

Last night, Kathleen put that question to George. He replied, "Don't feel sorry for Jason. He didn't marry the woman for her brains."

They were puddled together in the center of the bed that had been Mama and Papa's, and before that Grandmother and Grandfather's. The privacy they took for granted seemed hard-won on this occasion. George was tentatively stroking her breasts, as though making their acquaintance for the first time. "Gertrude's are bigger," he murmured, which, for some unfathomable reason, made Kathleen's respond to his touch quicker than usual.

"Since you're such an expert, what size were Rhoda's?"

"Don't recall ever noticing," he said, his hands continuing to explore the territory they knew so well. "Rhoda wasn't my type."

"And Gertrude is?"

"Heck no. She reminds me of a statue, like those carved figureheads on old ships." This was an imaginative speech for George, though he didn't intend to start a conversation; his thoughts were on taking his pleasure and giving Kathleen hers. He had positioned himself above her, as though he were a circus daredevil preparing to dive into a tank. This was not the time to accuse him of ogling Lola during supper.

Afterward, a rhythmic sound like the back and forth of a rocking chair came through the ceiling. George said softly, "They're going at it up there. I told you he didn't marry her for her brains."

Kathleen could not imagine Gertrude and Jason—or Gertrude and anybody—doing what she and George had just done. He was stroking her back, as though she were a horse that needed calming after a run. She has tried to explain to him that she doesn't need calming; she likes to stay in that exalted place, by herself, for as long as possible. George finished breaking the spell with the boyish whine he uses only when he's fearful (and to give him credit, that's not often): "Jason may want to divide the land now."

She rolled to the edge of the bed, away from the dampness of him and his pungent, sour odor that was no longer an aphrodisiac. "Why now?"

"The reason it's remained in your mama's name is because one of the daughters was missing. If the estate had been divided among the three of you and Rhoda returned, she could have made trouble."

Kathleen knew that, of course, but she had never thought of Rhoda's having that kind of power. She wondered if she was glad Rhoda was dead, or if she should feel guilty because she never spent one moment being sad that Rhoda left. Truth was, she hasn't missed any of them, though there was a certain satisfaction in knowing at that moment that all her sisters were accounted for. One never left Hackberry Hill alive, and the other two turned up yesterday very much in the flesh.

The grandfather clock had chimed on the dot of five, as if announcing their arrival. They'd have come sooner except for that roadside stop for water, which must have cost them half an hour. The last thing George told her before he went to sleep last night was, "Your brother-in-law doesn't have the practical sense to operate machinery, not even something as uncomplicated as an automobile. He didn't think to fill up his water canister when he started out."

"That's as stupid as starting out on a marriage without respect for the person you marry," his wife said, but the hateful words went over George's head.

The problem was hers, not his. Kathleen has learned to value him, and not just for the energetic activity he never seems to tire of that vaults her into blissful oblivion. She seldom thinks of the shame connected with the first time, which took place in the dark, feathery hayloft of the barn. Boys at school had never singled her out to josh around with like they did Rhoda, or to gaze at in awe, as they did Gertrude. George was the first male to notice her, though she lusted first and contrived to let him know it. That he was the hired man made it easier for her to be forward. She likened what they did to the whispered rumor that certain boys at school would screw farm animals. Her animal had hair like a crow's wing and skin so darkly smooth its pigment could have come from a tube—burnt sienna, or copper glow. He certainly caused her to glow. She thought she might burst into flame at his touch.

If Mama hadn't been preoccupied, she surely would have stopped what began right under her nose. Eventually, Kathleen transcended the shame. She knew that what they were up to was acceptable on a higher level and that, without their intending it, a baby was in the making. At least she wouldn't be an old maid.

After the second child was born, she prayed not to have another unless it was a girl. She didn't conceive again, and her monthly periods ceased when she was twenty-seven years old. Grandmother—Miss Kitty—told Kathleen in a dream it was her doing. In the years since that blessing, Kathleen and George have elevated to an art form the ritual that entrapped them. When she teaches herself to sculpt, she will make an entwined image of the two of them in fired clay, to remind her when she's old and he's gone to death or some other calling, of what they had, because the memory of making love does not keep well. What she recalls most clearly of those sessions in the hayloft is not the rippling pleasure or the fear of being caught, but the guttural approval of pigeons that watched from the rafters.

She awoke this morning feeling as though her hands were tied; she won't be free to wield a stick of chalk or a paintbrush. George arose with his usual quietness (while she, as usual, played possum), dressed, retrieved the lidded chamber pot from beneath the bed for emptying, and left the room, all in painstaking quietness. He is a considerate man. Mama probably never recognized that quality in Kathleen's husband, not having had it in her own. Papa dealt her fits, even when they were young. Mama seethed when she had to take orders from Grandmother, who was gentle with her only when Mama's babies died, and then not for long. They were never friends. After Mama supervised the washing and laying out of this mother-in-law for viewing before the burial, she became positively cheerful. She was as radiant at Miss Kitty's funeral as she was at Gertrude's wedding.

Kathleen thinks she and Gertrude are lucky that they never have had to contend with the mothers of their husbands. Lola's of the new breed of female who won't bend to a husband's will, much less a mother-in-law's. She announced at supper that she was "passionate" about securing the vote for women: "I've been incensed since the Senate rejected President Wilson's suffrage bill last year, and four women were arrested, actually given jail terms, for picketing the White House. At least women in New York State can vote. Have you been to any meetings, Kat?"

Kathleen had never given that ballyhooed subject a serious thought. "I haven't heard of any militant women's organization around here since the original Temperance Society became a social club."

"Was Grandmother active when it was militant?" Lola asked.

"I suppose so, but I doubt she took the temperance issue seriously. Miss Kitty loved her daily nip; it's just as well she didn't live to see this state pass a prohibition law. I seem to recall hearing she was among the group who marched, with hatchets, from the Grange Hall to the saloon."

"Really?" Jason sat up straight. "What happened then?"

"The men took the hatchets away from their wives," Kathleen guessed, "and the women went home to cook supper."

Jason laughed, to Lola's consternation. She said, "Well, this is a different time and a different issue. Wives may have to stop cooking supper in order to show their husbands how serious they are."

"If women could run for office, I would appreciate the opportunity to cast a ballot," Kathleen said. "But why bother, if we can only vote for men?"

"That will come later. First things first," Lola said airily. "I belong to the Felder Feminists. You should get something started here. You could call the group the Hackberry Hill Hackers. Do it, Kat. I'll send you some literature."

"You'll be wasting your time. I'm not a joiner, much less an organizer."

Before the boys left to spend the night in the mill, Harold said to her, where no one else could hear, "I think women should be allowed to vote, especially in light of what all y'all have to do."

Oh, what a lucky woman, whoever she is, who marries my Harold. I hope it won't be that spoiled twit, Daisy Whitney, who acts as if she's royalty, when there's no telling whose bastard she is. How can I be so mean? Am I getting to be like my mother?

9
Gliding Lightly

LAST NIGHT, HER DREAMS SEEMED TO OCCUR SIMULTANEOUSLY, as if in a triptych. She was riding a tandem in Felder Park with Rob, who had on a hospital gown, and she was a child wading in Turtle Creek, looking for swamp lilies to put on her mother's grave. The third scenario was the nightmare: at Rhoda's request, Lola vacated her body so Rhoda's skeleton could move in.

She awoke confused. Was this a new day, or a day left over from her earlier time here? Whichever, she felt she must glide lightly through it.

He's as handsome as ever, despite the gray in his hair and mustache. Gertrude greets him formally: "Dr. Whitney." It seems stilted.

"Peter," Lola says experimentally.

He ignores her outstretched hand to squint owlishly at her over pince-nez spectacles, then disillusions her further by exclaiming, "Don't tell me this is little Lola Holloway, all grown up!"

Jason, coming into the hall, booms, "None other," and grins as though accepting an extravagant compliment. "Lola completed her baccalaureate summa cum laude at Judson this past June, and has a position on the faculty of the Felder High School." Reminded by her cool stare that she is not an inanimate object, he changes course. "Jason Howard, Peter. It's good to see you again." This time, the man permits his hand to be shaken.

In a shiny, paper-stiff dress, her golden hair standing out from her head and crimped so strangely Lola wonders how in the world she accomplished it, the doctor's daughter waits to be acknowledged. "Hello again, Daisy Whitney," she says. "Last time we met, you were in a Rolls-Royce pram." She stops short of describing Daisy's tender little self shielded by a swath of mosquito netting.

"Indeed, it has been a long time. I'm delighted to be reacquainted with you, Miss Holloway." Before she finishes that pretty speech, her gaze swivels from Lola to Harold; it's his approval she wants.

Oh, gosh. She's head over heels, and he's oblivious.

"Daisy, may I present Miss Gertrude and her husband, Mr. Howard?" The man, in his eagerness to show off his daughter, makes the introduction improperly. Gertrude smiles indulgently.

"Good morning, ma'am, sir." The girl curtsies self-consciously.

Kathleen herds them into the front room, where Mama's curtains flutter like nervous hands in the breeze that sifts through the window screens. Gertrude chooses the lady's chair. She places her hands on the antimacassar-covered arms, then clasps them together in her lap. It's unusual for her to show anxiety. Daisy is perched on the edge of the prickly horsehair couch, watching Harold. The discoverer of the bones is expectantly alert. His cowlicked brother stands just inside the doorway, poised for flight. Kathleen shifts her position in the rocking chair that was Grandmother's throne. Standing beside his wife, George cracks his knuckles. The tension is contagious. Lola has a hard time keeping her right foot still, and she's salivating for a smoke or a stick of gum. Three years ago, the ingenious chewing-gum manufacturer Mr. William Wrigley sent samples of his product to every address in every telephone directory in the United States. Gertrude refused to even taste that free Juicy Fruit. In her view, anyone past the age of twelve who chews gum is common.

Jason booms into the awkward silence, "The ladies are aware of the situation, Peter." He cocks his head in Daisy's direction to suggest the girl be dismissed before the discussion gets under way. Peter seems not to pick up that signal. Lola's foot begins to swing again; she senses that Jason is willing her to keep her mouth shut.

It's obvious Peter has dreaded this moment. He begins calmly, but one eyelid twitches. "The framework Harold has reassembled for the most part by himself—it's a fine piece of work, worthy of an advanced medical student—appears to be that of a girl beyond the onset of puberty, but not fully mature. If I had a record of Rhoda's height when she was twelve or so, or even as young as nine or ten, I could determine whether what we have conforms with projected measurements for her at fifteen, the age Rhoda was when she disappeared. But unfortunately, I don't have such a record." Of course he doesn't. Most of the time, one exception being Lola's broken collarbone, Mama doctored them with turpentine, splints, plant poultices, Vicks salve, castor oil, quinine, boiled needles, and soapy-water enemas. Brown paper placed in the roof of the mouth stopped a nosebleed; essence of wintergreen calmed an upset stomach; baking soda and tobacco took the swelling out of bee stings and insect bites.

He continues, "Remains of this nature can sometimes be identified by teeth. When I told Kathleen one of the incisors was missing a corner, she recalled that Rhoda had a chipped front tooth. That is the basis for assuming the bones found in the pond are those of your sister."

Lola says hotly, "Kathleen is mistaken. There was nothing wrong with Rhoda's front teeth."

"Perhaps you were not as critically observant at the age of six as you are now," Jason remarks gently.

Gertrude says, "I don't recall Rhoda's having such a blemish either."

"That's because it happened shortly before she left here, and you weren't around then," Kathleen explains.

"But I was," Lola says obstinately.

"Perhaps the family portrait will tell us." Gertrude takes the centennial photograph from the mantelpiece's bric-a-brac.

Grandmother, Papa, and Mama are seated in dining-room chairs in the front yard, the girls grouped around them. A traveling photographer hid his head beneath the cloth of a big tripod camera and squeezed the magical bulb that froze them in that moment. Penciled across the photograph's wine-colored pasteboard mounting are the date "January 1, 1900" and an explanatory sentence in the same confident, masculine script (Papa's?): "The Holloways Of Hackberry Hill Welcome The New Century And Bid Reluctant Farewell To The Old." Gertrude, who would have been on the reluctant farewell side—she still keeps one foot in the nineteenth century, as though she can choose which era to inhabit—examines the picture through Jason's mother's lorgnette, which she keeps handy on a narrow neck ribbon.

While Gertrude holds the photograph, Lola looks over her shoulder at it—first at herself, the pouting toddler in Mama's lap. Wearing a high-necked, long-waisted white dress and a ribbon bow atop her head, Gertrude stands with both arms looped possessively around Mama's neck. Kathleen, outfitted identically to Gertrude, stands behind Papa but doesn't touch him. Rhoda, in a dress dark as a scowl, leans into his shoulder. She's the only child not in white. Her stockings are wrinkled; her lips are not parted. No one's smiling. Kathleen's sporadic feather-dusting hasn't shifted the unframed photograph from its original placement between a glass-domed bouquet of dried flowers and a conch-shell souvenir of Grandfather's visit to the Gulf of Mexico. Rhoda said Lola, if she believed, could hear the ocean in that shell; if she closed her eyes at the same time, she could see the foaming, crashing waves. And she was right.

"Everyone's toothless," Jason pronounces, after Gertrude passes the picture to him.

"There was at least one other family grouping," she says.

"You may be thinking of the wedding picture Grandmother didn't want on display because Papa appeared to be inebriated. I have no idea where it is." Kathleen shrugs. "Anyway, Rhoda wouldn't have been in it."

"There were other photographs of her." Lola has one in a gold locket she hasn't looked at since Gertrude told her to forget her early years. She sees that image now as though she holds the open, hinged heart in her hand: Rhoda's expression is one she wore often; no teeth are bared in that Mona Lisa smile.

"I don't know of any. A camera wasn't a household item while we were growing up."

Jason snorts into his handkerchief (which gets him the floor) and addresses Peter. "As a physician and the county coroner"—he emphasizes the last two words as though ridiculing the designation, which Lola is sure is not his intention—"are you aware of any reason why we should not conclude these devitalized remains are what's left of Rhoda Holloway?" It's called badgering the witness, and Jason's very good at the technique.

"I feel certain in my mind that we've made the correct identification. But if you are asking me to provide a death certificate, I must tell you I would not feel comfortable signing such a document."

"Are you saying certification of death is required for a skeleton?"

"I bow to your opinion on that legal point."

"Well, I say it's not necessary for what we plan to do here today."
Jason rubs his hands together briskly. "George and I have decided that
the remains, found on family property and deemed to be those of a
family member, should be put to rest while the family is together."

"Put to rest?" Peter Whitney echoes.

"In the church graveyard. Where is the subject now?" Jason glances
around the room, as though he might have missed it.

"Still in my laboratory, where we arranged the bones in some semblance of the creature they once . . ." The doctor coughs to avoid using
the word *inhabited*, then takes a different tack. "When we got most of it
assembled, I reported Harold's discovery to the sheriff. Upon finding no
mention of an unsolved missing-female case in the files, he concluded
that the remains were those of a transient, probably a trespasser who
drowned accidentally."

"The sheriff didn't look back far enough," Lola says. "Rhoda should
be on record as a runaway."

Kathleen shakes her head. "Mama would never have reported her as
missing. She would have told any officer of the law who came snooping
that it was family business, and none of his."

"Has the sheriff been informed that a girl left here fifteen years ago
and was never heard from again?"

Peter says quickly, "Not by me. I wasn't present when George showed
him where the bones were found."

George turns red. He hasn't mentioned that part to Jason. "I didn't
see it was my place to tell Phil Watkins about a disappearance that occurred before he moved here. The man who was sheriff when Rhoda ran
away fell off a fishing pier and drowned. Nobody saw it happen, but it
was a known fact that the fellow liked to fish and drink at the same
time, so no one tried to make a criminal case out of that drowning."

"Good point. There is no reason to arouse public interest in this private scuttlebutt either." Jason adds quickly, to forestall any further observation from Lola, "Peter, your expertise and guidance have been invaluable. If you'll bear with us awhile longer, I'd like to come by your place and see what you and young Harold have put together." He turns back to George. "Have you had a look?" It's as though this thing they're calling Rhoda is a sideshow fetus in a jar of formaldehyde.

"Haven't and don't care to," George answers. "I'm willing to accept whatever's on Doc's table as the remnants of the drowned sister, and I'll offer the services of my boys to dig a grave or a hole big enough for a bag of bones. As I've mentioned earlier, I have a pine casket available."

"Excellent." Jason beams. "How long will the dig take?" Now, it's an archaeological expedition.

"Two to three hours for a full-sized grave. They won't dawdle."

"So we could put her away around noon. The boys might go ahead to the cemetery and get the project started."

Kathleen asks, "Which is it to be? Croker sack or coffin?"

"We should take a vote," Jason concedes. "I'm in favor of keeping the skeleton intact, as it seems a pity to dismantle all that fine work. And it would be my privilege to pay for the coffin."

"I'll make you a good price." George looks around. "Can someone tell me where those boys have got off to?"

Daisy can. "Ray left with Harold, who's gone back to his precious discovery. That's all he's cared about for the past week." She adds quickly, "Sorry. I didn't mean to sound disrespectful of the dead."

"Don't worry about it." Lola absolves the girl. "This family honors disrespect."

"That was uncalled for, Lola," Gertrude says.

"Since the boys are already there, you can ride to the doctor's with me, George." Jason opens his watch and speaks as though reading from it. "While we're gone, Gertrude, Kathleen, and Lola will decide on the format. In the absence of clergy, I suggest each of you select a passage of Scripture to read, and perhaps a bit of secular verse."

"That will not do, sir. The church cemetery is hallowed ground. A man of the cloth must officiate." Gertrude uses *sir* to soften the blow of wifely contradiction.

"Sanctioned or not, this family's had at least one funeral without benefit of clergy," Kathleen says. "When Grandfather died, the Reverend McLarty had malaria, and Grandmother refused to let the Presbyterian preacher conduct the service. Miss Kitty spoke over the casket herself. McLarty's not available now either. He's close to a hundred and dotty as a June bug."

Gertrude doesn't give up easily. "Who supplies the pulpit?"

"A young seminarian was here for the summer, but he's likely gone back to school. Even if he's still around, I wouldn't want to ask him to participate in this underhanded procedure."

"Underhanded!" Gertrude enunciates each syllable as though it's a spelling assignment.

"Maybe crazy would be a better word." Kathleen turns her cool gaze on Jason. "Are you sure we don't need official permission to inter human bones?"

"The coroner is present." Jason waves a hand toward Peter.

"But he doesn't wish to be accountable," Kathleen says.

Peter responds icily, "What is it you wish me to account for?"

Jason sighs. "We would like you to assure us Rhoda was not murdered."

The sharp intake of breath Lola hears is her own.

"I can't provide that assurance."

"Rhoda talked to strangers. She was asking for trouble." Kathleen pulls her apron strings loose and flings the garment aside, as though the gesture can liberate her forever from the humbleness of domesticity. She reminds Lola of the warrior-maidens in a series of illustrated books on Wagner's *Ring of the Nibelung* that Jason gave her on her tenth birthday. At this moment, he is regarding Kathleen with heightened interest;

Kathleen would be competent in the courtroom! Lola feels a swift, intense jealousy.

"Oh, Sister, what a thing to say." Gertrude clasps her hands, then lets them fly apart and back together again, like birds in midair.

"Don't you 'Oh, Sister' me. I'm sick of this pretending you don't remember what life was like here. Even for you, the fair-haired daughter, it was no bed of roses."

Gertrude is hyperventilating. "Should I get your smelling salts?" Lola asks, hoping the answer is no. Lola doesn't want to miss something while she's upstairs retrieving Gertrude's nostrums bag.

"No, thank you." Gertrude doesn't want to miss anything either, and the salts make her woozy. "I shall rise above Kathleen's judgmental remark."

Jason says, "Let's keep to the task at hand. In my opinion, launching a full investigation into what might have happened years ago could be more harmful than useful. After all this time, there are no clues to track."

"That's right. No shoe prints or bloody hand prints, no weapons or any indication that a weapon was involved. There was no corpse to autopsy." The doctor explains excitedly now. "Of course, a cleaved skull or badly broken bones could suggest foul play, but the only significant traumas were the chipped tooth and hairline fractures in the occiput and one femur, all of which could have been caused by a fall from the wheel or earlier accidents. It was not possible to determine whether she'd been smothered, strangled, shot, stabbed, or poisoned." Jason clears his throat to signal Peter that he's going on unnecessarily, but the man's too wound up to stop. "A young girl who leaves her circle of protection is particularly vulnerable to mayhem." His swift glance at Daisy reveals his vulnerability to the thought of something happening to her. His resolve to keep his precious child close strengthens in that moment.

"The mayhem, if there was such, happened right here," Lola says. "Hackberry Hill is no idyllic oasis of safety. The unexpected could happen in town, in the woods, the churchyard, a barn, this house, or your own." Instead of convincing the man he can't protect his daughter by holding on to her, Lola has alarmed them both. Daisy's eyes widen. Her father's face turns ashen. She slides closer on the couch toward him; he places a protective arm around her shoulders.

Where was our papa when Rhoda needed him? Or when I needed him? Lola hears her voice as though it's someone else's: "Whether her death was accidental or deliberate, Rhoda was a victim, because she's not out there somewhere having herself a wonderful life."

Kathleen's arms enclose her. Overlooking Lola's emotional outburst is a kindness on Gertrude's part, since she disapproves of such display. Jason watches with evident concern but doesn't take a step toward them; comforting is woman's work. Lola leans into a cushion of femaleness that seems as familiar as her own body. If she had stayed here, would Kathleen have shown her affection and nurturance? As though in answer, Kathleen withdraws from the physical contact.

The doctor says quietly to Jason, "I'll go along now and expect you shortly."

"Right away," Jason says.

"Only the men have voted," Lola reminds Jason, after Peter and Daisy have left. "I cast mine for the casket. Whoever this relic is, she should not be buried in a sack."

"The casket." Gertrude raises her hand to be sworn in.

"Make it unanimous," Kathleen says, then turns to George. "Did you tell them the inside of the casket is raw wood, without padding?"

"I don't have a woman to do the sewing."

"He has a woman, but she doesn't sew," Kathleen clarifies.

Gertrude opines, "Our mother was so artful with thimble and thread. Lola and I have no real flair for needlework, and if you didn't inherit her talent, Kathleen, then it must have gone to waste."

"Maybe Rhoda got it," Lola says, although she never saw that sister involved in anything as ladylike as stitchery.

Gertrude exclaims, in her startled manner, "Oh, but Mama's talent could not have passed to her."

"Gertrude, this isn't the time for idle chatter," Jason says.

Kathleen overrules him. "I want to hear the rest of it."

"I can't remember what I was going to say." Gertrude is seldom flustered, and Jason seldom chastises her in the presence of others.

"Rhoda wouldn't care whether or not her casket is padded. She once told me she'd as soon sleep on the floor as on a corn-shuck mattress." Lola doesn't have to remind them that Mama had the only feather bed in the house.

Jason pulls out the watch again. "Let's go, George. Ladies, don't forget, you must select the readings."

"In the rush to get off yesterday, I neglected to pack my Bible," Gertrude confesses.

Kathleen says, "You must feel lost without it."

"Not really. I know several passages by heart."

"You mean from memory." Before Lola became a teacher, she never would have corrected anyone's manner of speech, especially Gertrude's. She wishes she hadn't now.

As Lola is thinking she must not let herself become a spinsterish pencil of a woman, Gertrude pulls her up short: "To know Scripture by heart implies more than rote memorization."

The men have left. The square room seems to expand with the freed space, yet Lola misses the musk of masculinity. Kathleen has staked out what must be her usual place, in Grandmother's rocker. Gertrude's glance travels slowly from one corner of the ceiling to another, as though searching out cobwebs. That there are none is rather remarkable, as Kathleen has made it clear that housekeeping is not among her interests.

"Penny for a random thought," Lola says, although the silence seems blissfully harmonious.

"Was Rhoda adopted?" Kathleen's calmly stated question is not for her.

Gertrude says, "Whatever gave you that idea?"

"Two things. You just said she couldn't have inherited Mama's talent for sewing. My earliest memory is of seeing Rhoda for the first time, and she wasn't an infant." Kathleen presses her hands on either side of her forehead, as though to firm up the vision. "It was Christmastime. A cedar strung with cranberries and popcorn took up part of the front hall, which was cold from a blast of outside air. Papa had just arrived from a trip; he was wearing his topcoat, and particles of snow that looked like goose down clung to it. A miniature stranger stood in front of the tree, reaching for the candles."

"Perhaps you've called up a cumulative picture of several Christmases."

"No, Tru. This recollection is my first awareness of a lighted tree, as well as my first awareness of Rhoda, which may be why it's very clear."

"That makes sense, Kat. Go on," Lola prods.

"I felt threatened by the interloper."

"Who else was present?" Gertrude asks.

"You, Mama, Papa, as I've said, and Grandmother. We were all watching the small child in the red coat. Dark hair peeped out beneath a tam, also red, and she could walk. She was barefoot, which surprised me, because Mama never let us go without shoes in winter, even in the house."

"She believed we could catch pneumonia through the soles of our feet," Gertrude explains. "And as usual, she was right. I have never had pneumonia."

"According to what we were told and the record pages in Grandmother's Bible, Rhoda was born in 1888," Kathleen continues. "In this memory, I see her as perhaps a year old, so I would have been three."

Lola says, "That you don't recall her as an infant doesn't prove she wasn't born here."

Kathleen's eyes do not waver from Gertrude's face. "You would have been old enough to form a clear recollection of this important event. Was Rhoda left in a basket on the front stoop? Did Papa find her there and bring her inside? Or is it as I seem to recall—he brought her home from one of his trips?"

"I don't care to continue this line of conversation."

"You don't have to. Now I know how it was. They didn't want Rhoda to learn she was adopted, so Mama swore you to secrecy. It never occurred to me that Rhoda wasn't born in this house until that single flash of an incident long past began to take shape in my mind." It's obvious from Gertrude's expression that Kathleen has discovered one truth about Rhoda's origin: she wasn't born to their mother.

"When did you first have this recollection?" Lola asks.

"After Rhoda was away for long enough that I began to think she really was gone for good. Must have been at least a year after she left that note in the sugar bowl. I thought of asking the doctor or the Reverend McLarty, as either of them might know if Rhoda was adopted, but I didn't."

"Why ever not? I would have asked everyone who knew Mama and Papa back then."

"Then I have failed to teach you the significance of family pride and loyalty, Lola," Gertrude says sadly.

"What you taught me is that it was in my best interest to forget I ever had a life here," Lola retorts. "You made me pretend I avoided infancy altogether and sprang into being at the age of six." Then, at the pain on the other's face, "I'm sorry. That wasn't fair." The rest of the apology sounds as if she's purloined it from a dime novel, but it's quite sincere. "Forgive me, dearest Tru. I can't imagine where I would be without you."

"You'd likely be right here," Kathleen says.

"I wish you two had drawn straws to see who took me. I wasn't old enough to make that choice for myself."

"We were hardly capable of making adult decisions then either. Gertrude and I were married off as soon as we were weaned."

"Not literally, of course," Gertrude amends.

Kathleen comes up with another recollection. "You were horrified that Mama put you and Jason in her room on your wedding night."

Gertrude takes up the thread. "I begged her to let me go upstairs, as usual. I had no idea what was expected of me. I could hardly believe it when she said I must put on my nightgown and sleep next to Jason."

Lola laughs. "You were deflowered in Mama's bed?"

"No, indeed. That would have been sacrilege. Fortunately, Jason understood and did not insist."

"Consummation of marital vows is not sacrilege." Lola speaks as though she knows.

"Though sometimes it's rape," Kathleen says. "Did you let him do it the next night?"

"Heavens no! We were on a train. The consummation . . ." Gertrude pauses to lick her lips. "That word sounds genteel. Like *consomme.*"

"When did it finally take place?" Kathleen's eyes widen. "Don't tell us it hasn't!"

"Of course it has. I couldn't have held a man like Jason if I refused him his entitlements. The act was completed in a hotel bridal suite on the third night after we were married. And it was ghastly."

"In what way?" Lola asks casually, hoping not to dispel this rare candor.

"I thought I was hemorrhaging. Jason had to explain to me that the show of blood was the natural course of events. I wondered why Mama hadn't warned me."

Kathleen says, "She probably thought if she told you what to expect, you wouldn't go through with the marriage."

"I very well might not have. Of course, the act got easier and easier." Gertrude sighs pleasurably.

"My friend Maggie says coitus, though it sounds like a disease, is better than gin and cigarettes."

"Your *friend* says!" Kathleen exclaims. "Lola, don't tell me your rose-bud is still intact."

"In the dormitory, we referred to it as a cherry, and yes, indeed, mine is more or less intact, because my boyfriend declined to take full advantage of my offering before he went to war."

Gertrude's confessional blush is back full force. "Your offering? Well. I have failed to bring you up as Mama would have."

"Why blame yourself for what Lola's done or wishes she had done? Mama never blamed herself when one of us took a misstep. I should know."

Lola yearns to tell Kathleen she admires her for making the best of her shotgun marriage, but she doesn't know this mature version of her sister well enough to risk opening that private door. "It's obvious you've done a fine job with your sons. They reflect well-being and confidence in who they are."

"Thank you for observing." She's not being sarcastic. There's grati-tude in the sudden smile, which also reveals Kathleen's best feature, a garden of pearly, even, unchipped teeth. From whom did she get those? Papa's were crooked and tobacco-stained, the only feature that marred his handsome face. Lola can't picture Mama ever revealing hers; those compressed lips barely moved when she spoke, and smiling was not in her repertoire.

Gertrude asks, "Do you go to church regularly, Sister?"

"No."

"That's a pity. Our grandfather gave the land whereon it's built."

"And our father tried to void the gift. When Papa couldn't regain title to the land, he started calling it 'My Own Little Church in the Wildwood.' You should remember that Sunday morning, as we were about to leave the house, when he said, 'Girls, I think I'll join you for worship today.' He hobbled out of his room in his nightshirt and a top hat, brandishing his best cane and whistling the tune of 'Little Church in the Wildwood.' Rhoda egged him on. The rest of us didn't dare." Kathleen adds, "Mama had no sense of lightheartedness. She couldn't admire her husband's ability to look for humor in most situations."

Now Lola knows where she gets her bothersome, persistent optimism. The idea that Papa lives in her will take some getting used to.

"Our mother did the best she could under the circumstances, which were trying much of the time."

"Tru, you sound just like her," Kathleen says. " 'Under the circumstances' was one of her expressions. I used to wonder if circumstances were pieces of furniture or a species of tree."

"I cannot condone criticism of my mother," warns Gertrude.

"No more squabbling." At Lola's sharp command, they look as chastened as students. "Let's go back to the subject Kathleen introduced. Kat and I are entitled to whatever information you have, Tru. Was Rhoda any kin of ours, or a child of the limberlost?"

"It's as Kathleen said. Papa brought her home from one of his trips." The scenario that Kathleen's account conjured becomes richer, more detailed, as Gertrude continues. "I was allowed to go out that afternoon to collect a bowlful of the first snow I'd ever seen, and Mama made us a pudding from it with raw eggs, vanilla flavoring, and sugar. It was nighttime when I heard him stamp his boots on the porch and fumble with the door latch. Then he was inside, with sprinkles of the frozen vapor on his hat and coat, even in his mustache; he looked like a foreigner, as though he had come from wherever the unusual whiteness had. He carried a small girl garbed in a vivid scarlet coat and bonnet. It wasn't a tam, Kathleen; the bonnet had a brim and tied under her chin. Her hands were encased in mittens looped together by a braid of yarn, and her cheeks were quite rosy—chapped, probably. She perched on Papa's arm and surveyed us. Grandmother said, 'I'm glad you're home, Son,' and raised her cheek for his kiss. Timidly, I inquired whose child this was. Papa said, 'She's ours. I've brought you a sister.' " Gertrude sighs and glances at Kathleen. "I'm ashamed to admit that I burst into tears and sobbed, 'I don't want another sister.' "

Kathleen shrugs. "At least you had the gumption to protest."

"Papa said the child was called Rose. Then Mama spoke for the first time: 'She'll not go by that name in this house.' "

"What objection did Mama have to her being called Rose?" Lola asks.

"She had to object to something," Kathleen says. "Mama wasn't one for surprises."

Gertrude has a rapt look on her face now. "Grandmother took the child from Papa and said, 'From now on, this girlie will be Rhoda Carson Holloway.' Carson was Grandmother's maiden name; Rhoda was for her sister."

"Papa might have met a Rose on one of his trips to Montgomery or Atlanta or New Orleans, who subsequently gave birth to the child he brought home that Christmas. In which case Papa was Rhoda's father, and we would be her half-sisters."

Gertrude glares at Kathleen. "What a preposterous idea."

"Did Rhoda realize she wasn't Mama's natural daughter?" Lola asks quickly, before Gertrude gets into a pout.

"Not that I was ever aware of. The day after she came to live with us, life resumed as usual, except there was one more at the table and clinging to Mama's skirts. The only other thing I recall about the incident is that Grandmother gave Mama a long talking-to behind a closed door."

Kathleen says, "I'm not surprised Grandmother was in on the arrangement."

"Arrangement?" Lola and Gertrude echo simultaneously.

"Papa would have contrived with the woman who bore his bastard to let him take the child, once she was old enough to be housebroken, to live with his legitimate family. Or maybe the woman died, and he had to own up to his responsibility."

"Sister, it grieves me that you could think our dear papa fathered a child out of wedlock—"

"The hypothesis makes sense," Lola interjects. "He brought her home as a Christmas surprise, and his mother backed him up, except for letting the child keep the name she came with. Grandmother was puritanical enough to disapprove of that red flag's being waved in Mama's face."

"Maybe he wanted Mama to think he had a mistress. He was capable of that kind of devilment. On the other hand," Kathleen reflects, "Papa had a natural sweetness about him. Remember the time he made a splint for a wounded robin?"

"No," Lola says with regret.

"No," Gertrude echoes flatly.

"Here's a more acceptable theory. Somebody told him about a poor, homeless child. Orphans were a dime a dozen in this part of Alabama then—in fact, they still are. He decided, on the spur of the moment, to add her to his own household." Kathleen doesn't care what Tru thinks; she watches to see how Lola takes to this scenario.

Not well. "You mean Rhoda is not even our half-sister?"

"I don't mean anything. I'm conjecturing."

"She was not baptized," Gertrude informs them. "That fact came out when the service was arranged for you, Lola. Mama was recounting to me how many of us had worn the christening gown. I was the first, then Kathleen, then the baby boy who lived a few months. When I asked her if Rhoda had worn it, she said 'No, circumstances didn't permit it, and there'll be no more discussion on the subject.' " Gertrude takes a deep breath, as though it might be her last conscious one for a while.

"Rhoda must have known she missed out on that sacrament as an infant. Not long before she left, we were at Turtle Creek one Sunday afternoon while a colored church was staging a baptism. Rhoda got in line, and the preacher immersed her."

Kathleen regards Lola skeptically. "You witnessed it?"

"Not up close. She made me stay on the bank. We'd gone to the creek to look for shiny rocks, and we couldn't come home until her clothes and hair were dry. I promised Rhoda I wouldn't tell Mama, and I never did."

Gertrude stands and takes a careful step forward, as though getting down from the witness stand. "I'm going to get a drink of water."

After she leaves, Kathleen confides, "It's just as well that Christmas memory didn't surface while we were growing up. If I'd had the least inkling that Rhoda wasn't really one of us, I'd have taunted her with the knowledge."

"Mama may have told her after Papa died, in which case Rhoda might have decided to return to wherever she came from."

"Papa didn't get away often enough to keep a mistress in one of those cities. The other woman must have lived hereabouts; the woods are full of secluded houses. Or she might have been with a Gypsy caravan that camped on the riverbank." Kathleen adds softly, rising from her seat, "I could believe Papa had something going on right under Mama's nose, and that Rhoda was a love child."

"So could I." Rhoda's fantasy of being born far away—which, along with the piano, Lola has been keeping for her—dissolves like Alabama snow.

Grandmother's rocking chair begins to move back and forth. Kathleen stops the motion with one foot. "Time to see to lunch."

"We're supposed to select Scripture," Lola reminds her.

"That won't be necessary." Gertrude sails into the room with renewed energy and composure. "We'll recite the Twenty-third Psalm in unison. Sister's right. We should get started on the picnic fare."

In fragile camaraderie, the three of them form an assembly line in the kitchen. Gertrude slices pink slivers from a fragrant ham for Lola to place inside biscuits left from breakfast. Kathleen peels and halves hard-boiled eggs, then mashes the yolks. They work in silence that seems companionable, yet Lola fears the void of talk will make them pull apart again. She likes the unusual sensation of being the middle note of a major triad, so she thinks up innocuous chatter that won't disrupt the harmony. "We'd make an efficient team in a munitions factory. Is there one in Hackberry Hill, Kat?" When Kathleen shakes her head, Lola says, "Not in Felder either. I wish I were employed in the war effort instead of as a teacher of spoiled adolescents."

The ringless fingers of Kathleen's left hand—Lola doesn't recall that she's ever worn a wedding band—fan out in a gesture of repudiation. "I don't let myself feel connected to this war. George is safe from the draft, but Harold won't be if it lasts much longer. If my son's life is taken on a faraway battlefield, that will be my punishment for having conceived him out of wedlock."

Gertrude places the carving knife on the platter before she speaks. "You mustn't punish yourself with such a thought."

"I can't control my thoughts."

"Oh, but you can learn to, Sister. All it takes is systematic, penitent, petitioning prayer. If you like, I will provide suggestions to get you started."

Lola nips that in the bud. "Finish slicing, Tru. I told Jason we would meet them at the cemetery."

"Why, when we could ride in the automobile?"

"I want the three of us to walk the path Rhoda and I used to take. I'll hold the strands of the barbed-wire fence while you crawl through."

Kathleen says, with a lilt of pride, "No one will have to crawl through. George built a stile over the fence, because I like to visit the cemetery."

"Well, I'm pleased to know that," Gertrude says.

But she's not pleased; she's jealous. If Mama is watching Kathleen make pilgrimages to the family plot, who's the favored daughter now? Kathleen picks up on Lola's thought and smiles, displaying her lovely choppers.

"There wasn't a broken tooth in Rhoda's head," Lola tells her.

"You were blind to her imperfections."

"No, I wasn't. Like most children, I was keenly observant. Rhoda's teeth were not crooked or misshapen. Had so much as a tiny fragment been missing from an incisor, I would have noticed, and pestered her to tell me how it happened."

Kathleen wipes her hands with a damp rag. "The day before she left, Rhoda and I had an altercation. It didn't last any time, and I landed the final blow. I aimed for her chin but hit her mouth. There was some blood; she ran off to get a towel. She didn't make an issue of being hurt, but I avoided looking at her for the rest of the day. The next morning, she was gone. I thought I had caused her to run away. I didn't tell anyone, not even George, about the fight. When Peter mentioned the tooth with a missing corner, I figured I had inflicted the injury on her last day with us."

"That's not enough to base a positive identification on! If you had caused real damage, the Rhoda I knew would have got even with you before she ran away."

"Hear what I'm saying: I want that grisly discovery to be Rhoda. Not knowing her whereabouts, I have worried that she would reappear and make my life miserable."

The dialogue is punctuated by a solid thunk each time the knife blade travels through the firm, mauve flesh to the marble biscuit board. Gertrude, the executioner, speaks without looking up from her task, and without elaboration: "I, too, want it to be Rhoda."

Kathleen says, "That leaves you, Lola. Even if there's no way to know for sure, can't you—"

"Go along with this deathly charade? I suppose so. But part of me will continue to believe she's above ground, leading the life of her intention."

"Intention is a powerful word." Kathleen points a yolk-encrusted fork at Gertrude. "Mama had such specific, unwavering intention for you that her vision materialized. You couldn't have planned your life better yourself."

"I admit I am quite pleased with my situation. I wouldn't change anything." This is said so complacently Lola wonders if Mama neglected to put a desire to produce offspring on the life map she created for Gertrude.

"I wish I could be that content," Kathleen says. "I feel I must strive to accomplish something beyond the quotidian routine of my life."

"Such as?" Lola prods, as Tru puzzles over *quotidian*.

"I want to reproduce, on paper or canvas, what I see in my mind."

"You're an artist? How wonderful!"

Kathleen corrects her swiftly. "I'm not an artist, but I may be past the dabbling stage. After I stopped school, I began conversing with myself, mainly to put into use words and definitions I memorized from the dictionary. Seven or eight years ago, one of my inner voices—the confident one, with the most assured vocabulary—told me to buy a paint box and get to it. I've been at it since then."

Rhoda's fingers could fly from one end of a keyboard to the other; Gertrude might have had an operatic career, had she been motivated enough to defy Mama; Kathleen can express herself on canvas. "My ultimate goal is to write for publication," Lola announces.

Gertrude reacts as though she's said her ultimate goal is to rob banks. "Oh dear. You have always put too much emphasis on books, no doubt because you learned to read at too young an age."

Kathleen asks, "Would you use a pseudonym, or call yourself 'Anonymous'?"

"Oh, I'll definitely write under my name, whatever it happens to be.

176

Though Lola Castleman sounds like a romantic non de plume. What do you think of Holloway Castleman?"

"It has an androgynous ring, if that's what you want."

Gertrude wonders, but won't ask, whether *androgynous* has to do with some form of perversity.

Now that she knows she won't be patronizing, Lola implores Kathleen to show them her work.

"All right." She takes a key from a cupboard drawer and unlocks the room off the kitchen that Papa moved into. Lola braces herself for an assault of the old smells, but there's only a faint odor of turpentine. Papa's cot is covered with art books and supplies. An easel holding a roughed-in preliminary sketch of grazing cattle is set up near a window that faces east, to take advantage of the morning light. Originally a sewing room, then a servant's room, then a sickroom, it's now a studio—though, to judge from the subject matter, Kathleen must do much of her painting outside. The finished pictures are spaced about the walls from just above the wainscoting to near the ceiling. Most are on stretched canvases, unframed, though several are bound in imitation gold-leaf moldings and varnished strips of oak. Lola knows without asking that the frames were made by George. The largest is a thickly daubed landscape featuring the barn in a more vibrant shade of red than the actual structure has ever worn. A sketch of the house with its dipping roofline and mantle of vines is a true representation, though it seems caricatured. On an elongated panel of canvas, the mill rises from an ethereal mist of lavender and pale green; Lola is reminded of the deceptively light renderings by Howard Chandler Christy for Sir Walter Scott's *Lady of the Lake*. The perspective is from their fork of the road, not the Whitneys', so the waterwheel doesn't appear in the painting.

"Gosh, Kat. These are really good."

Gertrude is impressed, too. "Oh, Sister," she breathes, "Mama would be so proud of you." Lola is proud of Tru for producing that accolade.

"Do you think so? I thought she'd be irritated with me for spending time this way, when I should be sewing or cultivating a flower garden."

"She might have been at first," Gertrude admits. "But she would want these on display."

Kathleen flushes at the tribute. "Two of my most recent are in the parlor."

Lola failed to notice any additions to that room's gallery, although she should have spotted Kathleen's portrait of her sons. Actually, it's a threesome: Harold, Ray, and a horse that doesn't look like Demon Rum or Whiskey. "It's wonderful of both boys. I take it you're familiar with Picasso's *Boy with the Horse*."

"Yes. I'm a shameless copier. Most of what I know of technique has come from imitating the masters. Helen Akers, who operates the lending library, orders art books with me in mind."

Gertrude says, "Helen was three classes ahead of me. When her mother died, she went to live with an aunt, who sent her to be educated in the East. Did she marry?"

"No. It's a typical sad story. She came back to take care of an ailing father, who finally died. The local bachelors weren't educated enough for her. But she's not the typical dried-up spinster. According to rumor, in the last couple of years, she and Peter Whitney have become close. He deserves some respite from crazy Coralee."

Gertrude passes up the chance to express disapproval of Peter's clandestine romance, or of Kathleen for repeating the rumor. Instead, she returns to the subject of Kathleen's art. "This is quite remarkable, Sister. You've captured your sons in an unrambunctious attitude."

"She means that as a compliment," Lola assures Kathleen.

The other painting is a slightly less than life-sized head-and-shoulders image of her husband, modeled on a Van Gogh self-portrait that hides the missing ear. This curious choice for emulation makes Lola wonder what's missing with George. It isn't the sex drive; Kathleen looks as though she's been gratified quite recently. (Maggie has taught her to recognize the signs.) Lola can almost hear herself informing Rhoda, *After all these years, Kat and the cow-pie man are still taking their pleasure with each other.*

The mill scene may be the best of what she's shown them, but Lola would not choose that one. "Please paint something for me. Name your price. If it's too much, we'll haggle."

"I've never sold a picture. At Helen's request, I did a pen-and-ink of the Grange Hall for the lending library, but I wouldn't let her pay me for it. That's the only one I've given away. I've thrown out a lot."

"I see nothing wrong with selling what you create," Gertrude says magnanimously. "Our mother used to hemstitch and embroider cup towels for the dry-goods store. She bought me a winter coat with the earnings from her handiwork."

"I don't recall her ever buying me a coat," Kathleen says.

"I should have said she bought *us* a coat. I wore it two winters, then it came down to you."

"And then to Rhoda, and then, in tatters, to me," Lola says. "Kat, I want to be your first client. I want to pay something in advance, so you'll consider whatever you paint next as a commission."

"I won't take your money before the fact. I'll send you something when and if it seems right."

Kathleen sees it coming and tries to sidestep the hug, but Lola doesn't let her. "Thank you, thank you!"

"Lola, you're being too effusive," Gertrude reproves.

"I'm not averse to effusion in small doses," Kathleen says, and hugs Lola back for all of two seconds.

10
Whippoorwill Plantation

His gas pedal near the floorboard, Jason says irritably, "Good God, George. Why do you suppose the man's going so doggone fast?"

"To show you his ten-year-old wood-framed flivver is as good a machine as your steel Packard."

"I wouldn't argue with that. The Model T is an American phenomenon. I've heard it gets an easy forty miles to an hour on a flat stretch. Our newspaper carried a photograph of a Lizzie hitched to a plow, and a young rascal actually drove one up the front steps of the high school in Felder, so Lola reported."

"She see it with her own eyes?"

"Says she did."

"Is Lola a truthful sort?"

"As women go." He grins as though they've shared a dirty joke.

"She's better-looking than I ever thought she'd grow up to be." George doesn't know why he said that. He's never given a thought to how his wife's baby sister would turn out, but if he had, he would have been surprised. When she lived here, Lola reminded him of something hatched from an egg, scrawny and pitiful and big-eyed. "It was good of you to give her a fine raising with proper advantages."

"Thank you, George. I'm sure you would have done well by Lola, had she remained in your household, but it was Gertrude's place, as the oldest, to take responsibility for the orphaned sibling." He pauses as though George will add something to that. When George doesn't, Jason continues. "Rearing the girl as though she were our daughter has been a joy and a privilege, especially as Gertrude and I have not been blessed with offspring. I knew this homecoming would be good for Lola, even under the sad circumstances. Gertrude balked at coming. Women can be difficult."

"Can they ever," George agrees. "It's a shame your wife and mine haven't made an effort to get on with each other. I expect they come by the stubbornness naturally. In my observation, their mother belonged to that category of women who are known for being highly opinionated, headstrong, and ornery."

"What was your impression of their father?"

"I had few dealings with him. The lady ran things, although she pretended everything had to go by him for approval. He was a figure-head, so to speak."

"My assessment exactly!" As Jason turns his face toward George, the latter thinks how this road has enough ruts to flip a car in a second of such inattention. Now, Jason's eyes are straight ahead again as he speaks. "Rayford Holloway showed evidence of having been a forceful person before he gave in to his weaknesses. I'm not sure when that capitulation occurred."

"Pretty early on, apparently. Kathleen says the grandmother ran things until the day she died, and Miss Lucy chafed at the bit when she had to take orders from Miss Kitty."

"I've often wondered if there might have been a tug of war between my wife and my mother, had they lived under the same roof. As it happened, the latter passed away before I met the former." He maneuvers the car to a halt with more turns of the wheel than necessary. Doc's house is larger than George remembers. After they get out, Jason says, "What an impressive structure. Marvelous detail. That's as fine a fanlight entrance as I've seen anywhere."

"He keeps this place spruced up. Anytime painters and carpenters need work, they can get it from Doc."

"Impressive cotton crop, too." Jason whistles the way some men do when admiring a woman.

It comes to George then that the doctor's plantation is like a beautiful, well-pampered woman. The cotton fields are lush. It's close to picking time. He doesn't see any help around, but he and Jason are probably being watched by dark, smoldering eyes. The overseer, Jim Jackson, looks at George, when they meet in town or on the road, like there's something he wants to talk about. George has always been friendly to him, but the colored man keeps the exchanges brief and limited to the state of crops or the weather. George has even told Jim he's welcome to fish in the pond, but he's never seen him near it. It's said that some Negroes are so scared of water that they won't wade into a creek except to get baptized.

Jason is thinking about the gold mine in these white fields. "The Delta has nothing on this. I didn't realize cotton would grow this well north of the Black Belt."

"There's no finer soil for cotton than the area around Huntsville, which is as north as Alabama gets."

"What's that strange contraption?"

"A mechanical picker Doc bought a few years ago. He gets Jim to

try it out every year before they resort to picking cotton the only efficient way there is, which is by hand."

The overseer's daughter opens the front door and calls out in a mushy
voice that makes George think of hot, buttered sweet potatoes, "Doctor
says you-all come on inside, he'll be right with you." She herds them
into a wide hallway, then disappears.

Jason is taking in the bracketed wall lamps, the black-and-white
marble floor, the tall mirror with the heavy gold frame, and the curving
staircase, which Daisy comes down now. Something about her strikes
George as familiar, though he seldom sees the girl. She is plenty sure of
herself. He must warn his boys not to get involved with this princess!
Harold is the one who's over here so much. Such a misstep could be
ruinous for him. The thought makes him groan. Jason gives him a look.
"Twinge of headache," George says. "It'll pass." If they lived near a good-
sized town, he could take the boys to a whorehouse, get them indoctri-
nated into when and where to bring those mighty tools into action.
There are bound to be women in the trade around here, but he's had no
need to seek them out, as he's been blessed with a wife who likes a romp
as much as he does. Maybe Kathleen's already talked to the boys about
this important issue.

"Papa asked me to serve you coffee in the drawing room." The
doctor's daughter smiles openly at Jason, then glances timidly in George's
direction, as though she's scared of him. Good. He hopes she is.

Brother-in-law is swayed by the whole setup: pretty girl in a grand
country house amid acres of cotton and timberland. They follow her
into a bright yellow room with a big wheel-shaped gasolier hanging
from the center of the ceiling. George hopes it's firmly bolted; the prissy
chairs, one of which he occupies, are dead center beneath that fixture.
She pours coffee from a silver pot into thin cups that rattle in the sau-
cers like bones. Is that why they call it bone china?

Daisy offers cream and sugar. "Harold and Ray were here when we got home," she informs them. "Papa had Jim take them in our wagon to the cemetery. Jim got some shovels and picks and will help them get started, so it won't take as long."

"Well, that is most accommodating," Jason says, no doubt wondering why George didn't think to bring along implements for his own sons to dig the grave with. He's wondering that himself.

Doc comes in. "I apologize that Coralee is not able to welcome you."

"Sorry she's not well," Jason says, in what George takes as a response for him, too. "I've been admiring your beautiful home. The setting is so tranquil, although the house appears to be a good bit closer to the main road than . . ." He stops and gives George an apologetic look. He was about to say "our place."

"Now that you mention it, I believe it is," the doctor says. "This is a rare treat, isn't it, Daisy? Having some company."

"Oh, yes." She exhales these words through a mouth that could tease and nibble a boy until he didn't know which way was up. But if Harold were in that deep, he'd show signs of distraction. Damn it, he does show signs of distraction, which his father has attributed to all the heavy medical stuff he claims he's into over here. If George finds out Harold's been lying to him, and what he's really been into is this girl's drawers . . . She says, "I wish we could have real parties here, but since Mother is not in good health, we can't. Do you entertain with tea dances at your house, Mr. Howard?"

"The last such affair I recall was Lola's coming-out event a couple of years ago, when Gertrude had the floors waxed dangerously." The girl is eager to know more, but Jason takes out his watch and studies its face, then suggests they proceed to the purpose of this visit.

Daisy goes out with them. When they get to the low brick building that used to house sick folks, her papa tells her she can't go in. George intends to wait for them outside, but after Jason enters, Doc holds the door open for him.

George has skinned many kinds of animals, turned hogs into sausage, hauled off carrion after the buzzards finished with it—none of which has prepared him for the horror of that picked-clean bone girl reclining on a counter. There is no blood, no mess. What bothers him is that it looks so human. The head is positioned so that the dark caves where eyes used to be seem to stare at him. Through him. Jason peers and asks questions, which the doctor answers; their words are a blur against the roaring in George's ears. What he ate for breakfast rises to his throat, and he barely gets out the door before he has to toss it all up behind a bush. Doc follows him. As though George is some silly woman given to fainting spells, the doctor hands him a small, uncapped bottle and tells him to sniff it. George does as he says, and it works.

Jason comes out a couple of minutes later and asks George, as though unaware of the other's sorry performance, if the coffin will fit across the back seat of the car.

"Not without both doors open. We could strap it on top. But the simplest thing would be for me to hitch up the horses and haul it in the wagon."

"Fine. That's settled." Then Jason tells the doctor, "George and I will return shortly. I hope you plan to be with us for the burial service."

"I would very much like to, if it's not an intrusion."

Jason says it won't be.

The girl reappears. "May I come, too?"

Jason says, "Of course," as though it's a party and he's giving it.

At least this one won't be like most send-offs around here, where people grieve for days before and months after. Mr. Holloway's wife wore a mourning brooch made of a coil of hair from his dead head; it was on her dress when she was placed inside the coffin George made for her. Where George comes from, a corpse is buried quickly and soberly, without hypocrisy or excessive ceremony. The departed soul is bid a firm goodbye and is expected to leave friends and family in peace, so they can get on with the business of keeping themselves alive.

If these bones are what's left of Rhoda Holloway, then Jason's right, a burial is called for. George never cared to be close to Rhoda, but he liked to watch her from a distance. There was a natural gracefulness in the way that girl moved. He just hopes she'll do the graceful thing now and leave them in peace.

◎

The doctor's wife hears unfamiliar male voices in the downstairs hall. One speaks like a gentleman. Daisy converses with them in the charming cadence she squanders on any available ears. She's much too outgoing, and shows signs of maturity Peter doesn't seem to notice. He wasn't here that day two years ago when Daisy bled like a stuck pig for the first time and sobbed to the women servants that she must have something terribly wrong with her. After Hettie trussed her up, Coralee explained to Daisy that the curse of womanhood struck monthly until its victim was well past her prime (except during periods of gestation, should she be so blessed). Then she confided to her daughter her own mother's remedy to staunch the flow and stave off anemia: bed rest for a minimum of two days (the lower limbs elevated by means of an upended ladder-back chair), combined with frequent ingestion of calves' liver jelly, beef marrow soup, and sherry wine to replenish the blood supply. She gave Daisy some tincture of opium in the event the child suffered cramping pain, but Peter found out and was furious. Hettie must have told him, although she swore to Coralee she didn't. Neither Coralee nor Daisy has mentioned the indelicate subject again. Apparently, the girl would rather suffer than follow her mother's advice to give in to the sickness. Daisy is not as docile or as solicitous of her mother as she used to be.

Now, there's another voice, one Coralee knows well. Peter has arrived to play the genial host. The urbane manner of speaking he acquired in Virginia commands the respect of patients he doesn't care a whit about personally. He might just as well call them by their infirmities: Miss Pellagra, Mr. Gout, Mrs. Ruptured Appendix. At their funerals, his mournful demeanor comes not from the loss of human life, but because he must face the fact, if only briefly, that he is not God.

Once, a man with a gangrenous gunshot wound was in the infirmary. The poor soul needed to end his agony, but Peter kept trying out injections and poultices on him. The smells and sounds weren't contained in the building behind this house. Coralee's flower garden and the vegetable patch reeked with the odor of putrid flesh. Terrible moans floated in the bedroom windows, as though she were being serenaded by banshees. She prayed for the sufferer to die. After it happened, Peter scowled at her for days—not because he thought she had anything to do with it (if she did, it was one of the few times prayer has worked for her), but because it was Mr. Gangrene who expired, and not she.

Day after day, year after year, Coralee awakes every morning surprised that she is alive. The hot and humid Alabama climate has played havoc with her constitution. Now that he no longer requires her body for the gratification of his, she is treated with aloof disdain by the man who vowed, before God, to cherish her. His heart that has never opened to her opened like a rose to the foundling. It's as if Peter and Daisy are the married couple in this house and Coralee is a barely tolerated dependent—a spinster sister or an impoverished cousin.

She can never forget for a moment that Daisy is not of her own flesh. He has never told her whose womb the infant grew inside. Coralee was not even allowed to change the name the mystery woman gave her! Peter said she was not to inquire in the town about the poor widow who couldn't afford to keep her newborn. He said the woman was not of these parts. She used to ask him, timidly at first, then boldly, if he had sired Daisy. "Don't be ridiculous," he would say, or "Keep your voice down. The servants will hear you." The last time Coralee asked the question, he said she was deranged.

At first when she didn't conceive, he was kind about it. Which is not to say he was kind during the act of trying to implant his seed. Once, after he'd forced himself upon her in the afternoon, causing her to cry out in anguish, Hettie came to her room, wiped her face with a wet cloth, and said, "Honey, if you let yourself relax and get used to it, you might learn to enjoy it." Hettie was wrong. Coralee never got used to being brutalized, much less learned to enjoy such treatment. Eventually, whenever he planned to assault her, he would give her a dose of laudanum beforehand. Finally, Peter decided her womb was undeveloped and she was therefore barren. After they got the orphan, he ceased to bother her in that way.

As Daisy grows and changes, Coralee searches for signs of Peter in the girl. Daisy doesn't take after him in physical attributes, but the way she uses her hands and cocks her head when she speaks—are these mannerisms inherited or parroted?

One of the men downstairs must be Gertrude Holloway's husband. Peter told her the Felder entourage might stop by, but that he wouldn't expect her to play hostess. Fine, then. Coralee Whitney will not show her face.

The Holloway girls' mother worked them like field hands. Rhoda was the most rebellious and seemed the hardiest. Such an amusing sight she was, prancing around on that big wheel as though it were a stage and she a trained performer. Coralee's view was from the tower room, a pellucid aerie where light streamed through the walls even on sunless days. Climbing the steep back stairs was a challenge that set her heart aflutter, but once there, she could pretend she was the wife of a ship's captain, come to watch for his return from a long voyage. The faintly visible river, blue in the distance, seemed a mirage. From that dizzying height, through glass as wavy as water, even close-by scenery seemed unreal, as though it were rendered by an Impressionist artist. The Holloways' secretive, willow-misted pond was a subject worthy of Monsieur Monet.

As though they were invincible water sprites, Rhoda and Lola would splash in that weir, plunging beneath the water and bobbing up again. Coralee watched the antics without worrying that they would get too close to the waterfall. Their welfare was no concern of hers. Later, when she heard the older of that pair had run away from home, she was pleased, thinking of Lucy Holloway's humiliation.

The last time she went to the tower room was the day Daisy came to live here. Soon after Peter and Hettie brought the infant to her—it was still early in the morning—Coralee took Daisy for her first stroll in the Rolls-Royce pram. Near the arbor, she had a sense of imminent danger, as though someone were watching them. She hurried back to the house and turned the baby over to Hettie. A few minutes later, she went to the tower to calm her agitation. But the familiar, tranquil view altered in a split second. A figure was on the stationary waterwheel; the wheel became a whirligig, and the person—or, more likely, the apparition—disappeared. The sight was so unnerving Coralee ran from the room and has never been back. Before that day was done, she came to believe the morning's scenario was hallucination brought on by the excitement of becoming a mother at last. She has never related anything about this unsettling episode to her husband.

She certainly will not tell him now that she knows he's keeping a list of her aberrations to use against her. He hasn't mentioned the subject of "rest cures" in a while, as he knows she will never go willingly to such a prison. Recently, Coralee overheard Torey whisper to Hettie, "If her mind gets too fuzzy, the doctor could have her committed to the Hospital for the Insane in Tuscaloosa. All he'd have to do is sign some papers." But tender-hearted Daisy will never allow that to happen.

After Jason and George leave, Daisy ensconces herself on the screened veranda with a flimsy periodical that looks, to Peter, to be mostly illustrations. He may ask his friend at the lending library to suggest light fiction of merit that will be appropriate for a young girl who doesn't care much for reading. Perhaps he'll take Daisy along next time he goes there. "Have you looked in on your mother today?"

"No, sir."

"Then you should," he says, though he wants her to stay right there with her Dresden figurine beauty set off by the fan-shaped chair of woven wicker. After she departs to do his bidding, Peter resists the impulse to place his palm on the warm depression in the chair's flowered cretonne cushion.

From the first moment he saw her, this child curled up like a cat in his heart. He has lived from that day with the foreboding that he won't always be there to protect her. He doesn't worry over illness as much as accident. He has brought her safely through measles, the whooping cough, and chickenpox. So far, she's been spared diphtheria, mumps, malaria, scarlet fever, and appendicitis. Thank God, the paralyzing, infectious poliomyelitis that came out of the blue two summers ago has not yet reached Hackberry Hill. He hasn't allowed Daisy to ride horseback. (One of his earliest defeats was not being able to save a child who'd been thrown, dragged, and kicked by a Shetland pony.) With great relief, by the time she was six or so, he realized Daisy was not inclined to be a tomboy like her natural mother. She was docile, cheerful, friendly, and obedient.

Coralee used to ask him the name of the woman who had this child, and if he had sired her. The projection led to a question he still puts to himself: If Rhoda Holloway had come to him with the suggestion that he implant his seed in her, would he have?

He'd hardly slept the previous night. The soft voice in his head had urged him to confide in Gertrude's husband—now, while he had the chance. Peter wasn't ashamed of this feminine alter ego. A physician who relied on textbook knowledge without heeding his intuition was a fool.

Torey appears in the doorway. "Mr. Howard's back. Should I take him to the parlor?"

Peter is surprised the noisy approach of a motorcar hadn't flagged his attention. "Bring him out here, please. And some coffee, if it's freshly made." Of course, it will be; Hettie boils coffee several times a day. "If Daisy comes downstairs, please tell her not to disturb us."

After Jason has admired the flagstone floor, the settee and chairs enameled a glossy forest green, and the lush potted ferns that emit a woods-and-earth scent, he says, "The casket's on the buckboard, which will go directly to the cemetery. I've come alone to collect the remains."

Peter frowns at this development. "I intended shifting the skeleton directly from the worktable to the coffin. Some of the smaller pieces are missing, but we assembled about a hundred and seventy bones on a cloth sheet, which would help keep the wired arrangement intact in the transfer. To save time, some components, such as the skull, were quite loosely attached." He waits for the other's reaction. Some men do not care to hear about procedures of this nature, even the bloodless kind.

Jason isn't squeamish. He just wants to get on with it. "Can't we ease the sheet with its contents onto the back seat of my car?"

"The figure's approximately five feet, eight inches in length."

"Hmm. That could be a problem, unless we crunch her down a bit."

Torey comes in with a tray of coffee already in the cups. Peter waits for her to leave before he says, bad-humoredly, "The whole thing's become a hellacious problem."

Jason takes out his cigarette case. "Will you join me in a smoke?"

Peter shakes his head, affronted that the man hasn't asked his permission. Doesn't he notice the absence of ashtrays?

Jason didn't brandish the holder when smoking with George the night before, but the current company should appreciate that refining touch. He puts a flame to his cigarette and inhales deeply. "So far, the women are handling themselves well," he says. "I hope this funeral charade doesn't start any hysteria. Now, that's an interesting word, and uniquely feminine. No doubt, you know its root is the Latin *hystericus*, or 'suffering in the womb.' "

Normally, Peter would relish a discussion of word derivation, but this is not the time. Since the moment he shook hands with Jason Howard earlier today, he has wanted to bare his soul to this man. He plunges ahead now, before he can change his mind. "I have a particular interest in this unfortunate matter, as Rhoda Holloway was the natural mother of Daisy, my adopted daughter."

"Ah," Jason says, as if exclaiming over the fragrance of the coffee.

"Rhoda came to me when she was over four months pregnant, but being rather tall—"

"Approximately five feet, eight inches, judging from the skeleton," Jason murmurs.

"—her condition was not blatantly obvious, although I was surprised Lucy hadn't noticed. The other person responsible was a boy Rhoda's age, Sam Holcomb, who had been killed while walking on the railroad tracks two months before. Rhoda said the act had occurred only once. They were not sweethearts, and she wouldn't have wanted to marry Sam. Neither the lad nor his family was aware of her predicament. The Holcombs moved to Mississippi soon after the boy died." Peter takes a sip of coffee. "Had Rayford been alive, he would have shown great compassion and support for his daughter. I can hear him saying, 'There's always room for one more here.' But Rhoda made it quite clear to me she had no desire to keep the baby."

"She came to you for an abortion?"

"No, I don't believe that idea occurred to her. For years, my wife had let it be known that she wanted a child. Rhoda came to offer me the one she was carrying."

Jason frowned. "For a price?"

"She didn't name an amount. She asked for enough to tide her over until she located elsewhere and found employment. What seemed of utmost concern to her was making a good arrangement for the infant that she would, of necessity, leave behind."

"Rhoda struck me as something of a sophist, despite her sequestered upbringing. Although detectives I consulted assured me most runaways of tender age are either found or come back home within a month, I wasn't surprised that this one had planned her departure well enough to leave no trail. I believed her quite capable of surviving, even thriving, in some urban environment far away from Hackberry Hill, Alabama." Jason strokes his chin, hoping the stubble isn't as obvious as it feels. He did not shave this morning. Gertrude packed his soap mug and razor, but no one brought him a kettle of heated water.

"Of course, the girl was technically a minor, and Lucy Holloway should have been informed of the situation, but Rhoda insisted her mother must never know. It wasn't hard for me to accept her terms. I very much wanted the child whose heartbeat called out to me through the stethoscope." Peter clears his throat, aware that this man whose face reveals nothing (other than a faint stubble) is taking in every muscle twitch, as well as weighing the inflection of his every word. "She never wavered from her plan to leave the vicinity after she had the baby. I would have taken her to a train station in another county, even across the state line had she wished, but frankly, I was relieved when Rhoda insisted she could depart in disguise from the Hackberry Hill depot, and that I should not see her off. She projected a maturity and confidence that belied her tender age." Peter is surprised at the catch in his voice. "As I gave that brave young girl an envelope of paper money and bade her goodbye and Godspeed, my feelings were a mixture of sadness and relief." He closes his eyes, remembering Rhoda's look of surprise at the heft of that envelope. He had calculated a sum that was more than enough for one person to live on comfortably for at least a year.

"Did you expect her to contact you for more when the money was gone?" Jason asks.

"I left that door open. She agreed to respect my wish that there be no communication between us unless she was in need. That I've not heard a word from her supports the hypothesis that she met her death on the day she was to embark on her journey."

"Indeed it does," Jason says. "I assume you arranged for the girl to be secluded while she waited to give birth."

"On the day she left farewell notes at her family's house, Rhoda moved in with my employees Jim and Hettie Jackson. Jim is my overseer; Hettie is our housekeeper. Their only child, Torey, brought the coffee in to us."

"That young woman has an intelligent look about her."

"She's also steady and reliable, as are her parents. After Torey graduates from high school next summer, I will provide her with the opportunity for nurse's training," Peter says. "The Jacksons occupy an isolated, comfortable log house beyond the woods at the back of my property. My pioneer ancestor built that house and lived in it when he arrived on this frontier. It's amazing how indestructible some of those primitive structures are."

"Reminds me of the old-timer's saying, 'You can't kill a log cabin.' "

Peter has no penchant for levity. "Rhoda kept her promise not to let herself be seen. This meant she could not leave the premises of her confinement."

"But word must have leaked out that she was still in the vicinity for several months after she went missing."

"Not to my knowledge. I had complete trust that Jim and Hettie would not utter a word. For their complicity in harboring Rhoda during those crucial months, I gave them the deed to the house and some surrounding acreage."

"A prudent move that would ensure their silence."

"I thought of it not as a bribe, but as a gesture of gratitude. Occasionally during the first two or three years, a rumor would surface that Rhoda Holloway had been spotted in Mississippi, or Tennessee, or Georgia." Peter pauses. "While Rhoda was living with Jim and Hettie, I occasionally stopped by the Holloway place, although Lucy made it clear she did not wish to consult me about her deteriorating health. Kathleen seemed stunned by her change of status from schoolgirl to wife and mother. It was obvious to me that Lola keenly missed Rhoda, her companion sister. After Lucy died, I would have taken that little girl in, if she'd been available. I was glad to learn that she would make her home with you and Gertrude." Peter's gaze shifts from his guest's unswerving stare to a cotton field that looks like washed fleece. "I made an entry in my medical journal of Daisy's birth and adoption. I also drew up a document with the basic statistics and signed it as delivering physician and adoptive parent. Rhoda signed Rose Hanson—a name she made up, as far as I know—to a statement that was partially true: She was a widow who, while passing through this area, came to me for her delivery, and allowed me to adopt the infant. Those papers are in my strongbox."

"I take it the adoption was not formally processed."

"I didn't want to put the details into the public record. My will names Daisy as my only child. Of course, people in the vicinity, including those in residence at the Holloway house, were aware we had taken in a foundling. No one asked where she came from."

Jason stubs his cigarette in the rich, black soil of Coralee Whitney's prized bird's-nest fern. "Since you didn't inform me back then—when, as the eldest sister's husband, I would have expected to take on the responsibility for Rhoda and her child—why do you tell me now?"

"At the time, I thought I was doing you a favor not to get you involved. Also, Rhoda expressly didn't want any member of her family to learn of her predicament. I've told you now because I hope you will make Rhoda's sisters aware of their relationship to my daughter."

"My friend, I very much doubt that Gertrude or Kathleen will respond to such news as you might wish," Jason says. "On the other hand, I believe Lola will be delighted to know of the existence of a charming niece, and will extend to Daisy her loyalty and affection."

Peter's eyes fill with tears he doesn't know what to do with. He hasn't cried since he was a boy, not even when his parents died. "I can't begin to tell you how much that means to me, that one of them, at least . . ."

Jason says, "Does Daisy know she was adopted?"

"Apparently not. I assumed that sooner or later, she'd hear something and ask me. But she's never mentioned the subject."

"It seems to me the full disclosure would be a heavy dose at this tender time of her life."

"Yes, I've considered that. But since Harold found those pitiful bones in the pond, I have felt as though I owe it to both Rhoda and Daisy to bring this secret into the light."

"Well, you've enlightened me. I propose you have your lawyer draft a document that will lay out the facts as you've just related them. At your death, the revelation will be part of your legacy to Daisy. And also at that time, my wife, Kathleen, and Lola will learn of their connection."

"But assuming I live even a few more years, Daisy will grow into maturity without knowing she was born into a loving family."

Jason splutters a mouthful of coffee. "A loving family? Gertrude and Kathleen showed their lack of affection for each other by entering into mutual estrangement more than a decade ago. I'm ashamed to admit I have allowed my wife to deprive Lola of contact with Kathleen since that time, until now."

"Kathleen should have had Lola in the summers," Peter says. "Children thrive in country air."

"As far as I know, Kathleen never extended an invitation."

"I should tell you I've never revealed the identity of Daisy's natural mother to Coralee. I think it best she not know."

"If I dared to present Gertrude with a foundling, she would prefer to think the infant was left on the stoop with the morning paper," Jason says. "I'd like to know more about the Holloway household during Gertrude's formative years. She doesn't talk about that time."

Peter takes his first sip of coffee and finds it as cool as his guest's reaction to his request. "I well recall one of my first impressions. Soon after I returned home to take over my father's practice, Rayford sent for me to help Lucy through a delivery. She insisted those tiny girls, Gertrude, Kathleen, and Rhoda, remain in the room during a birth which turned out to be anything but easy. The infant—a boy, their brother—was born severely clubfooted and died some months later. Those children watched and heard everything and never flinched."

"That could explain why Gertrude has an aversion to childbearing. Not that she would recall the event, if I asked her about it. My wife has a talent for forgetting what she doesn't care to acknowledge."

Peter says eagerly, "There's an accepted theory that painful or horrifying experiences are stored on the deepest levels of the subconscious mind. Though seemingly irretrievable, such a repressed memory could come boiling to the surface at any time."

"Ah, yes. The so-called talking cures. Time will tell whether the European psychiatrists' methods hold water; they certainly sound far-fetched to me. You were saying, about my late mother-in-law?"

Peter is put off by Jason's dismissive assessment of methods he himself finds intriguing. "I think I was about to say that Lucy was despondent from the moment she saw the boy's deformity. After his death, she would not accept the elixir I offered for her melancholia." The doctor pauses to flex his hands; the power of suggestion in the form of a sugar-based placebo works on most of his arthritic patients but doesn't make a dent in his own pain. "I wasn't called in when she had the next one—another male who didn't live long—although a year or so later, I was summoned when Lola was coming breech."

"Lola, a breech birth? I never knew that. There was nothing wrong with her, was there?"

"I recall my own relief that this one was perfect."

"She still is." Jason adds, "Gertrude once let slip some reference to her mother's having delivered babies. Do you know anything about that?"

"Before I came back to Hackberry Hill, Lucy began dabbling in midwifery, which Rayford told me she learned from watching Negro women deliver each other's babies on her family's plantation."

"You said mid-*wif*-ery. I'm curious about that pronunciation, since midwife uses a long *i*."

"One of my professors explained the second syllable in the longer noun rhymes with *if*."

"Interesting. Of course, the word resonates with meaning—women helping other women through that painful travail. Well, this is all very good, but we'd best get to our task. Since there might be some difficulty loading the remains into my automobile, I suggest the head travel separately."

"Separately?"

"In your lap."

"Oh." Peter leads the way to the laboratory and unlocks the door. The skeleton reclines like a patient used to being poked and prodded. The decapitation is a matter of untwisting some fine wires.

Jason touches the fringe of a pink blanket that lies lightly across the rib cage and pelvic structure. "A modest touch."

"It was Daisy's idea to cover the poor, naked creature for the viewing. Hettie supplied the blanket."

"Does this woman, Hettie, know who we think this is?"

"Yes. Hettie provided the identification. I brought her in for a look as soon as we had most of it together. She spotted the chipped tooth without my calling it to her attention, and related the mishap had occurred at their house not long before Rhoda gave birth. Rhoda was there alone chopping wood—which, of course, she should not have been—and the ax flew back and lopped a corner off the incisor. I wasn't informed, because they knew I would be upset that this girl, who was carrying my child—that is, the child she had promised to me—was doing something as dangerous as chopping wood."

"But you can't cite Hettie's word as proof, because your housekeeper isn't supposed to be that familiar with Rhoda."

"Right. It was by the grace of God that Kathleen somehow 'remembered' Rhoda had a broken tooth before she left home." Peter adds, "One feature that marks a female pelvis—which I didn't point out to my young assistant, his parents, or the sheriff—is the presence of parturition pits that would result from tearing of muscular insertions and tendons attached to the surface of the bone. In other words, this young female had given birth."

"So there's no doubt. She really is the missing sister." Jason leans down and stares boldly at the skull on the counter. The lower teeth remind him of his wife's. He shudders at the thought of Gertrude minus her sumptuous flesh. "I've seen photographs of skeletons with long hair. What do you suppose happened to Rhoda's glorious mane?"

"Fish, turtles, frogs would take care of it. Birds collect hair for nests. For years, I've seen a blue crane—could be more than one, but I think the old bird's a loner—dipping into that pond, as do the cowbirds that George's herd has attracted."

Jason values this opportunity to familiarize himself with the framework of the human body. He has never been involved in a case of medical jurisprudence, but the day might come when this experience will prove invaluable.

Peter says, "Try to keep the cloth taut as we lift it. Ready? One, two, three."

The makeshift stretcher comes to rest on the back seat with a delicate clacking noise. "Sounds like the bamboo wind chimes in my wife's rose garden," Jason says, hoping to introduce a fresh and ungruesome topic of conversation for the ride ahead, but the remark elicits no response.

As he gently manipulates the feet so the rear doors can be shut, Peter thinks of Lucy's clubfooted infant. He goes back into the laboratory to get the skull. "Considering the head usually accounts for approximately twenty percent of a grown human's weight, what we have here is amazingly light," he says, noting for the first time that Harold, without asking his permission, has cemented the occiput to the cranium. He gets in the car with the object cradled in the crook of one arm, as though it is a football.

"Twenty percent!" Jason whistles. "That's for the average human, I assume. For one of unusual intellectual capacity, would you say the statistic might be twenty-five percent? Thirty?" A twist of the ignition key produces a sound remarkably like human regurgitation. "Son of a bitch." He strikes the steering wheel with his open palm. Peter is sympathetically silent. After a few more tries, the engine catches, and Jason announces jubilantly, "She's humming like a top. Let's go before she changes her mind."

"Papa, you said I could come with you!" Daisy, shouting at the top of her healthy lungs, has planted herself in the car's path.

If he has any doubt, the girl's audacity convinces Jason she is Rhoda's offspring. Now, if he can just convince himself that Peter Whitney is not Daisy's natural father. At least he'll give the doctor the benefit of the doubt. Jason suggests, "Since the back seat's taken, will you allow her to ride on the running board?"

"Heavens no. Not even with a competent and careful driver such as I'm sure you are. Daisy and I will go in my car." Peter positions the skull in the center of the seat he is vacating. "We'll have to use the road. The shorter trail runs into an ungated fence at the churchyard."

"I'll wait for you to take the lead."

Jason keeps his feet firmly on the clutch and brake pedals and wills the engine not to die. The car quivers and snaps like a hound held back from the chase. He notices, with irritation, that Peter Whitney has no problem with engine start-up, although his flivver has to be hand-cranked. Just ahead is George's horse-drawn hearse with the empty casket traveling upright. Jason eases up on the gas pedal. The speedometer slips from fifteen miles per hour to less than ten. He is bringing up the rear of the shortest, strangest cortege he has ever been part of.

11
Digging the Grave

RAY PICKS UP ROCKS FROM THE GRASSY AREA staked out with string and sticks by Harold and the colored man. He wears a bandanna tied across his forehead to keep the sweat from his eyes. When he has the chance, he reassures himself that the plug of tobacco he took from the doctor's laboratory is still in the deepest pocket of his overalls. Nobody witnessed this act of thievery but the bone-girl, and she's not about to tell. He asks his brother, "You ever done this before?"

"What do you think?" With a booted foot on top of a straight-edged spade, Harold makes the first cut.

"I'd say you haven't. I've never even been to a funeral."

"I must have been taken to Grandmother's, but I was too young to remember it."

Ray feels a stirring of remorse as he gazes at the headstone with two names. He wishes he'd known the man he was named for. Mama has said Rayford Holloway's cane with the silver knob—it's still in the umbrella stand—will be his one day. Ray hopes he'll never have to use that cane.

The doctor told Harold their grandfather suffered for many years from an ulcerated cancer on his left leg. Harold can hardly wait to start learning all about that dread disease. Finding a cure for cancer is one of his ambitions.

Jim hums as he wields a rust-coated shovel, taking care not to get within range of the new, shiny pickax Ray has chosen. On the ride to the cemetery, Ray tried to pry conversation from the dignified dark-skinned man, but without much luck. He hasn't been around colored people enough to figure out why they are so close-mouthed. There was only one interchange. Ray asked if the reason the doctor's wagon didn't squeak was because the axles were greased frequently. "It don't squeak 'cause it's new," Jim replied. Ray couldn't believe he failed to notice they were riding in a spanking-new outfit. He will have to pay more attention to details if he expects to amount to something. And he does expect to, although he doesn't have a blueprint for his future, like Harold does for his.

Ray dislodges a clod of grass-choked red earth the size of a cannonball. He hacks out another, and another. Power surges from his shoulders into his arms with each swing. Harold is chipping the dirt out in smaller increments. Ray is embarrassed at the prissiness that comes on Harold sometimes, like now. He wonders if the colored man notices. "Are you sure you laid this space out right?" Ray asks his brother gruffly.

"Yes, I'm sure," Harold says.

The family plot is boxed in by an iron fence low enough to step over. "Looks like there's room for at least a dozen more. There aren't that many of us. The hoity-toities from Felder won't care to be buried here."

"I wouldn't say they're hoity-toity. Lola's really friendly. So is Uncle Jason. It's just Aunt Gertrude who's kind of aloof."

"Aloof, huh? You been stealing words from Mama's dictionary again."

"It's a way to better myself."

"I think I'm good enough as is," Ray boasts. "Ain't nobody in this world any better than I am." He glances sideways at Jim for some hint of corroboration, but doesn't get it.

Harold says, "There's no such word as *ain't*."

"Don't tell me how to talk. How'd you like a crack upside of your head?"

"Do that and you'll have to dig my grave by yourself, before they put you in jail for life."

Harold can always outsmart him with talk. Jim pretends he doesn't hear this last, like the colored man has been doing all along. The three of them work awhile in silence. When the grave is two-thirds dug, Jim lets them take swigs from a water jug and tells them he'll be getting on back. "I was just supposed to start you off right. Don't forget to return our tools."

They take a rest after he leaves. Ray pulls out the plug of tobacco, breaks it, pops the larger piece into his mouth, and offers Harold the other.

Harold sniffs it. "Where'd you get this?"

"None of your business."

"If you found tobacco in the doctor's laboratory, somebody left it by mistake, or in appreciation for his services. He never touches the stuff. Doc says it rots teeth and makes canker sores in the mouth. Mama said her mother used to put it on wasp stings to draw the poison out." Harold gingerly bites off a corner and works it around inside his jaws, getting used to the texture and the strong taste before he concedes, "Chewing tobacco's probably better for you than snuff or cigars or cigarettes."

"What about pussy? I've heard that's better for you than anything."
Every time he sees a cat or kitten, Ray thinks how much he'd like to see
the girl-thing that goes by the same name.

"There you go again on your favorite subject."

"It ought to be yours, too."

"I don't let myself think about it. You should put your mind on something else."

Ray aims an arc of brown spittle into the rectangular hole. "Shit.
You remind me of a preacher or a dried-up old-lady schoolteacher." He
wishes Harold would get mad enough to come at him, so they could
have a good, rolling-around-on-the-ground fistfight. But Harold ignores
the insult.

They have just finished the task they were sent here to do when the
women arrive. The visiting aunts carry baskets; their mother totes a quilt
roll. Ray watches them come single-file over the stile, each with her
skirt bunched on one side like a bouquet. His pants front rises in swift
salute to those tantalizing glimpses of female leg. Last year, for a bag of
marbles, a boy swapped him a collection of dog-eared photographs of
French high-kickers doing the cancan dance. Something is really, really
wrong with him, that he can think the same way about his aunts—even
his *mother*—as he did those foreign hussies. He wishes he could ask Harold
for medical advice on how to deal with the problem, but he's too
ashamed.

Harold lopes over to the women. He's almost a head taller than
their mother, who looks up at him like a girlfriend might. Lola is ogling
him, too. Harold basks in the admiration; if he had a tail, it would be
wagging. After allowing him to relieve her of the picnic basket, Aunt
Gertrude ignores Harold and daintily picks her way through the meadow
grass, hoisting her skirt a minimum. She is absolutely ladylike, which
Ray suddenly realizes his mother is not. Lola's not old enough yet to be
considered a lady, and she may not make the grade because she seems

too fun-loving; ladies aren't supposed to be carefree in their manner. Aunt Gertrude fits the bill, all right. Ray watches as his mother and Lola flank Harold possessively, like floozies.

As though she knows he's jealous, Lola leaves his brother and comes right up to Ray, grabs his face, says, "Hello again, you," and plants a kiss close to his mouth. Ray is aware that he reeks of sweat; he wants to die. She glows a bit, too, after that walk in the sun, but on her it's like dew. She smells like a gardenia bush. He holds the pickax in front of him, in case anyone's watching. Aunt Gertrude sure isn't. She's inspecting the tombstones, her hands folded in a prayerful attitude. His mother is spreading quilts on the bare, shady ground beneath the popcorn tree he and Harold used to climb, when they were old enough to meander off by themselves and still young enough that their time wasn't one hundred percent parceled out to school and chores.

"Do you boys know what the agenda is?" Lola fastens on Ray as though he's the one to ask. He's trying to figure out what the word *agenda* means when Harold takes it upon himself to answer her.

"Doc wanted Papa and Uncle Jason to be present when he placed the remains in the casket, which is likely why they aren't here yet."

"You did a fine job, boys. The edges are nice and straight," Kathleen says. She strolls past them as though she's out for a walk.

⊚

Kathleen prefers being alone in this place, where she sees the familiar in new, grotesque ways. Occasionally, the small stone angel on one of her infant brothers' graves will show her a leer of pure evil, though now its carved expression is merely insipid. Someday, she will capture the church steeple at the moment it becomes a phallus mired in deep purple shadow. She will call the painting "Unenlightenment"—unless by that time she's been enlightened.

Gertrude, standing under the dogwood tree that was rooted from a switch by Lucy Holloway, tries to ignore the gnats around her face and the strident mother-calls from a nest on a bough above her head. She looks forward to the time, surely not too far off, when her youngest sister is married. Then it will be the husband's responsibility to keep Lola's demons at bay. She wishes she'd brought a magazine to leaf through while she waits for her husband to arrive. He'll be irritated that they didn't select several passages from the Bible. Perhaps a secular poem would be more fitting than the Twenty-third Psalm—something uplifting, such as Mr. Wordsworth's "Daffodils," that everyone would know.

Lola wanders through the maze of horizontal tablets and upright stones without reading inscriptions. She must not open the sluice gate of emotion; she chooses that metaphor from her own time here, though she would not have understood its significance then. Now, the implications ripple forth, as though supplied by a source outside her consciousness: open the sluice gate, deflect the dam, interrupt the flow, redirect the course of events. This particular event must be handled in a lighthearted manner, as Rhoda would wish.

The younger boy, showing off for Lola's benefit, tries to spar with his brother, who brushes him away as though he's a pesky fly. In less than a month of teaching, she has learned to recognize the tangled yearnings of adolescent males, who focus one minute on girls their own age, next on women old enough to be their mothers—or, in this case, on an aunt who's not old enough to be their mother. She ambles back to them. "Bet I can guess, in one try, what you're thinking about."

"Go ahead," Ray dares.

Sex. "Your sweetheart."

"Heck, I don't have one. Ask Harold about his."

She turns the smile in the other boy's direction. "Let me guess. Your special love has the name of a flower."

Harold says stiffly, "Daisy's just a friend."

"So you said last night, and it's none of my business anyway. Either of you want to pose a question to me?"

"Would you tell us what Aunt Rhoda was like?" The question comes from Ray.

"She was a sport and a chance-taker. Her natural curiosity made her restless. It was as though she looked for ways to get into trouble. But most of the time, she was clever enough not to get caught."

"What kind of trouble?"

"By her own admission to me, Rhoda smoked rabbit tobacco at the age of twelve. By the time she was thirteen, she had learned to dry the leaves and was selling it on the sly. A patch of the weed flourishes conveniently behind the barn, which I'm sure you've discovered."

"Corn is the only crop behind the barn now. Pop must have cleaned the rabbit tobacco out before we were old enough to know what it was."

Lola would not be surprised to learn that George had found out about Rhoda's little business and put an end to it. That would explain why Rhoda had taken a dislike to him.

Ray asks, "Did it occur to anybody back then that she might have left with the Gypsy caravan? She could have hidden in a tent wagon."

Lola is touched. The boy speaks as though he'd like to think, as she had until last night, that Rhoda made a successful getaway. Lola says, "The part I found impossible to imagine is how she got from our place to some distant locale without someone spotting her. I could visualize her playing a piano for a vaudeville act or a picture show, or riding an elephant in a parade. Whenever I travel, I watch for Rhoda. Once, in Nashville, I caught a glimpse of someone who looked just like her, but a moment later, she vanished."

Harold says, "My father has arrived with the, uh . . ."

"Catafalque."

He will learn later this day, on looking up its definition, that Lola used the noun loosely.

Ray must follow his brother to be of service to their father, but for one instant, he stands straight and still, his right hand across his heart, because Lola has just ennobled that old wagon and its cargo and this occasion with a word he won't remember and will likely never hear spoken again.

"Rhoda would have been crazy about you," Lola tells him with her mouth close to his ear, imparting a warmth that spreads to the roots of his hair.

12
Death Is a Picnic

GEORGE BRIDLES THE HORSES and leads them, stamping and snorting, from their stalls. He allows each in turn to nibble sugar lumps from his hand before he harnesses them to the wagon. The brother-in-law hasn't been a lot of help. The man was peeved that the box would not fit in the narrow space between the seats of the surrey, which would have been more dignified for hauling folks back from the funeral. While they were in the carriage house, Jason noticed the surrey's top was worn through in places and asked if the local harness shop could repair the damage.

"I'll look into it. Likely, he'll tell us the top should be replaced. Leather doesn't come cheap."

"I'll provide additional funds for the incidental expenses account if necessary."

That response from Jason is responsible for George's high humor as he climbs onto the driver's seat and sings out in the confident twang he's forgotten he possesses, "Oh, I wish I was in the land of cotton; / Old times there are not forgotten: / Look away! Look away! Look away! Dixie Land." He doesn't have the sentimental tie to the War Between the States that folks around here do—he comes from the one county in Alabama that did not secede from the Union—but he likes the spirited songs from that time. The new ones generated by the current war make him uneasy, especially the feisty, jubilant "Over There." What's so damn cheerful about sending boys who are needed at home to fight on foreign soil? He resents the command on the latest red, white, and blue poster displayed at the post office: "EAT MORE Corn, Oats, and Rye Products, Fish and Poultry, Fruits, Vegetables and Potatoes, Baked, Boiled, and Broiled Foods. EAT LESS Wheat, Meat, Sugar, and Fats, TO SAVE FOR THE ARMY AND OUR ASSOCIATES." Associates! He doesn't trust those Frenchies any more than he does the Huns.

George turns to look at the rest of the procession. Two motorcars in tandem are noteworthy traffic for this road. Doc's is ahead of Jason's. No doubt, they are impatient with the pace set by Demon Rum and Whiskey. The old buggers ought to be retired and replaced with a couple of hardy mules or, even better, a motorized truck.

He flicks the sensuous rumps (unlike women, horses don't lose their best curves in old age) to hurry things along past the millpond, which, due to a temporary mantle of pond slime, is the color of new leaves. If Harold had asked him, George would have told the boy not to waste his time cleaning the overshot wheel. There's little call for milling now, but occasionally, George releases the sluice gate to set the wheel in motion and dislodge any accumulation of trash. He had found the blended sounds of the waterfall and the wheel's rollicking rotation soothing until the time—must have been fifteen or sixteen years ago—the wheel started up mysteriously of its own accord. That particular morning, he hadn't intended going to the mill unless someone came with a load of corn and rang the big bell. He was repairing a pump at the house when he heard the thing whirling hell-to-breakfast, with no sign of a wagon out front. By the time he got there, the movement had ceased. The strange occurrence has never happened since, but from that day on, George has regarded the waterwheel with wary respect.

The boy first thought the heavy, saturated, reddish brown bones must be those of an Indian, until the doctor explained the color was just stain from pond mud. When he asked to borrow George's carpentry drill, he described to his father how he had scrubbed the bones gently, then laid them in the sun to dry. The bones had bleached out to a pale gray and were much lighter to handle. "We are basically something like ninety percent water, so when the water's gone, the rest doesn't weigh much at all," his son told him. George had nodded appreciatively, though he'd just as soon not know that kind of stuff.

The doctor had seized on Kathleen's suggestion that it could be Rhoda; George was surprised when the man hedged this morning on making the identification official. Jason, a man of law himself, was clearly relieved that the local law hadn't got involved. Jason's and Peter's less-than-aboveboard attitudes have convinced George that higher education may not be such a good thing. He could teach Harold an honorable trade, like that of cabinetmaker, which would not require a man to put on a cunning face. But the boy has his heart set on making a doctor. In George's opinion, doctoring is every bit as conniving a profession as lawyering.

Except for the bell spire, the church is not visible until you get right up on it. The building, the clearing, and most of the cemetery are hidden by a dense stand of mature, potentially valuable timber: oak that's impervious to termites, as well as the easier-to-work-with pine and poplar.

Rayford Holloway tried, without luck, to retrieve the acreage his own daddy (thinking, no doubt, to lay up for himself treasures in heaven) had deeded to the church. Last night, when George asked Kathleen if her brother-in-law knew Rayford had been caught attempting to falsify land records, she said, "Of course not. Gertrude would never tell Jason about that peccadillo."

"Pecker what?" George asked.

Kathleen laughed. "Get your mind out of your trousers. A peccadillo is a petty sin. It's the word Papa used to talk his way out of a fine or a jail term. Rhoda eavesdropped outside the courtroom window. She said he was really magnificent."

George climbs down, ties the horses to a fence post, and motions the motorists to park close to the fence. His moist and glowing sons hurry to help him unload the container. Lola saunters over to say, though she's not lifted a hand, "I cannot believe we're actually doing this." George's feelings are hurt; she's taken no notice of the casket. The head end is a half-hexagon, and the sides taper to a narrow, squared-off bottom, which is why it's called a pinch-toe coffin. The lid has a beveled lip. The solid-brass hinges were special-ordered from Baltimore. With each wiping of varnish, he followed the grain of the wood. Bricks of gold or a woman's hair couldn't gleam more than this example of his handiwork.

At least the doctor comments on the fine quality of the casket as he directs its placement on the ground beside Jason's car. George averts his eyes so he won't get another glimpse of the fleshless corpse that weighs hardly anything. He walks away wiping his hands, which are sticky from the frayed reins, on his best trousers before he remembers that Kathleen tucked a white handkerchief in his pocket this morning.

Kathleen has not come forth to greet him; she's waiting for him, though. Her lips are parted as if she expects him to give her a big, juicy kiss right here in front of others. Of course, he wouldn't, though he quickens at the thought. "Got here as soon as I could," he tells her anxiously, when he is close enough to detect the rich, animal scent that comes on her during the middle hours of the day, after she's put forth some energy.

"We haven't been here long." Without looking at him, she trails the fingers of one hand over the front of his pants just to the side of the buttons. He acknowledges the gesture by allowing his thumb to graze a nipple (which he's relieved to note is not visible through the cloth of her dress) until it firms up like a walnut. She closes her eyes and inhales sharply, then breaks the spell by moving away from him. She is a strange and unpredictable woman, but she's not a cuckoo bird like her older sister. He glances around to see if Jason is getting such a welcome and is pleased to note that he is not. Just the opposite: Gertrude appears to be giving the man almighty hell about something. Her chest is thrust forward. George wonders if she stuffs them into one of those newfangled contraptions he saw a picture of in a magazine Kathleen brought home from the lending library. When he asked her if she intended to get herself a brassiere, Kathleen laughed at the way he pronounced the strange word—"brasher"—and also at the very idea of such a thing. He loved it when she answered, "No. Mine like their freedom too much to be cooped up."

A pleated rice-paper fan flutters about Gertrude's face and neck like an agitated bird. "Please get this over with as soon as possible," she urges when Jason is close enough that she can speak softly, so the others won't hear.

"Am I to take charge?"

"Of course. Who else possibly could?"

"I had dared to hope some man of the cloth might be on the premises."

"Heaven forbid!" Gertrude snaps the fan shut. "This cannot be a religious ceremony."

Jason frowns. "Are you saying that heaven forbids it?"

"I'm saying it would be sacrilege to give the final rites of Christianity to a schoolboy's anatomy project."

"I see," Jason says, trying to. "So how do you suggest we handle the burial of what may be your sister?"

"With shovels and silence."

"Hmm. Have you discussed this idea with Kathleen and Lola?"

"Must I?"

"You're becoming rattled, dear. Close your fan and take several deep, slow breaths."

Gertrude obeys. "That does help. You always know how to deal with my upsets." She leans forward to kiss him chastely on the cheek—and to press an unbrassiered bosom against his forearm in such a manner there can be no doubt the gesture is intentional.

Jason gasps. *"Dearest!"*

"I know. That was naughty of me." The fan whips open to hide her face.

Her feigned embarrassment thrills him as much as her inappropriate show of ardor. Last night had been an unexpected boon. About once every fortnight is the routine that works best; he'd snuck an extra one in. He is very fortunate to have found and rescued this unusual creature. Not every marriage is made in heaven, as his was. Jason feels sorry for George and Kathleen, the mismatched pair who, from all appearances, take no pleasure in each other's company.

Now, Jason turns his attention to Lola and Daisy, who are conversing in quiet animation, as though oblivious to the casket a few yards away. No doubt, Lola, who by nature is perceptive and considerate of the feelings of others, realizes the young girl should be distracted. Jason's heart swells, as it often does, at the sight of his ward. The affection he feels for her deflects nothing from the profound man-woman love he has for his wife, although ever since Lola attained puberty, he's had to be extra cautious not to give Gertrude the slightest cause for jealousy.

At this moment, he wishes he could enfold Lola in a fatherly embrace and tell her everything will be all right. Now that she is no longer a child, he must not touch her at all, other than to assist her into and out of conveyances and, on formal occasions, to waltz with her at arm's length or let her gloved hand rest on his as he presents her to society.

Lola tries not to watch what is taking place behind this girl who plies her with naive questions about Felder and life in general. If she didn't know better, Lola might assume Peter Whitney and Harold are moving a tablecloth filled with kitchen utensils from the back seat of Jason's car. Jason and George have paired off with their wives, though not necessarily in domestic docility. Both couples appear to have their minds on something other than the reason they are here. But what? Lola often wonders what married people say to each other day in and day out, month after month, year after year. At first, according to Maggie, all they talk about is how much they adore each other's bodies. After a few weeks, it dawns on them they have to find other topics of mutual interest. And, Maggie admits, that's not easy, unless the girl likes base-ball and the man likes to shop.

"When it came time for you to go to college, did you have a hard time choosing which one?" Daisy's eager questioning reminds Lola of her own natural curiosity, which Gertrude has warned her comes dan-gerously close to rudeness.

"The choice wasn't entirely mine. Jason talked of Goucher and Smith, but Gertrude wouldn't hear of my going beyond a hundred-mile radius of Felder. Judson College was the compromise. Jason was impressed be-cause that institute for females was founded in the 1830s, in the wilds of Alabama, by an educator who later became the first president of Vassar College. Gertrude liked the fact that Judson, which is named for the first woman missionary, has strong Baptist ties; it is her opinion that Baptists have more moral stamina than Methodists and Episcopalians. Fortunately for me, my best friend, Maggie Cartwright—Cooper, she is now—was matriculating at the same college, and I knew she'd find a way to break some rules."

Daisy whispers, though no one is close enough to hear, "Is it true they put special powder in the food to keep girls from getting passionate?"

"That's the rumor. I never detected anything strange in the food, but for days before a dance weekend, there would be a telltale white sediment of saltpeter in the glass carafes of water on the dining tables. Maggie and I didn't see how in the world our yearning to cuddle with the opposite sex could be quelled chemically, but we weren't about to take chances. For at least a week before the big event, we would drink no water, coffee, or tea in the dining hall. The other options were milk and prune juice, which, we learned the hard way, had to be kept in perfect balance. Too much of one, we'd get constipated; too much of the other, we'd get the runs."

Daisy puts her hand up to squelch a laugh, this being a solemn occasion. She then composes herself to ask, "Were you required to wear uniforms?"

"Yes, indeed. You're looking at one. Gertrude packed for me yesterday, and this is what she selected." Lola brushes dandelion fuzz off the pleats of her navy-blue serge skirt. "I had five, a fresh one for each school day. Some of the girls had only two and had to scrub or iron one every night. I should get rid of these relics; I could never wear a girlish middy blouse to work."

"If I should go to the same college," Daisy says, "I would be delighted to wear your hand-me-down uniforms."

"Aren't you the sweetest thing! Remind me again how old you are."

"Going on sixteen."

"Speaking of hand-me-downs, would your mother object if I sent you a slinky party frock? Every now and then, I've managed to slide a racy little number past Gertrude."

"I could slide it past my mother easy as pie."

"Then be on the lookout for a package soon. You and I are about the same size, except you may be an inch or so taller. Of course, skirts are getting shorter. A word of advice: if you keep shooting up, be proud of it. The goddesses were never midgets."

"Was there ever such a thing as real goddesses?"

"Yes, if you believe in the power of myth, as I do. I took an honors course in Greek and Roman mythology."

"I'm anything but an honor student." Daisy sighs and tosses her hair back from her shoulders with both hands. To Lola, the mannerism brings a fleeting memory of another girl and another time. Daisy says, "You look like you've seen a ghost."

"For a moment, you reminded me of Rhoda, because she was about your age the last time I saw her." Lola changes the subject. "Tell me how you feel about Harold. Is it a crush or the real thing?"

"The real thing on my part. At least I think it is."

"If he doesn't wake up soon and fall at your feet and let you know that, more than putting pieces of a skeleton together or anything else in this world, he desires to plant kisses all over you, then take my word for it, he's not the one, and there are other fish in the sea." Although Daisy's face closes against this advice, Lola persists. "It's better to walk away from an unreciprocated love than it is to run away from yourself."

"Do you think your sister Rhoda was running away from herself or from a boy?"

"Rhoda didn't care a twig about any boy. She was running away from a mother who had no affection for her and from me, who needed her too much."

"Maybe she returned to get you and then had the accident before anyone realized she was home." Daisy turns to look at the coffin just as the lid comes down with a solid thud. Harold kneels beside it to fasten the clasps. Daisy wants to leap on his back and pull him down and make him roll on the ground with her until they're covered with leaves and invisible.

"Or maybe this whole thing is a farce, and Rhoda's in Maine or Massachusetts or California," Lola says briskly. "It could be we're about to bury Chief Red Eagle's mother in the Holloway plot. It's the least we could do to make up for Grandfather's having wiped her off the map." The sardonic laugh turns into a sob. Daisy croons nervously and pats her on the arm. From the corner of a weeping eye, Lola sees Jason sprinting across the graves to get to her.

For the first time since she had her growth spurt, her guardian angel brother-in-law puts his arms around her, strokes her hair, and says, in his slightly nasal voice that reminds her of a baritone horn, "Rhoda wouldn't want you to be sad for her now. We're putting her where she belongs."

Daisy's face crumples in what she supposes is a sympathetic reaction to Lola's grief. What reason has she to weep for some girl she never knew? Within seconds, she has a masculine shoulder to cry on, too. Lola is right; she must never, ever run away from home. The one she would hurt the most would be her dear papa. He would never get over it. She hugs him fiercely and feels his heart beat next to hers.

Gertrude moves away from the disgusting sight of older men embracing young women and, inadvertently, toward Kathleen and George. Kathleen asks her, "What's all that about?"

"Lola has a tendency to be overly emotional, and apparently Peter's daughter does, too. It's not surprising in a girl with an unstable mother like Coralee Whitney, but I can't imagine where Lola gets that weakness. As you know, Mama never wept for any reason, not even when Papa died. Did she?"

"Not that I recall. Mama had the dry eye, all right." Kathleen smiles.

Finally, they have agreed on something.

Gertrude suggests, not in the least overbearingly, "Should we set the food out now?"

"I assumed we'd get the sad part over with before eating."

"There doesn't have to be a sad part. We can pretend we're planting a rosebush."

Kathleen says wonderingly, "Tru, do you realize you're crazy as a loon? And have been since the time your fever shot up to 106 degrees."

"I have no idea what you're talking about."

"You don't remember having typhoid fever? You were out of your head for three weeks. You were supposed to die."

"Who made that pronouncement?"

"Grandmother, for one. It got so bad the doctor was summoned. You stayed downstairs on a cot in the hall. Mama was smocking a silk dress made from her own wedding gown for you to be laid out in, and her tears spotted the fabric. Grandmother told her to either stop sewing or stop bawling. I was wrong just now. Mama cried when she thought she was going to lose you."

"I don't recall ever wearing a smocked silk dress."

"After you got well, Grandmother burned it. She said it would be bad luck for any of us to wear a dress that had been made for a shroud."

"What a waste. It would have been a more appropriate wrapping for the skeleton than a crib blanket and an old sheet." Gertrude continues dreamily, "Which reminds me of the first moving picture to come to Hackberry Hill, in the summer before I went away to school. There wasn't a nickelodeon in town then, so the Edison Company's *Great Train Robbery* was projected onto a tacked-up sheet in the Grange Hall. The audience screamed when the outlaw shot straight at the camera."

Kathleen says, "The whole family got free passes because Rhoda was asked to play the piano during the projection. After that, Rhoda used to brag that she could get rich providing accompaniment for moving picture shows in a big city, while I could only be a poor 'hoe-er' in the country. By the time she left, Rhoda was tall enough to pass for grown, and she would have had no compunction about lying about her age to get work."

Gertrude agrees. "Yes, Rhoda was woefully short of compunction."

George observes in amazement. Now, these two chat as though they're the best of friends, and a moment ago, they were about to get into it.

His wife resumes the reflection. "Whenever a traveling tent show comes to town, I half expect to see Rhoda among the troupe, and worry over what I would say to her."

"I came close to fainting once when I thought I saw her among a throng at the Memphis station. I'm ashamed to admit, had Rhoda ever approached me publicly, I might have cut her dead with a glance of nonrecognition and sailed right past."

"At least you didn't really kill her. If there were an investigation, you'd not be the least bit suspect, because you were in Felder when she disappeared."

"Sister, do you believe Rhoda was the victim of foul play?"

Kathleen shrugs. "She wasn't the suicidal type."

"But if she was play-acting on that wheel, which she was wont to do in defiance of Mama, it must have occurred as Peter said: she fell and then drowned while she was unconscious, and her body was wedged by roots or rocks beneath the mill. It makes perfect sense."

Kathleen says—sarcastically, to George's consternation—"Maybe we should take a vote on what happened, and then it will be settled once and for all."

Jason can't hear their conversation, but from the steely expression on Kathleen's face, the flush on his wife's, and the alarm on George's, he knows it's time for intervention. He leaves his footprints over the graves again, calling out as he approaches, "The boys have worked up an appetite. Kathleen, could we have lunch before the burial?"

"Fine with me."

She kneels and opens the large hamper. Gertrude begins to take things from the smaller one. Lola and Daisy come to help. This is women's work. The men stand aside, then murmur appreciatively—like field hands accepting lunchpails at the back door, Kathleen thinks—as they are handed plates heaped with ham-filled biscuits, deviled eggs, potato salad, sweet pickles, and thick chunks of pound cake the color of jonquils. There is room on the quilt-spread ground for everyone to sit without being crowded, yet there is a palpable closeness, as though no one would think of leaving the group without the permission of every-one else. Daisy likes that feeling. Ray sits next to her, near enough to smell, but Harold, whose scent she'd rather breathe, is on the other side of her father. Kathleen passes around punch cups of heavily sweetened tea. The block of ice she placed in the jug before they left the house has melted and weakened the brew, but it's nicely chilled. Lola presses the cup to her forehead before taking a sip. Eating is accomplished with efficiency and without conversation (to Gertrude's relief, since she loses her appetite at the sight of partially masticated food in an open mouth).

They are wiping crumbs from their faces and fingers with Lucy Holloway's threadbare napkins when Jason realizes no blessing was spo-ken over the food. He doesn't mention the omission; it saved time, and there'll be Scripture later. The plates are scraped near the fence (to pro-vide a feast for the birds and squirrels), then packed with cups, forks, and napery inside the hampers. When everyone is standing in expect-ant, respectful silence, he asks Peter discreetly, "Would a viewing be in order?" The closed coffin is adjacent to his automobile, palled by its shadow.

"Of course. The remains are not as precisely positioned as they were on the counter, but the result is presentable. We've left a small blanket over what would have been the torso, and the sheet's tucked around it."

Daisy elaborates. "The blanket was a baby gift for me, but Hettie doesn't remember who made it." From the sudden flicker of Peter's eyelids, Jason deduces that Rhoda made the covering as a parting gift to the child she couldn't keep.

Lola scribbles on a small notepad. She tears out the sheet of paper, folds it in triplicate, and asks Harold, who stands beside the coffin as if he's been appointed to guard it, "Could you slip this inside for me?"

"Sure." Harold lifts the lid slightly and, without looking, manages to tuck Lola's missive into a rudimentary hand. He reminds the doctor, "I brought a can of sealant."

"Does anyone wish to view the remains before the lid is secured?" Peter's demeanor reminds Jason of that of a first-rate mortician. When heads shake mutely, resoundingly, Peter nods toward Harold to proceed with the sealing.

Minutes later, Harold and his brother on one side and Jason and George on the other lift the box and carry it to the opening. *Plop.* It's in there, a close-enough fit that it's a wonder they didn't get scraped knuckles.

Jason takes a few steps forward, but before he opens his mouth, something so unanticipated occurs that everyone gets goose bumps. Everyone except Gertrude, who, hands clasped in front of her, has begun to sing: "Beautiful dreamer, waken to me . . ." The exquisite coloratura careens through lyrics and branches of trees. Daisy is poised to clap at the end if anyone else does, but there is no applause other than a collective sigh of approval, or embarrassment. Then Lola says (and Kathleen realizes she is sincere), "That was the perfect tribute, Tru."

Gertrude invites Lola to recite a bit of verse.

"What comes to mind is a jingle Rhoda taught me: 'McKinley's elected, / Bryan's a fool, / Sitting on a haystack, / Looking like a mule.' "

"Well, it was instructive at the time," Jason says. He fingers his watch but tries not to look at it. "I suggest we say, in unison, the Twenty-third Psalm or the Lord's Prayer."

"Why not both?" asks Kathleen, who likes funerals better than other religious occasions.

Gertrude answers, "Because this is not a sanctioned service."

"Are you saying we can have one Christian element, but not two?"

"Let's not get into that again." Lola darts between them like a referee. "One's sufficient. Rhoda would prefer the Psalm." She pitches her voice to schoolteacher level: " 'The Lord is my shepherd; I shall not want.' " The others join in. Some funeral, George thinks. Where he came from, sounds of mourning would be bouncing off that distant mountain by now.

Jason is poised to pronounce a benediction when Lola says, "We should talk about a headstone."

"Give me an idea of size and shape, also what you want it to say, and I'll attend to it," George offers. "There's only one stonecutter in the area now. The other fellow moved to Sylacauga to work at the marble quarry."

Jason says, "It should be unobtrusive. A small, flat tablet inscribed with a brief, impersonal sentiment such as 'Beloved of God,' instead of a name."

Lola is weaving the stems of wild daisies together. "Why have a grave marker, if it doesn't identify the occupant?"

"Good point," Jason concedes. A no-name tombstone would arouse curiosity and possibly trigger a belated investigation. "The inscription should be her name with no birth date, since the date of death is unknown."

Lola notes, contrarily, "She didn't much care for the name Rhoda. She planned to change it to Rhododendron when she was old enough."

"But she never got old enough," Kathleen says.

" 'Here lies Rose,' " Gertrude intones. "That was the name she arrived with."

"Arrived with?" George echoes.

"Rhoda was adopted into the family," Lola explains offhandedly. "Gertrude has kept that secret until today."

George is giddy with revelation: The girl who came uninvited to his bed all those years ago was not his wife's sister, which means he did not commit the other sin, the one he doesn't even know the word for.

"In all likelihood, Rhoda was Papa's bastard," Kathleen says quietly, as though she's read his mind.

So she was his wife's half-sister. The adjustment does not dispel his sense of reprieve.

Gertrude's eyes are closed as she concentrates on dispelling the words "Papa's bastard."

Jason is relieved that Peter Whitney and his daughter didn't hear this latest exchange. As soon as the discussion of a headstone began, Peter had steered the girl away, to give the family privacy. It occurs to Jason that the doctor may believe Rhoda was born to Lucy Holloway while he was away at school; he may not be aware that Rhoda, like her daughter, was given up by a birth mother. "Let's not digress from the subject of the marker's inscription. Rho-da Hol-lo-way." Jason enunciates each syllable carefully, as though George is hearing the name for the first time. "Not R-o-d-a. There's a silent *h* in there: R-*h*-o-d-a. Simple block letters on a first-quality, plain block of marble. No little carved thingamajigs." Later, Jason will give George a packet of greenbacks rolled tight as a cigarette, enough to pay for Rhoda's stone and another just like it with the name Elvira Perkins.

The Whitneys have strolled over to their own family plot, where Peter's grandfather's memorial, an elaborately carved double arch of granite, glints sturdily in the sunlight. Like many others in this cemetery, the grave is also marked with the scythe-and-square Masonic emblem and the iron cross that signifies military service in the Confederacy. Peter wishes he had not allowed Daisy to come to this fiasco of a funeral. She's confused by the lack of reverence and structure. It had seemed appropriate to allow the child that Rhoda Holloway brought into the world to be present here. Daisy should have some exposure to these women before she is informed of their connection to her.

She's eager to rejoin the others. As they approach the group, Peter sees what he's never noticed before: the shape of Daisy's eyes is similar to that of the younger boy's. The prominent cheekbones are somewhat like Harold's. Yet these features are not from their mother's side. Peter swivels his neck in the direction of George Craven. *Of course. Especially the cheekbones.*

He is aware that the group is dispersing, except for the boys (who may be his child's half-brothers!). They are to stay and dress the grave. Kathleen, carrying the folded quilts and the larger of the hampers, is headed to the wagon; she seems so of a piece with these items that no one springs forward to help her. Her husband—he of the darting, slanted eyes, angular face, and rotten morals—uncoils the reins from a fence post. The horses, realizing the siesta is over, toss their heads and stamp their hooves. Jason has handed Gertrude into the front seat of his car and is trying to get Lola's attention. Having placed her daisy wreath at the head of the grave, she can't seem to take leave of Daisy. Peter comes to her aid. "Thank you for being so kind to my daughter. I hope you'll allow us to call on you in Felder."

"I would adore it. Let us know when you plan to come, so we can stir up some entertainment." Lola presses her cheek to Daisy's and whispers, "Be on the lookout for a package." She would like to make a gesture of affection to Peter, but it might embarrass him.

As they bump along the road in Peter's car, Daisy asks, "Did you really mean it?"

The exchange of farewells with Jason and Gertrude was brief and perfunctory. Peter avoided saying goodbye to Kathleen and her husband, as he could not bring himself to shake George Craven's hand.

"Mean what?" He won't look at the girl's face, for fear of seeing that man there again.

"When you said we would take a trip to Felder."

"Yes, indeed. Perhaps we can go one weekend soon."

"Papa, I love you to pieces." Her head comes to rest like a dove on his shoulder. A rosebud breast presses innocently against his arm. Yes, he is her papa. No one can take that from him.

Ray stomps the clods he's shoveled onto the casket and pretends he is dancing on a stage. He might travel the world with a vaudeville show. He wouldn't mind blacking his face and playing for an appreciative audience. He steps from that dream to undisturbed ground and instant deflation. There's nothing more to do here. The others departed half an hour ago. "Damn it all, we got to walk home."

"It's no great distance." Harold has smoothed the sides of the grave as carefully as though the job will be inspected, though he knows it won't. Periodically, Harold and Ray are sent to scythe the meadow grass and tidy the church grounds, including this graveyard; the old clergyman never comes out to approve or pass judgment on their work. Payment is left on the church steps in a sealed envelope addressed to Mr. George Craven. Harold has no idea how much it is. Pop says the money will help send them to college.

They amble in silence. Ray decides he will not say another word. Let Harold start some conversation for once. When he realizes that's not going to happen, he asks, "Which one did you like best?"

"Which one of what?"

"The aunts."

"I liked them the same. Lola was friendlier, but I admire Aunt Gertrude's reserved demeanor."

"Demeanor, huh? Is that French for her behind?"

"No, jackass. It's English for the way she comports herself." Harold wonders why he likes womanish words such as *demeanor* and *comport*, and why he winces to hear himself say something like *jackass*, which comes so naturally to other boys.

"I'll take Lola any day. I like those nice little tits, and the way she switches her hips. I bet she let her sweetheart do it to her every night for a month before he left for overseas. Poor guy was so tired out he had to spend the trip over catching up on his sleep."

"That's no way to talk about your mother's sister. Show some respect."

"Aunt Gertrude has a pair of jugs on her I could be respectful about. Do you suppose Uncle Jason ever gets to lay a hand on one? Or better yet, his . . ." Ray sticks out his tongue.

"You're disgusting."

They toss the implements over the fence. At the top of the stile he helped his father build, Ray announces to his brother on the step below, "I've made an important decision. Which is, I'm going to pole ol' Daisy. Since you won't do her that favor, it might as well be me."

Harold shoves him with both hands. Then he has to convince a howling Ray that the ankle the latter landed on isn't broken, though it may be sprained. The injury slows them down considerably. Ray uses a shovel as a crutch; Harold has to support his other side and carry the rest of the tools.

When they arrive home, the Packard automobile and the visitors are gone. Harold is inexpressibly sad, as though an important segment of his life has ended. For almost twenty-four hours, his world expanded— new faces, new minds, new words—into a kaleidoscope of possibilities. Now, it's back to normal. "I hoped they would stay another day," he says sadly to his mother.

"Your aunt Gertrude has to sing a solo in her church tomorrow morning. The service couldn't go on without her."

Harold wishes she wouldn't be sarcastic.

"Dang it, I never got a ride in Uncle Jason's fancy car," Ray says.

"Are you really limping, or just pretending?" Kathleen is perched on her painting stool, which used to be her milking stool before she turned that chore over to Ray. A big pad of thick, unlined paper bought last week from a door-to-door salesman rests on her knee. The tablet cost as much as a new dress. The little paint pots and colored chalk are mail-order items. She goes through those luxuries like another woman would diminish an expensive box of chocolates. She pays for her art supplies from a packet of paper bills in ten- and twenty-dollar denominations that she found years ago. The bills were in a pocketbook that was bundled with a calico dress, a sunbonnet, and a pair of shoes, all seemingly new, in the crotch of a willow tree on the pond bank. She didn't spend any of it until she began painting. When George began to wonder how she paid for her art supplies, she told him she'd found money in her mother's trunk.

"Shouldn't you share that money with your sisters?" he asked.

"Not according to the rule of finders-keepers," she replied. He never asked her how much was there, and he's never mentioned the subject again. So far, she hasn't gone beyond the smaller bills. The bulk of the money, which she's saving for the boys' education, is hidden in Grandmother's dressmaker dummy in the room behind the kitchen. The mannequin wears the dress, and the bonnet hangs on a hook above it. Sometimes when she enters the room, Kathleen is aware of a benevolent energy emanating from this female presence she has created.

Ray tells his mother that he fell off the stile, but she doesn't seem to hear. With quick, definitive strokes, she is sketching the Bantam rooster that struts and pecks a few feet away. An arc of tail feathers streaks from the charcoal in her hand onto the paper. Ray thinks, crossly, that his mother is like that chicken, as her head bobs up and down from her subject to the paper. Chickens are never concerned with anything but themselves. His mother is the same way. She thinks of herself all the time now.

George doesn't seem concerned about his younger son's hurt ankle either. Whistling softly, he gazes down the road where, less than an hour ago, the big black-and-blue car gathered speed and disappeared in a backlash of copper-colored dust. Jason thanked him profusely for replenishing the fuel tank and the running-board canister but stopped short of offering to pay for the gas. Instead, he took out the foppish cigarette case to offer George a smoke, and found it empty. "I keep a spare pack in the dashboard pocket," he said hopefully, and a few seconds later, dejectedly, "Gertrude must have found that one."

"Does she smoke?"

"Only with quiet fury over the fact that I do. I told her early in our marriage that I'm happily addicted to tobacco and would tolerate no discussion about it. So from time to time, she confiscates a package, and it turns up a few days later in the same place I left it, but with the cigarettes shredded." Jason seemed more morose over this situation than he did over the one that brought him here. "The other possibility is that Lola, who puffs on the sly, helped herself when she went out before retiring last night. Yes, I expect that's what happened," he said, brightening.

"I'll give you a few for the road." George carefully extracted three cigarettes from his pocket without producing the box that held them.

"Thank you. Did you roll these yourself?"

"No. I never acquired the knack of licking the papers so they'd stay stuck. Also, like you, I prefer store-bought. These are Carolina's Brightest. Not Virginia's finest, but they should do in a pinch."

Jason lit one, inhaled, and pronounced George's brand every bit as satisfying as his own.

The man seemed reluctant to take his leave. When he grasped George's hand in farewell, he said, so low the women couldn't hear, "This place has great potential for a first-rate resort. The gristmill could be fitted out to accommodate vacationers who yearn for the quiet, scenic vistas of field and forest. It shouldn't be too difficult to roll out a clay tennis court near the muscadine arbor. Ideally, we should widen the pond and build a landing for canoeing. That knoll behind the house would be just the spot for an open-air pavilion. Of course, the cottonwoods would have to be cleared off. Now, if we could just come up with a few well-placed mineral springs. Give some serious thought to the idea. I'll be in touch."

George nodded noncommittally once or twice during that soliloquy. He waved Godspeed to his guests like a real host. As the car rose to the occasion—it actually seemed to shimmy for an instant before taking off—Lola gazed through one of a pair of small, nonopening rear windows. George didn't flatter himself that he was the object of her interest. It was this place. She was looking back at what she'd left behind all those years ago and was leaving again.

On the way back from the burial, Kathleen had said, "I hope they don't stay another night. I've had enough of this invasion of my privacy." Not *our* privacy. Her self-containment frustrated him, yet the air of mystery it gave her kept his appetite whetted. He had never felt any desire to be with another woman since he married this one.

When the group returned to the house and Jason announced that they would pack up and depart, Kathleen had let out a sigh of relief that embarrassed George as much as if she'd passed wind. While the car was readied, she remained on the porch. Her farewell was simple and heartfelt: "Goodbye." At least she didn't step back from Gertrude's pretend kiss and Lola's hug.

George sees that Kathleen has put the intrusion from her mind. Her concentration is on copying that midget rooster. Now is not the time to tell her Jason has grandiose plans to turn the place into a watering hole for idle city slickers.

13
Keeping in Touch

MIDWAY THROUGH THE REVERSE JOURNEY, a sudden shower made it necessary to fasten the side curtains, which caused the interior of the automobile to become hot and humid, which in turn caused the laryngitis that has Gertrude spending this Sabbath morning not in the choir loft, but propped on pillows with a mustard plaster on her throat.

As she composes a note to Kathleen thanking her for her hospitality under severely trying circumstances, Gertrude is surprised at how much she has to say beyond the bread-and-butter part. Such as, Lola was uncharacteristically moody on the ride back and even declined to take the wheel when Jason offered, though her spirits revived on finding a letter from her fiancé in the Saturday mail. Lola has accompanied Jason to church, after which she will spend the afternoon with her friend Margaret Cartwright Cooper. "Maggie," as she's known, is from one of Felder's finest families and has married into another. But Gertrude has belatedly learned that this young woman was rumored to be a bit fast when she and Lola were in college together—and maybe before that, perish the thought! She prays Lola's reputation has not been tarnished by the association. Last but not least, would Sister please retrieve Gertrude's china-head doll from Mama's trunk and send it to her?

After filling both sides of the fold-over stationery (which is discreetly embossed with the Howard coat of arms), Gertrude wonders if Kathleen will read the thing all the way through. She underlines the postscript: "The enclosed dollar bill should defray costs of packaging and postage. My doll has on an emerald-green frock; yours is the one in blue."

The Tuesday following their return from Hackberry Hill, Lola boxes up some clothes to send, as promised, to Daisy. When she asks Jason at dinner to post the package, he replies, "You can give it to her yourself. Peter Whitney called today to say he and his daughter will be in town this weekend. I hope you will show the girl around some on Saturday. We'll take them to dinner and the theater that evening."

Lola agrees without protest, as he knew she would. Jason makes a mental note to see about tickets. Normally, he would turn that detail over to his capable amanuensis, Miss Frances Leverett, who is also his third cousin, but there is no need to rekindle her curiosity. When Peter called the previous Friday, Frances had covered the mouthpiece with a hand and whispered importantly to Jason, "This is the handsome man who gave the bride away."

"What bride?"

"Yours. It's Dr. Whitney, calling from Hackberry Hill." Frances attended Jason's wedding all those years ago; the occasion was a highlight of her unremarkable life. After she handed him the receiver, she made a point of leaving the room and closing the door; she would never intentionally eavesdrop.

Fortunately, Frances had stepped out to do an errand when Peter called on Tuesday. Although this message was not ominous in content, Jason detected an underlying urgency. He hopes the man isn't about to become a client.

⊙

Jason learns from the desk clerk at the New Exchange Hotel that Dr. Whitney and his daughter checked in the previous afternoon. It was considerate of Peter not to mention that he would be in Felder on Friday. As it is, the man will take up the middle of Jason's Saturday, plus several hours of the evening. Gertrude thought it presumptuous of the doctor to solicit any attention from them, especially so soon after they've been together. However, when Jason reminded her that Peter escorted her down the aisle at their wedding, Gertrude reversed her attitude and offered to have the man and his daughter to the house for a light supper before the play.

Jason has secured a well-placed table in the dining room when Peter arrives and greets him warmly. "It's very kind of Lola to show Daisy around Felder. They left a few minutes ago. And thank you for suggesting this hotel. Our suite is quite commodious."

"I thought you'd be comfortable here, although it doesn't pretend to be as grand as its predecessor. In the 1880s, after a renovation, the Old Exchange advertised its boudoirs in metropolitan newspapers throughout the country as being 'fit for an Egyptian queen.' That one was torn down several years ago, when the owners decided to rebuild with modern conveniences." He recommends the Dozen on the Half Shell as a starter, and assures his companion the oysters have traveled fully iced all the way from Mobile.

Hardly have they dug in before Peter puts down his tiny fork, grips the corners of the table, leans across it, and says, somewhat louder than necessary, "I have reason to believe George Craven is the natural father of my daughter."

A slippery crustacean makes its way toward Jason's throat. He reaches for his water goblet.

When the crisis is over, Peter asks, "Are you all right?"

"Yes. But you sure startled the hell out of me."

"Sorry. I thought I should tell you before I confront the man."

"Let's hope it doesn't get to that. How did you arrive at this idea?"

"Until this past Saturday, I never doubted Rhoda's statement that the boy who was killed on the tracks got her pregnant. While we were gathered in the cemetery, I was struck by a physical resemblance between my daughter and that man. Daisy has Craven's cheekbones, and there's a strong resemblance in the shape and placement of eyes. My hunch was so strong I almost became physically ill."

"Supposing it's true, just imagine George's dilemma at the time. Married, or about to be, to one sister, he couldn't make an honest woman of the other. What a position to be in!" Jason pauses to fortify himself with more water. "However, without corroborating evidence, a confrontation with George would likely elicit an indignant denial and foster ill will between neighboring families. If he admits to being the girl's father, he might try to take her from you."

Peter's face turns white. "That possibility had not occurred to me."

"Of course, as long as you believe there's even the slightest chance that my nephew Harold and your daughter are more closely related than first cousin, you would do well to put some distance between them. Have you thought of sending her away to school?"

"Yes, I would like for Daisy to have that broadening experience. But I also like having her at home." Peter adds dejectedly, "All I wanted was for Daisy and Harold to wait until they're more mature to become romantically involved. Now, the very thought that they might be headed in that direction . . ."

"I still think you've jumped the gun. George is a definite brunette, as was Rhoda. Wouldn't it be highly unusual for the progeny of two dark-haired people to be blond and fair-skinned?"

"Children can take characteristics from grandparents and remote ancestors."

"So Daisy could have inherited her cheekbones from an aristocratic ancestor," Jason beams, as though Peter is responsible for this idea. "Whereas, from what I know of George's background, his facial angularity is likely due to insufficient nutrition during his formative years. I'll wager the young fellow Rhoda told you got her in trouble had coloring similar to Daisy's."

"I have no idea what the boy looked like. I didn't know the family."

"In my infrequent dealings with my brother-in-law over the years, he's impressed me as a forthright, industrious, and quite decent fellow. I hope you can put this notion out of your mind."

"I hope I can, too."

Jason waits until they are almost through the hefty servings of pot roast and picks a moment when the doctor has nothing in his mouth to drop his own bombshell: "Are you aware that Rhoda was a foundling?"

"I've never heard that before. Are you sure?"

"According to Gertrude, her father brought Rhoda home from one of his trips. Lucy wasn't happy about taking a strange child into her brood, but she did it. Kathleen and Lola didn't know until recently that Rhoda wasn't born into the family. Nor, as far as I can tell, did Rhoda know."

Peter says, "While I was away receiving my training, Rayford Holloway was elected to the state legislature. I recall a letter from my father in which he alluded to Rayford's having himself a high time in the capital city, but there was never any mention of his bringing home a love child."

"Ah. I'll admit to drawing the same conclusion that you do, but my wife would never entertain the thought of her father's siring a child outside his marriage."

"So you're saying Gertrude could never accept Daisy as a niece?"

"That's not what I'm saying. Rhoda was brought up as a sister of Gertrude's. Therefore, blood kin or not, a child of Rhoda's would be Gertrude's niece. My concern is that Gertrude would be utterly devastated to learn that one of her sisters secretly bore a child out of wedlock and allowed that child to be brought up by people who lived next door. Frankly, I see no reason for my wife to be put through that wringer, as no good whatsoever would come of her knowing."

"But you said Lola would welcome Daisy."

"She and your girl seem to be quite congenial. Let's give them time to get to know each other naturally. I would like to think that when Lola and Daisy learn of their connection, each will realize she's been aware of it all along, on some level."

The answer seems to satisfy Peter. He relaxes for the first time since they sat down and turns his attention to the warm, fragrant wedge of apple pie that has just been placed before him.

After coffee is served, Jason says, "Back to Rhoda's status in the family. You may know that, except for some household goods and personal effects, Lucy Holloway's property has yet to be divided. The main assets she had to pass on were what she received as her husband's sole beneficiary—the land with its structures, livestock, tools, and vehicles. There was very little on bank deposit in her name. I suspect she had cash reserves hidden somewhere, but as far as I know, nothing has ever turned up other than a handful of bills and coins in a sugar bowl."

"They always seemed to live pretty much hand-to-mouth."

"I suggested to Lucy that the runaway share with the others if she returned home within a certain length of time—say, two years from the date of her mother's demise—but Lucy was adamant there be no reference whatsoever to Rhoda in her last will and testament. It was as though this daughter never existed. However, Rhoda's status as a member of the family is recorded in at least one place: she's listed in the 1900 census with the other daughters in the household."

Peter says, "Poor girl. That would have been the final blow, to come home and find she'd been left out when the pie was cut."

"As long as the property was intact, I knew the others could be talked into doing the right thing by Rhoda. When I first observed those four girls together, each seemed to be distinctly her own person, yet there was an almost visible bond that linked them. I don't know that there's any other category of women quite as special as that of sisterhood." He sighs as though reliving some pleasant memory, then frowns as he gets back to the subject. "Another reason for postponing settlement is found in Lucy's own wording. The three daughters she named were to share as equally as possible, 'being mindful of each other's needs.' Gertrude and Lola have had no pressing need to divide the land that provides Kathleen's family's livelihood." Jason opens his cigarette case. "Do you mind?"

"I have no objection." At least not here, where there are ashtrays on the tables.

The waiter darts over to light Jason's cigarette. After the brief pause, during which a noxious cloud of smoke drifts toward his companion, Jason continues. "Before we left Hackberry Hill last Saturday, I suggested to George that we might turn some of that agricultural hodgepodge into a pastoral retreat for urban dwellers—cottages, tennis and badminton courts, a croquet lawn, a riding stable, plus a pavilion for shuffleboard, band concerts, and dancing by the light of rice-paper lanterns and harvest moons. I don't mean to bore you."

"You're not. It's an interesting concept. What would happen to the Cravens then?"

"They could run the resort. If they don't want that kind of responsibility, George could keep the house and the best pasture land for his cattle and spend more time on his woodworking hobby. The Holloway acreage should be parceled out before somebody else dies." He means before he himself dies. Jason shakes the glum thought by changing the subject. "Good news from overseas. On September 13, the day you summoned us to Hackberry Hill, the Second Battalion of the Alabama regiment went over the top, crawled through the barbed wire into no man's land, and captured the chateau which had been the German Army Corps headquarters."

Peter has also stayed abreast. "But they're saying fifty percent of the Rainbow Division's manpower is lost. I believe the figure includes the recovering wounded."

"Lola's young man would be in that group. Robert doesn't dwell on the state of his health in his letters to her, which she takes as a sign that he's rapidly on the mend, and I take as his showing a stiff upper lip by not complaining. The lad's father vented his frustration to me recently. Castleman wants his boy home, so he can buy him the best of medical care. He says military hospitals are no better than prison infirmaries."

"The crowding and shortage of drugs are the real problems in the military hospitals. This is the first conflict to involve medically trained nurses; some of our finest surgeons have heeded the call to overseas duty. And with refrigeration, blood transfusion has become an option." Peter's face becomes animated; this is his territory. "It's been reported that one hundred percent of all foreign substances discovered by x-ray are removed. What x-ray doesn't reveal, often the fluoroscope does. Of course, I would never minimize Lola's fiancé's situation."

"My friend, you and I may consider ourselves lucky not to have sons between the ages of twenty-one and thirty. Whenever I put my signature to a draft notice to call up yet another able-bodied young man, I feel as though I may be issuing his death warrant."

When they part outside the building, Peter decides to walk a block to pay a first-time visit to the wholesale pharmaceutical firm that for many years has filled his mail orders so efficiently. At six o'clock, he and Daisy will take a cab to the Howards' Garden Street residence. He hopes he will remember to buy a bunch of flowers from the stand in front of the hotel to take to Gertrude. His considerate friend Helen offered that suggestion. His wife suggested he rot in hell for leaving her ill while he introduced their sweet, innocent child to the pleasures of city life. He wonders if Hettie has been able to coax Coralee out of bed since they left.

Despite the heavy meal that rumbles inside him like a locomotive, Jason feels lighter than he has all week. Whether or not it is true, Peter Whitney's theory that George Craven was the root of Rhoda's trouble has rendered null and void his own suspicion that the doctor himself might have played that role. Certainly, it would be easier to excuse George for such behavior than Peter. In Jason's book, any man who took a vow to adhere to the ethics of an honorable profession yet would compromise a vulnerable, under-aged girl, particularly the daughter of a deceased close friend, was downright despicable.

Lola can hardly believe Daisy has never seen people playing golf before. Daisy can hardly believe it herself. (Maggie has insisted Lola use her car to take the visitor to the country club for lunch: "Keep it as long as you like, and show the little mouse a good time." She promised to make a fourth in her mother's bridge game and so can't join them, which Lola thinks is just as well; Daisy might not be ready for the likes of Maggie.)

Daisy hopes she isn't talking too much. Lola is such an attentive listener, not preoccupied like her papa and Harold; she smiles and nods her head or shakes it vehemently. At intervals, she exclaims, "You're absolutely right, Daisy"; "Really!"; or "Then what did you do?"

Daisy can't resist confiding her newest resolution, which is not to chase after Lola's nephew. "I used to seek Harold out at school or in Papa's laboratory, and I would endeavor to walk home from school with him and Ray. Now, I walk by myself."

"Good for you. Don't be too easy to get. Would you like to taste this shrimp?"

"No, thank you. The chicken is delicious. For some reason, shrimp make me think of your family's pond."

"You don't like the pond?"

"I get a funny feeling about it sometimes. When I used to swim there with Harold and Ray, it seemed as though there was something beneath that calm surface that could pull me under."

"Well, it wasn't one of these little critters," Lola says, popping another shrimp into her mouth. "I didn't care much for the gristmill. Especially the wheel."

"You must have been glad to leave Hackberry Hill."

"I was bereft. Rhoda had run away, and my mother had died."

Daisy asks timidly, "Has Mrs. Howard been like a mother to you?"

"She's done her best. Gertrude voluntarily matured beyond her years to fill that role for me. And her husband has been all I could wish for in a father figure."

"Harold told me two days ago, before I resolved to avoid him, that his father has placed the order with the stonecutter. I know you're anxious for your sister's grave to be marked. I'll write you as soon as the monument is in place, in case Mrs. Craven doesn't."

"Please do. It may not occur to Kathleen to let us know."

Daisy doesn't tell Lola that the previous Sunday, after church, she took the daisy wreath from the fresh grave to hang in her bedroom. When Torey asked why she wanted that dried-up thing, she said truthfully she didn't know; she just did.

Lola must have realized today was the first time Daisy had been to a department store. Her papa had given her more money than she'd ever had before, with no restrictions on how she could spend it. Lola thought the girl's idea to do some Christmas shopping was excellent. Daisy bought a rabbit-skin muff for Torey, paisley shawls for her mother and Hettie, a garnet stickpin for her papa, and a handkerchief for the lady at the lending library who, just this past week, found some literature for her that wasn't too taxing. When Lola selected a bright blue sweater for her fiancé, Daisy resisted the impulse to buy one like it for Harold.

They found a dress for Daisy, and when she couldn't make up her mind about another, Lola reminded her, "I'm sending some things back with you. Whatever you don't want, just give away or drape over a scarecrow." She got a faraway look. "I used to be terrified of the scarecrow in our cornfield. I wonder if it's still there."

"I don't believe it is." Daisy said what she thought Lola wanted to hear. Other than a mass of tall, dense stalks that people could get lost in, she had no idea what was in that cornfield. She wished Harold had taken her by the hand and led her into it.

After lunch, on the way back to the hotel, Lola says, "You and Harold have known each other since you were babies. He's bound to feel affection for you, but if it doesn't ripen into romance, don't allow your heart to be broken. Tell it—your heart—that someone wonderful is waiting to give you the attention you require. Keep this thought, and the someone will appear."

"Not in Hackberry Hill," Daisy sighs.

"Good point. So ask your papa to send you to boarding school in a distant city."

"I will." The words are strong and clear, like a wedding vow. Yet a month ago—even three days ago—she would have been devastated at the thought of leaving Harold.

Lola and Jason are at Union Station to hear from one of Alabama's recovered wounded, who has been sent back early to tour with the Liberty Loan Committee Trains. From the observation car's platform, the hero with a patch over one eye and an arm in a sling reports the Rainbow troops "are known for daring bravery and skillful handling of the bayonet, and for taking very few prisoners. The cowardly Germans have to be manacled to their guns to make sure they'll stick." After the inspiring speech and enthusiastic applause, Lola asks the first question: Does Sergeant Smith happen to know Lieutenant Robert Castleman of Company E? No, ma'am, but he's sure heard that name.

On the way home, she asks Jason accusingly, "Why wasn't Rob chosen to come back early for this tour?"

"My dear, I have no idea how the selection was made. That was quite a turnout. I hope Gertrude doesn't hear we were in a crowd."

"I'll not tell her." Lola has promised Gertrude she won't go to any more picture shows until the plague of Spanish influenza is past. Rumor has it the germ was released in this country by German spies. So far, the outbreak in Felder has been mild. A special emergency hospital is equipped to handle up to five hundred cases if necessary, and masks are to be worn on public conveyances. Gertrude believes staying inside one's home is the way to avoid La Grippe, even though the bulletins advise wearing loose clothing and spending as much time as possible in the open.

Acting on that advice, Lola and some of her students ride bicycles the following mid-October Sunday afternoon in a leafy park. Rather to her surprise, the boys ignore the occasion's opportunities for flirting with her and the young girls who flutter around like butterflies. These beardless males are obsessed with the idea of joining up. One tells Lola— passionately, his face close to hers—that he hopes the war won't end before he gets in the thick of it.

The next day, she reads her civics class a newspaper version of an Opelika soldier's letter about the war his unit is waging against "cooties," due to lack of bathing opportunities in the trenches. "Sweetheart," she writes Rob, "if you've had to play host to those nasty little creatures, thank you for not telling me. I'm so relieved you're out of that arena. As long as they keep you clean and comfortable, I don't mind if the nurses see you naked before I do."

In the same communication, she airs some grievances of a general nature. (The morale bulletins suggest every letter should contain items of local color.) Felder's fine new YMCA is fitted out with a gymnasium and swimming pool. Of course, the "Y" is a worthwhile organization that actively promotes the morale of the armed forces in this country and abroad, but that ill-timed fund-raising is bound to have hampered local participation in the United War Work Campaign and the War Stamp, Liberty Bond, and Red Cross drives. In protest of such costly municipal embellishment while the country is *at war*, Lola has declined the invitation to the opening gala. Although Jason won't boycott the event, he admits she has a point. It is also irksome that the Young Men's Christian Association receives so much more publicity than the Young Women's. Lola's only recently learned that last March, a YWCA volunteer from Iowa became the first American woman to lose her life in active service. The heroine had an arm blown off by a German artillery shell, died in a French military hospital, and was buried as a soldier. Lola doesn't have the stomach to be a nurse, but she would be a great canteen girl. Damnation, she should have defied Jason and the federal government and shipped herself to France.

About the time she mails this letter, Rob's reply to her lengthy outpouring arrives. He says he would give anything to have known her sister Rhoda, and that he looks forward to meeting Kathleen and the other relatives. Just by reading (and rereading) Lola's descriptions, Hackberry Hill had become a special place to him. They will visit there often after they are married. There's no mention of when he might be headed home. Maybe Rob intends to surprise her, in which case he will thwart

Lola's plans to surprise him with a prearranged, prenuptial honeymoon.

◎

Kathleen complies promptly with Gertrude's request and dispatches both china-head dolls, tying a note to one tiny, rigid hand: "These girls have been together so long it would be cruel to separate them now. Congratulations, by the way, on what you've done with Lola. She's a work of art." Gertrude cuts out the compliment and tucks it in her bedside Bible.

Lola informs Kathleen that Gertrude suffers from what appears to be morning sickness, and that Jason wears a fatuous expression. Maggie says she shouldn't ask, that she must wait to be let in on their secret, then act surprised and thrilled to pieces over the news, even though—of course—she's mortified that these long-married dears are just getting around to having a baby. It's as though they've just discovered sex. What on earth have they been doing all these years?

But Lola is proud of them for this feat, and relieved that they will soon have something—someone—to attach their hopes to besides her.

◎

The new time change set by the president is due to start on October 27. Daylight Saving Time will have everyone up an hour earlier than usual. Maggie refuses to alter her clocks. She's vowed not to give up a single hour of beauty sleep until Ted is safely home. Lola is optimistic about the time change. The combination of words is symbolic: it's time for a change, time for the war to end and the fighting men to come home and pay attention to women (for a change). Just after midnight on the appointed day, Lola sets her bedside clock to the new time and tells Rob, wherever he is, "Good night, my love. I embrace you in my dreams and in yours. If you hear a rapping at the window nearest you, open the latch and let me in."

October has been more golden than blue. The maple and oak trees

245

on Garden Street have outdone themselves in color. On the first day of November, the leaves begin to fall. Also on that day, a telegram from George Craven arrives informing Jason that Coralee Whitney has passed away. The funeral will be at noon two days hence. Jason decides he can catch an early-morning train, attend the service, pay his respects to the bereaved, and be back in time for dinner. "I really think I should make that effort, since we've recently had contact with Peter Whitney and what's-her-name, the daughter." God forbid he should ever slip and refer to that girl as Rhoda.

Gertrude says, "I hope you're not asking me to accompany you."

"My dear, I wouldn't dream of it."

Lola learns of his plans that evening and assumes she will be going to Hackberry Hill with him; she will request a substitute to take her classes that day. Jason tells her that will not be necessary, as his appearance will be sufficient to represent the family.

"But I want to see Rhoda's marker." Daisy has sent her a forlorn snapshot in which the stone's inscription is shadowed by a tree limb.

"Lola, I would rather you stay here, since Gertrude is in a delicate condition."

"Oh. So it's been confirmed?"

"Not officially. She's not ready to endure any probing by a physician, having heard somewhere that medical examination can cause miscarriage if performed in the first weeks." Jason is embarrassed to hear himself discussing such a topic with anyone other than his wife. Actually, he was embarrassed when Gertrude told him, as was she. They blushed together, then clung to each other and cried with happiness. At least he did. She may have been weeping over what lies ahead for her. He certainly wouldn't blame her.

Lola says, "Tru may have heard our mother or Rhoda say that. Mama sometimes took Rhoda with her to deliver babies."

"But not Gertrude?"

"No. Not Kathleen either. Just Rhoda. Mama and Rhoda had strong stomachs."

When the service at the cemetery ends, Peter asks Jason to stop by his house before leaving town. After dropping Kathleen and the boys off, George drives him in the surrey (to Jason's consternation, the new top makes the rest of it look shabbier than ever) to Whippoorwill Plantation. Jason says, "I'll not stay long. You may prefer to wait for me outside." George knows he's been given an order but isn't offended.

The doctor takes Jason into his study and closes the door. The man is composed, but like many in the aftershock of grief, he has a need to talk. "It's ironic, to say the least, that Coralee, who had not ventured beyond the grounds of our home in months nor been around anyone except Daisy, the servants, and me, fell victim to this virulent malady. The only explanation, and one that grieves me to admit, is that I brought the germ home to her, though I took all the mandated precautions—gauze masks and rubber gloves worn around all patients, scrupulous extra washing of hands and clothing. . . ."

"I'm sure you complied to the fullest." George's telegram had not stated the cause of the woman's death, and Jason hadn't been curious. According to Gertrude, Coralee had been sick with one thing or another ever since she came to Alabama. Nor did the wire include the information that Hackberry Hill was under siege by the flu. Jason has his handkerchief ready to press over his nose and mouth if Peter gets too close.

"By the time I'm summoned to a house where the pestilence has struck, usually the patient is beyond help," Peter explains. "The mystifying disease is violently capricious. Some throw it off in a few days, while others who are seemingly no worse afflicted succumb to death in a matter of hours. Some survivors are treated at home with folk remedies such as kerosene on sugar and goose-grease poultices. At one house, I saw a corpse with a camphor ball around his neck. We keep the few who are brought to the hospital in quarantine. All we can do is provide calomel purges, aspirin, and gargles."

"Well," Jason says heartily as he edges toward the door—the small room seems very warm all of a sudden—"you've been of great service to your community during a time of crisis. I hope the epidemic has about run its course here."

"There've been no new cases reported in the past few days. The last death I recorded was poor Coralee's. Alfred Hixon, the undertaker, brags around town that he could buy an Oldsmobile with his profits from the Spanish flu. I wish now I hadn't given the scalawag my business. But not having completely come around to your persuasive defense of George Craven, I couldn't bring myself to buy a coffin from him. To George's credit, he didn't try to sell me one. He and Kathleen were the first to come by to pay their respects, and he offered the services of his boys to dig the grave. However, Jim Jackson had asked to perform that labor, as his tribute."

Jason breaks eye contact to study his watch. Regrettably, such rudeness is sometimes necessary to get free.

But Peter just speaks faster. "I've been looking into boarding schools."

"Excellent." Jason reaches for the doorknob. He will wash his hands thoroughly before he gets home.

"Daisy admires Lola and enjoys their correspondence very much. With Coralee gone, there's no reason in the world for my little girl not to know who her real mother was."

Jason says gently, "It's your prerogative to tell her whenever you wish."

"Lola is the vital link. Please, won't you . . .?" Peter holds out his hands imploringly.

"All right. You have my word that I will reveal all to Lola within the next months, and instruct her to pass it on to your girl. Surely, you agree that Daisy should be over the shock of losing the woman she knew as her mother before she gets this one."

Peter smiles tremulously. "Yes, you're right. I leave the matter entirely in your hands. Thank you."

Neither Jason nor George feels any need to converse on the short ride to the station. Jason doesn't have the heart to bring up the subject of dividing the land and turning some of it into a resort. He also doesn't have the heart to heap any emotional burden whatsoever on Lola. Yet she'll never forgive him if he doesn't share whatever he has learned about Rhoda.

After he's on the train, he realizes he forgot to scrutinize George's cheekbones.

The trip back seems to take much longer. The squeaking and clanking of gears sound like human groaning. The dimly lit car is almost empty. The other passengers gaze out darkening windows as their bodies jiggle with the motion of the train. Jason imagines he feels his bones rattling. During a fitful doze, he senses that Gertrude needs him.

He recognizes the somber black automobile parked in front of his house as that of the physician whom Gertrude has not yet been ready to consult. *Oh, dear God.*

Bag in hand, the man meets Jason in the foyer and quickly explains that he has been summoned by Gertrude not for herself, but for her sister. The younger woman learned approximately an hour ago that her fiancé had perished of influenza on the ship that was bringing him home. The doctor has given Miss Holloway a sedative and is on his way now to administer the same to Robert Castleman's mother.

The women are seated close together on the couch across from the fireplace. Gertrude's arms encompass Lola like wings. Jason can see that they are weeping, but there is no movement or sound. In the portrait above the mantel, his mother wears an expression of empathy that he's never noticed before.

Jason lets her drive his automobile to the Castlemans'. He and Gertrude were not included in the invitation, which, to Lola's relief, was for sherry and not dinner. She will be gone before night adds more shadows to this house of sadness.

As their almost but never to be daughter-in-law, she is led into the overfurnished, intimate sitting room (which reeks of African violets, old cigars, and grief) where Rob, at different ages, smiles from every surface. Encased in convex glass and a wide oval frame with a faux mahogany finish, his most recent and only unsmiling photograph—a tinted, enlarged image in military regalia—glows darkly over the mantel. His father says he will have the picture retouched to change the bars from gold to silver, to reflect Rob's battlefield promotion to first lieutenant. Beneath the solemn gaze of her dead fiancé and the reproachful frown of his mother (*Why are you alive and my son isn't?*), Lola feels obliged to exclaim over every open-faced sandwich and sugared pecan on her plate. Jason has warned her that more than one glass of wine will affect her driving, but she gulps down two before she remembers that. All through the painful munching and swallowing, she is silently beseeched (not to abandon them, or to stay out of their sight from now on?) by these pathetic dears, who have aged a decade in the weeks since the death of their only child. On the way out, Lola remembers to return the ring she declined to wear. As Bertha Castleman's hand closes over the little velvet box, she dismisses her guest with finality and a blessing: "Goodbye, Lola. God be with you."

Rob's father walks her to the curb. Before she drives away, he hands her a cord-tied packet of her letters to Rob. He says, "His mother is not aware that these were in the trunk which was returned to us. I don't believe she would read private correspondence, but I didn't want her to be tempted. I've never shared with her the letter Rob wrote to me, after his first battle, in which he described his fear with near-poetic imagery.

The machine guns sounded like wasps. As the enemy routed them from the trenches, my boy thought he was stumbling over logs, until he realized the obstacles were bodies. Aside from that one, his reports were cheerful and manly."

That night, Lola confides in a letter to Kathleen, "It was all I could do not to jump out of the car and cleave to that man. Not so much to comfort him, but for me. I wanted to pretend, just for a moment, that he was his son. . . . I'm sorry we can't come for Thanksgiving. I was present when the doctor told Gertrude she mustn't travel in her condition, which was music to her ears, as she doesn't like to travel in any condition. Please say that you, George, and the boys will join us here for Christmas."

14
A Holiday Reunion

GEORGE TRIES NOT TO SHOW HIS ANXIETY. If for some reason the brother-in-law isn't there to meet them, he will hire one of those motorized taxis that congregate around big terminals and give the driver the address he knows by heart from having mailed reports to it. The train ride seems swifter than it is. Kathleen seldom looks up from the book she is reading, but he and the boys gape out the grimy windows at whatever there is to see—whiskey-colored creeks, woods without color save for the pines, fields that are like mattresses stripped of their bedding, and frost-singed meadows, some with haystacks. Distant barns look like they are made of pasteboard, like a tornado would carry them off. Ray keeps count of the times he spots pairs of tall, brick chimneys without a house between them. "There's another one burnt clean to the ground," he announces, as though it is good news. The cattle (many with ribs like birdcages; none as well-fed as George's) are so used to being stared at from whizzing windows they don't bother to stare back.

As the train comes to a halt, George spots Jason looking anxious himself. He probably figured they would manage to get themselves lost on the way (though there was only one stop, at which Kathleen told Ray in no uncertain terms he could not get off and look around).

Jason kisses Kathleen on the cheek and shakes hands with George, then with each of the boys, which turns into a lesson. "Always give a firm grip. That's right, Harold, you've got it. Not quite that hard, Rayford; you don't want to break a fellow's fingers. If a lady offers you her hand, of course, you must be gentler."

It is a dream come true. Finally, Ray will get to ride in that Packard. Now he'll know what he is talking about when he brags to his buddies. He and Harold stash the wicker cases according to their uncle's directions: two on the running board, one on the floor of the back seat.

Kathleen has an expression on her face that says as clearly as if spoken, "No, we don't own leather luggage. Why would we? This is the first time we've gone anywhere that requires a change of clothing." She apologizes for not having shipped the paintings. Jason assures her that is no problem whatsoever. He arranges for the cargo, which has been carefully crated by George, to travel in a cab that will follow them to the house.

Harold doesn't jump around and make comments every five seconds like Ray, but he is just as excited. As they ride through the business district, he absorbs details (self-assured pigeons darting around the feet of pedestrians on the sidewalks) and sounds (an almost harmonious meld of horns, brakes, wheels, horses' hooves, whistles, trolley bells). While the car is stopped to await a policeman's go-ahead, a small group of carolers sings "Joy to the World" as a uniformed man rings a bell over a wash pot. Two men wearing hats and topcoats like the doctor's drop coins into the pot. A gloved lady with fox skins around her neck does the same. Harold is glad his relatives live in a city where people are considerate of those less fortunate then themselves.

It is the first time they've been invited to Felder. The reason for it, according to Gertrude's letter, is to provide a united family atmosphere at Christmastime for Lola, who is despondent over the loss of her intended. Kathleen dreads the visit. It will be excruciating to watch her brood try not to embarrass themselves or her. She can't remember when, if ever, she has told either of her sons she is proud of them, yet the satisfaction of having them hums inside her like a motor.

The house doesn't appear nearly as large and formidable as it did in a description Gertrude wrote years ago in a homesick letter to their mother shortly after her marriage, and it sits closer to the street than Kathleen would have imagined, if she had ever bothered to try to. She allows Jason to assist her from the car, so she won't trip and fall on her face.

Lola comes toward her with tears in her eyes. Kathleen finds herself crying. Lola quickly wipes Kathleen's eyes and her own with a handkerchief and says resolutely, "No more of that. You're here. You're all here"— George and the boys are sucked into the whirlwind of that radiant smile—"and we're going to have a wonderful Christmas."

"Yes, indeed," Jason says, as he mentally implores Gertrude to come out from wherever she is. At that minute, she appears in the doorway in one of the full, ugly dresses that are supposed to hide her increasing bulk but instead, in his opinion, call attention to it. (He was greatly relieved when, soon after purchasing a gestation corset, she pronounced the thing not worth the three dollars it cost, and placed it in the trash bin.) Not that there could be anything ugly about Gertrude's astounding condition. Just last night, she allowed him to press an ear to that hillock of flesh and hear what may have been a tiny heartbeat. He and his wife are both convinced the infant will be a girl. Not that he would object to a son, especially now that the War to End All Wars is past.

After they troop into the house that is heady with the fragrances of spiced eggnog and the cedar tree Lola has hung with tinsel and painted ornaments, Gertrude says, "Sister, I hope you remembered to make candied grapefruit peel."

"I carried it in my lap," Kathleen says, handing her a yarn-tied box. "Merry Christmas, Tru."

It is Gertrude's time to shed a tear. "And it's really from Mama's recipe?"

"I didn't deviate so much as a teaspoon from her directions. It's not tinted red and green, as you suggested, because food coloring hasn't arrived yet in Hackberry Hill."

"That was a whim. I'd really rather have it just as Mama made it."

Jason and Lola exchange glances of relief. Gertrude is putting forth her best foot.

◎

The next tears come the following day, Christmas morning, after George has carefully pried open the carton that contains Kathleen's gifts, which were framed by his own hands. Gertrude weeps, though not with joy, when she realizes she and Jason are the recipients of a painting Kathleen showed her and Lola at the homeplace. Jason is delighted and expresses enough gratitude for them both. He's had a fondness for the Holloway mill since the first time he saw that handsome old building; Kathleen has captured its very essence. Gertrude says briskly, "I'll have to give some thought as to where to display this impressive gift." (After the Cravens depart, it will be hung in a back hall, away from the light of day, where Gertrude seldom ventures. She doesn't care to be reminded of Hackberry Hill.)

Lola pulls the wrapping paper off the other simply but elegantly framed canvas. She knows immediately who the figure in the painting is, though the eyes are hidden by a bonnet brim; that is fortunate, as Lola doesn't think she could bear the force of that gaze. The curve of cheek, the generous mouth, those long fingers, the graceful slouch, the strands of dark hair that won't stay tucked into the bonnet—all are

255

Rhoda. Rho would never have worn such a getup, but she looks very much at home in it.

"I call this one *Girl in Sunbonnet and Old-Fashioned Dress*." Although Lola's thanks is rather subdued, Kathleen can see she really likes it.

Later, when they have some privacy from the others, Lola asks, "Kat, how did you decide on the subject matter of my painting?"

She didn't. Such decisions are made by the subjects. The gristmill had asked to be painted, and so had this creature who came from her imagination. But these explanations would sound silly, even to Lola. Kathleen says, "Shortly after Mama died, I found a dress and sunbonnet with a pair of shoes, all seemingly new, in a tree near the pond. No one came by asking for these things. Eventually, I draped the garments on the dressmaker dummy in the room where I paint. Maybe I've been saving them for my old age—all but the shoes, which happened to fit, so I wore them. After you said you wanted a painting, I made several starts, but none seemed right. Then, a couple of weeks ago, as I was blocking a scene framed by the open window, a breeze puffed out the bonnet and set that long, full skirt to dancing, so I quickly sketched in a figure to wear them. Don't ask me how, but I knew this one was for you."

"That's because she's Rhoda. You've given her back to me."

"Well, believe me, it wasn't intentional." Once she is finished with something, she doesn't try to analyze it. "If she's Rhoda for you, and you like having her around, that's fine with me."

"Actually, I can see something about the sunbonnet girl that's like Daisy Whitney, too."

"Oh, please," Kathleen says. "Not her."

"You should have a special fondness for that child, who nursed at your breast."

"Maybe that's why I've never had any fondness for her. Daisy Whitney thrived on the milk my firstborn couldn't. It didn't seem fair. Everything she could ever want, Peter gave her."

"Except the one thing she most wants."

"Which is?"

"She's love-struck over Harold, but she doesn't think he feels the same way about her."

"George had a talk with Harold recently in which he ascertained the boy has not been messing about with the doctor's daughter or any other girl. The idea that a son of his could be a late bloomer in that department mystifies George, who was probably diddling with females by the time he was ten. But I'm glad Harold is not allowing lust to complicate his life. Even so, I was eased to hear from Helen Akers that Peter has arranged to send Daisy off to school next fall, in New York City."

Lola had received that news the week before, with a Christmas gift from Daisy. She suspects the pearl-and-sapphire brooch was Coralee Whitney's. "I'll be going to school in New York, too. We haven't told Gertrude yet, but Jason has arranged for me to take postgraduate courses at Columbia University. I won't be permitted to study law there, but the extra education will put me in good stead to storm the bastion of the University of Virginia Law School, which Jason has learned through his grapevine is on the verge of admitting women."

"I'm happy for you," Kathleen says, meaning it despite the flat inflection she hears in her own voice. "You need to spread your wings."

"I plan to relocate in the early summer, after Tru has the baby. The Howards and their wee one deserve some privacy, and I'm itching to begin a new life. Another new life. Will you come to visit me in New York?"

"Of course. Now that I own a splendid suitcase with my initials on it, I intend to make use of it." Jason selected that gift, as he had the books for the boys and the monogrammed cigarette case for George (who was so touched he was speechless).

"I hope Peter and Daisy aren't having a bleak holiday," Lola says. "I wanted to invite them to join us for Christmas dinner. They could have stayed in a hotel. But Jason said we should keep it a family affair." What

Jason said was that it would be hard enough on Gertrude having the relatives; he wouldn't saddle her with any more guests. Not that the Cravens' short stay, which will end the next morning, has created any work for Gertrude. Maud has cooked everything ahead of time. Lola and Kathleen have gotten the meals together and cleaned up afterward, while Gertrude has sat in her special chair beside the fireplace, knitting baby booties beneath her mother-in-law's protective image.

Kathleen says, "Helen invited Peter and Daisy for Christmas. The surreptitious friendship that began in the lending library has blossomed into open courtship. Peter's lucky, and so is Daisy. Helen will be a positive addition to their lives."

"Is something wrong? You have that troubled expression I remember."

"Thank you for not calling it a scowl, as Rhoda used to. George calls it my decision-making expression. I've decided to tell you what else I found in the willow tree."

"A dead owl?"

"Something that might smell just as bad. With the clothes was a brand-new handbag that contained over two thousand dollars in paper money. No one came around looking for it, so after a while, I stuffed the packet of bills up inside the dummy, about where a womb would be. I've dipped in occasionally but could pay that back if I had to."

"Kat, you must have a fairy godmother."

"Seriously. Do you think I'm the same as a thief, for not turning the money over to the sheriff?"

"Heavens no. Why should a sheriff get to decide what's done with it? If the loss was reported, you'd have heard. I think you were meant to find it; somebody wanted you to put that money to good use."

Kathleen says, "I hope you don't mean giving it to the church. I've planned for the bulk of it to go on the boys' education."

"That's putting it to good use."

"What if I let George have a hundred dollars for a down payment on a truck?"

"That's even better use. The boys will get educated; I'll help, and so will Jason. Why not just outright buy George a truck?"

"I'll have to think on that. I don't want to make it easy for him to leave me." Kathleen smiles. The troubled expression is gone.

Their parents get a guest room, but the boys spend both their Felder nights on the Howards' sleeping porch, which Uncle Jason notes was built for warm-weather habitation. "But we're having a very mild winter, and the shutters will keep most of the draft out."

As they lie beneath layers of thick wool blankets on narrow, iron-framed cots like the ones in the jailhouse at home, Ray says, "I thought we were going to be in the lap of luxury this Christmas. Hell, this is almost as bad as the damn mill."

"Not as scary, though," Harold says.

"I didn't think you ever admitted to being scared in the mill. As I recall, it was you who used to say, 'There's no such thing as the Holloway ghost.'"

"*Scary* wasn't the word I meant to use. *Melancholy* is more like it. I get a melancholy feeling in the mill."

"There you go, showing off again." Speaking of melons, Aunt Gertrude's are past the size of cantaloupes and headed toward watermelon territory. But he won't waste that one on his brother.

"Mama seems to be having a good time," Harold says.

"Pop's sure not. I could see he was pissed off about that sissy cigarette case he'll never use."

"I wish he would quit smoking."

"He can't sell the thing, because it's got his initials on it."

"Uncle Jason thought he'd like it."

"Yeah, I know. Well, Uncle did fine by me. I like my books." Ray has read enough already in the first one to see the main character is someone he'd like to know. He wishes Penrod were a real boy and lived in Hackberry Hill.

Harold's gift, the *Complete Works of William Shakespeare*, will make him wish he lived in England, and back then.

There is an hour to kill before they leave for the station. Lola is teaching the boys to play whist; Jason and George are in the study with the door closed. Gertrude takes Kathleen to see her garden. "Of course, there's nothing blooming this time of year, but I wanted to speak with you in private."

Kathleen braces for whatever is coming.

"Mainly, I wish to thank you for your thoughtful gesture yesterday, when Lola bemoaned the fact that her fiancé would never have a grave. As Jason said, your idea to place a commemorative marker for Robert in the Holloway cemetery plot was truly inspired."

Kathleen feels her face warm, but not in embarrassment or anger. "I'll see to that right away. Tru, I think you'd be impressed with how the family plot looks with the addition of the Rhoda and Elvira stones." The simplicity of those flat rectangles adds dignity to the fanciful scrolls, lambs, and cherubs.

"Perhaps you could send us pictures."

"Perhaps you could come see for yourself. After the baby's born, I mean."

"Sister, please come to stay with me for a while after that event. I don't believe I have a talent for comprehending infants. You could advise me as Mama would have."

Kathleen evades. "Well, we'll see. When is it to be?"

"By my calculations, the date of birth will be Friday, June 13, which is nine months from Friday, September 13. Conception occurred while we were at the homeplace. I'm neither superstitious nor mathematical, but it stands to reason those unlucky Friday the 13ths will cancel each other out."

"They will, absolutely. Don't give that another thought."

"Jason has agreed if we have a girl, she will be named for my mother. I hold his late mother in the greatest esteem, but I don't care for the masculine-sounding name Alfreda. A boy, of course, will be Jason Howard IV. However, I'm confident my child will be a female, as I don't see myself being a mother to the opposite sex."

"You might surprise yourself." But Kathleen pities any boy child who might have the ill fate to be born to Gertrude.

"We have tried to suppress our elation around Lola. She has liked being the only child in this household. Soon after she came to us, Jason explained to me—I doubt I would have observed for myself—that Lola was an emotionally wounded child who, in order for her spirit to heal, would require constant, loving affirmation, as well as firm moral guidance. I don't believe I ever had that sort of neediness as a child. I wanted our mother's approval above all else, but constant loving affirmation was too much to presume to expect, busy as she was."

"It's too much to expect of any woman. Jason's mother must have been as unusual as her name."

"He admits to having had more than his share of parental attention and affection. That's probably why the nurturer's role comes so naturally to him. With Lola, I have followed his lead in this area, and expect to do so with our own child. But I shall welcome your suggestions as to how I can be more relaxed and confident in my approach to motherhood."

"You'll do fine." Kathleen takes a breath so deep it causes her a flicker of pain. But then, in her experience, commitment is a painful thing. "Count on me to come and stay however long I'm needed when you have the baby."

15
Hettie and Jim

HER MOTHER-DEAR USED TO SAY, "Death makes a whooshing noise when it enters the house. The sound doesn't stop 'til all the air is sucked from the lungs of the one it's after. Best to guard your breath, put your hands tight over your mouth, lest Death make a mistake and get you before your time." The day it came for the doctor's wife, Death must have got to that house right before Hettie did. She hopes it took its victim by surprise, so the poor thing didn't try to resist. Mother-dear said it was best to go peaceful. Hettie never even heard the whoosh, but suddenly that morning, all normal sounds—the ticking of the hall clock, the comforting din of livestock, men singing at work in the fields—just shut off, as though someone had stuffed cotton in her ears.

The doctor and Daisy had left together, for the hospital and school.

Torey was in the service yard clipping the first load of wash to the line. At half-past nine, Hettie went up with Miss Coralee's toast and coffee and tapped on the door. The lady didn't respond, but more often than not, Hettie would have to jostle and sweet-talk her awake. The closed-up smell wasn't unusual either. Miss Coralee was so scared of what might be outside she wouldn't leave a window more than cracked at night, even in the warmest weather. Hettie set the tray on the bedside table and, guided by trickles of sunlight around the window shades, moved through the sticky darkness toward the outside wall, eased the shades up part way, then raised each window. She tapped Miss Coralee on the shoulder before she looked at the lady good in the still-dim room and said, quietly but firmly, as worked best, "Wake up, sugar, here's your breakfast." The thin shoulder was still warm. The blue fingers were crimped like a bird's claws; the eyes and mouth were open. A stream of black vomit drooled like a curl of hair across one cheek and down her neck. Hettie got on her knees beside the bed and said the Lord's Prayer. He told her none of this was her fault.

Hettie took Miss Coralee's silver-backed brush and worked it gently through the tangles, careful of that tender scalp, as though the lady could still feel it. She pulled a lavender kimono wrapper around the lady as best she could without forcing those frail, stiff arms into the sleeves; she smoothed the lace-trimmed sheets and the candlewick counterpane. Figuring the doctor should see what came out of his wife's mouth, Hettie didn't wipe the mess off. She took the breakfast tray and a vase of shriveled stalks from the dresser—yellow-button chrysanthemums from Hettie's own garden, so fresh and bright when she brought them the day before—and hurried downstairs. She rang the big bell to summon Jim, who rode at full gallop to the hospital to summon the doctor. Neither Hettie nor Jim knew how to call out on the telephone. The doctor said later he couldn't imagine why he had never thought to show Hettie how to do that.

During one of the last conversations the housekeeper had with Miss Coralee, the lady said, "I think you know the name of the woman who gave birth to Daisy. Why won't you tell me?"

"Honey, you're her mother. Anybody before you don't count." Miss Coralee hadn't asked her that question in a long time.

"Please, Hettie," she said in the most piteous voice.

"Can't tell you what I don't know." In exchange for the deed to her house and five acres, Hettie's lips had been sealed on this subject for fifteen years. So were Jim's. Hettie did the best she could and tried not to stray from the truth, but sometimes there was no other way.

"Was it Rhoda Holloway?" Miss Coralee spoke so softly Hettie hoped she didn't hear the name right.

"Makes no nevermind who it was. You been that child's mother since she was three weeks old."

"She came here the morning we got the baby. I had taken Daisy outside for her first stroll. As we neared the dovecote, the baby heard the pigeons cooing and began to imitate their sound. I was entranced. At that moment, I felt she was really mine. Then, suddenly, there was that wild-eyed, wild-haired girl, staring like an animal."

"Who?"

"Rhoda Holloway. She was at the edge of the woods, looking straight at us. After a moment, she disappeared. But you see, she wasn't supposed to even be in the area. She had run away from home months before."

"Sugar, I expect you're remembering the time wrong. If you saw her, it must have been before she left home, because she never came back, not even for a visit."

Miss Coralee was twisting her handkerchief into a rope. "I've seen her in dreams, and I could tell she's not of this world."

"Hon, the medicine is what makes you have strange dreams." She'd been of a mind for some time to step out of her place again and suggest to the doctor that he lower his wife's dosage. The last time she did, he told Hettie his wife would climb the walls if she couldn't get what her body had become accustomed to.

"A short time later that same morning—the day we got our baby— I saw the same girl fall off that big wheel. She didn't bob up in the water. She sank like a rock. And I never told anyone."

"You were there, at the Holloway mill?"

"Of course not. I watched from the tower room."

"Miss Coralee! Why didn't you tell the doctor, or me?"

"The more I thought about it, the more it seemed to be a hallucination. When I heard about the bones being found in the pond, it all came flooding back. I couldn't tell my husband then; he would berate me for not having done so at the time. It didn't seem to make any difference anyway. He'd already decided his skeleton was Rhoda Holloway. I used to beg my husband to tell me who gave birth to Daisy. He could have made up a name." Speaking about things she'd wrapped too long in silence, Miss Coralee sounded strange, not like herself. "But he said I had no right to the information, that he was ethically bound not to reveal her identity."

"I expect the doctor did what he thought was best for you and Daisy and the woman who gave birth to her. Whoever she was."

"I hate him," she said in the same way she might have said, "I love him."

"No, you don't, hon. Next time Rhoda Holloway crowds your dream, tell her you want her to be at peace, and for her to leave you in peace."

She said with her old haughtiness, "Hettie, you should refer to her as Miss Rhoda or Miss Holloway." Hettie was reminded of when the lady told her she should begin calling the child "Miss Daisy." Daisy was five years old at the time. The doctor disabused his wife of that notion then and there.

Rhoda didn't expect or want to be called "Miss." She cleaned Hettie's house while Hettie was cleaning this one. Rhoda even scrub-boarded and ironed their clothes. She said she was used to working and couldn't sit around doing nothing. She promised she wouldn't let herself be seen by anyone other than the doctor and the Jacksons. She wasn't to go near her people's place or try to see her little sister, though she keenly missed that child. She begged Hettie to leave Torey at home to keep her company. The doctor put a stop to that because his wife might wonder why Hettie didn't have to bring her child with her to work anymore. The lady wouldn't have, though. Miss Coralee never had any curiosity about what went on in her housekeeper's life.

Hettie still thinks of her as though she's alive. It's been a month since the funeral, and she's not finished packing away the lady's personal effects. Hettie thinks she will be with them awhile yet. She hopes Miss Coralee will leave before the doctor's new lady moves in.

Rhoda gave birth in the Jacksons' house as planned, only two weeks before it was calculated to happen. Hettie wondered, but didn't ask, if the girl took something to make the baby come early. Rhoda seemed to know a lot about birthing. She told Hettie she'd gone on midwife calls with her mother. The delivery was fast and easy. Jim rode his mule through the tall pines by moonlight to get the doctor. All that man had to do was clip and twist the navel cord and wipe the mucus from the baby's mouth. Hettie was proud for Rhoda, that she did it without his help.

Hettie knew from the start that once she got the first taste of being a mother, that girl would not want to leave without her baby. She was to stay on a while to get her strength back and nurse the infant. Hettie feared Rhoda might sneak off from their house with Daisy, and that the doctor would blame them. Hettie prayed about it every day. When she prays, she hears herself think the words; sometimes, like the day she found Miss Coralee dead, she hears the Lord answer.

Hettie grew fond of Rhoda Holloway, but she didn't want that girl to cause them trouble by taking back what was hers in the first place. It was a dilemma, all right.

There was another dilemma. When Mrs. Lucy Holloway passed on, the doctor came to tell Rhoda. The girl didn't shed a tear. All she said was that she wished she could stand a ways off and observe the funeral.

"I must insist you stay completely away," the doctor said. "Think how shocked and embarrassed your sisters would be, should you be seen as you are." Rhoda's belly had mushroomed since she'd moved in with the Jacksons. Before that, she admitted to Hettie but not to the doctor, she'd starved herself and bound her midsection with strips of tightly wound cloth, so her mama wouldn't suspect.

As far as Hettie knows, Rhoda kept her word and didn't go to her family's house or anywhere near town while she lived in hiding at the Jacksons' little house. Hettie never heard any talk that Rhoda was spotted around town either. People took it as fact that she'd run away, like she said in the notes she left her family.

The doctor came for Hettie and Daisy early that morning. The baby had just finished her first feeding of the day—and the last she'd have from the breast of her true mother. He arrived with a satin-lined basket and finery that Miss Coralee had ordered through the dry-goods store. He waited outside while Rhoda dressed Daisy and wrapped her not in the blanket he'd brought, but in the one she had made. Hettie wished she didn't have to see that sadness. She asked the doctor if she could stay home for a while with Rhoda that morning. Hettie could see the girl was wretched. But the doctor said Hettie had to ride with him, to hold the baby. She, Jim, and Torey usually walked together to his house on the needle-strewn path through the forest that whispered encouragement and closed around them like loving arms. The doctor said the path was made by the Indians who used to live here. He has never cut the tall pines that have been here forever, so it's like these woods are hers and Jim's as much as his.

Nothing's ever been harder than leaving her house that day. Jim had already left; he didn't want to be around for the sad part. The doctor gave Rhoda an envelope thick with paper money, spoke quietly to her for a few moments, and kissed her on the forehead. Hettie had made her goodbyes to Rhoda Holloway before the doctor arrived. She didn't look back at the white face that she knew would watch from the doorway until they were well into the woods and out of sight. The trees bent down to get a look at the baby in the basket on Hettie's lap. Torey crouched by her feet on the floor of the doctor's buggy.

Rhoda was supposed to leave the same day, on a train that hauled mostly freight. The doctor told her she might be the only passenger boarding; not many people came to or left Hackberry Hill on any given day. He had bought her a ticket ahead of time, and the plan was for Jim to drive her to the station. But she said she was up to a good walk, and that nobody would look twice at her in her "disguise." Hettie had found her a long-sleeved calico dress, sturdy high-top shoes, and an old-lady handbag at the dry-goods store. Rhoda made the curved-brim poke bonnet that would hide most of her face. Doctor brought her a pair of eyeglasses with darkened lenses, like near-blind people wore. Sure enough, when Rhoda tried it all on, not enough of her was showing to tell who she was. She planned to buy some clothes when she landed somewhere. She told Hettie to make dust rags out of the few she'd come with, and Hettie did.

When she returned home that afternoon, Rhoda was gone, the cabin swept clean of her presence. On the mantel, Hettie found a note with the knotted handkerchief of coins Rhoda had when she came to them: "Thank you for watching over our darling Daisy. With love and trust and gratitude, R." Hettie spent the coins. The handkerchief is in her keepsake box. Someday, she will give it to Daisy, even if she can't tell her whose it was.

As soon as they read the note, Jim threw the scrap of paper into the wood stove and forbade Hettie to mention anything about "that business" to him ever again. "It never happened. No white girl lived with us and had a baby here. You won't ever hear from her. The doctor paid her to get lost for good."

Hettie didn't think Rhoda would stay away more than a year and was surprised—and also sad and relieved—that the girl didn't write to her for news of the baby. After two or three years went by with no word of or from Rhoda Holloway, Hettie figured Jim must have been right: she'd lost herself on purpose. So Hettie prayed for her and tried to brush away thoughts of her—a young girl like that alone in the world, without friends or family—coming to harm. She got the courage once to speak about it to the doctor. He said, "Rhoda's instinctively resourceful. She can take care of herself." Hettie wondered if it ever occurred to the doctor that Rhoda's pregnancy was not an accident. She didn't put it past the girl to scheme that baby into being, to provide a means for her escape.

Torey had her third birthday while Rhoda was with them. That was too young to form a memory. So it hit Hettie like a bolt of thunder when her daughter later asked, "Isn't this the blanket that white girl made when she lived with us?" Daisy had sent Torey to ask Hettie for something to throw over the skeleton they were about to bury in the white folks' cemetery. As soon as the doctor had asked Hettie to look at the poor thing, even before she recognized that broken tooth, she knew, in her own bones, whose bones were laid out in his laboratory. Yet when her hand went to that little blanket on a shelf of the linen press, Hettie wasn't thinking of what it represented.

"You been dreaming," she told her daughter as she gave her the blanket. "Watch your mouth. Don't be making up things."

She had brought Rhoda the scrap of chamois cloth from stuff Miss

Coralee didn't know she had. It was the only time Hettie ever stole. She wanted that infant to go to her new home wrapped in her real mother's love.

⬭

When the doctor asked them to shelter Rhoda Holloway, they couldn't turn him down. It wasn't as bad as Jim thought it would be. She acted as though there was no difference between her and them. It bothered Jim that Torey took to Rhoda. His baby didn't know how rare it was for a colored child to be rocked to sleep in a white girl's lap. He's afraid all it will take is a friendly word for Torey to forget her place, especially now that the doctor's got her reading his books and training to be a nurse. Rhoda taught Jim's child to read better at the age of three than he can now—and to trust white folks more than he ever will.

The worst part was being scared the whole time the girl's mother would find out she was still around, and that she was living with a colored family. The doctor told him that would never happen. Rhoda promised the doctor she wouldn't get near his place, or her folks' place, or the town, and he took her at her word. Jim never thought she'd stick to it. For one thing, she had too much energy to stay put.

Not long after she came, he looked up from bossing the field crew one morning to see something move near the edge of the woods. The man next to him said, "Was that a deer or a girl?"

"Keep your head down to the task I gave you," Jim told him.

That night, he told Rhoda she better not show herself over there again, else they'd all be in trouble.

"I just wanted to get a look at where my baby is going to grow up," she said.

"You never been to the doctor's house before?"

"Just once," she said. "Mama scrubbed my sisters and me so hard she almost took a layer of skin off us. The doctor's wife and Mama sat on chairs that didn't look big enough for grown people, and we sat on the floor, trying not to spill lemonade on the Turkish rug, which I stared at until I memorized the pattern. I could draw that rug for you right now. Miss Coralee and Mama seemed to have nothing to say to each other beyond how unbearable the climate was and how they wished they didn't have to live in Alabama. The only sounds came from the rattling of their teacups and some yellow finches in a gold wire cage." She frowned. "Hard to imagine a child of mine growing up in a house where you're not supposed to touch anything."

"The girl's having second thoughts about leaving her baby with the doctor and Missus," Jim said to Hettie in private.

"No, she's not. Rhoda knows she's found the best possible situation for her child. She's just chafing at the bit, 'cause she's anxious to get clean away. Girl's been miserable at home since her papa died."

"Expect she's mad at whoever poked her, too," Jim said.

"She never talks about that part. You heard the doctor say it was the boy the L & N train cut in half. The engineer didn't see him walking on the track."

But something told Jim that dead boy wasn't the one. The doctor wasn't the poker either. He came to their house to check her over and to bring her books from the lending library. He gave Hettie money to buy Rhoda whatever she needed. But he never messed with that girl. Jim would bet his life on it.

After the birthing, Rhoda stayed on as she'd agreed, to nurse the infant for a few weeks. Jim had no wish to see a white girl's breasts, but he shouldn't have to avert his eyes in his own front room. The doctor came by every day then. He was as anxious to take that little bundle away as Jim was for it to be gone, but he wanted the infant to get a good start with mother's milk.

Rhoda convinced the doctor nobody would look twice at someone in the old-woman get-up she and Hettie put together. Jim was relieved she didn't want him to drive her to the station. He didn't want to be anywhere near that depot when that white girl went missing for real.

On the morning the doctor and Hettie brought Daisy to the planta-tion—the same day Rhoda was supposed to leave—Jim spotted her near the arbor. The other men were working the field near the main road, so he didn't have to worry that they'd see her. The doctor had left to make his sick rounds by then, and Hettie was inside. Here came Miss Coralee, pushing the shiny black carriage with gold striping that came in a crate all the way from England. Jim was afraid Rhoda would dash out and snatch up the baby. As though she picked up on his fear, Miss Coralee jumped up from the arbor bench and started rolling the contraption lickety-split back to the house, like she was in a goat-wagon race.

Rhoda kept moving along the edge of the woods, into and out of his view. When she got level with the clothesline hedge, Jim stepped from behind it and said, "Girl, what you think you're doing?"

She had on the bulky, shapeless dress Hettie had got for her, but her hair was hanging loose. She swung the bonnet that was supposed to hide it in one hand and the pocketbook in the other. "I'm headed over yonder"—she tossed her head toward the Holloway property—"to get my little sister. Lola's got no mother now, so I can't leave her behind. She won't be as much trouble as an infant."

"You're supposed to stay away from your family's place."

"I'm not going to the house. I'll meet up with my sister on her way to school."

"What about Mr. and Mrs. Craven?"

That girl could smooth-talk her way out of anything. "I'll leave a note at the mill explaining that I came back for Lola and have gone again."

It wasn't any of his business.

"This time, it really is goodbye."

She held her hand out, but he pretended not to see. He never once touched the flesh of that white girl. He mumbled "Good luck to you" for the second time that day, turned, and walked away. Then he counted to a hundred before he let himself look back.

Here is what Jim Jackson saw. She had shed the dress and shoes and was taking a shortcut to the gristmill, straight through the pond. When she reached the wheel, the water lapped at her shoulders. She pulled herself up on the spokes, wet undergarments sticking to her. "Oh, Lord," he groaned aloud.

Jim turned his back again on the sight of Rhoda Holloway. He was not about to watch her climb to the top of that waterwheel, then into the mill through a window to meet the man who had planted that seed inside her. The man who was married to one of her sisters.

"Surprised to see Missus took the baby outside," Jim said a few minutes later, when he went to the kitchen on the pretext of needing a dipper.

Hettie said, "They didn't stay out long. She's started to worry that somebody will try to steal the child."

"Who does she think would want to?"

"Didn't say. Now that the anticipation's over, she's back to acting peculiar."

"Maybe she thinks Rhoda will come here to snatch the baby."

"She has no cause to think that. Miss Coralee has no idea Rhoda gave birth to Daisy. Before the sun sets today, that girl will be looking out a train window on new sights."

He didn't tell his wife that Rhoda was at the Holloway mill right then, and likely up to mischief.

The afternoon of that same day, Jim spied Rhoda's little sister riding home from school in the buggy with the doctor. Over the next days and weeks, he listened in town for news of another Holloway girl's disappearance, but he never heard any. After a while, the doctor started bringing that child home to play with Daisy. So Rhoda had made up the part about taking her little sister with her, just like she made up the part about a boy who didn't have enough sense to dodge a train being the daddy. The only reason she went to the mill that day was to taste forbidden honey-love one last time.

When the doctor sent him to help that man's sons dig a grave for the skeleton, Jim had a fresh thought as to what might have happened that long ago day when he turned his back. Craven wanted to be rid of Rhoda once and for all, so she wouldn't make trouble for him. When she reached the top of the wheel, he leaned out the window and hit her over the head, then saw her get swallowed by the water and not bob up. The doctor said the body could have been snared by roots or something, so it never floated. If it happened that way, Craven must feel the deed was justified somehow, because he doesn't seem like a man burdened by guilt. He has the easy appearance of one who's satisfied with his situation in life.

As overseer of Whippoorwill Plantation, Jim Jackson orders other men around. Most of the time, Craven has no one to boss but his sons. If they had skin the same color, and if Jim could convince himself the man didn't kill Rhoda Holloway and take the money the doctor had given her, then he expects he and Mr. George Craven could be fast friends. But as it is, Jim has one more white folks' secret to take to his grave.

16
Neither Wax nor Wane

DOWNTOWN FELDER HAS NEVER BEEN MORE SPECTACULAR. There are red, white, and blue banners everywhere; flags on every building, some pleated like fans; huge arches across Market and Commerce Streets. The fountain is festooned like a Maypole with garlands of greenery. Beside it is a specially constructed wooden platform for the band. The trumpets, trombones, woodwinds, and drums are almost drowned out by the cheering throngs when Alabama's Rainbow warriors, the brave 167th, come marching from Union Station in formation behind Colonel Screws. After months of keeping the peace in the new republic of Germany, Rob's comrades in arms have finally come home. Lola tries to forgive him for not being with them and can't. But anger seems preferable to agony.

That night, she packs his letters from Washington and Lee and the war in the first heart-shaped Castleman's Valentine box Rob gave her, which Gertrude almost didn't let her keep because, at thirteen, Lola was too young to be courted. (Even though Rob got boxes of candy free and gave them to lots of girls back then, Lola knew, if he didn't, that she was The One.)

The next weekend, which marks the end of her tenure on the faculty of Felder High, she and Jason go to Hackberry Hill. While Jason confers with George about dividing the land, she buries the keepsake box beside a block of marble that Kathleen has inscribed, beneath Rob's name, "Brave Beloved of Lola Holloway." Nearby, Rhoda's stone glints in the last-of-spring sunshine.

Lucy Margaret Howard is born as her mother predicted, on Friday, June 13. Soon after Kathleen comes to be of assistance during Gertrude's confinement, Lola leaves for New York. The first communication to arrive at her new address assures Lola she will be officially on record as a godmother, even though she will miss the baptism, at which Lucy Margaret will wear the christening gown made by her grandmother of the same name. Kathleen has threatened to ship Mama's trunk to Felder, but Gertrude hopes she isn't serious. Jason is right—those old pieces belong with the house. She wishes they had not taken the piano. Sometimes, as she passes it in the back hall, she can hear the strings humming, and she'd just as soon not. If Lola has no objection, she would like to donate the instrument to the Sunday school. When it is time for Lucy Margaret to be exposed to music, they will get her a Steinway baby grand.

Along with the christening gown, Kathleen has brought the wedding gown and the veil with the mother-of-pearl comb attached, as she has anticipated (correctly) that Gertrude will want Lucy Margaret to wear those family heirlooms someday. "Of course," Gertrude assures Lola in precise slants, "you will wear them before your niece does. Darling, I pray that your heart is mending. Jason believes it is, but I know you better than he does. Women sense things about each other that men cannot penetrate. Remember what I told you, Lola: If a strange man looks at you lasciviously, or dares to touch you—Recently, I heard a story of an unaccompanied woman having her bosom pinched on a crowded bus—remove your hatpin and give him a good jab. And never hesitate to scream. God gave women high-pitched voices for their protection. Do I sound like our mother? I hope so."

❧

Lola goes on a dinner date with a former shipmate of Maggie's husband, Ted. Despite his somber surname, John Graves is good company. She calls Maggie on the landlady's telephone to report on the evening. Lola confides in a strident whisper through her cupped hand, the bell-shaped mouthpiece, and a cloud of static, "No, I was the one who made the pass. It was a long cab ride to my lodgings, I was tipsy from imbibing a smooth new cocktail called a Martini, and I needed affection."

There is no need to keep her voice low when she calls Jason and Gertrude, since she recounts activities they and her landlady will approve of, such as the time she took the ferry to Staten Island to visit a fresh-air camp for consumptive children. On that occasion, Lola took scads of notes and pictures for an article she planned to submit to the *Illustrated Daily News*, a new tabloid modeled on London's *Daily Mirror* that uses human-interest pieces with photographs. It won't pay much, but at least she will have earned income. Jason seems both miffed and pleased that she hasn't asked him for an increase in allowance.

As the Cravens have no telephone, Lola writes often to Kathleen, who responds at her own pace. Lola is delighted to learn that Jason has arranged a show of Kat's works at the Felder Art Museum, which is mainly a repository for old spinning wheels, tattered flags, Confederate sabers, and ghosts.

The *Girl in Sunbonnet and Old-Fashioned Dress* lends an air of grave dignity to Lola's small, prosaically furnished Morningside Heights apartment, which she was lucky to find. It's within a brisk walk of the university (where she has all morning classes) and an easy bus ride of the home for abused women and children (where she spends three afternoons a week). Her new friends are impressed that she owns an original work of art. She is glad Kathleen and George have no objections to Gertrude's and her portions of the family land being made available for sale through the government allotment program for war veterans. Jason hopes someone who sees its possibilities as a quaint inn or a handsome country manor will buy the mill. He was impressed when George said he intended to expand his casket-making enterprise and had no interest in running a resort; Jason appreciates a clear focus. If Lola's share doesn't turn over quickly, he has offered to buy her out, so she'll have a financial cushion while she's in school.

In mid-September, around the time they all gathered to bury Rhoda's remains a year ago, Lola writes briefly, "Kat, I love the snapshot of you in the new Ford truck, and am relieved to know you've put the rest of the found money in a savings account, and that you've told George the truth about it. Isn't driving exhilarating? I told Tru she should at least give it a try, but she says there's no need for her to learn, as Jason has hired one of the returned heroes as a chauffeur."

17
Moving On

L OLA WATCHES FROM A DISTANCE as Daisy Whitney, in a flood of just-arrived passengers, enters the terminal's main waiting room. The Beaux-Arts splendor that humbles even jaded New Yorkers is the perfect introduction to this wondrous city. She wants the girl to register her first impressions of Pennsylvania Station without distraction, so that years from now, Daisy will look back on this moment as a metaphor of her life-expansion. Lola is discovering the importance of metaphors in literature classes at Columbia, and learning about life-expansion from social reformers at the settlement house and an avant-garde enclave of would-be writers and philosophers who gather in a cheap, cozy restaurant to expound and argue.

Daisy is sufficiently awed by the pink marble walls and the vaulted ceiling (which reminds her of a gigantic, upended egg carton) to be relieved when Lola emerges from behind an enormous column. She almost doesn't recognize the svelte figure in the dark gray, mannish-tailored suit, head-hugging felt cloche, and the high-heeled cordovan oxfords. "It was most kind of you to meet me," she says, holding on to her Charlotte Corday hat through Lola's greeting, "especially when you're so busy with your studies and working on behalf of abused women and children." She isn't sure what that word *abused* signifies; Helen instructed her in what to say.

"In New York, you'll soon find, as I did, that time stretches to accommodate whatever you really want to do," Lola says. "By the way, I hear your school's pretty swell, and not as much of a lockup as your papa thinks it is."

What impresses Daisy more than the station's vastness and grandeur is the way Lola quickly commandeers a porter, then a taxicab, when there doesn't seem to be enough of either to accommodate all who want them.

"I promised Jason I would personally turn you over to your new keepers, so I hope you don't mind if I accompany you," Lola says.

"I'd be crushed if you didn't."

Mrs. Graham's Finishing School occupies a three-story house on Eighty-second Street, which is within a stone's throw of Riverside Drive. When Lola reassures Daisy that she herself lives only a dozen blocks away, Daisy smiles wanly; her papa warned her not to expect to see much of Lola in New York City. Minutes after the headmistress receives them in one of the pretentiously furnished twin parlors, Lola, having told the driver to wait, blows Daisy a kiss and vamooses.

Several of Mrs. Graham's relatives are in residence at the school. That contingent plus servants outnumber the students (sixteen girls at the start; two decline to return after Christmas). The faculty includes a genuine mademoiselle whose specialty is conversational French and whose last name Daisy never learns to pronounce to the woman's satisfaction; a fencing master whose tutelage Daisy avoids; and a frail, young English instructor who stares at her for overly long intervals. Flighty forays into higher mathematics and the rules of etiquette are conducted by Mrs. Graham's sister, a failed Southern belle who reached the age of forty in Savannah without snaring a husband, and therefore had to move to a vaster, distant locale in order to save face.

Daisy is the last student to arrive for the fall term. Eleanor and Eloise, mop-haired twins from Connecticut, stare at her new, royal-blue redingote (which has the Betty Wales label "Made Especially for College Girls") and giggle behind their hands. *Can it be out of style already?* But she soon realizes it is not her clothes they are making fun of, but the way she talks.

"Why do you say you're 'fixing to' do something?" asks Eloise. "Hey, y'all, what does 'fixing to' mean?"

Daisy replies sweetly, "I'm fixing to sock you if you don't shut up." They will become her close friends.

Papa emphasized that she must know what to do in the unlikely event she becomes separated from a chaperoned group. She can ask policemen or bus drivers for directions but must never speak to any other male to whom she has not been introduced—and she should be wary of those she's met. She should never smile at a man she doesn't know well, lest he infer the wrong idea. Her papa dispensed the advice mechanically, as though she were a patient, as he drove Daisy to Felder to catch the New York and New Orleans Limited, which would take her over a thousand miles away from him.

They arrived at Felder's Union Station comfortably ahead of the 8:15 A.M. departure time. Mr. Howard was there to see her off. Daisy wondered if he had stuck that red carnation in his lapel to add a touch of festivity to her leave-taking, or if he wore one often. When it was time to board the luxurious, varnished-vestibule, Pullman passenger train, her papa hugged her quickly, then turned away with his hands over his face. Mr. Howard came aboard to inspect her accommodations. He had already introduced her to a Mrs. Barksdale, who was traveling to Washington, D.C., and would be happy for Daisy to share a table with her in the dining car. (The lady assured Daisy they would visit the observation car together. The club car, of course, was off-limits to respectable females.) And it was Mr. Howard who smiled and waved encouragingly to her through the train window during the increasing momentum and excitement of exodus.

After her mother died, Daisy and her papa had become self-conscious with each other. It would have been better if Helen had come with them to Felder. However, the new stepmother didn't wish to intrude on what she called "a special father-daughter time."

The first night in Mrs. Graham's establishment, Daisy waits for sleep on a narrow bed in a room that is about the size of the Pullman compartment where she'd spent the previous night. Both are smaller than Hettie's pantry at home. She already misses Hettie and Torey. What in the world could she have been thinking of, to commit to nine months of boarding school in the nation's largest city?

That afternoon, in the scooting taxi, Lola had pointed out various landmarks, such as the nation's tallest skyscraper, the sixty-story Woolworth Building. They might as well have been picture postcards. Daisy tried to be impressed, but she felt most peculiar. She chalked it up to the vibration of the thirty-hour rail journey and the sudden dizziness from looking up at the train station's ceiling, which, according to Lola, was a hundred and fifty feet from the floor.

When the disoriented feeling keeps recurring over the next weeks, she realizes she suffers from homesickness, a malady akin to grief. Indeed, it's worse than when her mama died. On a school outing to a museum that seems bigger even than Pennsylvania Station, a wave of homesickness assails her in a long room filled with grandfather clocks. The clocks remind her of the Civil War veterans who were fixtures on the porches of Hackberry Hill, and though she'd never bothered to learn their names, she misses those old heroes. Hearing the new popular song "Alabama Lullaby" brings tears to her eyes and memories of being rocked to sleep in Hettie's lap. In the quiet darkness, her only solitude, she thinks about the secret Torey told her all those years ago, when they pressed their bleeding thumbs together and became sisters for life.

The letter Lola will never know how much Jason dreaded writing arrives with October and starts out just as breezily.

My dear, dear girl:

What a delight, to see your charming script on the topmost envelope in today's stack! I am touched and flattered at being singled out for a private communication. I'll not mention the letter to Gertrude, however, as nothing in it would have particular appeal to her.

I never felt you'd really left the nest while you were at college, as we got an occasional glimpse of you then. Now, it's been almost four months since we've seen you, and I find myself increasingly given to nostalgic reflection about the little maid who bravely chose to leave the only home she'd known to live with her eldest sister and the sister's husband in Felder. What a privilege it has been to have you in my life.

I can assure you Gertrude misses you as much as she worries about you. Do keep in mind that we're just a collect call away—it doesn't have to be just on Sundays—and that a letter mailed in New York City on Monday can reach Felder by the following Thursday. Since the First Class Washington-Franklin stamp backed off a penny to the pre-war rate of two cents, the cost of keeping up with faraway friends and family is very reasonable indeed. I understand the new Air Mail Service won't be available in this part of the country anytime soon, but if there's someone in Chicago or Washington you'd like to touch base with, you might give it a try. However, a twenty-four-cent airplaned letter, which includes special delivery, may not reach its destination any sooner than regular mail, as (justifiably, in my opinion) some pilots refuse to fly if the weather's the least bit iffy.

Indeed, I understand your "outraged feeling of betrayal" that your home state did not endorse voting rights for women. I, too, was disheartened that ours was not among those to ratify the Nineteenth Amendment to our U. S. Constitution. Yes, it's true: The Alabama Legislature voted nay—or "neigh," as befits that bunch of jackasses—on September 22. Your late father was a forward-thinking man. Had he been a member of that Legislature, I have no doubt he'd have made an impassioned speech on behalf of your worthy cause. I've often thought if Rayford Holloway had held on to his health and his elected seat, he would have helped draft the Alabama Constitution of 1901, in which case it would be a better piece of work. But this is a temporary setback. When you feminists get your Amendment ratified by the necessary thirty-six states—and indications are it's in the bag—Alabama women will have the right to vote in spite of these unenlightened statesmen.

Do I detect a slight veering off the charted course now, toward a career in social work, instead of the law? If so, I applaud that decision. You're aware that I've had reservations about your entering the dog-eat-dog profession, although I would be immensely proud to hang your shingle beside my own. (Actually, beneath it, until you become a partner. It has nothing to do with your being a woman; the same standard would apply to a male associate.)

Your sister prays on her knees daily that you will come to your senses and return to us. I'm not sure she was relieved, as you know I was, when you stopped seeing the local rascal who rushed you too soon and too fast after the shock of Robert's death. It's well you put an end to that churlish chase (although you certainly took your time about it). By the way, Ted Cooper told me at the Commercial Club meeting that a well-heeled friend from his Navy days, a New Englander who's making a name for himself on Wall Street, has been squiring you about.

Ted assured me this fellow is a true gentleman who realizes Southern women should be treated like fine crystal. He sounds most agreeable to me, but I'll not mention the subject to your sister, lest she pray the fellow right out of your orbit. Gertrude would have you marry a Felder bounder rather than a suitor with excellent credentials who might keep you above the Mason-Dixon line.

Lola, I would prefer to tell you the following in person. I thought of coming to New York to do so, but although I do intend to look in on you in the not too distant future, I can't leave the new mother and babe quite yet. I suggest you sit down before reading the next part, which may come as a bit of a shock.

According to Peter Whitney, his adopted daughter was born to your sister Rhoda, who named a school mate, one Sam Holcomb, as the biological father. The poor fellow was killed by a train less than a month after they made love together for the only time (so Rhoda claimed to Peter). Not long after that tragedy, the boy's family moved away.

Your father had died, and Rhoda didn't dare confess her predicament to your mother. I wish she had confided in me. However, it was fortunate and with some logic that Rhoda turned to the man who had been her father's closest friend. The good doctor was entirely sympathetic to her plight. He arranged for her to spend her confinement well-hidden, in the house of his employees Hettie and Jim Jackson. Peter was happy to adopt her offspring and provide Rhoda with funds until she could find work elsewhere. She assured him she wanted to relocate in a distant city. Rhoda, in some manner of disguise, was to leave town on a train the same day the baby was turned over to the doctor. Peter assumed she followed through with the plan. He never saw her after that day, and as you know, there was no word of or from her. My efforts to locate her were fruitless. Alas, now we know she made a fateful decision to test her skills on the waterwheel one last time, and the wheel won that dangerous game. It is my firm belief that no other person was involved in Rhoda's swift and untimely demise.

You should know that positive identification of the remains was made by Hettie. The mishap that took off a corner of a front tooth occurred at the Jacksons' house shortly before Rhoda gave birth.

For some time, Peter has wanted Daisy to know she has family besides him. However, he cannot bring himself to tell her the story of how she came into the world, and so has avoided the subject altogether. The girl doesn't know she's adopted. I would prefer that Gertrude not learn of this connection anytime soon, if ever, and I question the wisdom of telling Kathleen, sensible though she appears to be. As for you, Daisy would gain an aunt (or half-aunt, though I see no reason to impart that distinction) who's already her devoted friend. Peter seems happy in his new marriage, but the business of Daisy's being oblivious of her origin sticks in the man's craw, and he wants someone to take this cup from him. May I tell him you will be the cup-bearer? Think about it awhile before you give me your answer.

With affection and admiration as always,

Jason

He's unloaded a secret Lola would never have surmised and in the same breath—same letter, that is—put her in charge of relaying this information to the person who will be most affected. She will have to deal, alone, with a vulnerable child who's just had the props knocked out from under her. Lola is delighted to know that Rhoda left such a legacy, but she doesn't for a minute believe a "school mate" was Rhoda's lover. Jason knows the identity of the real guilty party but is keeping that part from her.

She informs Jason crisply that she will pass on the information "when and if the spirit moves me. The revelation is bound to devastate her. I can see the telegram she'll fire off to Hackberry Hill: DEAR PAPA STOP HOW COULD YOU KEEP THIS FROM ME ALL THESE YEARS

STOP I HATE YOU STOP LOVE DAISY. Seriously, Jason, why should I be the one to tell her?"

The day after Lola posts that riposte, the spirit moves her, and she knows Jason is right. She should be the one to tell Daisy.

They are shopping, Daisy's favorite pastime. In Wanamaker's, a young woman plays unobtrusive classical music—MacDowell, Lola thinks—on an ebony spinet that's almost hidden from view by a semicircle of potted palms. Rhoda would have thumped out something catchy, like "Alexander's Ragtime Band" or "After You've Gone," the new hit tune Lola danced to the night before in the Persian Room. Rhoda would have taken to nightclubs and jazz like that blue crane took to the pond.

Lola lures Daisy away from a hovering sales clerk and toward the revolving door with the promise of an ice-cream soda. When they are served (at a table whose surface is smaller than some of the hats they've just tried on), she asks casually, "Have you ever wondered if you were adopted?"

Daisy replies as though she expected the question. "Torey and I swore on blood, when she was ten and I was seven, to tell each other our most important secrets. Mine was that I wanted to marry Harold someday. Hers was that I was born in her parents' house. Torey's memory was hazy on the subject, but she recalled that the doctor took me home with him and that my real mother, who had long, dark hair, went away the same day. Torey said if I ever asked Hettie or Mama or Papa about it, she'd be in awful trouble. So I never have."

Lola glances around to be sure no one is within hearing distance. The druggist behind the counter frowns at her, as though he knows she's about to shatter this child's heart. Then she realizes he's registering disapproval of the cigarette in her hand. The ashtray on the table is for men. The cigarette is not lit; she doesn't recall taking it from her purse. It's just something to hold on to while she finishes this assignment. "I have recently learned that my sister Rhoda gave birth to you when she was fifteen. According to Jason, your father wants you to know but couldn't bear to tell you himself."

Daisy twirls the long-handled spoon, as though blending the chocolate syrup in the bottom of the glass with the whipped cream on top is what's important here. Seconds pass before she looks up. "So I have two dead mothers and a stepmother."

"Plus a trio of lively aunts. However, Gertrude and Kathleen are still in the dark about this. Shall we tell them or not? It's up to you."

"Let's not," Daisy says without hesitation. "I don't think Mr. Howard's wife would take happily to the notion, and I would be self-conscious around the Cravens, especially Harold, if they knew. Being able to have you as close kin is enough." The smile is a heartbreaker. Lola wonders how in the world her nephew resists this adorable girl, then thinks it's just as well he does, since they're half first cousins. Daisy adds, "When I took the wreath you made for her grave, I must have had a hunch your missing sister was connected to me."

Kathleen had sent Lola a photograph she'd come across of Rhoda's ninth-grade class. After receiving Jason's letter, she dug it out and took a close look. The students' names were noted in pencil on the back of the photograph. Lola saw Daisy in this image of Rhoda at the same age, but there was no resemblance between Daisy and Sam Holcomb, who was also in the picture. *Oh, Rhoda, whom were you protecting when you named this poor dead boy as your lover?*

Now, Lola takes a duplicate she's had made from her mesh handbag. "I thought you might like to have this. Rhoda is second from the left on the back row."

The girl scrutinizes the picture for several seconds, then asks offhandedly, "Do I remind you of her?"

"Yes. Not so much in looks—you're prettier than she was—as in gesture. You lift your hair and toss your head the way she did. And I've seen you hold your elbows and twist around suddenly, as she used to."

Daisy's expression freezes. "Do you think one of these gangly boys in the picture could be . . . ?"

"No. Rhoda never had a sweetheart at school. I believe your papa really is your papa." Lola convinces herself as she tells Daisy how it might have been: "Rhoda didn't get on well with our mother, but she adored our father. When he died, she grieved harder than the rest of the family. It was natural that she should turn to her father's best friend for comfort—a man who was a compassionate healer of others but had needs of his own." She places a hand over Daisy's. "Their mutual need resulted in a love child. To avoid scandal, your father took every precaution to guard their secret. Of course, he wanted the baby they made together, as did she. But Rhoda could not bring you into our family, nor could she stand by and watch another woman be mother to the child she'd given birth to. Her solution, or at least her intention, was to go far away, in order that you might grow up amidst the love and advantages the doctor and his wife would provide for you. Your father and the Jacksons, with whom Rhoda lived during her months of seclusion, assumed she had departed, as planned, the day you were taken to his house. They had no idea she would indulge herself in a farewell fling with the waterwheel." She lights the cigarette, takes a puff, and flicks the ashes on the floor, as Rhoda would. "You can see how embarrassing and painful it would be for your father to reveal this sequence of events to you."

"It would be painful and embarrassing for me as well. I'll never broach the subject with him. But thank you for letting me in on their secret—his and Rhoda's. I had no idea the story of how I came to be was so tragic, yet so romantic." Daisy's eyes are moist and starry.

Lola crosses her fingers in case she's just told a whopper.

On the first anniversary of the armistice, from the balcony of the Knickerbocker Hotel, a world-renowned tenor sings "Over There" over a Broadway parade. Lola searches the rows of marching men. It could have been a mistake, a mixup of identification; someone else succumbed to the influenza and was cast into the sea; Rob has amnesia. She thinks she's spotted him and waves frantically, but the stranger smiles apologetically and doesn't break rank. That night, she dreams of him for the first time in months, but when she wakes, there's nothing to remember. He's becoming more and more ephemeral.

But one memory is so crystallized she doesn't have to invent a single detail.

Mantles of snow, the first she's ever seen, adorn the stately houses and deep front lawns of Garden Street in Felder. The white substance caps iron fence palings and makes lacy shawls on matronly humps of shrubbery. She builds a snowman near the gazebo and practices the art of lip-kissing on his cold, artificial face.

That evening, as the stuff has begun to melt, Rob Castleman calls for her. They walk a starlit block to the gala in honor of Maggie's sixteenth birthday. Since Rob is almost a college man and therefore may have advanced ideas, Jason has forbidden him to drive Lola in his father's car and has set her curfew for 10:15, fifteen minutes after the party ends. She wears a long, sapphire velvet cape over an off-the-shoulder gown of magenta peau de soie. Her hands are tucked inside an ermine muff. Rob carries the satin drawstring sack that contains her party slippers.

Inside the Cartwright house, pocket doors have been opened to combine the parlor and a sitting room. Rugs and some of the furniture have been removed to free the floor for dancing. Gaslight flickers through hurricane shades of frosted glass, casting a rosy glow over faces and walls. The female guests perch like Cinderellas on gilded chairs in the hall, while kneeling housemaids replace the wet boots and galoshes with demi-heeled kidskin pumps.

As the Victrola churns out the first wobbly strains of "Peg o' My Heart," Lola moves into Rob's arms. She's danced with boys in ballroom classes, but this first time with him is different. Their bodies blend together with no awkwardness. As his thighs graze hers through layers of worsted and silk, she knows they will leave the party early enough to stand pressed against each other on Jason's darkened side porch and kiss until their mouths are bruised and satiated.

On that night, she never imagines that her most often wished wish will not come true.

18
Ever After

THE DAY OF DAISY'S ARRIVAL IN NEW YORK, Lola suggested she form the habit of solitary walks along Riverside Drive, which is within a stone's throw of Mrs. Graham's Finishing School. Taking this advice to heart, Daisy enjoys daily constitutionals, even in inclement weather, until she leaves New York two years later for nurses' training in Richmond, where she will live for the rest of her life. The young doctor who will become her husband reminds her only slightly of Harold Craven and, as time goes on, more and more of her papa. For the first three years in Richmond, Daisy has the assurance of knowing Lola is only sixty miles away, in Charlottesville.

By the time Lola obtains her LL.B. degree from the University of Virginia Law School, she has come to agree with Franz Kafka that "studying law is like chewing thousand-year-old dust." She elects not to hang her shingle below Jason's or anyone else's. Instead, she becomes a journalist and lives in several cities, including London and Paris, before marrying for the third, last, and happiest time. The man proposed to her in New York the year after the war ended but wasn't willing to wait indefinitely for her to make up her mind. When their paths cross again twenty-five years later—toward the end of World War II—John Graves is a widower with a grown son.

Lola has no children of her own, but she maintains a lively interest in the progeny of her kin. Daisy has twin boys; Ray and his wife have produced two of each gender. Harold has adopted a son and daughter in Formosa, where he is a medical missionary. (That Harold doesn't marry, especially after taking in those almond-eyed orphans, puzzles his father but not his mother.) Lola is closest to Gertrude and Jason's Lucy Margaret, who reminds her temperamentally, hauntingly, and sometimes heartbreakingly, at every stage of development, of herself.

After the girl elopes in 1942, just before her soldier fiancé ships out, Gertrude sends the wedding gown and veil to Hackberry Hill by Lola, who is making one of her whirlwind Alabama visits. "These should go back in Mama's trunk," Gertrude writes in the note to Kathleen, "until one of your granddaughters has occasion to wear them." Lola and Kathleen decide they will get to the bottom of that trunk. The only real surprise is a small, unlocked diary that neither recalls having seen before. Most of its pages are empty; others contain cryptic references to daily routine. Kathleen recognizes the resolute penmanship as their mother's. Lola reads the contents aloud and imagines she is hearing the words spoken by their youthful author: "Today I watched Tot birth a colored baby and didn't faint. She said white women have theirs with lots of blood-spilling too. Tot says she will instruct me how to keep from sprouting a watermelon in my belly, but if I don't provide my husband with a son or two, he'll turn from me to other succor."

The last entry is dated May 14, 1880: "Tomorrow I will marry a stranger and go to make my home in Alabama, which some say is a wilder state even than this one. I shall miss my mother and Tot and this familiar place so much I cannot bear the thought. My tears are blurring this ink. But the man God has chosen for me has a fine face and a quick smile, and he can whistle a right merry tune. I shall do my best to be a good wife."

On the morning of her thirty-fifth wedding anniversary, Kathleen wakes with a gold band on the third finger of her left hand. She sighs and wishes George had been so thoughtful, but she knows he hasn't. Miss Kitty has finally located her lost ring and bestowed it as a farewell gift. The house will be lonely without her. Lucy left long before; she must have figured out how to get back to that Georgia plantation. And if Rhoda is around, she doesn't come inside.

Kathleen uses the last of the found money to visit New York City— Lola meets her there—and the Metropolitan Museum of Art. (The boys were educated on George's earnings and the sale of the pecan orchard.) The experience convinces her it is pointless to imitate genius and that she should follow her own instincts in style and craft. For several years beginning in the late 1930s, Kathleen and other gifted members of the Dixie Art Colony make annual retreats at a former Indian campsite they call Poka Hutchi, a Creek expression that means "Gathering of Picture Writers."

"Craven & Son, Fine Caskets" has expanded from the barn into a new building next to it. Ray has no problem relinquishing his dream of returning the Holloway land to its former status as a cotton plantation. There is always a market for coffins, even in the Depression. The gristmill is not turned into an inn or a residence. No one wants to buy it except Jason, and Gertrude refuses to sell or give the property to her husband, because she doesn't want him to get all wrapped up in that place. As a concession, she moves Kathleen's misty painting of the mill from the back hall to the dining room.

At least the old gristmill will survive as a landmark, Jason sanguinely points out to Lola; an edifice constructed of stone will neither burn nor rot. People traveling on the newly paved highway recognize it as a piece of history that can tell a tale or two.

Without being asked to by Jason, George runs the machinery occasionally to keep it from seizing up. Each time, the wheel seems a little less rollicking. He recalls when it was feisty and confident and randy, the way he himself felt back then. But he isn't complaining. Every week or so, George and Kathleen turn to each other in the dark and find the old fire still there between them, just waiting to be ignited.

At Lola's instigation, during his term as mayor (before he follows in his grandfather's footsteps and gets himself elected to the state legislature), Ray Holloway Craven installs bronze signs where the city limits of Hackberry Hill begin and end:

HACKBERRY HILL, ALABAMA,
WAS ONCE CALLED SEHOY
IN HONOR OF A PRINCESS
OF THE NOBLE WIND CLAN.

Coda:
The Memory That Never Surfaced

She walks in the middle of the road, where it's highest and rounded. Her mama would have switched her for this infraction; Rhoda would have made her take a close look at some maggot-infested carcass of an animal that was in the wrong place at the wrong time. But her mama's buried in the cemetery, and Rhoda has gone away, and the only conveyance she's likely to meet up with is the doctor's buggy. He'll spot her sooner in the middle of the road and have plenty of time to stop the horse before he runs her down. He might even offer her a ride. In the months she has been without guidance, she has learned to plan out things for herself.

Her best thinking is accomplished on the way to school. This morning, she left the house earlier than usual. Her intention is to be the first one there, so she can read the teacher's new copy of Goody Two Shoes before the blissful aroma of printer's ink on unsmudged pages is overwhelmed by the smells of crusty overalls and bare feet. As she walks, she conjures up pictures of Mr. Howard's fine brick house. Gertrude has said she will have her own suite. (She understands the meaning of that word but doesn't yet know it's spelled differently from sweet.) She has a whole creaky upstairs to herself now. In the dark of night, she wishes someone were up there with her besides the dead-baby angels and the wandering grandmother. She hopes they won't follow her to Felder. Rhoda would tell her not to worry, that ghosts can't cross county lines. If Rhoda were still around, she wouldn't be moving away. No, sirree, not even for the luxury of a private, chain-flush commode and a glass-front whatnot filled with china-head dolls in flounced dresses.

The waiting is more than half over, but the days crossed off the calendar she made have passed slowly. She pretends she is on the way to her new life now. Today, she may just bypass the schoolhouse and hike to the loading platform, where she will sneak past the ticket agent and on to the passenger car while the conductor looks the other way and sings out mournfully, "Last call for all aboard!" Gertrude and Mr. Howard will be amazed, shocked to pieces, that she could get to Felder by herself. Of course, she is only play-acting. But she could do it, if she had a mind to. Rhoda had never been anywhere until she lit out on her own, and God knows where that girl has got to by now.

Beyond the curve, the mill starts to blend in with its surroundings and doesn't look so forbidding. There's no sign of activity. George is back at the house, repairing a broken pump.

When she came downstairs this morning, her weary sister, who seems like a stranger, was still asleep; baby Harold has his days and nights mixed up. She didn't take time to boil herself an egg, but pocketed a cold, hard biscuit and some shriveled crab apples to have for lunch at school. In place of breakfast, she will help herself to peppermint stick candy from the big jar George keeps in the mill for customers. That's if the door's unlocked—and hooray, it is! If Mama were still alive, he wouldn't be so careless.

She feels the empty, cavernous building's aloofness, as though it's a grown person who intends to keep her at a distance. She's been here with Rhoda, who came to pester George, but this is the first time she's been inside the mill by herself. Yellow motes—residue from yesterday's grinding—swirl like gnats in blocks of sunlight let in through skinny windows. "Corndust." She whispers the satisfying word she's just invented and wonders if she will ever have occasion to use it in her new, citified life.

The mill's interior is quiet and spooky, like the church used to be when the family was the first to arrive, which they usually were. Kathleen doesn't think it's necessary to go to church every week, or even every month; they've been only twice since Mama's funeral. When Rhoda was teaching her to swim in the mill-pond—Grandmother had called it a weir; Rhoda said the old lady would roll her tongue around that r like it was something tasty—the musical rumble of the waterfall masked its danger. Rhoda scared her so about the rock dam and the big wheel that she's never been tempted to get close to either. The steep wooden steps to what George calls the loft remind her of a Bible picture: Jacob's ladder to the stars. The big grinding stones bring to mind another: Abraham about to roast his little boy on a slab for God to have for supper. Fortunately for that child, in the nick of time, God changed his mind.

She holds her breath as she surveys the vastness of the second level, where she's never been before. Though the fixtures are strangers, she recognizes the function of each. The milling operation is one of the few topics of conversation at the house. In the place of prominence beneath the oak center beam is the bucket elevator, which has a wide belt with square metal containers that move grain from one level to another. Next to that is the bolter, which sifts and refines the coarsely ground meal. Flat bags made of unbleached muslin are stacked near the window; a couple of filled ones, larger than bed pillows, are on the broad sill. The two-hole corn sheller, painted fire-engine red, is the most fetching piece of equipment. It's just as well there are no ears of corn lying about; she'd be tempted to mess with this contraption. In one corner are a narrow cot and a washstand. Before he married her sister and moved into the house, George must have been lonely up here at night, the silent machinery his only company.

She scoots back down the steps. An iron lever on the wall catches her eye and dares her to try to move it. She stands on a chair, takes a deep breath, and puts her weight and will into the effort. The lever flies forward. Seconds later, she hears a whooshing sound as water hurtles down the millrace into the stilt-raised wooden trough—what George calls the flume. Oh, Godamighty, Jesus, Moses, and Abraham, she has opened the sluice gate! Like a surprised Jack-in-the-Beanstalk giant, the cumbersome wheel lurches into action. From the corner of an eye, she sees something—a bag filled with meal?—hurtle swiftly past the window. She runs out the door and around the side of the building, where the huge caster spins merrily now, showing off just for her, spewing froth that looks like the spittle of an overworked horse. Whatever fell has disappeared below the foam. She'll be in big trouble if George finds out she's wasted someone's provender. Creatures that lurk beneath the pond's surface—tadpoles, minnows, silver bream, whiskered catfish, bullfrogs, turtles, water moccasins—will find that cornmeal mighty tasty. She wills the thing not to rise. For several minutes, she watches the tailrace that takes off the torrent's excess. To her great relief, no clots of meal or loose grain appear in the runoff water. She hurries inside the mill to tug the lever back into place; her fingers ache with the strain. When the waterwheel obediently wheezes to a stop, she feels powerful and confident, as though she could halt and restart her own heart.

The candy is forgotten. She runs the rest of the way to the humdrum safety of school with a loose book strap switching her legs. The doctor does not happen along.

Returning from school that afternoon, as she nears the pond that harbors the morning's secret, she spots his phaeton just ahead, where the road divides like the curves of a heart between his land and theirs. He stops the horse, tips his hat as though she merits the courtesy, and offers to take her the rest of the way home. As soon as she settles beside him, he tells her, a new jubilance in his voice, that earlier this same day, he brought a baby girl to live at his house. The news fills her with jealousy and a quickness of hope. One orphan's fortunes have just changed for the better, and so will her own, very soon now. These last months of loss have taught her something: Whenever one part of her heart shuts down, another part opens up.

The doctor begins to whistle a cheerful song that everybody around here knows the words to. According to Rhoda, there was a time when their papa's whistling of the tune could make an out-of-sorts day turn around; even their mama would smile and tap a shoe at the sound.

She sings along lustily, somewhat off-key, which the doctor doesn't seem to mind, nor does the trotting mare who sets the rhythm: "Oh, Susanna! Cry no more for me; I've been to Cal-i-for-nia with my banjo on my knee. . . ."

The song ends, but her heart keeps on opening.

Acknowledgments

I am deeply grateful to literary agent Joelle Delbourgo, publisher Carolyn Sakowski, and editor Steve Kirk.

Walter Clement arranged tours of restored gristmills and came to my assistance several times during the making of this novel. Historian Wesley Newton advised me and entrusted me with a thick file of his notes on World War I. Gruesome questions were addressed by Dr. James Downs, director of the Alabama Department of Forensic Sciences, and Dr. Bill Cawthon. Photographs of 1917 Packard automobiles and relevant data were furnished by John Grundy; names of trains and schedules were provided by Andrew Waldo; Fairley McDonald III looked up laws and amendments; Jim Forte and Bob Swanson responded to my queries on postal history and censorship.

Issues of the *Montgomery Advertiser* from 1918, on microfilm at the

Alabama Department of Archives and History, proved very helpful. Other published works that inspired this re-creation of time and place included *The Way It Was, 1850-1930,* by Mary Ann Neeley and Beth Taylor Muskatt; *Alabama's Own in France: War Stories of the 167th Infantry,* by William Amerine; *Historic Mills of America; Wishes Are Horses,* the memoir of Fanny Marks Seibels; and *The Montgomery County Historical Society Newsletter.*

Although the fictional city of Felder is loosely modeled on Montgomery in the second decade of the twentieth century, Hackberry Hill is not based on a particular town, and I have found no evidence of a place in Alabama called Sehoy. The name belonged to three Native American women in successive generations who married prominent white men, yet retained their tribal affiliations. William Weatherford, also known as Red Eagle, was the son of Sehoy III and the great-grandson of the "princess of the Wind Clan."

The Second Thursday Book Club and Robert Wisnewski's discussion class keep me aware that a book takes on new dimension when readers bring to it their own perceptions and expectations. I am indebted to Jay Lamar and the Read Alabama Series for the opportunity to read portions of this book, while it was a work-in-progress, to a discerning audience; to the interesting, creative people I have met through writing, who have expanded my boundaries; and to the bright and entertaining women I go to lunch with.

Last but not least, I thank my family: Tommy, Fairley, Julie, Letitia, Pat, both Jims, Parker, Elizabeth, Anne Ferrell, and Charlotte.